THE
SECRET
AGENT

FRANCINE MATHEWS

THE SECRET AGENT

BANTAM BOOKS

THE SECRET AGENT

A Bantam Book / July 2002

Map by David Lindroth, Inc.
Book design by Lynn Newmark.

Library of Congress Cataloging-in-Publication Data
Mathews, Francine.
The secret agent / Francine Mathews.
p. cm.
ISBN 0-553-10913-8
1. Women private investigators—Thailand—Bangkok—
Fiction. 2. Americans—Thailand—Fiction. 3. Bangkok
(Thailand)—Fiction. 4. Fathers and sons—Fiction.
5. Missing persons—Fiction. 6. Grandfathers—Fiction.
I. Title.

PS3563.A8357 S43 2002
813'.54—dc21   2002018273

Published simultaneously in the United States and Canada

Bantam Books are published by Bantam Books, a division of
Random House, Inc. Its trademark, consisting of the words "Bantam
Books" and the portrayal of a rooster, is Registered in U.S. Patent
and Trademark Office and in other countries. Marca Registrada.
Bantam Books, 1540 Broadway, New York, New York 10036.

PRINTED IN THE UNITED STATES OF AMERICA

BVG   10   9   8   7   6   5   4   3   2   1

Dedicated with love to the memory of Kay Fanning,
Writer, Adventurer and Legendary American—
who once dined with Jim Thompson
at the house on the khlong

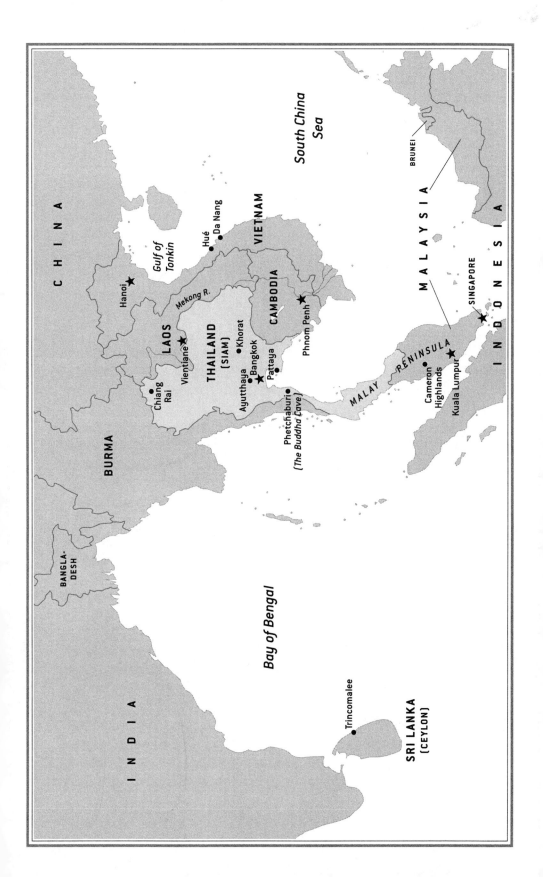

THE
SECRET
AGENT

THE
FINAL MEETING

Rose Cottage, The Cameron Highlands of Malaysia, March 26, 1967

He had never been a man who minded the heat.

In Bangkok he disdained air conditioners and forced his houseboy to cook nightly over a charcoal brazier, the flames flickering like knives on the man's burnished skin. By day he slipped through the sweltering streets when the sun was strongest, silk suit tailored close to his lean frame. His face was deeply tanned from sitting by the pool at the Royal Sports Club, his brow furrowed from staring into the light.

They called him many things in Bangkok: the Silk King, the Boss, the Legendary American. The braver ones called him Spy and Devil. He fashioned a life from myths and lies over the course of twenty years; he bought and sold entire villages, entertained everyone who stumbled into Southeast Asia, advised ambassadors and court potentates, dried the tears of women desperate for love. They had always whispered behind his back in Bangkok and the names they called him were proxies for one word: *Power*. He relished this about Siam the way he loved the stench of the khlongs and the liquid snatch of raw silk through his fingers: Siam was ruthless, Siam cared for no man not born of the River of Kings, Siam bowed only to secrets and the power secrets held.

He was a man who could buy anything with money; but secrets were traded in blood and that was why he cherished them.

This afternoon, alone in the blessed quiet that is granted to those who remain alert while the rest of the household naps, he sat on the terrace and turned a cigarette in his restless fingers. His doctor insisted that he quit smoking—but he was past sixty now and had lost too much in recent days to give up anything by choice.

The sun was fitful and the air was chill, six thousand feet above the Malaysian coast. He shivered slightly, closed his eyes, and thought of monsoons—of moist warmth, of stones steaming with fragrance. Of skin wet and shining in the garden torchlight, her head rising like a serpent's from the filthy water of the khlong—

He discarded the cigarette in a burning arc.

He was alone at last after the fuss and clatter of Easter morning, the service at the Anglican church in Tanah Rata, the picnic later on a distant hillside. He knew that his urgency had disconcerted the others—the way he hustled them through the meal, packing up plates and glasses as soon as the last morsel was consumed, shooing them back without explanation to the car. Was it a sign of advancing age, this lack of courtesy, a slip in tradecraft? He was stripped raw with tension, his ears preternaturally alert, a fine beading of sweat at the hairline—he, who had never minded the heat.

Tradecraft had got him this far. It would take him no farther.

He glanced at his watch. Time to rise and push back the chair, time to set off purposefully down the gravel drive toward a man he had not seen in years and might be forgiven for failing to recognize. It was his last possible chance at a meeting. He had cased the route earlier in the day, refusing the car that would have conveyed him to church, joining the others at the foot of the road that wound past the golf course. He would take nothing with him now but the briefcase brought from Bangkok—the briefcase, and every mortal lust or fear that had propelled him through two decades of life in Asia.

His eyes narrowed in the failing light. The road was deserted, the whole world asleep. He set off.

Later, they would admit that they heard him go. The girl he had brought with him from Bangkok turned restlessly in her sleep, arm lifted in a gesture akin to dancing. Her lips might have formed his name.

She slept on.

PART ONE

MAX

1

The Oriental Hotel in the heart of Bangkok is a name to conjure history. It recalls a time when tourists were travelers, when steamer trunks came by long-tail boat up the Chao Phraya, the River of Kings; when stoic male writers and legends of the Asian bush crawled out of the jungle to swap stories in the Bamboo Bar. Somerset Maugham almost died of fever there, in the 1920s, and Joseph Conrad tossed sleepless on a sweat-soaked cot; Hemingway ought to have seduced a legion of hard-drinking women behind the swinging shuttered doors, but apparently never did. During the Second World War the natives of Bangkok edged warily around the hotel, which had become an object of fear under the Japanese; and when Thailand capitulated to the Allies in September 1945, the Oriental turned hostel for U.S. and British officers.

They must have felt right at home, those Allied soldiers, between the French doors and the lawns running down to the swollen brown river. Orchids bloomed as profusely as English violets at the foot of the towering palms, and the whistles of the boatmen flew over the water like lark song. Under the drift of electric fans the officers drank deep of gin and Pimm's, composing letters to women they hadn't seen in years. They imagined themselves conquerors, without having fired a shot.

This is the sorcery of Thailand, and of the Oriental Hotel: to make a guest feel at home without ever implying he is anything but a guest.

But like all great hotels, the Oriental is a stage for public drama: it demands a decent performance from the people who walk through its doors. The right to enter history comes at considerable cost, and style is the preferred form of currency. Shorts and backpacks—those hallmarks of the indigent tourist desperate for an hour of quiet and air conditioning—are strictly forbidden in the Oriental's main lobby.

Stefani Fogg had stayed at the hotel before. She had read the dress-code notice etched politely near the revolving front door. But she was a woman who rarely apologized, particularly to the hired help. And so this morning she hitched her backpack higher on her shoulder and swung her long, bare legs out of the taxi.

"Welcome back to the Oriental, Ms. Fogg," the doorman said, and bowed low over his steepled hands.

She took the spray of jasmine he offered her and raised it to her face. The scent was elusive—the essence of untimely death. She nodded to the doorman, paid off the taxi and stalked inside.

She may have been conscious of the eyes that followed her as she crossed the spotless carpet. If so, she ignored them. She ignored, too, the soaring windows, the chairs swathed in silk, the towering arrangements of lilies, the four employees who bowed in succession as she passed. She ignored the powerfully built man with the gleaming black hair, who sedulously scanned his newspaper at a desk opposite the magazine kiosk, although he was the only person in the room pretending to ignore her and thus ought to have been alarming. Stefani was too tired to care. The rigid set of her shoulders and the thin line of her mouth screamed exhaustion. During the past week she had slept badly and in the previous twenty-seven hours, not at all.

"Mr. Rewadee," she said by way of greeting to the Manager of Customer Relations. Her voice was as frayed as a hank of old rope. The backpack slid from her shoulder to the plush carpet at her feet.

"Ms. Fogg! Welcome back to the Oriental!"

This phrase—or variations on the theme—was a gamut she was forced to run every time she reappeared on the banks of the Chao Phraya. But she liked Rewadee, with his correct navy suit and his beautiful silk tie, his smooth, tapering fingers; so she stifled her annoyance and forced a smile, as though her clothes did not stink of mildew or her feet require washing.

The manager's plum-brown eyes crinkled and he waggled a finger at her. "You're three days past the date of your reservation. We'd al-most despaired of you. We even went so far as to *talk* of calling New York."

"I'm sorry. I was trapped in Vietnam. A flood."

"I had no idea there was a problem. Typhoon?"

"Yes," she said abruptly. "You still have my room?"

"Of course. For *you—*"

Rewadee waved vaguely in the air as though to dispel doubt, or per-haps the odor of damp and decay that clung to her clothing. "I shall escort you to the Garden Wing myself."

He came from behind the counter, reached delicately for her back-pack, and hoisted it waist-high like a fish unaccountably snagged on his line. Stefani did not protest. The tension holding her upright had begun to dissolve in the jasmine-scented air, the hushed quiet of deep carpets. She followed Rewadee without a backward glance.

The powerfully built man at the writing desk folded his newspaper carefully as he watched them go.

The rain had started during her eighth day in Vietnam, after she left the Mekong Delta behind and headed north along the coast. Before Saigon there had been Vientiane, the backcountry of Laos, and the an-cient trade routes that once ran between Burma and Angkor Wat and were being painfully reclaimed for capitalism from the guerillas and the drug lords. It had been seven weeks exactly since her last stop in Bangkok, seven weeks of monsoon, not the best time of year to travel. Vietnam and Laos have no national weather services. Predictions are made on the basis of hope, not science. Stefani learned to judge the feel of the air against her cheek, the color of clouds in the sky, and to guess the degree of wetness coming, as people have done for millennia. She was alternately sweating under a humid sun or pounded by cloudburst.

The rain fell in torrents just south of Hoi An. She stared out the car window at the endless fields of rice, rainwater lapping the dikes where the local peasants buried their dead, the stone monuments solid and square among the feathery tips of green. Only one highway ran along the coast of Vietnam, a strip of macadam that uncoiled as innocently as a snare through the sudden peaks and dipping plains of the Truong Son Range. The South China Sea was creeping over the white strip of beach and encroaching upon the road; seawater licked at the hubcaps of her hired Mercedes. The car hood thrust through the small fry of pedal bikes and motor scooters like a blunt-nosed shark; enraged cyclists slammed their fists against the windows as she passed.

They pushed on from Da Nang, Stefani and her Vietnamese driver, through the water that flooded the coast road until it fanned from their fenders like a ceremonial fountain and the emerald rice paddies were entirely submerged. By the time they struggled over the Hai Van pass and descended into Hué, the ancient Vietnamese capital, it was pitch dark and the driver was swearing.

A sluggish current streamed before the reception desk at the Morin Hotel, then at the Century the entire ground floor was under water; and while she stood there on the soggy carpet, watching the rain drip from the ceiling tiles and gush down the banisters of the grand staircase, the first refugees arrived by boat.

After that, Stefani abandoned the banks of the Perfume River and sought out the private home of a man she knew, a surgeon in the hospital in Hué, who lived on higher ground. Though it was nearly midnight, Pho was standing outside his house as she approached, his wife and four children busy on the flat roof of the single-story dwelling. They had managed to rig a tarpaulin (old U.S. Army combat green), and most of their belongings were already piled under it. Stefani got out of the car and helped haul a basket of trussed chickens up to the roof.

Her driver dropped her pack on a plastic deck chair and wallowed down the hill in his flooded Mercedes, never to be heard from again.

"You will eat rice with us?" Pho's English was halting but thorough; at thirteen, he'd carried a gun for the South Vietnamese Army.

"I would be honored," Stefani replied.

Pho's wife boiled rainwater over a kerosene burner, and rice is what they ate for the next five days—rice and the few eggs produced by the querulous chickens, while the Perfume River engulfed the Imperial City. They were cut off on a shallow island without a boat, and the river kept rising.

That first night no one slept. Pho's wife strapped her youngest child tightly against the wet skin of her breast and rocked without ceasing as she hunkered under the tarp. Stefani paced off the roofline and found that the world had dwindled to eighty square feet. By day, they watched the houses of less fortunate lowlanders sweep by on the current. Boxes, rubbish, a flotilla of dead cats. Pho's neighbors called shrilly from other rooftops, traded rumors and news and what food they had. The children squabbled and fished ineffectually for the cats. Stefani tried to make a cellular phone call and found her battery was dead. By late afternoon, boats swamped with the homeless were poling through the flooded trees.

She scanned the skies for helicopters and saw nothing but layers of cloud. The sound of rain pattering on the tin roof under her feet was slowly driving her mad. No helicopters appeared. The surging current was only eighteen inches below the roofline. The rain went on. She fought the impulse to dive like a rat over the side of the sinking house.

A palm tree in Pho's front yard served as her high-water marker. When the flood began, two feet of trunk were submerged. At 2:53 A.M. on the third day, at the height of the typhoon, she shone a fitful flashlight on the swaying palm and guessed that eight more feet had vanished. Thirty-one hours later, when the river was within five inches of Pho's roof, the rain turned to drizzle; the water began to recede. Stefani thought of arks and of doves and of eating something other than rice boiled in rainwater. When the house's ground floor appeared thirteen hours later, she helped Pho sweep the stinking mud and three drowned chickens from his house while his wife burned incense to the river god.

That afternoon, Pho waded down to the open-air market and bought vegetables and more kerosene. Stefani went with him, sloshing through water that surged to her thighs and trying not to think of snakes. She watched shoe salesmen hose the mud out of ladies' pumps and men's sneakers; she watched hawkers sell plastic ponchos and tourists film the wreckage with Baggies strapped over their video lenses. The corpses of the drowned were beginning to surface. Children sold chewing gum and the more enterprising cyclo drivers charged journalists ten bucks apiece to view the dead bodies.

Later, she pressed two hundred and six dollars—all the hard currency she had—into Pho's palm and pulled her backpack onto her shoulders.

She fought her way onto a public bus and traveled south at a snail's pace, back to Da Nang, the only airport within reach that possessed a jet-length runway and a connecting flight to Bangkok. The trip usually took three hours; she stifled in the bus for ten. The narrow highway was still drowned under a yard of water. To the right she spied the railway line, whole sections of track torn off and dangling. There were rumors of passengers stranded for days in the packed train cars.

"Not your usual suite," Mr. Rewadee said now as he threw open the door, "but exactly like it in every particular. I've placed a bottle of Bombay Sapphire and several of tonic at the bar, along with some limes."

There were four rooms on two levels: a breakfast area near the pale green sofa, the bedroom and teak-lined bath up a short flight of stairs. Kumquats flushed orange in a porcelain bowl. She knew, now, that seven people could survive for days in a space eighty feet square. Maybe she should invite all of Bangkok in for a party.

"Mr. Krane has called several times," Rewadee observed delicately. "I would be happy to inform New York that you have arrived—"

"I left two suitcases with the bellman over a month ago."

Mr. Rewadee bowed.

"I'd like them brought up right away. Also a cheeseburger and a beer. And could you book me a massage for this afternoon?"

One entire wall of the room was glass. Stefani tugged open the raw silk curtains, saw the long-tailed boats churning across the River of Kings—and leaned her forehead against the window. Just what she needed. A view of the water.

"Welcome back to the Oriental, Ms. Fogg." Her personal butler held out a silver tray with a glass of orange juice and a copy of *The New York Times*.

Stefani Fogg was thirty-nine years old. She had a slight frame that encouraged most people to think she was frail. She was a pretty woman with the face of a pixie: like her body, it was a face calculated to deceive. Under the fringe of jet-black curls her brown eyes were assessing and shrewd.

"Wharton School," Oliver Krane had murmured over lunch at his corporate headquarters in Manhattan seven months before; "and prior to that, Stanford. I can see you in California, Stef—but *Philadelphia*?" He consulted no résumé; it was his habit to remember everything. The most secure intelligence network in the world, Oliver Krane liked to say, was the human brain—provided it was properly handled. "Iconoclast. You did the Lauder Program instead of a Harvard MBA. I like that about you; you never quite run to form. You speak German, I understand? Although you're said to prefer Italian."

She shrugged. "Better wine."

"Pity you didn't work up some Russian. Or Chinese."

"But then I wouldn't be just another pretty face, Oliver."

"Balls," he'd retorted sharply. "You don't run a fund for a major investment house—and get a seventy-eight percent return over five years—with just another pretty face."

He peered at her forbiddingly through his tortoise-shell glasses.

"I want you for Krane's, Stefani, and I'm willing to bet I've an offer you won't refuse."

"That's your job, isn't it?—predicting the level of risk?"

Oliver had done his homework, of course; he knew the precise extent of Stefani's personal holdings. Something under eleven million dollars in various funds; an eight-room co-op on Central Park; a summer place in Edgartown; a ski condo in Deer Valley. He would know that mere money wasn't enough to scuttle her present job. She'd had money for years: she found it boring.

The walls of the small dining room were lined with cobalt blue velvet. Only one table—theirs—was placed in the center of the maple floor. The view from the fifty-fourth story was blocked by sheer silk curtains that shifted under the eye like seawater; a screen, no doubt, for Oliver's varied electronics.

He had given her sushi, tempura prepared at the table, a fan of fresh vegetables and a glass of Screaming Eagle. When she had refused a passion-fruit flan, the head of the firm leaned across the table and ticked off his points in a voice that sounded pure BBC, though it was probably born in Brixton.

"Point the First: Stefani Fogg when she's at home. Likes to describe herself as bright but shallow. Raised comfortably in Larchmont, Princeton, Menlo Park. Father a chemical researcher and large-animal veterinarian. Mother rather determinedly hip. She's a clever girl, our Stef, but gun-shy where commitment is concerned. No lover, no child, not so much as a small white dog for messing the carpet with. Appears to choose men by their shirt size rather than their IQs—the odd fitness instructor or bartender, a hapless musician. In the past seven years, no relationship longer than four months.

"Frequently described by the admiring epithet of *bitch*. Roughly translated: she has committed all the sins available to a woman in a man's world. Restless, impatient, ruthless, ambitious. Sole weakness a reckless streak you could drive a semi through. Two hundred years ago, she'd have been burned at the stake as a witch.

"Point the Second: Stefani Fogg rumored to have turned down the chairmanship of FundMarket International last year, when it was offered her on a plate. Pundits confused.

"Point the Third: Stefani Fogg supposedly in play for CFO of at least three major multinationals, none of which succeeded in bagging her. Pundits agog.

"Point the Fourth: *Galileo Emerging Tech*—the fund Stefani Fogg manages at FundMarket—has lost nearly sixty-seven percent of its high-market value over the past three weeks. Rumors flying within Fund-Market and without: Fogg is slipping, Fogg is asleep at the wheel, Fogg will be out on her arse next Tuesday. Pundits immensely gratified."

He sat back in his seat and stared at her with satisfaction. "Missed anything?"

"About *Galileo*—" She toyed with the Screaming Eagle. "The tech market's volatile, Oliver. You want big returns, you run major risk. Sometimes that means short-term loss."

"And you've generally defied the odds, haven't you? So what's gone wrong this month?"

She didn't reply.

"I have a theory, old thing. I won't bother to ask whether you'd like to hear it."

"Well, you *did* give me lunch. I can spare you a few more minutes."

"Stefani Fogg is bored off her nut and desperate for fun," he suggested. "*Galileo* is sinking because Stefani no longer gives a diddly. I could offer the girl a spot of larceny or a fast plane to a desert island, and she'd snatch them both out of my moist little palm. Any sort of diversion would do, provided it were dangerous enough. She's toyed with electronic fraud, with faking her own death, with ripping off Tiffany's in a cat suit at midnight—but the payoff is never quite worth the risk. Our Stef knows that crime, however *séduisante,* can rather get one's hair mussed. Crime carries with it a measure of annoyance. There's the enforcement chappies, of course; there are turf battles between kingpins she doesn't even know, potentates she could easily offend. There's the possibility of maiming or a sordid public death. Our Stef's looking for bigger game. A challenge to match her peculiar wits. Am I right? Have I hit the target bang-on?"

She had gone quite still, watching him. He was a mild-looking man in his late forties: slim, loosely tailored in medium gray wool, his fair hair clipped short over the temples and rakishly long at the brow. The tortoise-shell glasses partially concealed caramel-colored eyes. Altogether a sleek kind of cat, his tail practically twitching as he surveyed her. He *had* done his homework.

"So you have the antidote to boredom, Oliver. What could you possibly offer that I need or want?"

"Fun, intrigue and high jinks on six continents," he shot back promptly. "A floating bank account accessible at all times for expenses that will never be questioned. Counsel from the main office whenever you want it, but no handcuffs or second guesses or attempts to drive your car from the rear. An unwritten brief. A handful of clients. Stimulation. A direct line to my desk, night or day. Gut decisions. Unlimited spa time in exotic places. *Power*."

"To do what, exactly?"

"Beat crooks at their own game. Much more exciting than joining them, I always think. Spy and seduce and manipulate empires—all in the name of defending commerce. With your talent and brains, Stef, you could write your dossier."

"But why *me*, Oliver? Why the bitch with the lousy returns?"

"Because they'll never see you coming, darling," he answered softly. "You're a bloody great gold mine. Smart and chic and too damn bored with your own wealth to be corruptible. You'll have your teeth sunk into their jugulars before they even catch your scent." His tawny eyes flicked across her face with brutal candor. "And there's the added advantage that I can *deny* you, ducks. As far as the world of High Finance is concerned, we've never even traded so much as an air kiss. I'm not offering you a title and a desk with a plastic nameplate. I don't want you on Wall Street. I want you bumming around the world on extended holiday."

"Anonymity and carte blanche," she mused. "A high-wire act without a safety net. If I fail, I fail alone."

"Where would the challenge be, otherwise?"

A silence fell between them.

"Don't refuse me before you've had ages to think," Oliver suggested. "It wouldn't be the first time a woman's done that, I admit—but for you, I'm willing to wait."

"Until *Galileo* craters?"

He smiled, and pressed an invisible button under the table. A waiter appeared within seconds, on soundless feet.

"You've had the glamorous turn, old thing." Oliver's voice was like a croon. "You've had the usual stiffs in the Wall Street clubs with their fast cars and limp members. Now you want to run with the wolves. Don't you? *Confess* it."

Krane & Associates was the foremost practitioner of a singular discipline known as risk management. The ignorant called it a security firm; the desperate called when any form of shit hit the most delicate type of fan. Krane offered all the usual security measures available to corporate clients—bodyguards, armored cars, internal surveillance and Internet monitoring. But these were mere party favors Oliver Krane tossed to the unwitting. Krane's true worth—the commodity that had brought the Forbes Five Hundred to their knees—was that he knew more about everything than anybody on earth. He had ears to the ground in Jakarta and Shanghai and Hampstead and Miami, he sold information to the highest bidders in Hong Kong and Dubai. Oliver screened private jets for sophisticated bugs, gave drug tests and polygraphs to suspect employees, retrieved information from computer drives that were supposed to have been erased, found fraud in the ledgers of the most venerable corporations.

Oliver took pictures of remote deserts from private overhead platforms. Oliver tracked arms shipments through gray networks. He could listen to lovemaking at a distance of two thousand miles, and sometimes did. Give him thirty-six hours, and Oliver Krane could detail every secret your competitors had purchased from your most loyal employees, and exactly how much they had paid for them.

His corporate motto was blunt: *Krane. Because what you don't know can kill you.* What he ran, in essence, was a crackerjack intelligence organization publicly traded on the New York Stock Exchange.

He was persistent in his patience, as Stefani learned over the next few weeks. He sent her birds-of-paradise in art-glass vases with smart-ass cards that were never signed. He sent her manila envelopes stuffed with newspaper clippings and transcripts of cellular communications and internal financial audits. He sent photographs of dubious personalities and a few cryptic leads in the research campaign she was conducting into his private life. Tidbits and come-ons and clues she couldn't resist—but he never sent them directly. They appeared on the seat of a taxi she had just flagged down, or folded into her morning paper. Once she was handed a spreadsheet with her oysters in the old bar at Grand Central Station. She knew she was being followed—surveillance was child's play for Oliver Krane—and the knowledge aroused her. She liked the thought of moving under a watcher's eye. She began to dress each morning with Oliver in mind.

More important, she examined Krane's stock as though it were under consideration for inclusion in *Galileo*, measuring its performance against those few risk-management competitors she could find in the marketplace. She researched Krane's corporate hierarchy and its promotion record for female employees; gathered press pieces from on-line databases that recounted Krane's most sensational cases; and checked to see what litigation the company currently battled. Her final gesture was to invite an old friend from Wharton for dinner. She respected Darryl Bainbridge—he ran a private investment firm for elite clients worth billions. He'd hired Krane the previous year to find an electronic embezzler among his handful of brokers.

When she asked Bainbridge what he thought of Krane & Associates, he cocked his head at her before replying. "Best-kept secret in the United States, but not for long. Buy all the stock you can—and keep it for yourself."

Oliver Krane's approach was unorthodox, and in a calmer frame of mind, she might have questioned why. Krane pursued her in the only way guaranteed to catch her interest: he titillated and teased, feinted and attacked. She began to test the city streets four times a day, smoking cigarettes she didn't really want in the vast granite doorway of FundMarket International. Nothing she could find in the office was half so intriguing as what might appear in the hands of a street vendor.

*   *   *

On the eleventh day following their private lunch, contact came in the form of an issue of *Ski* magazine and the Michelin guide to the French Alps. The section on Courchevel had been marked with a hot pink Post-it note.

This one has your name all over it, ducks.

Oliver's cramped scrawl.

A downhill racer tore across the glossy magazine cover, body crouched into the fall line. Above him rose a sheer headwall of black granite dusted with a filigree of white. Stefani frowned. She had skied enough—at Deer Valley and Gstaad and Kicking Horse—to know she was looking at a professional, and a rather famous one at that.

Max Roderick.

He'd won gold and acclaim at three different Olympics during the past two decades. He was known for hurling himself down World Cup courses with what looked like total disregard for his own neck and was in fact a calculated assault with a hairsbreadth margin of error. The press loved the way he clipped slalom gates so deliberately with his rigid shoulders and set his edges in a curve that would snap a lesser man in half. The media played up his effortless grace and tried to crown him king. But Roderick made it politely clear he didn't give a damn whether the cameras followed him or not. He abandoned Beaver Creek and the U.S. Ski Team for Austria; he trained alone. He granted few interviews. If he chased any women on either continent, he did it in places the press couldn't reach. He rarely drank and he went to bed early. Eventually the press got tired of Max Roderick—of a silence and a discipline they could not understand—and Roderick went on winning.

Stefani flipped through the magazine. *A skier's skier brings his knowledge to bear on the tools of the downhill trade. . . .* Roderick was retired, now, and living in Courchevel, where he'd won Olympic gold at Albertville in '92. He designed high-performance boards for a famed French manufacturer.

She glanced for a moment at the shot of his face, taken in the flat gray light of February, all color leached to monochrome and the angle of bone and landscape sharper for it. A palpable impression of intensity: eyes piercing and clear, with deep creases at the corners from years of staring at the sun. White-blond hair tousled by a ski helmet. The skin tanned and tough. It was a handsome face—one that had known pain, found it irrelevant, and pushed on.

Of course the press loved him. But he was not her usual type, Max Roderick. Loners made her nervous.

... appears to choose men by their shirt size rather than their IQs ...

She tossed the magazine into the trash.

Two hours later, she called Oliver Krane on his private line and demanded dinner.

Alone now in her elegant room at the Oriental, Stefani Fogg slid her filthy body into water so hot she winced. The first bath in nearly a week. She closed her eyes against the steam and the sharp bite of eucalyptus. And allowed herself, all her careful defenses down, to remember.

2

So what's wrong with Max Roderick, Oliver?"

Dinner that early spring evening six months ago was Indonesian takeout served on a linen-draped wrought-iron table in the walled garden of a five-story town house somewhere in the East Sixties. Stefani doubted that Oliver actually lived there—the place was devoid of such personal betrayals as photographs or magazines with address labels— but he moved from kitchen to terrace with such confident ease that it was clear he knew the house well. She imagined he kept a shifting roster of private haunts, visiting them as a lesser man might visit a series of mistresses; and indeed, wives and entire families could furnish the most obvious of them, without having any clear connection to Oliver at all.

In the past five days, she had determined that Oliver Krane's life was deliberately elusive and all but indistinguishable from his attractive camouflage. The background checks and financial histories she'd run had turned up conflicting story lines. One suggested he had been born in London and educated at a lesser British public school before reading law at Oxford; another, that he had once been named Czenowski and was pursued in his salad days by KGB recruiters; her favorite, that he was a foundling left at a Catholic orphanage who graduated from picking pockets in Bombay to dealing heroin in Hong Kong. In Oliver's fiction Stefani caught the scent of his fears and dreams.

"Max Roderick found himself smack in the middle of a sordid little murder a few weeks ago," Oliver informed her over a slice of pickled mango. "Our Max trotted off to Geneva to talk up the Swiss on the matter of skis, and damn if he doesn't find a pretty young thing sprawled in his bed one morning, strangled and no mistake. She was a Thai bar girl from the red-light district and all of fifteen. Max maintains that he had never set eyes on the girl and has no idea how her corpse ended up in his room."

"But she was in his *bed*."

"In a sequined thong, no less," Krane agreed complacently as he set out satay skewers like burnt offerings on a celadon plate. "When Roderick stepped into the bath at six-ten that morning, no strangled young thing where she ought not to be. When he appeared in his towel nine minutes later, there was the dead girl in the altogether. Superb skin and hair. I've seen the photos. Tragic."

"So he's claiming he was framed? That someone else murdered her? Do you believe his story?"

"I believe nothing I have not proved for myself. And yes, that includes the existence of God—Pascal notwithstanding."

"But is Roderick the sort of guy who'd hire a whore? Much less kill her?"

Oliver shrugged. "I know quite little about the man beyond the usual paparazzi pap. Max lives alone—the last woman in his life left him abruptly two years ago and sued for damages. No one has taken her place. Rumor also has it that Max took a mental dive when he failed to qualify for the '98 Olympics—and that he's been searching for his soul ever since. Physically, he's capable of strangling an adolescent. Whether he's *emotionally* likely to do so . . ."

"Have you met him?"

"Once."

"And?"

"He's attractive enough, though rather guarded—used to keeping people at arm's length. Difficult to read, as a result. But—"

"What?"

"He struck me . . . as a man in the grip of an obsession."

"About . . . ?"

Oliver shook his head. "That's just it, heart. I'm not entirely sure."

"Was he charged with murder in Geneva?"

"No. His personal lawyer—an old chum from the World Cup Circuit named Jeffrey Knetsch—ensured that the business was tidied up and presented by the Swiss police as a gross misunderstanding. Max was allowed to toddle home in all the sanctity of innocence. What are friends for?"

"I can't believe the Swiss police are pushovers."

"Nor are they," Oliver admitted judiciously. "They confessed that the case presented certain . . . irregularities. Even Max insists that the door to his bedroom was locked when he entered the shower that morning, which contradicts his protestations of innocence; but anybody possessed of ingenuity might have found a way to circumvent the electronic code."

"Is that what Max suggested?"

"His lawyer did. I shan't weary you with a recital of the hotel uproar and the subsequent investigation. Suffice it to say that the Swiss police applied latex lifts to the girl's neck and found not a single fingerprint. Her murderer wore gloves. No gloves anywhere in Roderick's room. Police reckon that if Max got rid of the gloves, he might as well have got rid of the body. Never mind that one's a trifle larger than the other; the elevator shaft adjacent would have done in a pinch. And why go to the trouble to suggest a crime of passion and then premeditate it down to the gloves? If Max was coldhearted enough to plan the whore's demise, he would hardly lose his head and discover the body next morning in his own room. Disordered thinking, what? Swiss can't abide that."

"A hotel employee ought to have seen her enter."

"Service lift," he supplied promptly. "Employees paid off. Wee hours of the morning. Probably already dead when she rolled down the hall on a breakfast tray."

"Can they trace Roderick to the girl's bar?"

"Of course. Roderick's Swiss clients took him there for a spot of fun after the day's meetings. An hour into the show, Max got bored and went back to his hotel. End of story—or Max's version of it."

"Oliver—if Max didn't kill the girl, who did?"

He gazed at her owlishly. "Don't admit, old thing, that you're jumping ship! You're never going to sell FundMarket down the river and throw in your lot with Krane?"

"I'm just interested in the story, that's all."

"Not good enough, ducks. Put out or get out."

She crushed a leaf of cilantro between her thumb and forefinger. A pungent scent, half pepper, half rain-wet asphalt. "Say I was considering a move . . ."

"That's why we're dining in this chummy fashion, I presume."

"Would I be working on Roderick?"

He rolled his eyes. "Have I said anything to suggest that the man is of interest to my firm? Krane's *never* deals in murder. Not the personal kind, at least."

"But is murder really the point?"

"Got it in one, Stef. Ever been to a shooting box in the Central Highlands? Walks along the loch? Salmon fishing? A round of bagging pheasant?"

"No. Why?"

"Thought you might look jolly well in oilskins, that's all."

"Oliver—"

His gaze turned bland, suggestive of the angelic.

"You sent me *Ski* magazine, Oliver. My name's written all over it, your note said."

"Something decorative to stick in your loo, darling, nothing more." He thrust his hand into the depths of the takeout bag and withdrew a sheaf of paper and a black pen. "Now, if you were to sign on the dotted *line* . . ."

Stefani frowned. "A contract? Somehow that seems . . ."

". . . Overly binding? Touchingly archaic?"

"I expected an electronic print of my voice pattern. A computer chip embedded in my scalp."

"We'll come to those," he said soothingly. "I *like* contracts, darling. Paper suggests history, somehow—the Inns of Court, the Magna Carta. The English bourgeois *will* rear his leonine head, despite all the money spent on Italian suiting. And besides—the payroll department insists. Something to do with the Internal Revenue Service. Your Social Security number, if you please."

"You've known it for ages," she said dryly.

"But I want it in *your* handwriting." He exited to the kitchen with a tray full of food. Whistling.

She scanned the contract. From its idiosyncrasies, she judged that Oliver had drafted the language himself. She was afforded full access (through Oliver) to Krane's staggering array of security resources without the slightest public affiliation, until such time as she and Oliver mutually agreed to disclose her employment. Her salary, a modest 1.5 million dollars per annum, was to be wired monthly to bank accounts of her naming. Oliver had elected to pay her exactly half a million more than her pre-bonus salary at FundMarket, she noted wryly. She could be terminated immediately at his discretion, with the benefit of a year's pay. True to his word, he had given her enough freedom and rope to hang herself several times over.

"You want a secret agent," she murmured, as he reappeared with a glass of wine. "Don't you?"

"I find, heart, that the cost of excellence is a certain amount of fame. I do my job too well. Any number of nasties and ghoulies can track my people coming and going. For this job, I need someone who's clean."

"Because a hooker died on Max Roderick?"

He did not reply.

"Who hired you, Oliver? The Swiss? Or Roderick himself?"

"Use the pen, old thing," he said gently. "The *paper*."

"You think I'm going to turn my back on all the security I've forged at FundMarket in the past four years? Walk away, just like that?" She snapped her fingers under Oliver's nose.

"No," he admitted. "I think you'll *run*."

"You flatter yourself."

He was whistling again, a hiss of air between his teeth. "I notice your pet *Galileo* is sinking further into the NASDAQ swamp."

Galileo. God, she was bored with *Galileo*.

Stefani uncapped the pen and scrawled her name on the contract. Boredom was the one sin she never forgave herself. "Now tell me who hired you."

"The Thai government, I think." Oliver said it doubtfully. "Though with the Thais, one can never be sure. Devious little beasts, behind their smiles."

"Surely they're not concerned about a prostitute murdered on a different continent."

"Particularly when they or their assigns might be responsible for killing her," he added pensively.

Her head came up at that. "Your clients? You think the Thai government may have set Roderick up? But what does an American skier resident in France have to do with Thailand?"

"Precisely what I asked Max when he rang me two days ago. He's also decided to hire Krane's, you see. Or rather, he's hired *you*."

A jolt of feeling shot through her like an arrow. Excitement? Fear? "—I being not *precisely* Krane?"

"Not yet," Oliver agreed cheerfully, "and not so's the Thais will ever notice, God willing."

"What am I expected to do?"

"Recover a fortune. Max believes he's owed one. The Thais disagree."

"And you've been hired to establish the truth of their claim?"

"Precisely. Spot of forensic accounting. Old hat."

Her shrewd brown eyes swept his face. "Are you also being paid to discourage Roderick?"

Oliver adjusted his spectacles with an air of distaste. "I am not a *thug*, my sweet, although on occasion I have employed them. At the moment, I've decided to employ *you*."

"You think I can get Roderick to take his ski boots and go home to France?"

"On the contrary! I hope you'll follow him right down into the crevasse."

She allowed Oliver to consume a remarkable quantity of Indonesian curry—to talk of Venice and the art trade in Stockholm and his favorite anchorage at Bitter End—while the sky overhead blackened to navy and the first warm wind of spring stirred the dead leaves. The roar of traffic throbbed beyond the enclosed terrace like a massive bloodstream. Stefani pulled a silk sweater about her shoulders and warmed her fingers at the candle flame. Oliver poured her a third glass of wine.

"What kind of fortune is the ski champ hunting?"

"A priceless Southeast Asian art collection, presently housed in

Bangkok's most elegant little museum. The museum itself is at issue, I might add."

"And why does Roderick care?"

"Something to do with blood, I imagine." The cool eyes were locked on hers. "Know anything about friend Max? Beyond the ski-circuit chatter, I mean?"

"You would hardly have hired me if I came with predispositions toward the case."

Oliver sighed. "Too bloody smart for your own good. Of course I knew you weren't acquainted with the man. He's not your type."

She shrugged.

"And yet . . . curiously compelling. So austere and shining in his self-isolated perfection, he's like the north face of the Eiger to an Aryan Youth: something to be scaled. Smashing muscle tone. You want to strap on your crampons and climb all over him, Stef. Admit it."

"The fortune, Oliver."

"Max Roderick is the last of a line of rather daring chaps who suffered difficult ends. His father, Rory, flew bombing runs over North Vietnam and died in the Hanoi Hilton. His grandfather was a true legend in Southeast Asia—an adventurer, a potentate, a glamorous rogue. Jack Roderick. He trained with the OSS during the Second World War then settled permanently in Bangkok in '45."

Stefani's eyes narrowed. "To do what?"

"Run agents for the CIA," Oliver replied carelessly. "Jack Roderick was Bangkok intelligence chief right after the war. Took to the people, the food, the khlongs like a duck. Found God a few years later and abandoned spies for Thai silk—he's credited with reviving the craft there. Started a company called Jack Roderick Silk, still famous the world over. Made a great deal of money. Bought or stole every Khmer antiquity on offer during the course of twenty-odd years. Stored them in his house—an antique itself, shipped down-river from the ancient capital of Ayutthaya—and when he disappeared one day without a trace, the Thai government seized the lot."

"Disappeared?"

"Like so much smoke," Oliver assured her. "Jack Roderick went on holiday to the Cameron Highlands—old British hill station in Malaysia— and took a stroll around cocktail time, all by himself. Never came back. Body never found."

The same surge of feeling—fear? excitement?—knifed through her again. "When was this?"

"Easter Sunday, 1967."

"The height of the Vietnam War."

"Hanoi declared son Rory dead two weeks after Roderick disappeared. No obvious connection."

"And his entire fortune was—seized?"

"The Thai government claims Roderick always meant to leave his personal collection to the people of Thailand. He'd burbled on about it quite often, apparently. His will—or should I say, his *first* will—provided for just that." Oliver smiled. "They're quite proud in Bangkok of having preserved the Roderick house and gardens—the whole kit and caboodle, including books on a bedside table—just as it was when he vanished in '67. Jack Roderick's House is now a major tourist attraction."

"And his grandson wants . . . what? Financial compensation? Or the collection returned?"

"Our Max wants everything, ducks. That's his opening bid. Everything that belonged to his grandfather returned with interest. Max claims, you see, to have found Jack's second will. Quite recently. The will leaves the estate to the Roderick heirs, and the lawyers are calling it good."

She expelled a deep breath. "Hence the Thai prostitute in Max's Geneva hotel room. A warning from your precious clients: Back off, Golden Boy, or you'll be mauled."

"If we believe Max's version of events," Oliver rejoined gently. "Which I'm not sure we do."

"Why should a bunch of American lawyers strike fear in the hearts of the Thai government, thirty-five years after Jack Roderick's disappearance?"

"Dunno. That's not my end of the deal, heart—it's *yours*." He was studying his chopsticks.

Stefani tossed back the last of her wine. "You talk about these clients as though they were a corporate entity. Whom do you really mean?"

"That," Oliver returned, "I cannot tell you. Compartmentalization is the first rule of warfare. Less said, the better for all of us."

"So you've arranged for me to work *against* Krane & Associates, on the basis of no investigative experience and partial information?"

"You're not the *enemy*, Stefani. You're just tackling one end of this naughty little problem while I manipulate the other. Experience is overrated, you know."

"I'd have to be mad to accept such an offer."

"You already did." A fingertip grazed her cheek, fleeting as a wasp's sting.

3

Krane & Associates engineered her downfall. That was part of her cover story—the complete disintegration of her public life, the end of Stefani Fogg as Wall Street knew her.

"I promised Max you'd arrive in Courchevel in a week," Oliver Krane mused. "That gives us very little time. It shall have to be Monday, I'm afraid."

Stefani arrived for work rather late that Monday and paid scant attention to the multibillion-dollar fund she was allegedly managing. She spent considerable time chatting up old friends on the phone and took a very long lunch. Then she pled an afternoon meeting with clients and went shopping at Bergdorf's. Oliver had mentioned Scotland. She figured she'd need some boots.

Two hours later she arrived back at her office with a Persian lamb coat, four pairs of shoes, and a hatbox dangling from her wrist. Sterling Hayes, the chairman of FundMarket International, was waiting for her.

"Stefani."

She had always despised Hayes—not simply for his expression, which was cadaverous, but for the caution that compelled him to wear braces embroidered with foxes and hounds.

"Sterling!" she cried gaily. "It's been *ages*! What can I do for you?"

He did not shut her office door, but stood uneasily before her desk like a paid mourner. "I've been talking to Oliver Krane."

She frowned. Set down the boxes and bags. "That awful pseudo-Brit with the security service? He went public last year, right? How's his stock doing these days?"

"I retained Oliver Krane thirty months ago when I took over the chairmanship," Hayes informed her dryly. "Krane designed the architecture of FundMarket's security system. It's highly sophisticated. We track electronic trades. Screen employee e-mail. Record phone conversations."

Stefani kicked off her shoes, opened one of the boxes and pulled out a pair of brown suede boots. "Yeah? So?"

"Stefani—" He hesitated, his eyes on her feet. She was wearing houndstooth stockings, expensive and transparent, a checkerboard haze over instep and ankle. "We record every phone call. Every trade. We analyze the tapes for patterns on a daily basis. It's the best defense we've got. You understand, don't you?"

She glanced up at him. "What are you trying to say, Sterling?"

"This morning, Krane showed me his computerized records. He made the case that you've been trading on inside information, Stefani. For at least three weeks. You've been trying to beat the system."

An appalled silence.

"I understand the pressure—your reputation, the *Galileo* slide—"

"There must be some mistake," she cut in.

"Krane doesn't make mistakes. I've seen his data. I can't turn a blind eye, even for you. I can't risk the SEC breathing down my neck. You know that, Stefani. You have to go."

She sat motionless, one boot on, the other dangling. "Over my dead body. Who the hell is this bastard Krane, that he can suddenly fire a major player at FundMarket International?"

"He's the bastard we pay to keep us clean."

"To do your shit work, you mean," she slashed. "You can't just throw me out like a used condom, Sterling. Fuck Oliver Krane!"

Hayes glanced apprehensively at the trading room beyond Stefani's door. Heads had swiveled in their direction. "Please. For the good of the firm . . ."

". . . You want me to roll over? Not a chance in hell, buddy." Stefani tossed the suede boot to the floor and stood. "What's really going on? Did Krane lose too much money in *Galileo* and scream for my head?"

"This isn't about Oliver Krane," Hayes told her quietly. "It's entirely about *you*."

"Right," she retorted with a harsh laugh. "Me, and Sterling Hayes. The Board almost handed me your job last year—remember? The Board *loves* me. One phone call to the right desk, Sterling, and we'll see who's walking out the door—"

"Don't make that call," he said abruptly. "Not if you want to retain a shred of self-respect. I shared Krane's report with the Board an hour ago. I've received full support for your resignation."

She stared at him, aghast.

"And that's what I'm *demanding*, Stefani." His voice was suddenly clipped, the skin taut across the planes of his narrow face. "You've played the princess too long. You flaunt your money, you talk a crock of sunshine, but you're not worth the desk space we give you, little girl. Resign within the hour or I fire your ass tonight."

He turned on his heel. The entire group of traders—twenty-three people in all—had risen from their seats and were gawking at Stefani's face. She had gone pale with rage. She picked up a glass paperweight—a Steuben rock with a silver sword thrust through its middle—and hurled it at Hayes's retreating form. Somebody in the outer room ducked.

She collected the scattered Bergdorf's bags, stepped over the paperweight lying like so much crushed ice on the industrial carpet, and went.

It was inevitable that one of the traders would talk. Traders live for the few moments of high drama in each boredom-riven day; they snort gleefully over the bones and flesh scattered across the corporate field. By the time she had dumped her clothes at the co-op, squeezed in a workout, changed for the evening and swished some Scotch around her mouth, the buzz had hit the street.

The party she planned to attend that night—a celebratory launch at the Plaza for some dot-com's IPO—was filled with guys in business suits who'd done well at school and risen fast, the safe models patterned on Sterling Hayes. There were a few visionaries, too, in charcoal turtle-necks and wide pleated pants, flown in from the Pacific Northwest. A scattering of women correctly suited in jackets and skirts to the knee. Stefani wore a sleeveless sheath the color of paprika. It outlined every vertebra and muscle of her body.

Half the heads turned as she appeared in the doorway; most eyes lingered. The hum of conversation faltered, then resurged more firmly than before. She scooped a drink from a passing tray and wove her way into the room.

Some of them were polite and approached by the back door: *How is FundMarket, Stefani? Tired of* Galileo? *Any thought of a change?* She laughed uproariously and told them lies. She threw her arms around mere ac-quaintances, stepped on too many feet, spilled a drink down a currency trader's blouse, slid her hand into a distinguished banker's pocket. She swayed and guffawed and called Sterling Hayes every kind of insult, to anyone who would listen; and when enough time had passed and the room had cleared an arc around her tidal wake, she found herself face to face with the man himself.

He was standing next to Oliver Krane.

"Ah, Stefani," Hayes said. "Enjoying your newfound freedom? Per-haps you should thank Mr. Krane."

Stefani tossed the last of her Scotch into Oliver's face.

She had no friend to take her by the arm and haul her into a bath-room. No man to carry her home in his polished black Audi. No one in the entire room who cared about her enough to protect her from her-self, or from the *Wall Street Journal* reporter covering the event. By the time the management called a taxi and ladled her into the backseat, Stefani Fogg had committed suicide in public several times over. No one waved as the car pulled away.

On her doorstep twelve minutes later, she found a pint of her fa-vorite Italian gelato—hazelnut—misting gently in dry ice.

Bravo, ducks, applauded Oliver's note.

He'd tucked it into a first-class ticket for Heathrow on Virgin Atlantic, with a connecting flight to Inverness. She glanced at her watch. She had barely fourteen hours before takeoff.

And then, because she had paid a fortune for the co-op and all the privileges that went with it—because she was free of Sterling Hayes and FundMarket and *Galileo*—she threw the terrace door wide open and screamed good riddance to Manhattan from the balcony's ledge, forty-three stories above the street.

She settled down in front of the VCR with a videotape Oliver had sent her—old Olympic footage of Max Roderick—and the pint of gelato. She felt like she was back in grad school; but homework had never been this much fun.

"... the determination to *succeed is a constant spur to this young man who has survived the worst that life can deliver: the loss of his Navy pilot father to the Vietnam War when he was barely eight years old, and then the death of his mother, Anne, two years later—a victim of alcohol and drug abuse. If the young Max Roderick was scarred by loneliness, he hid it well—driving himself relentlessly down the toughest courses in the United States and Europe at an age when other boys are busy learning to drive . . ."*

The image was seductive: a slow-motion arc of body and steel gliding effortlessly along the fall line of a crystalline slope at Albertville. The 1992 Olympics. On this practice run staged for the American viewing audience, Max wore no helmet. His golden head glinted in the sunlight, and as he vaulted through the starting gate he seemed transported, as though this precipitous flight was all he needed of heaven and earth. The sonorous voice of the background narration struck just the right note: Max Roderick was noble, Max Roderick had survived unimaginable pain—Max Roderick was the supreme gift his generation could offer the world.

Max Roderick, just possibly, was a killer.

Stefani fast-forwarded to a section of the tape that showed Max at rest—munching on an apple in his coach's kitchen, joking with the man the network called his surrogate father. He must then have been thirty years old; he looked like a fresh-faced kid, the eyes clear and light, the profile predatory as a hawk's. Taut, honed, purposeful, ingenuous, in his fleece sweatshirt and jeans. Everybody's All-American.

"*. . . Joe DiGuardia practically raised Max Roderick from the time the young ski phenomenon entered his Lake Tahoe program in 1966. DiGuardia, who took bronze at Lake Placid in the Men's Downhill, is a tough and uncompromising master—but he loves Roderick like a son.*"

Cut to Joe DiGuardia swearing viciously at a figure half obscured by dense snowfall and a starting gate. DiGuardia carefully waxing a pair of skis. DiGuardia hugging Max at the Innsbruck finish.

And then, replayed for all time on the eternal screen, the Men's Downhill: Sarajevo.

His frame was whipcord taut, powerfully muscled, bent into a punishing crouch as he hurtled over the ice-covered course in the red, white and blue Lycra racing suit. He caught air at the summit of one slope, took the most punishing curve at top speed, nearly lost an edge. The commentators gasped. Stefani gasped with them. She knew the end of this story—she knew the end of all Max's famous races—but still, the pure drama held her. The single man plummeting down the sheet of ice as though intent on suicide. The precision. The control. The ruthlessness in every line of his body.

"And that," she breathed, as Roderick crossed the finish line and raised his arms in triumph, "is all that really matters. That's what your body reveals. You'll stop at nothing to get what you need."

"It's a minor problem in the scale of things," Oliver Krane said thirty-six hours later, as he stood staring out at the rain sheeting down over Loch Lochy. "Max Roderick's, I mean. A disputed inheritance. New will, old story; and the claim's unlikelihood of success, given the Thai property laws."

He was studying the mist roiling off the lake. The brooding expression on his face was unexpected and thus unsettling. He was neat and compact in a cashmere polo and baggy flannel trousers, his hands thrust into the pockets. Heavy clouds had thrown a gloom over four o'clock tea; what Stefani hadn't expected was the sudden blaze of sunlight that forked periodically through the leaden sky, firing the gorse and broom on the hills rising above the lake's far shore. In those moments of illumination, every drop of water suspended in the molten air gleamed like an astral body.

Oliver had met her at the airport that morning in the predictable Rover, a black one equipped with global positioning, a laptop with wireless e-mail and a sherry decanter. He had driven south to Inverlaggan House, fed her smoked salmon and oat cakes, ordered her to rest for at least an hour and then had met her in the library. Her small frame was curled into a chesterfield, the brown suede boots discarded. She was suffused with well-being, exultant to the core; Oliver was still brooding.

"Unless you're born and bred a Thai, you can never really *own* anything in that country," he told her. "Fixed assets, I mean. You only *think* you do. Just try carrying them across the border."

"So why did you take this matter on?"

He shrugged.

"Not good enough, ducks," she mocked. "Put out or get out."

"Quoting the master already?" He glanced over his shoulder with the swift calculation she had come to think of as essentially Krane. "I should probably have passed, if you must know. But for the one thing."

"You wanted Roderick's autograph?"

Oliver snorted and moved away from the window. He fell into a chair drawn up near the fire, its leather worn to a temperate softness. Unlike the town house where they had eaten dinner or the corporate offices in the urban aerie, these rooms actually felt like they belonged to Oliver.

"I've had a spot of trouble in Asia recently," he replied. "An accidental death. Or perhaps I should call it *unexplained*."

"Someone you knew?" Stefani asked. A spate of rain dashed against the narrow windows.

"A rogue, a deceiver, a friend and a silent partner. Harry Leeds. We were at school together, Harry and I. I won't tell you which. We started Krane's together: my brains—Harry's bucks. There was a rough patch in the early days, when Harry was too much of a barrister and I, too much a beggar man thief; but by the time we were both thirty-five we'd settled our differences and pooled our winnings. Harry played godfather to my Hong Kong office, kept a string of polo ponies, clamped most of Asia under a network of spies and electronic surveillance for which he was exceedingly well paid, and asked nothing further from life. I stalked the rest of the world by turns, hired proxies in places I couldn't be."

"Is Asia important to Krane's?"

The tawny gaze flicked over to hers. "It's our bread and butter, darling. Every likely lad with tuppence in his pocket wants a piece of mainland China. Without Krane's, they'd all be rooked inside of a fortnight.

You can sell anything these days in Tiananmen Square—wireless phones, soda pop, a fresh-killed chicken or your youngest sister. Commerce thrives, there's no police force to speak of and the law is entirely theoretical. But I stray from the point."

"Harry Leeds," Stefani said gently.

Oliver sighed. "When I first learned of Max Roderick's problem—the dead whore 'twixt the bedsheets—it was through one of my clients, Piste Ski, the French company for whom Roderick designs his pricey little boards. Piste Ski was keen to learn whether Max Roderick was framed for murder. They suspected blackmail—debts—some sort of extortion. Although Max was never charged, Piste Ski was afraid of bad press and wanted the truth about our Olympic boy before his golden touch turned to lead."

"—Trust being a virtue the French hold in low esteem." Stefani uncurled her legs from the chesterfield and crossed to the fruitwood commode where Oliver kept his single malts. "What did you discover?"

"I nosed around Geneva first. Put my Swiss ears to the ground and loosed my trained dogs. I covered the police's tracks and searched for anyone who might have seen Roderick with the dead girl. It never occurred to me, I will confess, that the entire hit was Thai. But inside of twenty-four hours, I heard the faintest whisper that someone might have financed the job out of Bangkok. So I contacted Harry."

Stefani turned and studied him intently. There was something in Oliver's manner that suggested the confessional, as though all the blithe spirits and giddy talk of the past several weeks had been a type of mania designed to hold him back from the abyss. She remembered the elusive Catholic orphanage that had popped up in his background story. Had he often needed to invent a priest?

"Of course you called Harry," she said evenly. "It was the obvious thing to do."

Oliver was studying the flames with an absorption he usually reserved for golf magazines. "I sent Harry a report of the killing and subsequent investigation—*mine,* not the Swiss police's—via secure fax. I know from the office logs that Harry received it. Four hours later he was lying dead under the front tires of a Kowloon taxi."

"Jaywalking?"

Oliver's caramel eyes skittered away from hers. "Harry never *walked* anywhere. His bloody great Jaguar was a point of pride. Symbol of Harry's prestige. He was a Hong Kong *taipan* of the old order."

The Scotch felt like crushed velvet on her tongue. "And what did the police say?"

"Something bland and polite and regretful and obscene," Oliver muttered. "I do not accept it. I do not accept accident in my part of the world."

She set down the glass. The rain had settled in over the gorse and the milling sheep; rain spat and fizzled in the darting hearth. The early northern dark was falling.

"You believe Harry was murdered because you queried him about Max Roderick? But he might have died for any number of reasons, Oliver. Gambling. Drugs. A man he shouldn't have crossed. Or a woman. There must be things you didn't know about him. There always are."

"Harry was no fool. He'd lived in Asia most of his life and he understood the risks of our job. At Krane's we're paid a hell of a lot of money to walk around with bull's-eyes on our backs. We've got the world's nasties in our sights, and they mean to take us out before we take them down. But in thirteen years of adventure and high jinks, old thing, Harry never once faltered the course. He was sublime."

And now the wind is whistling over your grave, Oliver Krane, and what worries you is your own fear.

But instead she asked: "Did Harry know Max Roderick? Or anyone in the Roderick family?"

"I have no idea. Harry's lips, regrettably, are sealed."

"Have you told Roderick about Harry's death?"

"I chose," Oliver replied with heavy emphasis, "to keep my cards close to my vest. The connection between the strangled whore and Harry's hit-and-run exists, for the moment, only in my head."

So Oliver did not quite trust Max Roderick either.

"Why was Harry in Kowloon that day?"

He ran a hand over the back of his sleek head—a restless, futile gesture. "God alone knows. Presumably there was someone he wanted to collar—an informant, a friend. I imagine he was asked to meet there, on foot—and that's the sort of mistake a novice would make, never Harry. Harry knew that when someone hands you a meeting, first thing you do is turn it inside out."

"But instead Harry went to Kowloon," Stefani mused, "which means he was off-guard. He didn't see trouble coming. He believed in the friend he was meeting."

"Right again."

"And you heard no more whispers out of Thailand?"

"The trail, as they say in the best spaghetti westerns, has unaccountably gone cold."

"Except that Max has come to Krane's for help, and you're sending me to France. Where all the trails begin?"

For the first time, Oliver smiled. "Bloody brilliant, Ms. Fogg. See why I wanted you for this job?"

4

They said nothing more about Max Roderick that evening and avoided the subject of him entirely the next day, because time was short and Oliver had a great deal to teach. There were the obvious things, like Krane & Associates' operations worldwide, which Oliver summarized between brisk gallops through the fields of Inverlaggan House that first misty, exhilarating morning. He sat his mount with the incalculable air of having been born to a life of privilege that Stefani admired and deeply suspected was chicanery. He talked incessantly but to the purpose—imparting so much information, in fact, that she was glad she had tucked a voice-activated tape recorder in the pocket of her field jacket. She made no mention of the device and had almost forgot it when, at the end of nearly two hours' ramble amid the rowanberries and the spear thistle, Oliver told her gently, "I'll have that tape now, old thing, if you don't mind. What you can't remember don't matter a fig; and homework never was your style." He tossed the tape, recorder and all, far out into the lake and led her back to the house for breakfast.

By lunch, she was swimming in detail. There were all the subtleties of forensic accounting and of hard-drive analysis and file retrieval—which she gathered were pet topics of Oliver's and far too complex to master in a matter of hours. He threw them at her while they hunted for trout, adjusting the angle of her pole and advising her alternately on coarse fishing and sheltering assets.

"If you're in debt to the world and the world wants payment," he advised, "have your best friend sue for a shocking amount. Better yet, have your ex-husband throw the book at you. Fail to answer the suit, and he'll get a healthy default judgment. Then you file bankruptcy and the bulk of your liquidated estate goes to your detested former spouse. A few weeks later he'll hand it all back as per your previous arrangement—minus a bagatelle of a handling fee. You shelter the remainder offshore. Brilliant little game, because it's simple and goes almost unnoticed—except by those of us who think like the crooks do."

In between riding and fishing lay all the small matters Oliver was determined to teach her: how to search a room for bugs, a car for explosives or the exterior of a building for video surveillance. How to fire a handgun, which Stefani had never done in her life and hardly expected to enjoy so much; how to shoot a camera disguised as a cellular phone while poring over suspect documents. How to detect infrared barriers and circumvent the more predictable forms of electronic security systems. Over a smoky single malt in the fire-lit library one rainy afternoon, Oliver showed her how a hostile handshake could steal her identity across the Internet waves, and how to prevent it from happening in the future. He gave her phone numbers, security numbers and names in code: mental keys to a whole series of Krane's rooms she might never unlock, with no notion of what lay behind their doors.

He even taught her, during a stint in his cavernous subterranean gym, how to fall into the arms of a would-be attacker and flip him onto his back with a force that drove the breath from his body.

"We'll have to leave switchblades for another time," Oliver said regretfully as he picked himself off the mat with a lithe spring. "I've no one whose neck I can put to the knife at the moment. You'll have to rely on the C-clamp."

The C-clamp, she learned, was a rigid cupping of the fingers in the shape of the letter C. When jammed, hard, against an assailant's Adam's apple and shoved upward, it was capable of killing a man in three seconds. Oliver declined the experiment, however.

"Use the mannequin," he instructed with an airy wave at a life-sized Ken doll dressed in the requisite black. The mannequin emitted a high-pitched, mind-grating signal akin to a triggered smoke detector, setting nerves on edge and adrenaline pumping. Just to shut the thing up, Stefani lunged, grappled and shoved for all she was worth. Ken toppled backward with a satisfying thud, her hand still dragging at his plastic windpipe. It was unfortunate, she thought, that she had been forced to silence the only other person she'd seen in days.

Inverlaggan House was empty of life except for themselves. This was technically impossible, of course—someone prepared Stefani's meals and tidied her room. But except for a distant figure she once glimpsed raking leaves, the Highlands landscape was stripped of casual acquaintance. Either Oliver preferred to live in the illusion that he was self-sufficient, or his staff was under strict orders to give her a wide berth. Was this for her safety—or theirs?

Like everything to do with Oliver Krane, the atmosphere of Inverlaggan House—part James Bond, part Bertie Wooster—intrigued and amused her in a way that nothing had for months.

Every evening she curled up in her massive four-poster bed with a daunting collection of facts about Max Roderick: one hundred forty-three pages of names, dates and events in a very public life. It was, she thought, like studying an issue of *People* magazine devoted entirely to one person. The researchers at Krane's had included photographs and video stills: Max as a boy of ten, dressed in a blue blazer that looked two years too small for him, standing with bowed head by his mother's open grave. There were few other mourners: but Joe DiGuardia, the eternal ski coach, had his hand on the boy's shoulder. Max as a gawky teenager, his smile forced and his right knee in a massive brace. And finally, a much older version, the features of the face sharpened and intensified by years of discipline: Max looking vaguely hostile as he stared down the camera lens.

She glanced at the caption: 1999. The waning days of his World Cup career, after the failure to qualify for the Nagano Olympics. He was strolling through Gstaad, arm in arm with a spectacular blonde in a silver fox coat. Suzanne Muldoon.

Stefani flipped through the dossier and found the woman's entry. *Muldoon, Suzanne*—the only real love in Max Roderick's life. A downhill skier ten years his junior. She had shared his sport, his passion, his bed, for three years—and self-destructed in a bruising fall during a World

Cup final at Innsbruck. Knee ligaments detached in four places. She had been flown directly to the Steadman-Hawkins Clinic in Vail, where surgical miracles were routinely performed; and then—disappeared.

Muldoon parted from Roderick in an acrimonious and public battle over culpability for her injuries, the Krane dossier noted. *She sued for damages, citing deliberate and reckless endangerment due to relentless pressure to train beyond her physical capabilities. The suit was settled out of court. Muldoon never skied competitively again.*

Stefani reached for a pad of paper and pen she kept on her bedside table, and wrote in jarring red ink: *What else does S. Muldoon know about Max? Will she talk? Why has he been alone ever since?*

The piercing gaze of a hawk haunted her dreams.

Krane had suggested, back in New York, that Stefani's Scottish interlude would be a sporting one, and despite the wealth of information he managed to impart, they spent most of each day outdoors, in the bracing chill of a Highlands March. The shooting box, as he called it, sat in the southern end of the Great Glen, a flooded rift valley that split the Central Highlands from northeast to southwest. The high lonely reaches above Loch Lochy were sparsely populated, barring the occasional hiker toiling through the glen. The place was as different from Manhattan as a place could be. Half of Oliver's purpose in bringing her to Scotland, Stefani guessed, was disorientation.

Inverlaggan had been built on a rise above the loch, some five hundred feet from the shoreline, with a clipped green terrace and a field of boulders strewn in between. It was a pre-Elizabethan edifice that resembled a castle more than a house, with crenellated battlements and a moat that had long since been drained and graveled. A tower house, Oliver told her, in Scottish parlance—a thirteenth-century keep that had grown wings during the Renaissance. It had witnessed the Jacobite defeat at Culloden, not forty miles to the north, and harbored Bonnie Prince Charlie during his flight to the Continent; and when the tartan and the bagpipe and the clans were banned as a result of that failed revolt, Inverlaggan passed to English owners. Allied soldiers were garrisoned in its fastness during the Second World War, but since then, the place had fallen into disrepair.

"This whole bit of country round about Loch Lochy was used

for commando training in the last war," Oliver said as he tramped down the wild western shore of the lake in his dark green Wellies. "There's a memorial to them in bronze over at the foot of Spean Bridge. Parachute drops, live ammo, stealthy raids by night—assassins and decoder rings. Perfect setting for Krane and Associates' corporate training center."

"Walt Disney could not have done better," Stefani agreed. "But why the Highlands? Are your people Scottish?"

"Good Lord, no!" he replied in tones of shock, and heaved her booted foot out of a boggy patch with one hand placed deftly at the elbow.

"The will," he said two nights later, as he handed her a few sheets of paper, "direct from Roderick's lawyer, Jeffrey Knetsch."

The first thing she noticed was the date: February 12, 1967. Jack Roderick had drafted his final testament a little over a month before he disappeared. She shuddered involuntarily. She had never written a will. She was certain she would die if she did.

The bequests were brief and to the point. A few minor monetary gifts to persons of multisyllabic Thai names that meant nothing to Stefani—a collection of Bencharong porcelain to *"my houseboy, Chanat Surian, in recognition of his faithful service"*—and three hundred shares of privately held stock in the Jack Roderick Silk Company to *"my beloved friends, the Galayanapong family."* Midway through the first page, the document came to the point.

I, John Pierpont Roderick, being of sound mind and body, leave the residue of my estate and all my worldly goods and chattels, including thirty percent of total shares in the Jack Roderick Silk Company ("the Estate") to my son, Richard Pierce Roderick. In the event that Richard Pierce Roderick predeceases me, the Estate shall go in equal parts to his heirs and assigns.

She glanced over at Oliver Krane. "Richard Pierce, I presume, was nicknamed Rory?"

"The traditional diminutive of Roderick. Correct."

"I thought he died *after* his father."

Oliver shrugged. "Who's to say? Jack Roderick wasn't declared dead until a full seven years after his disappearance. No one can fix the time or place our Jack slipped this mortal coil. But Rory's death was witnessed—by rather a lot of his flying buddies. So the Estate ought to have passed directly to Max."

"I see." Stefani frowned over the document in her hands. "But this will was lost for more than thirty years? And then just . . . resurfaced?"

"Jack Roderick's sister Alice, who must have been ninety if she was a day, died quietly in Delaware last year. Her grandchildren subsequently cleaned out the matriarchal attic. In an old mailing tube—the sort that's used for rolled pictures—they found the blueprints of a house. Jack's house in Bangkok. The will had been slipped between two elevation renderings. He must have dropped it on the pile of blueprints by mistake, and sent it on to his sister."

"He doesn't sound like the sort of man to do anything by mistake."

"He was the soul of deliberate cunning. A.B., Princeton Class of '28, then University of Pennsylvania for graduate work in architecture." Oliver would know Jack Roderick's date of birth, his Social Security number, lifetime traffic violations and each specific of his Decree of Divorce—no matter how long ago they had occurred. "Our Jack was something of a Brahmin. A trust-fund boy. Spent the Great Depression squiring socialites around the New York party circuit, then dove into the war and the OSS. Given the funds he started out with and his success in Bangkok, there should have been a tidy little sum awaiting his heirs. But at his death, there was exactly three hundred and twenty-seven dollars in his bank account, plus or minus a few cents. Odd, what?"

"Think he had an account offshore?"

"He left no instructions to that effect."

"Maybe they were lost, too." Frowning, she flipped to the will's final page, where the signatures stood out in bold black ink. Jack Roderick had got his witnesses, at least. In that respect the will looked valid. "Who are these people? George and Richard Spencer?"

"Pair of Englishmen. Father and son. Roderick hired George in the early fifties to man the Bangkok store, and the Spencers gradually acquired twenty percent of the shares."

"Who owns the rest?" Shares—the trading power of percentages—was something she understood.

"The weavers," Oliver told her.

"The Weavers?" she repeated blankly.

"Silk weavers. Entire families, usually, who produced the hand-loomed goods. Jack Roderick Silk is a cottage industry, you know—or was. That was Roderick's brainstorm: place the power of production into the hands of the artisans. Pay them for whatever they produced. Offer them shares in the total profits. Give them incentive to control their own industry. They called him the Silk King in Bangkok but he's a Bloody Pinko Communist to you, and don't you forget it."

"How is the stock presently disposed?"

"Most of the original weavers made fortunes, sold their shares and set up in direct competition with Jack Roderick Silk; the cottage system is defunct; the company is centrally organized. George Spencer is dead; son Dickie is President and Chairman of the Board of Directors and holds fifty-one percent of stock. Spencer *is* Jack Roderick Silk."

"Never gone public?"

"Too small-time."

She waved the papers in her hand. "So how much is this legacy worth to Max?"

"Zero," Oliver answered cheerfully. "The three-hundred-odd dollars is long gone. When the Thai government declared Jack Roderick dead in 1974, his silk shares reverted to the company. Old Man Spencer snapped them up. To tell you the truth—with the house and the art collection in the hands of the Thais, and the silk company in Spencer's control—I'm not sure what Max is fighting for."

"And yet—you describe him as a man in the grip of an obsession. What does he really want? His grandfather's house? Or the truth of what happened to Jack Roderick? And why are you so uncertain whether Max is capable of murder?"

"Call it respect for what is brutal in the blood," Oliver returned. "Jack Roderick—however charming, however patrician—lived and died by his wits. His son was beheaded at the hands of his enemies. Max is heir to both men."

Stefani thrust herself restlessly out of her chair and stood near the fire, her expression hidden by the fall of dark hair. "There's nothing in that will to cause murder. No reason to strangle a prostitute in a hotel bedroom. No reason to send your friend Harry to Kowloon and run him over with a taxi."

"Then perhaps those deaths have nothing to do with Max's Thai business," Oliver suggested. "But his sudden appearance in Bangkok a year ago, armed with his grandfather's last will and testament, coincided with a good deal of bloodshed."

She glanced at him swiftly. "You think someone wants Jack Roderick to stay dead?"

"Why else have him disappear?"

"That presumes the disappearance was deliberate, and not of his choosing," she countered. "The man walks down a driveway in '67. He might have got lost in the Malaysian jungle. He might have met a tiger and been devoured."

"But if the fact of his death is sufficient reason to murder two people *now,* after thirty-five years—"

"It wasn't a tiger and it wasn't the jungle. Oliver," she said bluntly, "what do you want me to do in Courchevel? Prove Max Roderick a murderer—or a saint?"

"I want you to live high and drink deep. I want you to hire the best goddamn house in the Three Valleys and live like the French *expect* wealthy Americans to live. Wear outrageous clothes. Throw parties for strangers. It's high season, ducks: ski your ass off. Invite Max for dinner and breakfast. He knows I'm sending you and he knows not to blow your cover."

"My cover?"

"You're an old friend. Or an ex-lover. A cousin's discarded wife. Be a one-night stand he picked up years ago in Austria, if you must—who's to know whether it's true or not, in the middle of the French Alps? But you are categorically *not* to behave as though Krane and Associates is on your mental map. To suggest as much might be deadly. Don't even call me unless you use a public box and this number"—he handed her a small slip of paper inscribed with his tiny handwriting—"and identify yourself as Hazel. Phones are the very *worst* where security is concerned."

"Hazel," Stefani said mistily. "Of all things. Like a fat old terrier snoring on the rug. I believe you've grown fond of me, Oliver."

"Hell, darling." He planted a kiss on her wrist. "I *invented* you."

5

Jacques Renaudie swept the snow from his stone doorstep that morning with deliberate strokes of his short, muscled arms, a cigarette dangling absently from the corner of his mouth. He wore a blue fleece vest over a wool sweater knitted two decades ago by his wife, who had decamped for Paris last summer in a desperate bid for all she had never possessed in youth. Jacques sent her money from time to time and washed the sweater himself when necessary and did not ask his wife when she might return. He was a methodical man with a thatch of grizzled hair and a coarse-skinned nose. Although it was already past eight o'clock, he had not yet shaved. He had drunk heavily of schnapps the previous evening—a foul liquor he would never have touched had his wife been snug in the room upstairs. A faint odor of charcoal from the bar's open fireplace still clung to his skin.

Jacques's eyes were very blue and they were focused now on the hard, bright crystals at his feet. It had snowed during the night—dry powder, a near-perfect fall despite the lateness of the season—but he was considering not the untracked *pistes* of the Sommet de la Loze above him but his youngest daughter, who was destined like her mother for unhappiness. He had slept fitfully after closing his bar at two A.M., and by six o'clock in the morning when he gave up the battle, and rose with aching head to make coffee and send his ancient Bernese out into the drifts, Sabine had not yet returned from the party in Courchevel 1850. It would be that Austrian, Jacques decided—the young star of the ski team who had taken gold at Salt Lake, a boy with the slow stupid grin of all those who are named Klaus. Sabine would make a fool of herself just to prove she had value in *some* racer's eyes, even if it was not the one she really wanted. Jacques spat suddenly into the new snow and raised his eyes from his stoop.

It was then he saw the blond-haired man riding the platter lift up the length of Le Praz's main street, his gear strapped to his back and his helmet in his hand. Out of bitterness Jacques stood motionless, the broom idle, debating whether he should call out to this one, who was up before all the others in that exhausted town. He might offer him coffee. He might ask for the truth about Sabine and the Austrian named Klaus. But he knew Max Roderick would already have taken what was sufficient for the morning, and would refuse the day-old bread in Jacques Renaudie's larder. Max did not linger in doorways, growing cold when he might be skiing. He saved his conversation for the longer twilight of spring and summer, when the Haute Savoie emptied of the hungry-faced women from New York and Paris with their flowing fur coats, their brass-colored hair. By May the door to Max's workshop high on the hillside stood ajar each afternoon, and the effort of a hike through the meadow and wildflowers was rewarded with cold beer from the barrel he kept in the stone cellar of his old Savoyard farmhouse. There was a time when Sabine herself had begged to accompany Jacques, with no greater reward in view than to study Max's bent head in silence as he manipulated the images on his design screen.

To see him thus, profile turned toward the summit, new-minted skis making twin tracks through the powder, was a source of relief. The rumors, Jacques thought, must be wrong. Max had strapped a pack to his back along with a length of rope, a small ice pick and an avalanche beacon; he was intending, then, to venture off-*piste*. Risky, perhaps, so late in the ski season; the winter had been unusually mild, and the cornices in the high peaks trembled in sunlight, the avalanche cannon boomed at dawn and the thunder of sudden snow slides roared through the town most afternoons. Nothing Max had not heard before.

Jacques shrugged at nobody in particular—perhaps an image of his wife he still carried in his mind. If Max Roderick was in the very midst of Le Praz by eight-fifteen, then he had already shot five hundred meters down the length of Jean Blanc from his home in Courchevel 1850. Nobody but a true man of the Alps skied so purposefully, and with so much gear, at this hour of the morning. Unless . . .

Unless Max had spent the previous night in Le Praz itself, and was only now crawling back toward Courchevel 1850 and home. And what was more likely? Jacques's expression darkened. Max Roderick would never take the *piste* into Le Praz if he intended to ski the backcountry, as his gear suggested. Had he awakened in his stone house in the early hours of morning, and glanced at the fresh powder blanketing the peaks, nothing would have kept him from the tram that led to the heights of Saulire, the tricky demanding couloirs and the broad, flat bowls where he loved to test his skill and exhaust his strength.

Jacques watched Max disappear from sight, feeling a flare of rage toward the man. It was only a matter of time before Max abandoned Courchevel like all the rest; he had merely pretended, after all, to be one of them.

The rumors had begun four days before, when the Dash 7 from Paris with its forty-seven passengers overshot the runway that ran alongside the Boulevard Creux and ended, engulfed in snow from nose to tail, on the neighboring *piste*. This was not entirely an unusual occurrence. The runway was just slightly more than a thousand feet long and was set at an incline—downhill for takeoff, uphill for landing. Private planes, unused to alpine conditions and thin air, routinely ended nose-up in the groomed expanse beyond the altiport; for a Dash 7 to do so, however, was news. The miscalculation might potentially be called a *crash*.

Jacques had witnessed the affair himself from the comfort of Boulevard Creux, where he sat drinking a robust red wine from a local vintner and delicately considering the merits of a terrine. He heard the whine of the Dash 7's engines; from the corner of his eye, saw the clumsy shape descend like a falling house on the tilted landscape. The terrine, he decided, was not without merit but strove for too much. He pushed it aside and concentrated on a fine soft cheese from a dairy farm near Méribel.

Cries of horror and immense excitement—a woman's scream from the adjacent table—an overturned chair. Jacques stood, his napkin still tucked into the collar of his shirt as though he were a yokel, and not an institution in the life of the most glamorous ski area known to man—and stared out at the huddled mess of the downed prop plane. It had missed several late skiers by a matter of meters.

"*Sacré bleu,*" he'd muttered. "And how they will get that thing off the *piste* is anyone's guess. A tow will not do it. *Imbécile.*"

As he watched, the emergency door above the wing was thrust open. A long, booted leg in leopard-print velvet appeared in the black maw of the opening. Jacques swore under his breath. *This* type usually arrived by private jet.

She wore sunglasses under the mop of dark curls, although it was already evening and the light was alpine flat. A black Persian lamb coat, full and swinging. Suede gloves, and a leather backpack slung over her shoulder. She poised on the wing, jumped down as carelessly as though the entire life of Courchevel was not gaping at her from Boulevard Creux, and sauntered toward the altiport terminal some hundred meters back along the overshot runway. It was a good six minutes before the rest of the Dash 7's passengers found courage to follow.

Jacques continued to swear as he watched her go, with a fluency that did him honor. Not because the woman was a sensation—he was long jaded by celebrity and bravado and chic, he saw them all the time. Nor because her beauty was a reproach to a man abandoned by his wife. No, he swore because he had seen Max Roderick fixed like a stone to one side of the *piste,* just beyond the fallen plane, his weight well back in his boots and his poles thrust into the snow. Watching.

He made no move toward the Dash 7—he suggested not the slightest anxiety or concern for its occupants—but something in Max's expression, the arms folded tightly across his chest as he stared at the wing, told Jacques that Max had been waiting for this plane. For the appearance of this woman.

Although such an idea was impossible.

Impossible, Jacques repeated to himself now as he stood shivering on his own doorstep. There had been no welcome in Max Roderick's face. He had merely stared after the woman's figure while the sirens began to wail, then seized his poles, thrust himself cleanly down the *piste* and vanished from Jacques's sight.

Until he reappeared, so the rumors went, at a party in the woman's rented villa—here, in Le Praz—the very next night. The two had been inseparable in the few days since. The paparazzi—never far from *le pauvre* Max—were beginning to sniff the wind.

An old flame, declared Yvette Margolan with a knowing air as she handed Jacques his olives the following afternoon. *I saw her when I delivered the charcuterie. Not young, but* très chic. *She happened upon our Max unawares, after the passage of many years. It is Fate,* non? *He has been too much alone,* mon vieux, *since la Muldoon . . .*

But Max had not been unaware.

Jacques stood in the rising morning, his eyes fixed on the spot where Max Roderick had passed, riding the platter lift out of Le Praz at eight-fifteen on a Friday of new snow when he should have been aboard the tram for Saulire long since. The cold seeped through his vest and his ancient sweater and he shuddered suddenly, seized by the chill like a dog snapped on a too-short leash. Why should it matter to him, if Max amused himself with a hundred strange women? Was he, Jacques Renaudie, an old man now that his wife had run off with a banker to Paris? Never mind that he had known Max for more than a decade, and had never witnessed such slavish attention, such wholehearted indiscretion . . .

Curse all women and their heartless scheming, Jacques thought savagely. Where *was* his daughter, anyway? He should refuse Sabine the house when she finally came home. Jacques banged the base of the broom against the step and turned in search of the cigarettes he kept in his kitchen.

Max Roderick had not spent the night in Stefani Fogg's villa. She had slept at his home instead.

He had dropped down to Le Praz at first light in order to fetch some of her clothes—a change of long underwear, a fresh ski sweater. The rest of her gear still sat in the vestibule of his old farmhouse on the ridge just beyond Courchevel 1850, the highest of the ski area's four main bases.

She had hesitated when he invited her for dinner the previous night, and he knew that she was longing for a hot bath and an early bed. He had spared her nothing in the previous seventy-two hours: the relentless drops down the steeps of La Vizelle, the circuitous passage through the woods of Courchevel 1550; the nail-biting jumps from outcropping to outcropping in the rugged Grand Couloir; the moguls on La Combe de la Saulire. He had taken her into bowls far above tree line, so junked with crud they tore the skis out from under the best of amateurs. She was equal to everything but his pace.

That first morning they had stood together in the sharp, cold, early light on the knife-edge of Saulire's ridge, the far-flung Alps unrolling toward Switzerland. They were alone in a cruel and beautiful world of glacial ice. Wordlessly, he handed her the water bottle from his ski jacket. She tipped it to her lips and then said, "Follow me."

Before he could speak or move she was airborne over the cornice, eyes searching for landfall. She moved with a sort of reckless instinct he had not expected and found dangerously intoxicating. He threw himself after her, following precisely the turns she traced on the headwall's face. When at last she slashed to a stop and looked back over her shoulder, waiting for him, the two sets of tracks ran unbroken for nearly twelve hundred feet. A single clean run without pause or hesitation.

"You've skied this before?" he asked her curtly.

"Never."

"Your skis could be shorter, and they're all wrong for your center of gravity."

"I just got them last year."

"We'll switch them tomorrow. I can fit you from the stock in my studio."

"But I like my equipment!"

"You'll like mine better."

Did he intend to challenge her, that early in the morning on their first day? He wasn't sure. Max had skied with many women in his professional life—women from the U.S. Ski Team, and girls down the length of his long apprenticeship on a thousand mountains around the world. He was used to the tenacity, the aggressiveness, the naked competition of such women; he was used to precision and skill. What he recognized in this woman was a more elusive quality: joy. It showed in every line of her body when she turned downhill.

"Where do we go next?" she asked.

"You told me to follow you." Another challenge. She thrust her poles into the snow and went.

There are more than three hundred and twenty miles of marked runs in Les Trois Vallées, the three valleys of St. Bon, Les Allues and Belleville; to ski them all would require an entire season, but she made a game attempt. Each day she ascended from Le Praz to Courchevel 1850, met Max at the foot of the Verdons gondola and from there decreed their course: toward the villages of Méribel, Val Thorens or Mottaret. They skied hard and by unspoken agreement never referred to the business that had brought her to France. When they talked at all, in the spaces between runs as they climbed back toward the summit on a multitude of lifts, it was of the food or the sun or the terrain they had just conquered.

"Where do you ski in the States?" he asked her once; and abruptly, as though she did not like to think about it, she replied: "Utah."

"Deer Valley?"

She turned and gazed at him, her dark eyes unreadable behind her sunglasses. "Deer Valley. Is it so obvious?"

She wore a headband of carved and dyed mink, the glossy curls springing back like a wild fringe from her forehead. Her nose was red from exposure. Her jacket, incredibly, was of Italian doeskin the color of caramel and the texture of satin. Her ski pants were the same. "It saves time," she had explained, "après-ski. I'm already dressed for a party."

"You have the skill for Snowbird and Alta," he commented, "but you *look* like Deer Valley."

Her lips curled in contempt. "Deer Valley's *nice*, Max. They valet your skis when you come off the hill."

"They valet them here," he replied, "if you pay them enough."

"Don't let the skill level fool you." She avoided his eye, staring instead at the ridgeline. "I'm relentlessly shallow. I like pretty houses and pretty bodies wherever I go."

"How honest of you to admit it. Most people profess the opposite—and live out their days as liars. There's no Mr. Fogg, I gather?"

She shook her head. "I buy my own mink, thank you very much. The one thing money *can* buy, you see, is freedom."

He thought of Suzanne Muldoon, and the sweeping silver fox. She'd loved furs as much as he hated them, and so the coat arrived in tribute to their three years. Two months after he'd bought the thing, she'd served him with a lawsuit.

"Freedom," he told Stefani, "can be quite solitary."

"But loneliness, in my book, is always preferable to dependence. All relationships require *someone* to dominate, and the other to submit. That ain't gonna be me."

"Unless you pursue a man whose strength matches yours. An equal. What might happen then?"

"A fight to the death." She threw back her head and laughed. "Don't tell me you're a romantic, Max. I don't believe in them anymore."

He stayed off her private terrain after that.

She let him guide her through the bars and hostels of his adopted town; she drank Armagnac warmed over a candle flame and turned her toes toward the fire and paid lip service to his attempts to charm her. Max had been a celebrity for nearly twenty years. To be held at arm's length—to be treated as though he were nothing more than a guide to the terrain—was disconcerting.

What exactly did Stefani Fogg know about that moment in Geneva? The dead Thai stripper with her hair flung like raw silk across his pillow? What could—what *ought*—he to tell her?

That the girl's eyes had bulged obscenely in death? That as he emerged from the shower, he noticed first the way the early morning sun caressed her golden breast—how her fingers reached wantonly for air—and only a second later, the look of horror and denial in her face?

He could not find the words to describe what he had seen, nor the revulsion—the fascination—he still felt. He said nothing of the painfully young corpse or the red-sequined thong that left a raw band across her dead flesh or the flurried hotel manager or the correct little man with the Hitler mustache who interviewed him for the Geneva police, deferential as Stefani Fogg could never be.

She had asked him nothing about the murder. This woman sent out from New York to walk with him through the wasteland was clearly waiting for further developments. She seemed content to let him size her up for a few days on the slopes. Max knew that she was assessing his qualities in turn. He didn't stop to wonder how this test—for that was what it clearly was—might have been accomplished, if Stefani Fogg had never skied. She would not, then, have been Stefani Fogg. An entirely different set of assumptions would have applied.

And so that third afternoon, when the light had flattened at the high elevations and clouds had converged on the lower *pistes,* he turned to her as they entered Courchevel 1850 and said: "Have dinner at my house tonight. It's time we talked about Thailand."

"Then of course I'll come."

"You can see the place from here, if you strain your eyes. There's a platter lift to the top."

She followed the line of his hand, staring toward the lonely peak at the end of the ridge beyond the village and the stone house with its heavy cap of snow.

"It's exactly the sort of house you *should* have. Rooted to the earth. Beautiful in its simplicity. A house that knows who it is."

"The smaller building to the rear is my studio. You can come up now, if you want. It'd save you a second trip, in the dark."

"I will," she replied. "I want to see those skis you promised me."

They left their gear outside in the clear dusky cold. The hall was empty but for a painted Swiss armoire and a long pine bench; a faint scent of vanilla lingered in the air. The pavers beneath Stefani's toes felt warm, like the stones of a hearth.

"Glycerin," he told her. "Piped through the subflooring. Thicker than water and heat retentive. It warms the surface, then the whole house."

"I thought this place was an antique."

"It dates from the forties. I renovated a few years ago."

In 1996. The year after he'd settled in Courchevel and bought the farmhouse. She remembered the date from his dossier—those one hundred forty-three pages consumed before Scottish bedtime. She had most of the man's life memorized by now; none of it had prepared her for Max.

The videos had captured the cutthroat competitor, the inexhaustible energy. But there was a quality of refusal about Max in person—of disengagement from the world—that Stefani found intriguing and unnerving. He weighed every word before he spoke, as though the consequences of speech—of contact—of human emotion—might be irreversible. She suspected that yawning fear lay behind that reflexive control; but fear of what? Was he capable, as his air suggested, of living without a shred of love? Was his solitude the result of arrogance? A defense against pain? Or a calculated decision to take the best life could offer, and give nothing back?

"How did you manage to build up here?" she asked.

"It wasn't easy. In summer, the roads are accessible by four-wheel, but most of the lumber had to be lifted. Around June, the resort people pull the quad chairs off the cable and attach steel containers capable of carrying anything up the mountain. Whirlpool baths, caviar, goats seeking summer pasture . . . The usual mix of necessity and luxury."

"Max, why did you leave the States?"

The tousled gold head turned in the act of shedding its helmet. "That's the first personal thing you've asked me."

"I couldn't find the answer in my files."

"And do you like your data complete?" He studied her intently with those clear, light eyes. "Or are you trying to understand my soul?"

"I'm interested in French real estate."

It was not, Stefani thought, the truth. But she had kept Max at arm's length ever since she'd arrived. It was the one way she felt safe.

"I detest the American skier's practice of retiring to a resort as the local mascot," he said deliberately. "I have no interest in skiing once a day with a crowd of delighted fans or plastering my face across billboards. I don't want to make commercials endorsing watches or credit cards. I chose this place because I could *live* here, and do work that interests me. The French don't care what I eat or what I wear or who I sleep with. Courchevel is so public I can disappear."

Until, she thought, *a corpse shows up in your bed.* "Don't the paparazzi ski?"

His mouth twisted. "Not on my terrain. The last time they followed me, three guys and a woman had to be airlifted off the headwall. Like a drink?"

He had tampered with the old Savoyard structure in the main room; the far wall was glass instead of stone, with a view of the tramline. The lights strung from base to peak were sparks in the growing dark. She stood in the middle of the space—he was spare with furniture—and felt the loneliness. He probably slept with all his windows wide open. She shuddered suddenly.

"What happened to Suzanne Muldoon?"

"Your second personal question." His hands stilled over a bottle of

Bordeaux. "Once she got my check, she cut me out of her life. Is red wine okay?"

"Red's fine. Why did she sue you?"

"She could hardly sue Innsbruck. Or the World Cup." He concentrated on pouring her a glass. "When you race, Stefani, you face death every day. That's why you train so hard—it's the voodoo that keeps you alive. Suzanne was lucky. She kicked back—eased up on her training— partied too hard—and did a back flip over a course barrier. She got off with a blown knee. Could have been a broken neck."

"She claimed you drove her beyond her limits. That your coaching was relentless."

"Relentless? I didn't know Suzanne understood words of three syllables. But I wasn't her coach. She paid somebody else for that."

"So why sue *you*, Max?"

He set down the bottle and stared at her, his expression remote. "I think her dreams died hard. Somebody had to pay, and Suzanne figured she'd paid enough. Her career was shot. She'd lost her chance to medal, she'd lost the endorsements—she needed to clutch at something. Apparently it wasn't me."

Though you looked, in all those photos clipped from a hundred magazines, like a match made in Hollywood...

"A frivolous suit," she mused. "Impossible to prove. But instead of fighting it, you settled out of court. Pity?"

Max handed her the wineglass. "Failure is so goddamn tedious. I gave Suzanne half a million to go away. Do you want to see my shop?"

It was connected to the house's lower floor by a short passage, beyond an exercise room and a hot tub with doors that opened into the night. The workspace was spartan. A drafting table with color ads of ski gear clipped to its upper edge; a promotional poster or two tacked to the walls; a computer and a few chairs. But every square surface of the open area beyond was lined with prototypes of skis, red and black and strident yellow. Boots were scattered around the floor in various stages of assembly and the tools of the ski tuner's trade reared up like the medieval rack: vises, benches, warming pans for wax. Brushes. Spray cans. Flat-bladed knives. Buffers and drills.

"I hadn't realized this was so hands-on," she remarked.

"I test everything I make."

"But you don't *make* it, surely? You draw it. On that drafting table. The skis themselves are made in . . ."

"Lyons." He was watching her, checking off the facts she'd found in his dossier. "They send everything back for quality control and technical refining."

He crossed the room and chose some skis from the horde against the wall. "Here's the pair I thought might suit you. The Volant T3 Vertex. They're designed specifically for women and their marketing slogan is: *Weaker sex, my ass.* That suits, right?"

The skis were the color and sheen of stainless steel. A Bauhaus concept of a blade. The DeLorean of the slopes. "You didn't design these," she said.

"I don't design for women," he replied. "I can't test the skis properly. Women have a totally different strength-to-weight ratio. Your center of gravity is lower. You turn differently, carry your weight differently, bend differently than men. I can simulate that on the computer, of course, but not on the slope."

"I like my skis," she protested.

"Because you paid for them. You're skiing Vökls right now—and don't get me wrong, they're *great* if you're a two-hundred-and-twenty-pound guy. You handle them well, considering. But I'd like to see you on these."

She ran her eye down the surface. "Teflon?"

"Over a foam core."

"They're too short."

"They're perfect. I'm taking you into the steeps tomorrow. Off-*piste* terrain. Anything longer, you'll be sliding down the Alps on your backside."

"You'd make sure of that, wouldn't you?" She spoke with a trace of amusement. "If only to have the satisfaction of being *right*. You need to ski faster, live harder, think quicker—"

"Dominate," he agreed evenly, taking a step toward her. "It's my driving force. I dominate the people around me just like I dominate the mountain. Or so Suzanne always said. I pushed and pushed until she broke. And I feel not the slightest regret, Stefani. I always knew Suzanne lacked staying power. It was only a question of what and when."

He held her gaze as though daring her to challenge him, and Stefani resisted because resisting was her reflex in all such contests. *So it's true,* she thought. *You are relentless, and you don't give a fuck about any- body. I've been warned. But I'm not the kind of woman who breaks.*

"Poor Suzanne," she said dryly. "She must miss you awfully."

"She got the cash. That's all she really wanted."

"What did the Thai prostitute want, Max?"

He flinched. For an instant she caught the pain—or was it violence?— swimming through the green gaze.

"Did you invite her to your room? Did it get a little . . . rough?"

"No." His voice was quiet. "I haven't asked anybody into my bed for a long, long time."

He was close enough to graze with her fingertips and the air was suddenly charged. She was too conscious of the unblinking stare, sharp as a talon; the face that had lurked in her Scottish dreams. Something fluid and animal had entered the room.

This is why, she thought bitterly in the direction of Oliver Krane, *you choose men by their shirt size instead of their IQs. Because it never, never forces you to see the ugly side of yourself—the selfish, ravaging desire to rule.*

And then a drawling voice from the hallway said, "You should lock your doors, buddy. Valuable stuff must be hidden *somewhere* in this house, although I admit you hide it pretty well." A sharply molded head peered around the door frame; the dark eyes lighted instantly on Stefani. "How many more women have you stashed away beneath the floorboards?"

"This is Stefani Fogg," Max said. She heard the warning in his voice.

"I'm Jeff Knetsch." The newcomer extended a hand. "Max's oldest friend. Also his lawyer. Is there any more wine?"

6

Max had given her no warning of Jeff Knetsch's arrival in Courchevel—
though Knetsch had flown in from New York to assess this woman
who held her fork so indolently as she listened to his talk of the West-
chester suburbs and his passion for golf. She had taken the lawyer's appearance in stride; but Max suspected that she was on her guard. She
was too shrewd to mistake a business meeting for a casual dinner
among friends. The current between them had altered subtly: the dangerous intimacy of the afternoon had vanished. Now she projected a
cultivated intelligence that was as distancing as the cynical banter of
the chairlift. He understood how close he had come to the real woman
only once she was in retreat.

Max had known Knetsch for more than thirty years—they had cele-
brated their eleventh birthdays together on the giant slalom course at
Tahoe—and he knew the lawyer was on edge this evening. His deep-set,
hungry eyes roved constantly over the room, over Stefani Fogg's figure,
over the books on Max's shelves. He twirled his wine in nervous, long-
fingered hands. As Max watched, a thread of Bordeaux trickled down
the stem of the glass and beaded the table as with blood.

They ate figs wrapped in prosciutto and balsamic vinegar, goat
cheese drizzled with honey, and Moroccan lamb stew ladled over crisp

French bread. Dessert was a *tarte tatin* he'd bought from Yvette Margolan in Le Praz that morning; otherwise, he'd cooked the meal.

"I can hardly boil water," Stefani said as he poured her more wine.

"Freedom," he observed, "must buy a lot of takeout."

She looked at him then—hearing the afternoon's echo in his words—and for an instant, it was as though Knetsch had never appeared and they were alone.

"How long have you worked for Oliver Krane?" the lawyer asked her abruptly.

"Maybe ten days. But I thought only Max was supposed to know why I'm here."

"Max would never hire an outside consultant without my approval."

"Really?" She smiled. "I thought he already had. Do you get to France often, Jeff?"

"About four times a year. Whenever Max needs a friend."

"He's needed one quite a lot lately."

Knetsch raised a skeptical brow.

"The body in the bed," she prompted. "The Swiss police. A lawyer comes in handy, don't you think?"

What did the Thai prostitute want, Max?

He understood then that she'd been thinking about the murder in Geneva from the moment she'd arrived. She hadn't accepted his story.

"The Swiss police, thank God, know a setup when they see one," Knetsch said heavily. "Max was never in real danger of being charged."

"I find murder hard to dismiss, regardless of whether anyone's been charged. Why would someone frame you, Max?"

"For the negative publicity. That's been true all my adult life."

"There are sick people out there ready to ruin anyone's morning." Knetsch kept his eyes on the garnet depths of his wineglass. "Particularly our Golden Boy here. But that's not the matter you were hired to pursue, Stefani. You're here to help Max with his inheritance claim."

"Don't you think it's probable the two matters are linked?"

"Oliver Krane charges a goddamn fortune," Knetsch persisted. "He ought to have sent somebody with a bit more experience. It's obvious you can ski—but what else do you bring to the table?"

"Back off, Jeff," Max said quietly.

"As your lawyer—"

"—You're presuming on attorney-client privilege. I'm going to light the fire in the living room. Anyone want coffee?"

He was behaving, Max thought, like a maître d' in his own house—sliding among the difficult guests with his hope for a perfect evening. And yet he'd asked Jeff to come—he'd wanted his opinion. Why, then, was he so quick to defend Stefani Fogg?

The sky beyond the great room's windows was very black and punctured by stars only visible when the house lights were dimmed. They were dimmed now. She had draped herself across one of his leather sofas—that whipcord body a visual sketch of her mental strength: disciplined, precise, economical. When he looked at her he saw not the form in repose, but the tensed spring of scores of ski runs. He dropped an armload of firewood on the hearth and busied himself with kindling. Knetsch picked up where he'd left off.

"What do you know about Molly Sanderson, Stefani?"

"She was Max's first crush." Amusement in the velvet voice; but she was right. He'd adored Molly in the diffident, grudging fashion of five-year-olds, subjecting her to the tyranny of his rage as often as he hugged her.

"Molly was Max's nanny in Evanston from 1964 until 1966, when he entered first grade," Stefani said matter-of-factly. "She was nineteen when she started with the Rodericks and married two months after she left them. Now divorced and living in St. Paul. She remembers Max fondly."

"Joe DiGuardia?"

"Downhill ski coach at Squaw Valley. That was after Max and his mother moved to San Francisco."

"In what year?"

"Late '66. Max would've been seven. His mother rented an apartment in Haight-Ashbury, joined the antiwar movement, and discovered recreational drugs. She died of a heroin overdose in 1969, when Max was ten."

He was conscious of his hands, arrested in the act of laying the fire, his whole body tense with listening. Her voice was too casual; she must suspect how it affected him to hear such things on the lips of a stranger.

"Max was given the choice of moving to Chicago—his grandmother was still alive then—or to his great-aunt's house in Delaware. Joe DiGuardia, the ski coach, opted instead to act as guardian. Max stayed in Tahoe. He lived with DiGuardia, off and on, for the next decade."

"Doing what?" Knetsch asked, as though it weren't obvious. Max felt a spurt of anger toward his friend—toward the rigid stance he'd adopted in the center of the room, inquisitor to Stefani's languid heretic.

"Max trained with the U.S. Ski Team, competed worldwide, took his first Olympic medal at nineteen. He met *you* years before that, however, in 1970, when you were both kids in the Squaw program. You took silver twice—once at the World Cup and once at Sarajevo—but you were never quite in Max's class. Is that the basis of your friendship?"

Every relationship requires someone to dominate, and the other to submit.

Knetsch's face had paled. He set down his glass.

"Your racing career ended when you broke your femur at Jackson Hole," she continued implacably.

"—Saving *his* sorry ass, I might add."

"Max lost a ski in Corbett's Couloir. You went in after him. When you caught an edge and fell fifty feet, he crawled the length of Corbett's to get help."

That strange exhilaration as he inched his way down the sheer granite face of the most famous chute in North America. Clinging with his gloved fingers to an outcropping of granite, he'd kicked off his boots and felt with his toes for purchase in the ice. Knetsch was wedged between two jagged shafts of rock above, his teeth clenched and sweat already beading his forehead. The bone of his left thigh shafted through his ski suit's Kevlar. When the rescue team roped up an hour later and rappelled down the face to reach him, he had fainted. Max's feet were frostbitten from stumbling through the snow. What he remembered now was the fierce sensation of triumph: himself, alone against the mountain.

"He always was a noble son of a bitch," Jeff remarked carelessly. "What drugs were prescribed for my post-op pain?"

"I'd guess you popped Percocet, but my sources aren't telling." Her dark eyes shifted to Max's face; their intensity jarred him. "What I *don't* know is what you hope to gain by digging up the past. This isn't just a battle for misappropriated assets. Is it?"

He reached for a box of matches, averting his face. "I want the truth about what happened on Easter Sunday, 1967."

"Do you think the truth exists, after all these years? Everybody connected to your grandfather must be dead."

"Not everybody." He closed the fire screen. "There's me, for instance—and whoever's killing fifteen-year-olds and leaving them in my hotel room."

"So you agree. The two matters *are* connected."

"Of course. I didn't strangle that girl. Whoever did, meant it as a warning. *Let sleeping dogs lie.*"

"What dogs, exactly? I've heard a bit about your family—Jack's disappearance, your father's death as a POW. But no more than the bare outline. What can you tell me, Max? What do you think happened to your grandfather?"

He glanced at Knetsch. His friend rocked slightly on his heels in the center of the room, lips compressed. He didn't like this woman or her easy assurance. Knetsch wanted her bowing and scraping to them both.

"How much do you know about my grandfather?" Max asked.

"It's a pretty broad legend. Socialite, Brahmin, Silk King, spy—"

"Forget the first three and concentrate on the last. Jack Roderick, trained by the OSS to liberate Thailand in 1945, trained in intelligence and jungle warfare. After Truman drops the bomb on Hiroshima and the Thais capitulate to the Allies, Jack's made Bangkok intelligence chief for the outfit that eventually becomes the CIA. And then the spy story drifts into nowhere. Or more importantly, into Khorat."

"Khorat?"

"Northeast Thailand. A region that borders Laos and Cambodia, with soil so arid it's good for nothing but clay pots and mulberry trees and the production of silk. Jack went to Khorat in 1946 and fell in love with raw silk. By 1950, he'd founded an export company and set down roots in Bangkok. He led quite the glamorous expatriate life."

"The Brahmin, the Silk King, the art collector—"

"All cover," Max said flatly, "from start to finish. Gramps was a NOC—an agent of American intelligence operating under Non-Official Cover. Or so I believe. The CIA refuses to confirm or deny it."

Knetsch groaned and threw himself into a chair.

"A NOC," she repeated. "You mean—a businessman by day, spy by night?"

"It's the most dangerous kind of spying there is. You're not attached to the U.S. embassy, so you've got no diplomatic immunity. If you're accused and tried for espionage by your host country, nobody can save you. That's what my grandfather was doing. And that's why he disappeared."

"How can you be so sure?"

How to explain the sense of mission that had been growing in him for months? The certainty, akin to instinct, that guided him the way a sixth sense drove a sleepwalker through a darkened landscape?

"I've . . . examined the facts."

"Facts?" Knetsch snorted.

"It's obvious Jack was still working for the CIA when he set up the silk business. Otherwise, why bother with Khorat at all, right after World War II? The place was—it is—a goddamn desert. Other than a few Khmer ruins, it's got nothing to tempt a tourist. Even the Thai King has ignored it for fifty years."

"So?" she prompted.

"Jack went there about once a month. A fifteen-hour car trip, each way. He supposedly had a bunch of Laotian friends—but I think they were agents he ran for U.S. intelligence. He needed a plausible reason for all those meetings on the Laotian border, so he came up with the silk business."

"Okay." Stefani nodded. "I can accept that as a theory. But are you suggesting that these Laotians killed your grandfather? Or was it the Thais, pissed off because he was spying on their turf?"

He stabbed a poker at the burning logs, sending a shower of sparks up the chimney. "Stefani, what was happening in Southeast Asia in 1967?"

"The Vietnam War."

"The Vietnam War." He glanced over at her. "By the late 1960s, Jack's secret life began to catch up with him. Suddenly the revolutionaries in every former colonial power—the guys who were on my grandfather's side during World War II—are leading guerilla armies through the jungle and committing atrocities in the backyard. Suddenly all of Southeast Asia's exploding and my dad—the Silk King's son and heir—is trapped in the worst shithole in enemy territory. U.S. fighter jets are flying missions out of air bases in Khorat—Gramps's favorite playground—

and Billy Lightfoot is the commanding officer of U.S. Forces in Northeast Thailand. Too much coincidence, Stefani. Too much for me to swallow."

"Who's Billy Lightfoot?"

"A soldier's soldier. He trained my grandfather during the OSS days, and when Gramps disappeared, Lightfoot flew Army helicopters into Malaysia to hunt for him."

"Unsuccessfully."

Max nodded. "I tried to find Billy two years ago, to talk to him about Gramps. I thought he might even know something about my dad's execution. But Lightfoot had died of heart disease. His widow was senile."

"Your father was killed in North Vietnam, a few weeks after Jack disappeared. But he was a POW, wasn't he? A casualty of war?"

"My father was executed in front of all the American flyers imprisoned in the Hanoi Hilton." He tried to keep the bitterness from his voice; he'd been a kid of eight, for Chrissake, it shouldn't still matter so much. "He was beheaded. A vengeance killing. And I don't mean for the bombs he'd dropped."

"But why would Jack's work in Thailand—whatever it was—determine your father's fate in Vietnam? Where's the link between the two, Max?"

"She had to ask," Knetsch muttered.

Max ignored him. "During the Vietnam War, Thailand was the only country in Southeast Asia willing to give the United States legroom. Cambodia, Burma, Laos, Malaysia—all hostile, all fighting their own battles with communist insurgencies. Revolt was in the air. But Thailand was a democracy, in name at least, and canny enough to profit from the U.S. presence."

"And Jack Roderick brokered the deals? Is that what you're saying?"

He shook his head. "I think Gramps disagreed fundamentally with the Johnson administration's conduct of the war in Vietnam. I think that because Jack refused to support it, he was betrayed and silenced."

Her gaze was very steady as she considered the implications of what he'd said. "Silenced by the CIA? His own organization?"

"Why not? Who else is capable of keeping the whole stinking mess hushed up for more than thirty years?"

Knetsch groaned despairingly. "They murdered Princess Di, too. Drugged Dodi's driver and paid off the paparazzi. I read it in the Star."

But Stefani was still looking at him. "Even if I thought for an instant you might be right, I don't see how your father's execution fits the theory."

"The CIA always plays both sides. Maybe they promised something to the North Vietnamese. Maybe Gramps refused to deliver, and was eliminated as a result. When the deal fell through, the Viet Cong retaliated. They beheaded my dad."

"You sound like a raving conspiracy theorist."

"Maybe I am."

"Can you separate what you remember from what you've been told?"

"What do you mean?"

"You were a kid—eight years old—when your father and grandfather died. Whatever you believe about your family's past springs in part from memory, and in part from half-truths—things your mother may have believed and passed on, for example."

"And we know Mom was always high as a kite," he retorted, "and thus unreliable. But she didn't talk about Jack's disappearance—she'd never even met him. My father was reported dead two weeks after Gramps disappeared, and that news overshadowed everything else. Mom preferred to remember the good times—when my dad was alive. That's what she talked about."

"The good times?"

He studied the crackling flames, and chose his words well. It was important that she understand he had been raised in more than a shooting gallery.

"My mother was the only child of a wealthy Chicago banker. A leading debutante of 1956. She grew up with my dad, and they were cut from the same mold. Naïve, well-intentioned upper-middle-class Americans with bright smiles, whose lives were blown apart by a conflict they never chose. My father was barely thirty when he died. I've outlived him by a decade. I have no idea what he was really like. When I was little, he was the god in the helmet who flew the big jets—every boy's hero. But it's been a long, long time since I've seen him as anything but a victim."

"Of fate? Of U.S. policy?"

"Of his childhood. That, more than anything."

"Explain."

Max glanced at her. "We all want to be our fathers, Stef. Boys do, at least. My dad had a war hero for a role model. Jack was James Bond in a Panama hat. Dad spent his life living up to Jack's legend."

"And you?"

The question brought him up short. "I learned to ski at the age of six because it was the closest I could come to flying."

She reached for the warmth of the fire; light dappled the bones of her face. "Did you ever meet Jack?"

"Once. My father took me to Bangkok when I was four. In the fall of '63."

"He never came to the States?"

"Not in my lifetime." The bitterness crept in, despite his care. "Jack abandoned his family. Dad was about five when World War II began, and Gramps never really came back. Bangkok—the silk business, or the life of a NOC—always attracted Jack more than being a parent. Dad resented Gramps—his house, his art, his legend in the expat community. Resented it as much as he wanted to be a part of it. Could you blame him? I'm not really sure why he even took me to Thailand."

"What do you remember about the trip?"

He sighed and shoved his fingers through his hair, as though he might clutch at the past lodged somewhere in his skull. "Flood water in the streets. It was the end of the rainy season and we went everywhere by boat. Gramps liked the old khlongs better than the new roads they'd built for cars, anyway. He loathed progress. He still called Thailand 'Siam.' "

"You see?" Stefani countered. "Those are things you've been told. 'Progress' and 'Siam' aren't a four-year-old's words."

"Oh, *fuck* the words. You asked."

"Tell me about Jack."

He summoned the face—indistinct at best, retouched by later glimpses of photographs—that lurked always on the edge of his mind. "He was a big guy, but then I was quite small. He had silver hair that was always slicked back, and a white bird on his shoulder. The bird's beak looked exactly like his nose."

"Did you like him?"

Max shrugged again. "Do four-year-olds like anything?"

"What about the house?"

"God—the *house*." He smiled involuntarily. "A tree house made of teak. Leafy and cool. Rooms with dark floors I could slide across in my socks. Silk pillows. Lizards skittering along the walls. My bedroom was like a ship's cabin, small and wood-paneled. The smells of jungle and garlic and rotting fruit came through the open windows at night."

"For an all-American kid, that must have been a little weird."

"It was the most fabulous place I'd ever seen. Like waking up in Never-Never Land, surrounded by the Lost Boys. I didn't want to leave. When I toured the place again last year, I knew that I'd been trying to get back to that house all my life. Back to the garden, as Crosby, Stills and Nash would say, where fathers live forever and war never comes."

A swift glance from the dark eyes; something he'd said had hit home. "Do you remember anything else?"

"Waking in the night and being afraid."

"Bad dreams?"

"Noise. The kind you can't ignore. I got up from bed and walked out into the hall. Gramps was standing there, shouting at some guy who was running down the stairs. There was blood on Gramps's face and my dad was restraining him. They'd been fighting."

"Jack and your father? Or Jack and the guy on the stairs?"

"I don't know."

"Did you recognize him? The stranger?"

"All I remember is that I was afraid. They were angry and the talk was serious, something I shouldn't hear. I went back to bed and pulled the covers over my head."

"Could it have been a thief?" Knetsch suggested.

"He was a Westerner," Max replied, as though that made a difference. "He was tall and had a crew cut and wore some kind of uniform."

It was a memory he couldn't shake: broken sleep, shouting and blood, the tall, angry figures flickering grotesquely in torchlight. A nightmare that recurred over thirty years until it became the pivot for obsession: *I must know the truth.* Jack's will, the Bangkok house, the priceless collections, the stock in the silk company: were they all merely proxies? Did he just need to lay a ghost three decades old?

"Have you asked the CIA what they know about Jack Roderick?" she asked.

"I filed a FOIA request—that's the Freedom of Information Act. They sent back three sheets of paper blotted out with black ink. Told me squat. But they know more than that—I'm sure of it."

"Max, why did you hire me?"

His eyes slid over to Knetsch's. The lawyer stared implacably back. "I didn't. I thought I was hiring Oliver Krane."

"To do what? Storm CIA headquarters? Rifle old files in Langley?"

"You're a forensic accountant," he said, feeling his temper slip. "Find my grandfather's lost cash. Nose out the people responsible for stealing his house and everything in it. Help me and Jeff prove my claim."

"You haven't a shred of proof for a single thing you've said."

"Exactly. And that's why I've got to go back to Bangkok. *To find the truth.*"

Knetsch's wineglass tipped over and shattered on the stone-flagged floor.

"Bangkok?" she repeated dubiously. "That could be dangerous."

"I know."

The devil-may-care look resurged in her eyes; she grinned, and held up her glass in salute.

Not even death threats could faze this woman. Oliver Krane had known exactly what he was doing when he sent Stefani Fogg to France.

Around midnight, Max told her it was too late to ski to Le Praz, and offered her his guest room instead. She didn't protest—didn't fight her way past him to click into her skis, though the wine and the hours of talk had closed the distance between them and she had more than once caught herself wondering how the line of his jaw would feel under her fingers. While he went in search of sheets, she walked Jeff Knetsch to the door.

He was still uncomfortable in her presence; all the facts and the effort at professionalism had failed to make him her friend.

"What do you really think of Max's story?" she asked him. "Max's assassination theory?"

"All that crap about the CIA? I think he's got too much time on his hands."

Or the strong need for a hero. But which man does he want to redeem? Jack Roderick? Or Rory?

"And as for flying to Bangkok—"

"You're worried?"

The lawyer hesitated, one hand on the massive oak jamb of Max's door. "He's pissed off somebody with a lot of firepower. And it hasn't occurred to him that the strangled whore was just an opening shot. Next time, he could lose something he really values."

"Does he listen to you?"

Knetsch smiled wryly. "Max listens to nobody. Especially when he has paid for the advice. Are you skiing tomorrow?"

"Off-*piste*. Max wants to show me the backcountry. Join us, if you like."

It was her attempt at a truce. But wariness lingered in the eyes of Max's oldest friend.

"I know Max's backcountry. My leg can't take that kind of terrain anymore," he said curtly. "I'll meet you for a drink afterward."

"The Bateau Ivre," she suggested. "Four o'clock."

"Done." He turned away.

But as she shut the door behind him, she wondered what had inspired Knetsch's mistrust. Krane & Associates? Her credentials? Or the fact that she was a woman in Max Roderick's house?

7

Max lay awake well past one, feeling the turbulent night air shudder against the frame of his house. Faces swam in and out of his consciousness: Jack Roderick's eyes and sharp nose; his father's, a softer version; and Stefani Fogg's profile, half-averted. When he thought of her, it was always in profile—the slope and pitch of her facial structure like a *piste* he had yet to map. He had told her what he could of his family's past, not because he had paid Oliver Krane to send her here to Courchevel, but because he'd tested and liked her nerve. Max had learned much about the human spirit by watching the human body ski: three days' observation had shown him how little she feared.

Except, he suspected, deep emotion. Feeling that might cause pain, or chain her to another human being. Feeling that could wreck the perfect autonomy she'd crafted for herself.

He avoided the same traps. He'd been terrified of them most of his life.

Wind buffeted the house's peaked roof; the door to the balcony rattled faintly in protest. The fog that had blanketed the slopes at dusk had blown into Switzerland; the moon was setting. He rolled over, thrust his feet out of bed, and without turning on the light placed his hand on his viola where it sat in the corner of the room.

It is possible for one man to ski at world-class level or to play an instrument with orchestral precision—but not in the same lifetime. Max loved his viola with the passion he had long since lost for skis, in part because the viola had always denied him mastery. It submitted to nothing in his repertoire.

He took up the bow with humility, clutched the instrument by its throat and walked out into the freezing air. The wind was like a knife on his naked back; it pierced the folds of his pajama legs. He might be incapable of subjugating the music under his hands, but he could still subdue his flesh to the elements. He laid his bow across the strings.

A viola contracts in extreme cold, and the sound it makes is warped and distorted. A chord sang out from the shrinking wood, and then another—melancholy, haunting, a paean to the dying moon. It was as though the mountains themselves were bewitched to speech. And the stories they told were of a sort to terrify children.

Take good care *of your mother, pal.* The strong right hand felt like a heavy weight on his shoulder and there was a burning in his nose as though he might sneeze or cry, so he leaned into his dad's trousers and buried his face in the dress poplin. The whole Navy was watching from the pier, women holding babies and little kids dropping pebbles into the flat black water, the aircraft carrier's reflection wavering and dissolving with each *plunk! plunk!* as though it were insubstantial as air. Coronado, a breathless July morning, 1965.

You're the man of the house now, Maxie Max. I'm depending on you to keep Mom safe. You'll be in first grade soon, so once you know how to write I'll expect a letter every week, telling me how things are. Your house log for the S.S. Roderick. *Got that?*

He nodded up into his father's face, arms still clutching his trouser leg, but the sun behind Rory's head blotted out his features. The hand lifted from his shoulder, cupped his mother's chin—

Take good care of your mother, pal.

He had tried his best, using sheet after sheet of grade-school paper, his eraser tearing dimples in the flimsy stuff. He'd written about trips to Evanston and the big old house by the lake his grandparents still owned and the pounding rain on his bedroom eaves. He'd written about the dead snake he'd discovered in the cellar and the road trip he and his mom took to Lake Tahoe and how he'd seen a deer beneath Half Dome in his first Yosemite hike.

It was not the first time his father had been away on carrier duty. Max was used to living alone with his mother for months, used to the circle of closeness they pulled in like a tent flap against the lurking beasts beyond the doors, but this was the most dangerous tour his dad had pulled. At times his mother's expression grew distant, she took to ironing clothes relentlessly during the long winter afternoons. After one of these bouts when he was six, she drove Max into the hills and rented him skis.

There were hurried patches of leave during the two long years his father was gone, unexpected as Christmas. Phone calls knifed with static. Trinkets that arrived in crushed cardboard boxes covered with strange ink seals. TV footage of downed planes that Anne hurriedly switched off whenever Max entered the room.

Take good care of your mother.

When his father's A-4 fell out of the sky that January morning half a world away, he knew nothing about it until he found her lying in a stuttering coma, drunk as a lord, on the kitchen floor of the San Francisco apartment. By April, when they knew Dad was dead and no body was coming home, Anne began walking the streets at all hours, an old raincoat of his father's wrapped around her emaciated body. She burned incense and hung beads from the door frames and sang phrases of half-remembered songs under her breath, and when she looked at Max he was convinced she saw through him.

Take good care of your mother.

One night at three A.M., on his way to the bathroom, he tripped over her body in the dark. What he could not say to Stefani Fogg—what he could not find the words to tell anyone—was that thirty years later, as he'd stared at the expression of horror in the eyes of a dead Thai hooker, it was his mother's face he'd seen.

He awoke at dawn and drank his coffee in front of the living room's wall of glass. Snow had fallen sometime after he propped the viola back in its place and returned to bed. There would be a foot of powder in the glades, but most of the tourists would grab the tram to Saulire. The backcountry would be empty and quiet on this Friday, tracked only by local guides and the kids who cared nothing for avalanche danger. He felt his heart surge at the thought of it: silence amid the blanketed conifers, the mass of snow trembling above the trees like a wave poised to curl.

He set off alone with a backpack and his usual gear to the rented villa in Le Praz. Stefani had given him her key the previous night, and told him where to find a change of clothing. They both knew she was not the sort to rise early, even for the best new fall of powder in the world.

And so Jacques Renaudie saw Max that morning as he swept his doorstep, riding the platter lift out of town in defiance of all rumor.

"The concept of skiing within-bounds is pretty much an American one," Max told her somewhere around midmorning, as they paused for breath in their hike up a crevasse. Their skis were slung over their shoulders and in their packs they carried water, protein bars, ropes and picks and beacons. Stefani's back was aching.

"Boundaries exist for the National Forest Service—which owns the land most American ski areas are built on—and because too many skiers have died in backcountry avalanches." He wore his helmet again today, and had forced her to wear one as well. "If you map out your terrain, and fire avalanche cannon every morning in peak snowslide season, you can control the snow pack and fend off the worst disasters."

"Simple risk management." Stefani briefly considered the idea of Oliver Krane standing in the path of an avalanche. "Whereas in Europe, nobody worries about skiers dying?"

"In Europe, the *pistes* were carved by villagers first and by ski corporations only after World War II. Look at the concentration of houses. It seems random, but it's uncannily scientific. If you watch a tidal wave of snow churn down the mountain for centuries on end, you build where the wave never passes."

She gazed out from their perch—a small plateau perhaps twelve feet square in the granite face. From this distance, the map of the Trois Vallées was a storybook illustration—hamlets of stone and sloping roofs tucked into the clefts between the hills; deep forests of fir with heavy mantles of white; and the power cables of ski lifts soaring from ground to air.

"The closest you could come to flying," she mused. "A kid airborne on a pair of skis. Did your father ever see you race?"

"No," he said curtly, his eyes fixed on the landscape.

She spared little breath for conversation after that. She was too intent upon following Max's footsteps. It was important to pay attention to every toehold and outcrop that could be grasped with gloved fingers. She did not ask him where they were going; he had pointed upward to a rocky cornice three hundred feet above a glade. Higher still, there soared an open granite headwall flush with old hard-pack and new powder.

"Switzerland," he explained, "if you climb far enough."

She supposed that when they had skied down through the thick growth of trees that marched toward the valley below, they would turn around and repeat the exhausting climb. It hardly mattered. For now it was enough to track the man in front of her.

"Do you do this often?" she asked when at last they stood on the cornice edge.

"I've been up here three times this winter." He pulled his skis from the harness on his back. "Let me go first, and pick your own line later."

She was just clicking her boot into the bindings of her new T3s when the crack of a gun ricocheted off the headwall. The sound echoed, gathering force.

"What's that?"

Max's head was craned backward, his eyes fixed on the snow above them.

A second crack. Stefani heard, quite clearly, the bullet singing over their heads.

"Go. *Go, go, go!*" Max shouted, and pushed off the cornice as though a starting gate had sprung.

She dove after him, unable to look at the mass of white shuddering behind, the grip of fear suddenly at her throat. The silence before the roar of the snowslide was like an instant suspended, as she soared out into the air twenty feet before landing on the slope below, the sound of her own breath hideous in her ears. Max never looked backward, never spared so much as a glance for the massive sheet of snow peeling off the headwall; every nerve in his body seemed trained on the tree line below, on the heavy glade that might shelter them and impede for a few precious seconds the onslaught of the avalanche. She was incapable of thought or decision; she merely thrust herself forward, the technique instinctual, willing herself not to catch an edge and tumble headlong to her death. Willing herself to survive.

The snow's roar was deafening, now, and she could not help casting a hasty glance behind—the cornice, the chute down which they had raced, the headwall above: all blotted out in a screaming mass of white three stories high. She almost stopped dead from sheer terror but a faint shout from Max pulled her head around. He had halted near the edge of the glade some sixty feet away. *Waiting for her.*

She hurled herself forward through air dense with sound, her body wired for the moment when the avalanche would gather her up in its jaws and crush her. Max had moved farther into the trees and she reached them a mere instant before the wave of snow. She had once seen the path an avalanche could slice through a forest: trunks lying like spilled matchsticks on either side of the brutal swathe. But those had been aspen trees, frail wispy things with no roots to speak of—now she cut sharply around the massive bole of a fir and felt the earth shudder beneath her feet. The snow slide gobbled up the glade.

With a sound that might have been a whimper she forced herself deeper down into the trees, her eyes locked on Max's back. The firs behind her were groaning now like martyrs on the rack, bent unnaturally under the snow's weight, trunks snapping like twigs. There was no trail in front of her, nothing to follow down the mountainside but Max's flitting form, his turns powerful and unquestioning. *I've been up here three times this winter—*

A branch whipped across her shoulder and her skis slid out from under her. She fell, screaming.

Max careened around, poles stabbing for purchase. "Get up! Get up, God damn you!"

She forced her poles into the loose snow and heaved upward. His face was gray beneath the tan, his eyes fixed on something behind her. She hurled herself downward and saw that he was still rigid in the same spot. The roar made words impossible. In an instant she would be seized and bent double, spine snapping like the trees—

Max dropped his poles and caught her as she tore past. Her feet nearly slid out from beneath her again, but for the vise of his arm. His mouth was pressed to her ear. "That's the worst of it."

Only then did she allow herself to look behind. Twenty-five feet up the mountainside, the snow had come to a shuddering halt against the bulwark of the firs. A broad door had been punched through the glade, and a road half a football field wide spilled from it. Firs that had seen two hundred winters had been felled in a matter of seconds.

Max was still holding her. She began to tremble, so violently that she slipped through his arms and sat down on her skis. The massive weight of snow suspended against the sky, caught in the net of branches, was creaking eerily, like sails in high wind.

"We should get down while we can," he said urgently. "Can you make it?"

She looked up at him, her eyes wide, her face pale. "Hell, *yes*. That was the best goddamn run I've ever had in my life." A wild elation flooded her heart.

They emerged from the trees at the base of a valley, on the cusp of high alpine pasture. They shouldered their skis and began to walk down the hard-packed road that led to a small village, and forty-five minutes later stopped at the first tavern they could find. There was a fire and a few free tables amid the crowd of local patrons. In a heavy Savoyard accent a young woman offered them fresh bread and cheese and sausages; they drank Swiss beer and toasted the bread and cheese over the fire with long-handled tongs. Stefani was in tearing high spirits, she was giddy from cheating death; she flirted and charmed and had never looked more glorious. Max knew how a near-death experience could take some people and he waited for the after-effects of adrenaline to wane. He restrained the impulse to grasp her shoulders and pull her close. It was only after the pastry was offered and refused, and she had tossed back a brandy, that she voiced the obvious question.

"Who fired the gun?"

She said it quietly, so that the others who spoke English in the tavern would not hear. The *others*—had one of them hiked down from his perch in the hillside, after leveling his gun and firing two shots? Had the bullets been meant to kill them outright? Or merely to crack the headwall's face?

"Anyone who carries a gun and fires it during spring ski season is a fool," he told her. "You can be prosecuted for triggering an avalanche."

"If you're caught." She pushed her brandy glass aside; she was somber and thinking, now. "I'd like to believe it was an accident.

Teenagers—a prank. Or that sport nobody really does except in the Olympics—the biathlon. Skiing and firing at little targets in the snow."

"There's a course for that," Max replied tersely, "and it's not at the altitude we skied today."

"Jeff's right, you know. You're a target."

"A Thai gunman in the woods?" he mocked. "I don't think they ski."

"—Or one of their assigns, as Oliver Krane would put it. *Yes.* I think the firing of a gun while Max Roderick stood in the direct line of a backcountry chute will never be coincidence. That was a planned attack, Max. It very nearly succeeded."

"But we escaped."

"So what?" Her voice rose slightly and he saw her check her next words and regroup before continuing. "This time the hit was supposed to look like an accident. Next time, it'll be focused and deadly. You should leave Courchevel."

"I don't run away from problems."

"Why do men always consider a tactical retreat to be running away? And even if it *is* running away—what's wrong with survival?"

"I've been surviving since I was eight years old. I'm not willing to settle for that anymore."

Her eyes narrowed. "What the hell do you mean?"

"Do you know what it's like to be the last man standing?—The one who's left behind when the others disappear or fall out of the sky or die without a word to the people they love? It means you can never be too safe. You can never lose control. You've got to beat the odds that wiped out your forebears. You've got to rewrite history, prove it wrong. You've got to be immortal." He spat the word.

"You really believe that?"

"I've had it thrust upon me," he said bitterly. "I never had a choice. It didn't matter that my family was gone and that at the age of ten I was a free agent. The day I stood over my mother's grave I understood what the rest of my life was for. If the Roderick clan was to have a happy ending, it was up to me to find it. I've spent my life testing death every day. I study the odds, I perfect my skills, I hone my strength. And then one day, Stefani, I fail. I *fail.* I fuck up the time trials for Nagano and I get sent home for good behavior. And as I look at the life I've made for myself—all this space, all this surviving I don't know what to do with—I say: what is it for?"

She stared at him wordlessly.

"Have I been running from the past for thirty years? Have I avoided the truth—about Dad, about Jack—because it might just be too painful? Is it better to pretend that history means nothing?"

He glanced away, unconsciously searching the faces surrounding them for one that looked out of place, for a detail that betrayed a taste for murder. "I shouldn't place you at risk. I'm sorry."

"You aren't. Oliver Krane is—with my permission."

"Then you should understand that I'm not running anymore. I want to know the worst of what happened. I want explanations that have been too long denied me. I want retribution and truth telling and I want somebody to pay. God damn it—*I want the house.*"

"You've got a perfectly nice one," she observed.

He laughed despairingly. "You have no idea what you're talking about. To understand, you'd have to have seen the house on the khlong. You'd have to walk in your bare feet across the polished wood floors, stare up into the heart of those soaring rooms, and touch the face of the Buddha as it stares out over the garden. You'd have to feel the presence of ghosts—as I felt them last year. *He's still there,* Stefani. Jack is there. And he belongs to me. Not to the crowds that shuffle through his palace in their dirty jeans every day. *To me.*"

She nodded slowly, the expression in her dark eyes at once cool and compassionate. "So what are you going to do?"

"Fly to Bangkok on Monday. Come with me?"

To his surprise, she flushed. "Of course. Isn't that my job?"

He couldn't help smiling at her. "You skied your pants off today, you know."

"You *wish*, Roderick."

Flirting again, despite the knowledge of being watched, despite the gun. God, she had a brutal courage. And yet she looked so frail. He watched her stroke crimson lipstick over her mouth as coolly as though she were in an elevator in Manhattan.

"You saved my life," she observed around the lipstick. "Now I owe you. So fuck the apologies, okay?"

There was just enough challenge in her eyes. He leaned in and kissed her, hard, so that the careful application of red paint was pointless, a scrawl across both their mouths, now.

8

They made it back to Courchevel six minutes late for their drink at Le Bateau Ivre. Jeff Knetsch sat waiting for them at a table in the back corner, his ski jacket off and his restless fingers wrapped around a beer. He seemed engrossed in conversation with a woman slouched indolently in one of the chairs, her boots propped on the restaurant's blazing hearth. She had waist-length orange hair drawn up high on the crown of her head; her skin was tanned; her makeup perfect. She could not possibly have skied that day, Stefani decided.

"Oh, God," Max muttered in her ear. "Brace yourself."

At the sight of Max, Jeff's beer slipped from his hand and sloshed over the table.

"Darling!" The woman's legs dropped to the floor with a crash. She thrust herself out of the chair and hurried toward them. Brown eyes, almond shaped, with Asia in her bones. The accent, however, was pure Sloane Ranger.

"Ankana," Max murmured, leaning down to peck her cheek. "What a pleasure to see you in Courchevel."

"The most brilliant coincidence! Absolutely fabulous! I was standing in line for the tram—Saulire's smashing today, darling, you *should* have been there—and suddenly I was almost *run over* by poor Jeff! I was screeching obscenities at him before I realized who he was, of course.

And then I simply roared with laughter! Too bloody rich, isn't it? Running into each other this way? And all the while I thought he was in New York!"

She seized Max's hand and dragged him back to the table like a prize marlin.

"Ankana," Max said, "may I introduce a very old friend? Stefani Fogg, Ankana Lee-Harris."

"Charmed," the woman said patly, and fixed her rich sloe eyes on Stefani's face for a fraction of a second before dropping back into her chair. "How're tricks, darling? How's the divine stone house? Cleaned the hot tub since I was in it last? Got any more of your yummy Bordeaux?"

Max smiled tightly. "Have you been waiting long?"

"Two hours," Jeff told him. "I quit early. Leg's not what it used to be. Sit down."

Stefani felt Max's hand tighten on her arm. He pulled out a chair. "Just one drink, I'm afraid. We're both pretty trashed."

"Skied yourself to death, I suppose?" Ankana smiled. "Jeff tells me you abandoned him for the backcountry. Shabby treatment, Max—for shame."

"He was well out of it." Max scanned the room for a waitress.

"Heavy powder?"

"Mix of old crud and new corn. Demanding. Are you here long?"

"Just the weekend. Bobbie—my husband—is so vicious these days I had to flee. Desperate for a bit of fun. I'll be back in the trenches Monday morning, worse luck."

"How do you all know each other?" Stefani asked. Max had obviously decided to say nothing about the avalanche, and so she followed his lead.

"Oh, it's been *years*," Ankana declared tragically. "I was a World Cup groupie in my babyhood, and knew all the boys like the back of my hand." Bedroom eyes at Max. "But I lost touch once I moved to London. Then Jeff and I met by chance two years ago at the Met—I'm in public relations, darling, in the art world, and Jeff's on the Metropolitan Board. I couldn't believe it! So of course we've kept in touch."

"You live in London now?"

"Hampstead Heath. I spend every waking minute plotting methods of escape. And you?"

"New York."

"Jeff's backyard! Know Shelley and the kids, then?"

"Only by reputation."

"How in the *world* did you fetch up here?" The tilted eyes betrayed no suggestion of the intense interest Stefani detected in every line of the other woman's body.

"I'm spending my ex-husband's money," she replied coolly. "It seemed like the best revenge."

"How brilliant of you!" Ankana shrieked. "Then let's stiff you for the bill!"

"Jeff, I'm too tired to fight for a drink," Max interposed firmly. "I think I'll head home."

"I'll drop by later." The lawyer's face was pinched and white with exhaustion; his leg must be hurting him more than he admitted. "There are some things we need to discuss."

"Business? How *boring*," Ankana burst out. "Can't I snag some time in the tub while you two are nattering on? Max, you owe me an invitation. Admit it. It's been *years* since I've seen the inside of your place."

He stared at her, then shrugged slightly. "As long as Jeff pays for the damage."

"He always does!"

Another shriek of laughter, and they fled for the door.

"Explain," Stefani demanded under her breath as they picked up their skis. The frigid rush of air, smelling of new snow, was like a cleansing bath on her upturned face. "Who is she?"

"A leech," he said flatly. "A nightmare. No morals, no money and no mercy. Jeff's up to his neck for the rest of his stay."

"Is he having an affair with her?"

"I suppose they could have arranged to meet in Courchevel. But I doubt it. Jeff's family means a lot to him. Ankana's vice is usually more casual."

"You despise her."

"I don't trust her. She's changed her skin so many times in the past, I don't know who she really is."

"Asian?"

"By way of Heathrow. She's native Thai, married to an English peer with more money than sense."

"The public relations bit is bogus?"

"Oh, she has a job. At a museum in London—the Hughes Museum of Asian Art—but nobody's quite sure how she stays employed."

"Max"—Stefani stopped short at the parting of their ways, her *piste* leading down to Le Praz, his toward the house—"be careful tonight. A Thai woman appears two hours after you're nearly killed. I don't like the coincidence."

"Come with me and watch her yourself."

"I've got a phone call to make."

"Mr. Krane?"

She nodded. "I want his opinion on avalanches."

There was a phone booth in Jacques Renaudie's pub in Le Praz that looked primitive enough to be untraceable. Stefani had noted the spot during a pre-ski coffee run two days previous. At four o'clock that afternoon—nine A.M. in New York—she pulled the booth's door shut, fed a token into the ancient machine and requested an international operator. "Collect call from Hazel," she said, and pronounced one of the numbers that Oliver had given her.

As the call went through, she kept her eyes trained on the front of Renaudie's place. Local skiers thronged around the bar, ordering beer and hot toddies while insults flew back and forth in rapid French. Le Praz was a quieter village than Courchevel 1850, where Max lived; it drew few of the international jet set and more families with children. She had chosen the villa in Le Praz because it was less obvious than one of the four-star hotels near Max's home; but she was an oddity here, in her fawn-colored doeskin and her mink headband.

"Carlton Gardens," said a quiet voice in her ear. She jumped. How like Oliver to name his transfer service after a Monopoly card. The operator gave her name; the call was accepted. And there was Oliver at the speed of light—from his current undisclosed location. Stefani was fairly certain he was nowhere near New York.

"Hazel, darling," he cooed. "Drinking buttered rum and pining for your dear old uncle? How are tricks on the World Cup Circuit? Tell me everything. We're completely secure."

"Max and I were nearly buried alive this morning," she replied, "in an avalanche someone triggered by gunfire."

"Good lord. You *do* intend to go out with style. Any casualties?"

"None. We were alone—skiing one of Max's private spots. Whoever fired the gun knew we would be there. The attack was deliberate and targeted very narrowly."

"Then the field of suspects is similarly narrow, I presume?"

"I chose not to point that out to Max. But I want to know more about his lawyer, a man named Jeff Knetsch. He appeared out of nowhere last night, looked me over and hated what he saw. He had an idea where we'd be skiing. You'll find him in the dossier you gave me— but only as background. I need present-day stuff. His loyalties, his weaknesses. How much Max is worth in legal fees."

"Then you shall have it," Oliver promised briskly. "I think it only fair to warn you that Mr. Knetsch has been making inquiries of his own."

"Regarding . . . ?"

"*You*, love, naturally. He's gathered quite a bit of dirt."

Stefani digested this information in silence. "On Max's orders?"

"One would assume."

He takes nothing on faith. He trusts no one. Or is Knetsch acting alone, trying to undermine my job?

"Shall I finger anyone else's knickers?" Oliver asked mildly.

"It's a long shot, but there's a woman. Name of Ankana Lee-Harris. Born Thai, married to a Brit named Bobbie Lee-Harris. She surfaced with Knetsch today. Max didn't like it."

"Address? Maiden name?"

"She lives in Hampstead Heath and works for the Hughes Museum of Asian Art. That's in London."

"I *know*." For the first time since she'd met him, he sounded faintly annoyed. "Age? Coloring? Bank accounts?"

"I only had a drink with her, Oliver. She's about my age. Asian hair that's bleached orange."

"Right-o. Hazel—"

"Yes?"

"Enjoying yourself?"

He trusts no one—

For an instant, the memory of Max's mouth on hers forced her to close her eyes.

"Immensely," she replied.

9

Mademoiselle Fogg!" cried Yvette Margolan as Stefani strode into the charcuterie. "What a pleasure it is to see you! And how were *les pistes* today?"

"Thrilling. I practically threw myself down the mountain."

"The backcountry, it is always demanding." The Frenchwoman leaned engagingly across her glass countertop. "A joy, yes, like all of Courchevel, but *très fatigant*."

Stefani glanced at her shrewdly. "Is the backcountry written all over my face?"

"Max, he told me where he would ski when he came for my *tarte tatin* yesterday. I always ask where he goes, because he has the best nose for powder of any man on the mountain."

Which meant that anyone who talked to Yvette yesterday could have known where Max planned to ski this morning. Stefani felt the sharp stab of frustration.

"When one is following Max Roderick," Yvette prattled, "one must race as though the devil himself were at one's heels. I know. I have skied with him too many times to count."

"You've known Max a while?"

"As long as he has lived in Courchevel." Yvette gestured toward a framed photograph that sat above her cash register: four people laughing in the snow, Saulire in the distance. "We used to be so happy, Jacques and I and his wife and Max, when we hiked the backcountry together. But then . . ." She cocked her head at Stefani. "How is Max these days? He is happy?"

"I suppose so."

"You had not seen him for many years, I understand?"

The woman was settling in for a long gossip. Time to feed the rumor mills.

"We were quite close during the late eighties," Stefani offered recklessly, "but when I married, we grew apart."

"You are *married*?"

"Not anymore," Stefani lied smoothly. "My ex-husband was an oil man. I've come to Courchevel to forget him."

"Ah." The Frenchwoman scanned Stefani's exquisite clothing, then nodded sagely. "And Max, he has been too much alone. But enough, *bon,* you did not come into my shop to talk of *les amours.*"

"I thought we were talking of skiing," Stefani said innocently. "But you're right, madame—I'm here for that marvelous *tarte tatin* Max served last evening. Would you happen to have another?"

It was as Yvette was wrapping the confection in plastic and brown paper that the bells over the door jangled. A dark, lithe girl in a ski sweater and fur boots sauntered into the shop. She had glossy hair the color of sable; petulant, full lips; and gray eyes thickly lashed. A cigarette dangled from the corner of her mouth.

"*Allô, Yvette,*" she called. "*Tu vas bien?*"

"*Oui, comme toujours, Sabine. Et votre papa?*"

"*Ce con,*" the girl replied venomously, and ground the butt under her heel.

Yvette darted a worried glance at Stefani. "Thank you very much, Mademoiselle Fogg," she murmured, and handed the tart over the counter.

"Fogg?" muttered Sabine. "*C'est la putain américaine?*"

"*Zut, Sabine,*" Yvette hissed.

But the girl barred Stefani's path. "You are the woman named Fogg?"

"I am. And you would be?"

Sabine eyed her from head to toe, then smiled maliciously. "But you are so old! Max cannot be in love with you. You must be nearly forty!"

"Nearly. Are you out of diapers yet?"

Sabine tossed her hair and sauntered over to Yvette's counter, where she began to examine a tray of chocolates. "In France, *vous comprenez*, men prefer younger women. They use ones like you for tidying the house and ones like me for messing the bed."

"Sabine!" Yvette protested.

"Don't worry," Sabine tossed over her shoulder. "I am going. I have a date with the Austrian Ski Team. You can tell Max where to find me if he is lonely." She slid past Stefani and stalked out the door.

"*La pauvre petite*," Yvette mourned. "She has never understood the abandonment of the mother, you understand."

Stefani gathered her ski gloves from the shop counter. "Jacques Renaudie's daughter?"

"*Mais oui.* Her mama was head over ears in love with Max, once upon a time. But Max, he never saw Claudine as a woman—merely as the wife of an old *ami*—and she went off at last to Paris with a banker friend of Max's. I have not heard from her in some time." Yvette glanced at the photograph above her cash register. "*Cette jeune fille* will not be happy until she has punished them all for making her miserable."

When she reached her rented villa, Stefani changed out of her ski clothes and sat down to compose a secure fax for Oliver Krane. It was imperative she add a few names to his query list. Jacques Renaudie might look benign, but his estranged wife and bitter daughter were reasons enough to hate Max Roderick. Even the best of friendships might shatter under strain; the best of men strike a bargain with murder.

Jeff Knetsch splashed two fingers of whiskey into his glass and held it to the light. He was not the sort of man who drank to excess; but the impulse flared at moments like this, when events and people spun out of control.

Control. It was a byword of his, the defining concept of his life.

Control freak, they called him at Ballard, Crump & Skrebneski, the white-shoe law firm where he'd made partner seven years before. Control freak, and Mr. Anal-Retentive, and The Micromanager. Jeff had no quarrel with the names. His reputation began and ended with obsessive attention to detail.

As an associate he'd been praised for the immense tally of billable hours he'd racked up each year, for the burning focus he gave the most incidental problem. He led a blameless life in the suburbs of West-chester, where he served as a Sunday-school teacher at the Episcopal church. His wife, Shelley, never behaved inappropriately at firm functions; she dressed well, if conservatively; and if the pair of them seemed at times to be colorless—if their conversation was too safe, their opinions too predictable—this did neither of them any harm in the eyes of those who governed Jeff's career. He might not be a rainmaker—the sort of charming glad-hander who reeled in business by the fistful—but Jeff was *steady.* He was *dependable.* Jeff Knetsch, as partner at Ballard, Crump & Skrebneski, was given the difficult cases. The demanding and persnickety clients. The ones the firm could not afford to lose.

Had one of his partners studied him closely, however, as he made his way each day from elevator to office, Jeff's camouflage might have failed him. A nerve above his right eye twitched compulsively. His fingers were clenched on the handle of his briefcase. Discipline was no longer Jeff's tool; it was his prison.

He survived the tidal waves of life by keeping his thoughts and emotions in concentric boxes, nested firmly on the floor of his mind. Communication among them was strictly forbidden. One box held his past, and all the dreams he had nourished in late-night fantasies of glory and fame. In another box was the pain of profound physical injury and its recovery. A third held his law career. A fourth, his marriage. And in the fifth—

A whoop of wild laughter floated up from the hot tub one floor below, breaking into his thoughts. Ankana Lee-Harris was bathing nude down there, her golden thighs iridescent in the underwater lights, her eyes luminous as a cat's. She'd propped an open champagne bottle near the edge of the tub and one of Max's crystal flutes lolled in her taloned fingers. She showed no inclination to leave anytime soon.

Max hated having her in his house, and he'd let Jeff know it.

"Get rid of her."

They'd faced off in the kitchen, where the swinging door guaranteed a bit of privacy.

"I want her out in the next half hour."

"Max, I'm not sure I can—"

"If she's still here by three A.M., there will be hell to pay. And I refuse to argue the point with that woman in an advanced state of inebriation."

"It's only seven-thirty. There's plenty of time—"

"Jeff," Max muttered with contempt. "You've still got the backbone of a jellyfish."

His self-control beginning to unravel, Jeff had reached instinctively for the bottle of Scotch. A wave of vertigo, like a fever spike, and the Scotch sloshed wetly over his fingertips.

"I'll have to take her to dinner. Someplace expensive."

Max tossed him fifteen hundred francs. "Kick her ass-first into the snow. Rudeness is the only thing Ankana understands. You owe her nothing."

If only—Jeff thought now as he drained the Scotch in his glass—*that were true. If only I owed her and all the rest of them exactly nothing*—

He did not drink to excess or keep a mistress or live carelessly on credit cards—but he was prey to one imperious weakness. *The fifth box.* The box where all the risk and wildness dwelled, the box where chance gave no quarter. Jeff loved that box—loved the unpredictability, the sudden windfalls of fortune, the losses so absolute they could crush a man.

The gambler's box.

Everything was possible there, everything rosy, and he had begun to throw more and more money into games of chance with each visit to Vegas, each weekend trip to Atlantic City. He kept accounts with bookies under multiple names. He was adrift in a sea of Internet operations, all vaguely structured and probably illegal. He was in debt beyond his reckoning and the consequences had never mattered. To bet his life on the toss of a die was the ultimate intoxication. He was Fate's plaything.

"She's leaving Sunday morning?" Max demanded.

"So she says."

"Stefani and I are flying to Bangkok on Monday. You can head back to New York anytime you like."

Dismissed, Jeff thought, *like baggage. So much for old friendship. You fucking idiot, Max.* A wave of anger and fear, fueled by the Scotch, surged into his brain. "You invited Fogg to Bangkok—just like that?"

"Just like that. I've made my decision. This is why I hired her."

"I've been wondering about that. Why you hired her."

Max glanced toward the hallway—listening for Ankana? He did not reply. Eavesdropping at keyholes certainly numbered among her talents.

"Stefani's not the most qualified person in the world," Jeff persisted, "whatever Krane wants you to believe. She could do forensic accounting in New York as easily as in Thailand. Frankly, any competent paralegal in my own firm could accomplish about as much, at a fraction of the cost."

"Is that what this is about? Where I put my business?"

"Not at all. It's a judgment call. She's not worth her fees."

"What have you got against Stef? She's competent enough—"

"So it's 'Stef' now? Fuck competence if things have gone *that* far." He waved the Scotch bottle vaguely in Max's direction.

"You're pissed off about that crack she made. About your career," his friend said with a trace of amusement. "You don't like her because she refuses to kiss ass."

"I love her," Jeff retorted. "She's a gas. She looks at you with those melting eyes and lisps words of four syllables you can barely comprehend. That's why Krane sent her over here. He figures you won't balk at his bills if you're dazzled."

Max snorted.

"You wanted my advice," Jeff said impatiently. "*My expert opinion.* I say: Send the woman home."

"It's too late for that."

"Why? We were managing very well without Krane and Associates a week ago. Now you're flying Fogg into Bangkok. What's changed?"

Max threw him a level look, the sort he reserved for competitors he'd beaten. "You're not enough, Jeff. You're in New York, with a practice that goes far beyond my problems. No matter how much money I throw at your firm, that's not going to change."

"I'd be the first to admit I'm not God. I can't save every situation. But I *am* your oldest friend."

"You're closer than a brother." He said it without emotion, a bald statement of fact. "But that's got nothing to do with Stefani."

"I don't trust her. That should mean more to you than it does. You were nearly killed today."

When he'd walked into the house that night, Max told him how he'd survived the avalanche. Max and the snow, the ultimate gamble.

"She could have died, too."

"Some security expert! You were safe enough in Courchevel until her plane crashed on your doorstep. Max, what do you really know about her?"

"She's shrewd, she's thorough, she's got a hell of a good degree from a major business school and she's financially independent through years of hard work. She can ski like a pro. She's got courage and mental toughness. She isn't afraid to look danger in the face. What else is there?"

"She's been married and divorced," Jeff shot back, "twice. She's done a total of twenty-seven months of therapy and a variety of depression drugs. She's had three miscarriages and was arrested five years ago for possession of cocaine. Not the most stable woman in the world. Did Krane tell you why she left FundMarket?"

"No. Did you send out your firm's private investigator, Jeff, as soon as you knew her name?"

"Of course." He set down his empty glass. "I wouldn't be offering the best possible representation if I did anything less. She was fired from FundMarket for inside trading. She was one step ahead of an SEC investigation. The mutual fund she managed was in deep doo-doo. She was given the choice of walking out, or being thrown. The rumors have been all over *The Wall Street Journal*."

"Rumors?"

"It's always rumors until the SEC jumps."

"So you paid a private eye to tell you what *The Wall Street Journal* decided to print? Don't submit that cost in your next bill. *Please*."

"Krane can't know what he's sent you. He will, though, once I've placed a few calls."

"Why would you do *that*, Jeff?" Max's voice was strained. "—Sabotage a woman I hired?"

"Because your life is at stake, buddy," he shot back, "and you're thinking with your dick."

Max's face hardened.

"It's been a while since you've spent this much time with a woman. You get wood every time she brushes against you in her leather pants. Why do you think she wears them?"

Max looked abashed. He was considering the point.

"What if the Thais got to her first?" Jeff demanded. "The same thugs who dumped the whore in your hotel room? What if your *security expert* set you up for that avalanche today?"

"Why would she bother?"

"Krane's firm is FundMarket's watchdog, Max. Don't you understand what that means? Fogg traded on the inside and lost her job. *Krane's surveillance architecture is the reason why.*" He gripped his friend's shoulders. "Max, she's got a motive for revenge against Oliver Krane that's a mile wide. And she's using *you* to bring him down."

10

Max sat alone reading the private investigator's file. It was all there, as Knetsch had said—the dirty laundry of a forty-year-old woman's life, arranged in clinical order and looking all the more sordid for it. He digested detail after detail: names of husbands, boyfriends, doctors, attorneys; the dates of her detox treatment following the cocaine bust; items in society columns that suggested highly public rampages; car accidents; affairs. The worst time had been seven years earlier, when nothing but wild living seemed to matter, when even her image in newsprint photos looked blurred and indistinct.

He read in the brutal hope that the file would make it easier for him to sever his connection with Stefani Fogg. He read to justify his trust in Jeff Knetsch—and at the end of the exercise, he had achieved no resolution.

He'd skied with her, watched her outrun an avalanche and judged her accordingly. Were his instincts so wrong?

He slapped the file closed.

There was nothing in Jeff's report of the woman who had conquered the financial canyons of New York. Nothing of the brilliant mind and the canny judgment he was certain she possessed. Nothing of the courage that sang in her veins—unless it was the sort of bravado that tells the world to go to hell and lives with the consequences.

That, he understood.

"Jeff!" he shouted toward the downstairs passage where the hilarity, now, was at frat-house pitch and the slosh of water set his teeth on edge. "Get the hell out of my house! And take that woman with you!"

He was used to the pitch of Jean Blanc, the 3000-foot vertical drop between Courchevel 1850 and Le Praz; and at this time of evening it was utterly empty. He crouched low over his tips, turning with the curve of the terrain, at a speed that might have been clocked at sixty-five miles an hour, had anybody cared. All his life he had thrown himself down the sides of mountains; it was the surest antidote to pain he knew. Here he could be precise, powerful, focused, clean. *Trust your training, trust your equipment,* he heard his old coach say; *nothing else matters. Nothing else is real.*

He reached Stefani's villa at the end of one of the town's narrow, twisting streets just as most of Le Praz was settling down to dinner.

The house lights etched oblongs of orange on the snow packed around the entrance. He stared for an instant through the undraped window. She sat by a crackling hearth, a glass of wine in one hand. Unconscious of being observed, her eyes and mouth shadowed in the firelight, she looked older than the flirt he had taken to lunch. It was a hard, watchful face, he realized—a secretive face that she ruthlessly composed for public view.

He rang the bell.

She set down the wineglass before glancing toward the window. He knew from her look that she understood he'd been watching her. She did not move for the space of several seconds. As though a sort of menace would enter the house if she let him in. But her head was up, her eyes fixed on the window—

He rang the bell again.

"You're in time for a drink," she told him as she opened the door. "I'm serving white tonight. It pairs well with avalanches."

He stamped the snow off his boots and snapped open the clasps. "I never drink when I'm skiing."

"And you have miles to go before you sleep?"

"Something like that. I'll leave these outside."

Her dark eyes came up to his, openly assessing. "You've been talking to your lawyer."

"How did you know?"

"Oliver told me."

"Told you what, exactly?"

"That you'd ordered Knetsch to poke around my past. The people he hired—the methods they used—were appallingly obvious."

Was this mere bravado? A bald attempt to make him believe she was in Krane's confidence, when in fact she was out for her boss's neck?

"What Jeff did, he did on his own."

"How comforting." She held the door wider. "I'd offer you dinner, but I'm the sort of person who keeps nothing in her refrigerator but champagne and caviar."

"I didn't come for dinner."

"But you did ski all the way down here for some reason, and it's freezing. Come inside."

He stepped into the room. "Stefani, why did you leave your last job?"

"Surely Knetsch could find that out."

"I want to know if his story's true."

"There are always stories, Max." She said it quietly. "Jeff has a story—I have a story—but you'll still have to decide whom to believe. A woman you've known for days? Or a friend you've had all your life?"

"You want me to take you on faith, is that it?"

She shrugged and retrieved her wineglass. "Faith is just a word we use to legitimate gut instinct. I've acted on gut for years. A trader lives and dies by it. So does a downhill racer."

"Were you fired for insider trading?"

"Yes." She looked amused. "See what I mean? You're not much more advanced in your decision."

They eyed each other wordlessly. What impulse urged her to dodge the truth? He had the background report on his kitchen table. Her sole hope lay in pleading her case—persuading him to trust. Instead, she'd flipped him off.

Did she care so little?

Or too much?

She leaned back against her sofa, one cognac-colored boot propped on the table. Her legs were sheathed in velvet, and every honed muscle was outlined against the firelight.

"You should have asked a different question, you know. Something like: 'Stefani, did you use privileged information to buy and sell specific shares? And did you and your fund-holders benefit from that information?' To which I could have answered: *No*."

"Oh, Jesus. Why is it so difficult to get the simple truth?"

"You want the truth about your grandfather. The truth about me. The truth, even, about your friend Knetsch. Truth is, Max, that the truth is what we make it." Her eyes never left his face, but her expression was too indolent, too careless of the situation. Her sweater was made of some soft, caressing stuff the color of spilled wine and he wanted, suddenly, to take her shoulders in his hands and shake her.

"Then you can leave Courchevel tomorrow." He turned for the door.

"I hear some pretty interesting stories about you," she said thoughtfully to his back. "There's Yvette Margolan, for instance, and her story of Madame Renaudie—a pretty woman, from her picture. And then there's the story of the daughter, Sabine, who's pining for you and going down on the entire Austrian Ski Team. The whole thing sounds too much like a remake of *The Graduate* for my taste, but I'm not one to judge."

"No," Max said bitterly, "having failed twice at marriage and three times at motherhood."

He had opened the door and nearly stepped into the night when he caught sight of her face. She had gone dead white, her eyes blazing as though he had slapped her.

"You bastard," she said through her teeth. "What do you know about me?"

The simple truth.

Only the truth is never simple.

Faith is a word we use to legitimate gut instinct, she'd said. But was it gut, this time—or something else?

He walked back across the room, his legs stiff and ungainly as though still encased in ski boots; and when he stood over her, all the doubt and indecision and passion in his face, she reached up with both hands and pulled his mouth down to hers.

Violence in the parted lips, the taste of wine elusive on the tongue. Violence and challenge and rage at the stupidity of men—himself in particular—who should know better than to slam her for the sins of youth. Her fingers tore at his hair, at once claiming and fighting him, and he remembered what he'd said to her, one day on the lift.

. . . pursue a man whose strength matches yours. An equal. What might happen then?

And she'd replied: *A fight to the death.*

He felt the force of desire like a physical blow, and sank down between her knees—Max Roderick, who needed and wanted nobody very much. The tangle of emotion he'd kept at bay since outpacing the avalanche—the adrenal rush of risk, the fury of a threatened animal—torched like a flame inside him. *A fight to the death.* He cupped her face and forced her chin upward, his mouth at the hollow of her throat.

"God damn you, Max," she breathed. "God *damn* you."

She arched away from him, as though she would claw her way to freedom if she could.

"Stop fighting me."

"I can't. If I give way to you—"

I'll have nothing left? Was that the end of her desperate sentence? He slid both hands under the cashmere sweater and in one impatient movement pulled it over her head.

"It's always about winning, for you," she said. "Dominance."

"No, it's not. Most of the time, my darling, it's about fighting off fear."

He stared into eyes dark with comprehension—with the naked bruising of lost years—and his breath was suddenly shallow. "I don't want to be alone any longer."

"Alone's the only place I feel safe."

"You're too brave to settle for that. Safety's not worth a damn."

She closed her eyes, an expression of pain on her face.

"You know why I want the house on the khlong—what it means to me. The past regained. The wrongs set right. I want you in the same way. We need to take our happiness. I can't envision the future without you in it."

"Max—"

"You said something the first day we met. A challenge before you jumped. Say it again."

She lowered herself until her skin was flush with his, melting in the firelight.

"*Say it again,* Stefani."

Her mouth was against his ear, the words so faint he might have imagined them. "Follow me, Max. *Follow me—*"

Much later, when she dreamed again, it was of a house made entirely of snow, the windows blank and the door sealed shut. She was fighting to get out.

11

She slipped away from Max early the next morning and sat out alone on the freezing terrace, hoping the icy air and fathomless quiet would slap some sense into her skull.

The world at this hour was monochrome: black knives of fir thrust deep into the sky, white snow lapping at their roots. When the first sun slid through the woods, jumping from tree to tree like a spreading flame, the landscape surged into color.

A pad of paper and a felt-tip pen sat on the table before her. On the pad she'd written: *You've been a very bad girl. Whatever will Oliver say?*

It was not, perhaps, the sort of thing she ought to tell her boss—that she'd slept with a client—but then again, it was precisely the sort of outcome Oliver Krane might have planned. What had he said to her, a few weeks before? *You want to strap on crampons and climb all over him, Stef. Admit it.*

Oliver had seen more than she had, from the moment he'd sent her *Ski* magazine. She felt a sudden and hot resentment toward him for throwing her into Max Roderick's lap. Then anger gave way to the desire to run.

It won't last, she wrote as the sun fired the fir trees. *A hell of a good time, a few sleepless nights, and then—*

The memory of his mouth on the flesh of her inner thigh. His voice in her ear. The surging power of a body honed by years of punishing will. Max in the night was a kind of demon—controlling, demanding, impossible to deny. Even if she'd wanted to.

She dropped her pen, overcome by a wave of feeling so sharp and unexpected it was painful. It gathered her up in its velvet claws, tumbled her to the ground; she was gasping for air—

The avalanche.

What *was* it about Max she found so compelling?

The distance he kept from every living being—or the way he invited her suddenly into his soul? The doubts she still kept about his motives—or the absolute certainty she felt in his touch?

What did he find in her to love? She was cynical, tough, solitary, afraid. He challenged her to take herself as seriously as he did. If she accepted that challenge, she would get badly mauled. She had never allowed herself to feel deeply without facing significant pain.

Maybe I should just head back to New York right now.

She had thought to find a simpler man when she flew into Courchevel: one who'd liked speed and danger as a kid and had never grown up. But she understood, now, that Max had grown up way too soon. Death had snatched everyone he'd loved, and so all trust in love had deserted him. Was he asking her to save him? Did she want that burden?

He tells me he can't live alone anymore, she wrote on her sheet of paper, *but is he capable of anything else? He'll use his detachment—his perfect control— to learn the truth about the past. Will he use it against me, if I get too close?*

Was his lovemaking just a game, as deliberate as every other contest in his life? Had he studied her weaknesses—gauged her doubts—and outplayed her in the most brilliant way possible? Did he think he could win her absolute loyalty, and thus divide her from Oliver Krane? And would he drop her in the snow once he had what he really wanted—his Thai house, the key to his past?

At the bottom of the page she wrote in slashing script: *Remember: Not even Oliver is sure who Max really is. Trust nobody but yourself.*

"Coffee?"

She lifted her head and saw him framed in the villa's doorway. A sleek and compelling animal, even in repose. Eyes the color of moss. The hawkish molding of brow bone and temple, the willful set of the mouth. Had she been a fool or a child she would have worshipped him. Instead, she recognized him as the enemy.

"I'd love some."

His eyes lingered on the bright mask of her face. "Don't worry. I won't take over your house."

"It's not mine. I'm only using it for a while."

He ignored the implied insult and handed her a mug.

She drank deeply, hoping the coffee would steady her. He leaned on the deck railing and stared out at the firs. "It's a good house, borrowed or not."

With effort, she said, "I think I'd like to be alone today."

"I'm going to hit the backcountry again. While there's still powder."

"One avalanche wasn't enough?"

The corners of his mouth lifted. "As you said: It's a hell of a ride."

"Jesus, you're bad for me. You reinforce every reckless impulse I've ever had."

"You like danger." Gently, he took the mug from her hands and set it on the table. Traced the neck of her terrycloth robe with his fingers.

"I like peace and quiet. I like to be alone."

"Liar."

The cocaine belonged to Dennis, she had told him impatiently somewhere around three A.M., "who was a complete prick and a fuck-off and a guy who could disappear for a week every time I sent him out to buy milk. He left a little bag of powder in the glove compartment of my Audi and the cop who stopped me for speeding couldn't help but see it. Dennis should have been killed by the Colombians years ago and saved us all grief. I married him in my party phase—"

"Just a phase?" Max quipped dryly.

"—and he took me for everything I was worth. He lied about his job, he defaulted on his taxes, he screwed around with anything in a skirt, and twenty-six months after our wedding left me holding the bag he'd stuffed with his credit card receipts while he emigrated to Brazil. I spent five weeks in rehab I didn't need, sharing the denial I didn't feel. My wages were garnisheed by the IRS for three years, but I never declared personal bankruptcy."

Max finished the pâté she'd fed him in lieu of dinner and asked, "What about Tad?"

"Tad," she'd told him steadily, "was a mergers-and-acquisition guy who was worth roughly the yearly budget of the Three Valleys put together. He never moved without his cell phone, he was on call twenty-four/seven, he had one great passion in life and he respected my brains. I thought after Dennis, he'd give me stability."

They were camping in the middle of the living room floor, food and wine spread out around them, the fire nothing but a mass of embers. Max stroked her hair from her cheek. "And?"

"Tad had a different habit. When the pressure got to him—and it got to him every three or four days—he liked to practice kick-boxing on his wife."

The fingers curled convulsively at her temple and then relaxed—a movement so faint she might have imagined it.

"Max, I'm a lousy judge of character."

"Go with your instincts, perfect your technique."

The skier's mantra, the trader's ethic. Sometimes his comprehension of her thoughts was unnerving.

The miscarriages, he'd said somewhere near dawn. *Was Dennis responsible for those? Or Tad?*

She had pretended to be asleep. She never spoke of the lost children to anyone.

"Oliver," she said into the telephone receiver two hours later, "I'm going to Bangkok with Max the day after tomorrow."

"Are you indeed, Hazel my girl? And are you booking two rooms at the Oriental? Or one?"

"I always have my own room, Oliver," she replied succinctly, "in case I need to sleep."

"Bravo, ducks. And the sniper on the mountaintop?"

"—Could be anyone who learned where we skied from a woman grocer in Le Praz," she murmured with a glance at Renaudie's gray head across the pub. "The field is no longer narrow. Did you receive my fax yesterday?"

"And read it," Oliver said. "I have one thing only to tell you: Friend

Max sends Claudine Renaudie a tidy sum of five thousand francs each month, paid into an account in Paris. Is it from charity? Guilt? Or simply to keep her quiet?"

A chill curled along Stefani's spine. "Paying her to stay away, you mean? But why, Oliver?"

"No idea. Time may tell. Although time has a way of exploding our best prospects: until a few hours ago, Mr. Knetsch was emerging nicely as a villain."

The chill dissipated. "Tell me."

"He's wallowing in red ink, and he's made no less than thirteen calls to Bangkok in the last six weeks. I found that singularly odd, given that his firm has no Thai clients."

"Calls to whom?"

"The Ministry of Culture. The possibilities looked enticing, until I learned that Mr. Knetsch sits on the board of the Metropolitan Museum."

"So?"

"The Met is gearing up for a *pièce de résistance*. Two Thousand Years of Southeast Asian Art, or some such, with pieces loaned from all over the world."

She felt a pang of disappointment. "He's been talking museum business. Perfectly legitimate."

"The project could explain his chumminess with Mrs. Lee-Harris. She's arranging for the shipment of several Buddhas from the Hughes Museum."

"Public relations."

"Exactly. Liaison is Ankana's middle name. She works the networks, worldwide; none better. She's also desperately short of cash. That seems to be a bond between her and Knetsch. Neither has a penny to spare the pauper."

"Are they feeling pressure, Oliver?"

"Were I in either's shoes, I should be wincing from pain."

"Then they're vulnerable."

"To blandishments, blackmail and suspicious sums delivered in unmarked bags. All for services rendered, of course. Either might have sold our Max down the river. But there's no proof of it. Does Knetsch still think you're unsavory?"

"He tried to get me fired."

"Oh, well *done*, heart! Jealous of Max's luck, do you think?"

"Meaning . . . ?"

"The medals—the money—the adoring young beauties? All landing on Max's doorstep, while Jeff nurses his bum leg and ferries his dull kiddies to Sunday school? He'd have to be a saint not to repine. Not to wish their positions reversed. And he's not a saint—"

"—He's a lawyer. I suppose it's possible," Stefani mused. "Oliver, did the Met ever do business with your late friend Harry Leeds?"

"Now *that* is a question I had not thought to ask." Speculation knifed the urbane voice. "So Max is flying to Bangkok? Still determined to unearth old bones?"

"He wants Jack Roderick's House. That's the root of his obsession, Oliver—to him, that house stands for everything he's lost. His childhood. His innocence. The time when he could trust other people without question. He wants it all back. The inheritance is just a proxy."

"One would think," Oliver retorted with an edge of anger, "that when good men have died in the name of silence, silence would be observed. But no. We will have our truth, regardless of cost. I shall have to consider what this means for my clients."

"Oliver—whose side are you on?"

"My own, naturally."

That night Max carried her into the old stone house high above the glittering tram and deposited her in front of the soaring glass windows. He had rigged a tent out of parachute cloth and rappelling cords, a fairy dome suspended from the ceiling.

"When I was a kid in Evanston," he told her, "we used to sleep out in the backyard on summer nights. My father kept a tent there, and he'd lie in it for hours. He loved the sound of rain pattering on canvas. I can remember his hand on my rib cage, his utter stillness. The rain dripping down. All of us, my mother included, safe inside."

She looked up into the soaring yards of cloth. "Max, what happened to your mother?"

He took a moment to answer. "You'd have to know what she was like."

"Before 1967?"

"She idolized Jackie Kennedy. Wore pillbox hats. White gloves. Had a matching bag for every pair of shoes. She spent weekends at the Naval Academy and was married under an arch of crossed sabers. She joined the Junior League in Evanston, and wherever we moved after that—from port town to training base—she sent recipes for the annual League cookbook. *From the Kitchen of Anne Roderick.*"

"And after?"

"She lost faith in Camelot."

"So did Jackie."

"Things she'd believed, all her life—that her country was wise, that heroism meant something, that God looked after his own—meant nothing once my dad was murdered. She went in search of a different type of meaning: psychedelic drugs, Eastern mysticism, free love. She tried to reinvent herself, as though if she were a different person she wouldn't feel the pain."

"She should have thought of you."

"I don't blame her for it."

"She should have *lived* for you."

"But I failed her," he said brutally. "*Take good care of your mother—*that's what Dad said on the pier at Coronado. And I failed. I failed them both."

"Bullshit."

He stared at her wordlessly, the tram lights reflected in his eyes.

She reached up and pulled the tent down around them like a shroud.

Somewhere in the middle of the night she awoke to find that she was in his bed, and that his hand was resting lightly on her hip.

"Tell me," he commanded, "about the miscarriages."

"Why? Because it's a tidbit Jeff's spy didn't have?"

He got up and roamed around the room. He was comfortable in his skin—in the body that looked, in the snow-refracted moonlight, like chiseled marble. He reached for a black case that stood in one corner. The viola.

He turned the instrument in the soft glow from the window. Then he picked up the bow and raked it across the strings.

The feral notes shuddered through her body; an elegy for the night and its beauty, for the fleeting illusion of love. She lay motionless, the sheet drawn tight across her breasts, as though the slightest movement might break the spell of his playing. And when the bow fell and silence surged in around them, she said to his back, "They died inside me every time, no matter how hard I tried. I'm not a woman who's capable of sustaining life."

"Bullshit," he said, and bit the protest from her lips.

12

The March sun was just lifting into the sky when Max Roderick left his house. He snatched coffee for breakfast from a bar in town and took the first tram up to the top of Saulire, filled this Sunday with a handful of the one hundred and sixty passengers it usually carried. Courchevel was known for many things—its terrain, its crowd of beautiful young people, its state-of-the-art lifts—but not for its early risers. Heading out into the cold half-light of morning to carve first tracks was a habit Max had kept from years of hard training in the United States, a habit that marked him as a professional in this European playground.

He was carrying a pair of skis he had designed himself and intended to test that morning while he was alone and able to focus. The skis were fairly short for a man of his height, with flaring tips and narrow waists, designed for tight turns in the steeps and for whipping easily through the bumps. The bindings rested on a platform raised roughly half an inch above the ski's surface at the waist's midpoint—an innovation borrowed from downhill racers, who had been wedging their boots higher for years, now. The raised footbed encouraged a swift transfer of weight from one edge to the other, and thus, faster turns.

Max ignored the skiers in the tram: four tourists gawking at the spectacular abyss beneath the swinging cable; a couple locked hand-in-hand in the vast car's far corner; an elderly man nursing a foam cup of something hot. The latter had his eyes fixed on Max as though he recognized his face from Olympiads gone by—from Albertville, just a few valleys and a decade away. He was holding a pair of skis Max had designed three years before. Max allowed his gaze to drift past the man to the rock wall looming near the front of the tram. His spirits surged as they always did when the mountains seemed ready to fall into the fragile car.

It was eight-fourteen in the morning. By noon the chutes that riddled the backside of Saulire would be filled with cries of ambition and disappointment—but for this hour, at least, he would have them to himself. It was the last day of his ski season; the afternoon would be devoted to packing, and tomorrow he and Stefani would be bound for Bangkok. He closed his eyes and saw again the roiling brown waters of the Chao Phraya, surging through its banks; the elegant lines of the ancient teak house set into its garden; and dimly, as through the smoke of years, the tall man with the white bird on his shoulder. Stefani would love Bangkok—the bold ugliness, the striving squalor. She would wear nothing but silk. The damp climate would turn her black curls into a mass of wild softness, restrained but never tamed by a sprig of orchid—

After three good hours of skiing the steeps, Max decided, he'd head back to the old stone house for lunch.

She would be there—it never occurred to him that she might not. He had learned more about her in the past week than she realized; the truth about himself he had learned long ago. To strike the delicate balance necessary between two such strong tempers and wills would never be easy—but he recognized his luck in finding her. For the first time in months, something had gone right.

The tram slid into the cable house; the doors flew open. Max stepped past the attendant, clicked into his skis and skated three hundred feet toward the trailhead at the far side of the peak. The chutes of Saulire were vertical trenches cut into the mountain by eons of wind and weather. The deep snow that blanketed the gentler pitches elsewhere on the mountain was a scant dusting here, more ice than powder. Bare rock thrust outward, granite dark, the length of the couloir.

He wondered, for an instant, how Stefani would ski them—and was brought up short at the thought. He was no longer alone. The sensation was a strange one. In the midst of even his most demanding affairs—even with Suzanne—he had remained essentially solitary. Was it this loss—this invasion—that she fought, rather than him?

He settled the straps of his poles firmly in his palms, tightened his helmet and chose his line.

Like jumping down a ladder, whispered DiGuardia, his first and forever ski coach. *Except you're doing it with boards strapped to your feet. Trust your training, trust your equipment. Nothing else is real.*

It was the mantra he'd learned by heart, years ago, the half-uttered prayer to whatever god governed ski slopes. He studied the rock face falling away beneath him, bent his knees and sprang into the air.

Twelve feet below was the square yard of snow he intended to hit. The skis took the full impact of his two-hundred-pound frame, and with a metallic crunch that was audible for a fraction of a second, the right binding sheared completely off.

The ski flipped twice and fell in a gleaming arc some seventy-five feet below.

Max stabbed at the rock surface with his pole—fell forward over his remaining ski—and tumbled like a stone.

Jacques Renaudie skied only ten days a year. He never started earlier than ten o'clock, so that the rising warmth could soften the ice into something like half-dried cement, which tugged at the undersides of his skis so gently that his speed was broken without the slightest demand upon his aging thighs. He hated the layers of clothes dictated by January and February, and ventured up the mountainside only when he could slide down it wearing a heavy sweater and jeans. He rarely skied more than two hours at a time, taking the best of the midmorning and leaving the flat light of afternoon to the foolish and the avid. He was a Frenchman and therefore a connoisseur—of the *pistes,* as of everything.

In his day, Jacques had been a hellbent daredevil with a talent for bruising his way through a mogul field faster than any other man in Courchevel. He had worked the competitive bumps circuit at a time when the sport held little glamour and no Olympic slot. If he dallied in his middle age, it was in part because his knees could no longer support the punishment he longed to deal them. Thus two solid hours on the steeps of Saulire this warm March morning: a prize for good behavior.

He was worried about Sabine, who once again had been out all night and was threatening to join her mother in Paris. He thought suddenly of that woman's face—the American Max Roderick had picked up off the runway—with its milk-white skin and cunning black eyes. The Snow Queen, Jacques called her; the mythic witch who froze men's hearts to ice. How Max could turn from a girl like Sabine—

Jacques swore under his breath.

He stood at the mouth of his favorite couloir, one the locals called La Trahison. *Betrayal.*

A lump of ice the size of a walnut skittered past his ski tips and bounced off the rock walls of the chute, careening downward. He followed its fall idly enough while he adjusted his gloves, and then his eyes narrowed. Far below him like a discarded doll lay the figure of a skier—motionless against the rock—

Jacques went rigid, then craned his head for a better look. The suit was bright yellow, the helmet dark blue. A man, from what he could see at this distance, and facedown, his legs splayed at an unnatural angle.

Jacques's eyes traveled upward, found the ski poles twenty meters above, lying like bent hairpins. The skier had fallen, then, at the very mouth of the chute.

Mon dieu, Jacques whispered. *Le pauvre con* hadn't stood a chance.

There were rotors in the dream, a persistent hacking. Stefani scowled in her sleep and felt the coldness where Max had lain. She sat up abruptly in bed.

Through the windows she saw the tramline rising to the heights of Saulire—and something else: a helicopter beating its way steadily toward the peak. A Medevac chopper. Some fool had attempted terrain he couldn't handle.

"Max?" she called, and swung her legs to the floor.

The house threw back the stillness peculiar to empty space. She glanced at the clock on the bookshelf under the window. Ten-forty-three. Jesus—how had she slept so late?

She brushed her hair out of her eyes, took his robe from its peg and went in search of coffee.

It required three men traversing the rock face in crampons and ropes to reach the body where it lay. Forty minutes after Jacques Renaudie sounded the alarm—nearly three hours after the fall—the head of the Courchevel ski patrol bent down by his side and felt for a pulse in the neck.

"*Il vie,*" he said tersely. *He lives.*

The helmet alone had probably saved him; but from the angle of his head the three men feared for his neck. In the best of circumstances they might have encased him in a foam body shield and flown him immediately to Geneva; but he lay wedged into a sloping cleft on which only one other person could crouch. The last thing anyone wanted was a second casualty among the ski patrol. And yet, the victim must be strapped somehow onto a stretcher with skis, for transport to flatter terrain where a helicopter could land.

The head of the rescue team glanced grimly at the sheer concave wall of the chute rising six stories above. He had traversed the face with the stretcher strapped to his back and had found nowhere that three men, much less a helicopter, might stand. He glanced below, and saw that perhaps ten meters farther down, the chute widened. It would have to be enough.

"Two of us will have to turn him," he barked, "get him onto the stretcher, and slide him carefully to that spot. It's the only way."

His colleagues, roped together and then to the ropes secured at the couloir's mouth nearly fifty meters above, stamped their crampons into the ice. One drove the blade of his ice axe into the surface of the chute and clung to it while the other inched downward to help unstrap the bulky stretcher from the team chief's back. The chief stabilized the victim's head and neck as his colleague slowly log-rolled the inert form onto the gurney. The face was ghastly with bruises and cold; but it was unmistakable.

"*Merde,*" the chief muttered. "*C'est Roderick.*"

"Max Roderick?"

The name echoed against the stone. It sped upward to Jacques Renaudie like a well-placed bullet as he stood shivering in his sweater and jeans. He had removed his skis and propped them crosswise in the snow near the orange rope that cordoned off La Trahison. He heard the name, stood stock-still an instant, then shouted back down into the chute.

"*C'est Max?*"

"*Oui.*"

"*Il vie?*"

"*À peine.*"

Barely.

They were sliding the stretcher with great difficulty, now, to the point in La Trahison where the *piste* widened. Their progress was agonizingly slow. From above, Jacques could see nothing but the helmet and the dead weight of the man, a murderous burden to the team attempting to save his life. There was the stretcher poised on the bare ledge. The head of the ski patrol waved wildly to the chopper circling at a little distance; it zoomed nearer, the rotors beating painfully against the thin air. The ski patrol attached the stretcher to the chopper's line; all watched as it swung upward, into the gullet of the craft.

Jacques stood there, freezing, until the helicopter had ducked its nose and dropped turbulently away into the sunny March sky; then he stumped slowly back to the tram head. There would be a phone. It was his duty to call.

13

The monstrous titanium cage the doctor called a "halo" was bolted to Max's blond head. Stefani had arrived after the hideous procedure of driving spear-shaped pins into his skull; thankfully, he was so deeply medicated with morphine that he never flicked an eyelid as two surgeons worked simultaneous torque wrenches on the halo's bolts. Thirty pounds of pressure per square inch, at the thickest points of the skull, until his head was suspended in the cage and the mobility of his neck was arrested. He had fractured two cervical vertebrae—the C1 and C2—and lost all neurological function in his extremities.

"What does that mean?" she asked the trauma specialist who spoke to her in the waiting room.

"He's experiencing quadriparesis."

"He's completely paralyzed? From the neck down?"

"For the present. It is far too early, madame, to predict the outcome."

"I don't understand. If Max broke his neck—"

"Monsieur Roderick suffers from concussion, he fractured two vertebrae, his spinal cord is bleeding," the doctor explained. "He cannot feel his arms or legs, he has no movement in them—but the cord itself is only bruised, not severed. That is reason to hope."

The Medevac unit had intubated Max's lungs. He could not breathe on his own. His neck and head were in traction, now, and his limbs pinned to the surface of a rotating bed. Four hours after his arrival at the hospital, she stared down at the supine figure with rage in her heart. Max's eyes swiveled beneath his closed lids, lost in opiate dreams.

"You're saying this vertebral fracture could eventually heal?"

"Some do." The doctor's reply was careful. "Monsieur Roderick may require surgery to fuse the fractured bones. But the halo is there to encourage natural healing. He has already come far, madame—for left as he was, several hours on that mountain, Monsieur Roderick should have died. Ninety-eight percent of such victims would not have survived the Medevac flight. Of those that do, ninety percent will never walk again. But there are cases—"

Later, Stefani told Jeff Knetsch, "We're wasting time. We've got to get him to Paris, if it's a question of surgery. Every minute Max loses, the less chance he has of full recovery."

"He'd be better off dead than living like this," Jeff shot out wildly.

"Do you think it was an accident?"

"You tell me," he retorted. "You're the *security expert* . . ." with such malice that she understood, then, that he blamed her for everything that had happened to Max in the past few days.

Stefani pressed her palms against the glass that separated her from Max's room. Would anyone ever reach through the steel and tubes to touch his skin again?

"I intend to see his skis," Jeff muttered beside her. "I'll go over them with a fine-tooth comb. And then I'll *kill* whoever did this."

"If the skis were sabotaged, whoever did it is long since gone."

He laughed brusquely. "You're the only person who had complete access to his design shop over the past few days."

"Don't be a fool, Jeff. You've had access for years."

He seized her roughly by the shoulders with his long, nervous fingers. "I may not be a legend of the ski slopes who screws any woman he can get his hands on. But nobody's ever been stupid enough to call me a fool."

She grasped his wrists and stabbed hard at the pressure points, as Oliver Krane had taught her. Jeff let go of her shoulders with a rasp of breath and stepped backward.

"Bitch," he snarled. "You think you hold the world between your knees. But you don't hold me."

* * *

"Oliver," she said around midnight into the hospital's pay phone, "Oliver, Oliver, *Oliver*."

"You weren't sent out as a bodyguard, heart. Stop hitting yourself over the head for another man's weakness."

"Weakness? Good God—this wasn't human error. It was deliberate. We know now that Max isn't a murderer—he's a victim, Oliver."

"And we're all dreadfully sorry. But given what's happened to Max Roderick in recent days he should have examined his equipment like a commando," Krane replied callously. "Every five minutes. And at least before he trusted his life to it. He shouldn't have skied alone. All in all, friend Max looks like having a death wish."

"Knetsch has already called the ski patrol. They've recovered Max's skis. The screws securing the right binding were completely sheared off. So clean a break, the patrol said, that they might almost have been filed."

"Then they were. Any ideas?"

"Lots," she said succinctly. "Let's start with the equipment. He took out a brand-new pair of skis and bindings this morning. Ones he'd designed. He always liked to test his stuff in extreme conditions before it went on the market."

"Who in Courchevel knew that?"

"About testing the skis? Or which pair he planned to take?"

"Both."

"His work habits are common knowledge to his friends. But he has only a few of those. Off the top of my head I could name a local woman— Yvette Margolan. Jeff Knetsch. Jacques Renaudie. His daughter."

"The aggrieved Renaudies," Oliver murmured.

"It was Jacques who found him today."

"Peering over the edge of the couloir to inspect his handiwork? When he might have skied two hundred other trails that morning?"

"Coincidence?" she asked bitterly.

"Bugger coincidence."

Oliver's abrupt impatience. *I do not accept accident in my part of the world.*

"And then there's this woman," she added, "named Stefani Fogg. Knetsch is convinced that I want Max dead. That I came to Courchevel for no other purpose. That I'm some kind of black widow."

"She mates and then kills," Oliver returned. "Problem is, Knetsch has no motive. Why would *you* kill a client?"

"Revenge against Oliver Krane," she replied promptly, "for ending my career at FundMarket. I'm supposed to bring you down, Oliver, by destroying Max. Knetsch told me the story himself."

"Our Mr. Knetsch is a Machiavellian. We shall therefore include him in the suspect list. If he's flinging accusations, he must have something to hide."

"He's Max's oldest friend."

"He's also overdrawn in all his accounts and has a gambling habit that could sink Las Vegas," Oliver returned brutally. "Max supports his law firm to the tune of sixty thousand dollars a year. That's a nice little book of business, not to mention the prestige value of touting Roderick as a client. Knetsch might not like our competition; he wants his cash cow all to himself. He knew about the skis?"

"Possibly. But then, so did I. Max propped them by the door of the design studio last night—"

"Inside or outside?"

"Inside. But the door has a very simple lock. A credit card might spring it."

"Of all the bloody—"

"I know," Stefani interrupted. "He didn't take it seriously enough. This threat to his life."

"Bugger the man for an arrogant fool."

Suppressed violence, bitterness even, in Oliver's Etonian drawl; and she suddenly remembered his anguish over Harry Leeds.

"Have you seen Max? To speak to?" he asked.

"Briefly."

"And?"

"He could tell me nothing."

Impossible to explain to Oliver the crevasse that had opened at her feet, Max frozen on the opposite side. Max wandering somewhere beyond the halo and rotating bed, his eyes fixed on the line where wall and ceiling met. Max incapable of speech while the machines breathed for him. Max in the grip of despair so deep it might suffocate him entirely when no one was looking.

"There's rather a good man in Paris for this sort of thing," Oliver mused. "Strangholm. Makes the dead walk, so to speak. I'd be happy to call him myself, if you think you could persuade the powers-that-be to send Max there. He cannot do better."

"Give me Strangholm's phone number."

"You might face some opposition."

"Not if you could persuade Knetsch's firm to recall him immediately to New York."

"Ballard, Crump and Skrebneski. I once played polo with Ballard and dallied with Skrebneski's wife. I shall place the call immediately. We'll have friend Knetsch out of your hair in a trice. And ducks: this is not your fault. Not even remotely."

"Did you feel that way when Harry Leeds died?"

A slight check in the conversation, a palpable chilling of their mutual air.

"Chin up, darling. I'll call tomorrow with all the pertinent medical information."

But he still hadn't answered her question.

"The break in the vertebrae and the seepage of blood within the cord is causing extreme pressure on the spinal nerve." The head of the Moutiers orthopedic team looked ill at ease, Stefani thought, as though he was giving them data even he didn't trust. "We would like to send Monsieur Roderick to Paris for further evaluation."

"When?" Jeff Knetsch demanded.

"Within the hour, if possible."

"Which hospital?" she asked.

The orthopedist shrugged, his eyes flicking nervously from her face to Jeff's. "I thought perhaps l'Hôpital-Générale de Paris."

"I want him sent to Dr. Felix Strangholm, at the Clinique St. Eustache, 27 Rue Carnavalet," Stefani said. "It's a private spine center. You know it, surely?"

"As Mr. Roderick's lawyer," Jeff broke in quickly, "I must protest. Ms. Fogg has no authority to determine the nature of Mr. Roderick's care."

The doctor frowned. "I have heard of *monsieur le docteur,* of course—but am unacquainted with him personally. He is *très pressé.* I am not sure that he would accept another patient on such short—"

"He has already done so," Stefani cut in. "I received a telegram this morning from Dr. Strangholm authorizing the transfer of Monsieur Roderick to his clinic."

"You had no right!" Jeff pivoted toward the orthopedist. "I'm sure you know best where Monsieur Roderick should go. L'Hôpital-Générale de Paris will be perfectly acceptable."

"Do you have medical power of attorney, Jeff?" Stefani demanded bluntly.

He stared at her mutely.

"I thought not. Then we're at an impasse. Neither of us has the authority to determine Max's care. Which means that his doctor will have to decide."

"Madame, I—"

She threw the orthopedist her most impish smile. "Tell me, *monsieur le docteur*. If someone you loved were damaged as gravely as Monsieur Roderick, and then offered the chance to be treated by Felix Strangholm—would you send him to a nameless specialist at l'Hôpital-Générale instead?"

"I would not, madame. I would snatch at every hope and at the slightest possible chance. *Bon*. To Dr. Strangholm it is, within the hour."

Through the ICU window, she watched three male attendants disengage one set of tubes and connect another—these, the ones that would sustain Max's life while he hurtled through the air to Paris.

"I've been called back to New York," Knetsch told her savagely.

"Poor timing," she returned, "unless you've a reason to get out of France fast. Worried about those bindings, Jeff? Afraid they'll betray you?"

Without hesitation, he struck her across the face. She shoved his chest hard, forcing him backward.

"I wish to God he'd never met you."

"Oh, that's a nice touch," she said appreciatively. "Try it out on your bookie next time you need money."

The door to Max's private room was kicked violently open. He lay strapped to a cervical board on a rolling gurney. Stefani fell back against the wall, silenced by the sight of that motionless face, the ventilator taped into his mouth. He was headed for the helipad for the second time in twenty-four hours.

"You've been snooping," Knetsch muttered with suppressed violence.

"That's right, pal. And I've just gotten started."

14

Felix Strangholm was a rotund man with a bald head and penetrating green eyes. His plump lips were pursed contemplatively, as though he teetered perpetually on the brink of revelation. He was chary with words, which caused his colleagues to hang on his every syllable. When he entered a room, he commanded the most intense absorption—from his associate director down to the woman who cleaned his toilets. He wore a doctor's white lab coat over a cashmere polo and a pair of riding jodhpurs. He moved through the hallways in stockinged feet, the legacy of a period of Zen meditation. He was unfailingly polite. His appearance gave next-of-kin the flicker of hope that what was eccentric might indeed be lifesaving. At the very least, they assumed from his expression of acute attention that he listened when they spoke; they found this novel and comforting.

On the periphery of her mind, Stefani recorded these details of the man who now governed Max's future.

She had arrived in Paris eight hours after the medical helicopter landed on the roof of the Clinique St. Eustache. By the time she had checked into the hotel Oliver had booked for her on the Place Vendôme and taxied to the Rue Carnavalet, Max was already in fiber-optic surgery. Strangholm was *désolé,* the surgeon assured her three hours later, to find that the fragments of bone in Monsieur Roderick's neck had been allowed to exert pressure on his spinal nerve for more than a day. He had halted the internal bleeding, fused the fractured vertebrae, and prescribed massive steroids for swelling in the spinal column that he believed was responsible for part of Max's paresis. But even with the most assiduous intervention, Max's future was cloudy. Strangholm would do what he could, but those *imbéciles* in the Haute Savoie . . .

Strangholm furrowed his brow, pursed his lips and smoothed his palm across the polished surface of his granite desk. In perhaps eight hours—six, even—they should know a great deal more. Madame might hope to speak to monsieur after the doctor's rounds—at eight-thirty tomorrow morning, yes?

Stefani agreed. Her heart was suddenly pounding. She had not spoken a word to Max in two days.

The traction was gone. He wore a plastic vest, reminiscent of a full body cast, that supported the lower edge of the halo. A nurse had placed a cushion beneath his neck to ease the ache of his rigid muscles; but for the moment, he remained supine, staring only at the ceiling, unable to move his head. An IV feed was taped to one wrist; electrodes were gelled to his chest; socks cloaked his feet below the hospital gown. His legs looked chill and gray—the skin of a dead man. But the ventilator, she noted with a catch at her heart, was gone. This morning, Max breathed on his own.

If he heard her as she entered the room, he was unable to communicate it. "Max. Oh, Max—"

"Stef." The word seemed to cost all the breath he had. She reached out and gripped his arm.

"Ms. Fogg."

Strangholm was frowning at a series of magnetic resonance images clipped to a light screen. "In my office, please."

She followed him from the room.

"The news is both good and bad," he said without preamble. "The extreme paresis begins to recede. You will observe that Monsieur Roderick is able to breathe on his own, and that he has recovered enough strength to speak. Both functions tire him enormously, but with therapeutic practice he should manage them to admiration. Already when the skin of his back is pinched, he registers sensation. I expect him to recover feeling in his fingertips by the end of the week, and perhaps—with time—the use of his arms and hands. I believe that we have been able to halt the damage to the spinal cord occasioned by the fracture in his neck."

"That's . . . but that's *wonderful* news . . ."

Strangholm reached for his pipe and tamped its bowl thoughtfully. "However, I cannot hold out hope for a complete recovery. The time elapsed between injury and surgery was too long. We shall pursue an aggressive regime of therapy. Monsieur Roderick will remain in his halo for eight to twelve weeks, during which time he will be trained to use a wheelchair and, perhaps, a walker. But I cannot promise that he will ever regain the use of his lower limbs."

"There are worse things, I suppose. Does he know the odds?"

"It is utterly inadvisable to talk of permanent loss at so early a juncture. We must give him something to hope for, and he may, eventually, achieve a miracle. Let him grow used to his limitations only when he has no alternative. Until then—"

"I'm deeply grateful for all you've done," Stefani said.

The doctor inclined his head. "Monsieur Roderick may expect to remain in treatment for at least six months. You will wish to know what he will face in coming weeks, I am sure, and you will wish to make financial arrangements. I assume you will be able to conclude all this today, madame?"

"After I speak to Max."

They had rotated his bed, to prevent the accumulation of fluid in his limbs and to thwart the onset of pneumonia. His breath wheezed raggedly through his parted lips. Stefani walked toward him, wishing his eyes could focus on her instead of the ceiling.

"It's so good to see you," she said. "And you've got sensation in your back. That's marvelous."

"I would rather be dead."

"Don't say that."

A flicker of the eyelids that might have been anger. "That binding—"

She moved so close that his gown grazed her cheek. "The binding was screwed," she told him softly. "Someone got to your skis. This wasn't your fault, Max."

His eyelids closed. An expression of immense relief flooded his gaunt face. It was replaced swiftly by rage. A groan broke from his lips.

"Don't," she protested, anguished.

"Don't *feel*?" A harsh sound, bitter, like laughter. His eyes remained closed. She wanted to touch his mouth, his cheek, his temple—but the halo's bars kept her at arm's length.

"I'll never ski again."

"Yes, you will."

"Liar."

It was becoming his pet name for her. But, she reflected, hadn't she earned it? "Your surgery was successful. Your chances for recovery are good. You need extensive therapy—"

"Leave me."

"Strangholm is optimistic, Max. He says—"

"You've got to leave me. Now."

She drew a deep breath. "Fine. I'll be back in a few hours, after you've rested."

"Don't." The green eyes opened wide and fixed implacably on her face.

"Max—"

"A cripple. I won't let you. Throw yourself away."

"That's absurd. I'm here because I want to be."

"That won't last," he said clearly—the first few words he'd managed with force. "Go now. Before I hate you for leaving."

She returned to the clinic every morning and afternoon over the next four days. But each time she asked to see Max, she was told he refused to admit her.

"It is a natural depression," Felix Strangholm explained with awkward kindness. "He is at war with his body. As who would not be, who has dared what he has in life? He believes he is better off dead. And he does not wish to find you here out of pity. I would guess, madame, that as his strength and feeling return, so will his courage. You must allow him this period of selfish grief. Do not reproach him—even in your heart, *hein*?"

On the fifth day she found a familiar face outside the door of his private room. "Mr. Knetsch. Back from New York?"

"I wasn't really needed at the firm anyway."

"How sad. You like to be needed, I know." Stefani kept her voice carefully neutral.

"They seem to have done a lot for Max here." Knetsch said it grudgingly. "Nothing, probably, that they wouldn't have done at the General Hospital."

"I hope they'll be able to do much more, in time."

"I've been told to thank you," he added more briskly, "for . . . services rendered. And to say that Max hopes you'll have a safe trip back to New York."

"I'm not going back to New York."

"Why not?" He glanced suggestively at her crotch. "There's nothing for you here."

"Fuck off, Knetsch."

He pulled an envelope from his jacket pocket. "Here's a copy of the letter I faxed this morning to Oliver Krane, terminating Max's retention of his firm. Max is abandoning the Thai mess, for obvious reasons. You aren't needed anymore."

Stefani scanned the single sheet of paper, feeling her anger mount. "This was drafted by you, Jeff. Not Max."

"I've also revised the arrangements you made for payment to this facility. Max is fully capable of footing his own bills."

"Max told you to do all this?"

"Max trusts my judgment. I've known him all my life."

"And I've only known him a week." Stefani crumpled the letter in her hand. "I want to see him."

"That won't be possible."

"You can't keep me out of that room!"

"I'm afraid I can." He thrust his back against the door and smiled at her faintly. "I now have Max's power of attorney. He gave it to me this morning, when he told me to fire your sorry ass."

15

She flew out of Paris that evening hating all men with a vengeance, and especially their lawyers.

"Knetsch has a point, ducks," Oliver had said from the other side of the Atlantic as he consumed his breakfast. "Max hasn't welcomed you with open arms. He's been through a good deal, and has worse yet to face. For now, you must come home. As Strangholm said, it's possible that his feelings will change with time."

"I don't give second chances, Oliver," she raged. "Max has slammed the door. He's on his own."

"Second chances are merely a means of forgiveness, old thing," he warned her. "Fail to forgive, and you hurt only yourself."

She had considered those words during the sleepless seven hours of her westward journey, a period of extreme turbulence over the North Atlantic when even the flight attendants could be heard shrieking in their compartments. Her anger toward Max—toward Jeff Knetsch—even, absurdly, toward Oliver Krane—hardened into self-hatred. *I'm not a woman who's capable of sustaining life.* It was she, after all, who had given up: who had packed her bags and abandoned the man she believed she loved to face his hell alone. She who admitted to being shallow and avoiding pain. To pursuing frivolity rather than truth. Was it any wonder Max had told her to go?

She was still sleepless when the plane touched down. Oliver Krane, uncharacteristically silent, awaited her beyond the international arrivals gate. He bundled her into a sleek black car with a faceless driver, her luggage already stowed; threw a blanket over her legs; made soothing noises all the way into the city; and deposited her at her door without a word of commiseration.

She slept for eleven hours. As she stood once more before the wide glass doors that led to her co-op terrace, dusk fell over Manhattan. She cursed its beauty and heartlessness in fluent Italian just for the hell of it, then turned her back on Gotham.

She lay in bed, staring sightlessly at the ceiling or the heavily draped window, for three days. The phone rang periodically; she ignored it. Oliver left thirteen messages on her answering machine. She caught the note of worry in his tone; but she knew he was surveilling her apartment, and would know that she had not yet left the building. She had ordered no food, collected no mail. *I'm not a woman who's capable of sustaining life.*

When at last he threatened to blast her door open with a bit of wire and plastic explosive, she reluctantly picked up the phone.

"You need a sense of purpose, heart," Oliver said gently. "As a trial run at risk management, Courchevel was a bloody disaster. But I know your talents. You cannot return to FundMarket or any of its competitors. You're made for better stuff."

"Such as?"

She was established now in her living room, suddenly ravenous, with cartons of take-out Chinese spread about the floor.

"You might wet your feet in the intelligence pool," he mused. "Jaunt around the various continents with your head into the wind. Send back reports of an enticing nature. Krane publishes a weekly newsletter, you know, for select clients about the globe. Privileged information, for those who understand what it costs."

"I can't stay in the United States," she said flatly, "and Europe's out."

"Chile? Argentina?"

"Possible. Brazil is hopeless, of course."

"A carnival of thieves," he agreed. "I once tracked down the Brazilian treasury, you know, which had somehow ended up in its president's pocket. What about Australia?"

"I've never been there." Stefani's chopsticks hovered in midair. "What's in Australia?"

"Nice, safe telecommunications markets. Internet heists. A considerable number of tanned bodies. The food industry. Pharmaceutical supplies. You could mingle with the best set and keep your ears to the ground. And it's an excellent drop-off point for Asia—"

She stiffened. "Oliver—"

"The Indonesian political system is due to totter at any moment. And there's always Burma, of course, which must be monitored in the event it decides to join the twentieth century. It will never join the twenty-first."

"What has happened to your Thai clients, Oliver?"

"Made a noise like a hoop and rolled away," he answered. "Round about the time friend Max took his tumble. They left a great deal of hard currency in their wake, of course. Harry would be gratified to know that he died for the sake of my net worth."

The bitterness only thinly veiled.

"And you're willing to let Harry's death rest?" she asked him.

"For the moment, I regard myself as having no choice. But I am a quite patient man. I shall deal with Harry's killers in my own time and way."

"Asia," she murmured. "Not safe at all, is it?"

"Not so's you'd notice. I believe you're recovering apace, darling," he said.

And so had begun the odyssey of her last six months. Stefani had danced her way through Melbourne, through Adelaide and Perth and the Great Barrier Reef; through Port Arthur and Kuala Lumpur and Seoul. She had descended upon Rangoon at the behest of a furniture designer who had established an empire there, fingered lacquer boxes and wandered through sustainable-growth forests. She researched market conditions in Laos and copyright piracy in Hong Kong and police repression and child labor in the jungles of Malaysia. The substance of what she saw found its way into Oliver Krane's intelligence reports. After six weeks she began to enjoy herself—to be quickened by novelty, to revel in the warmth of strangers, to be humbled by all that she had to learn.

During her first visit to the ancient Vietnamese capital of Hué—a visit conducted sensibly in the dry season—she made fast friends with a surgeon named Pho, and learned from him that in Vietnam ear surgery was still performed with a hammer and chisel. Coagulant drugs were unknown in the operating room. Eyeglasses were never worn among the burgeoning population—which no doubt accounted for the hazards of motorcycle traffic in the city's congested streets. Eyeglasses, Pho explained, had once been deadly. They were worn by the intelligentsia, and thus branded those who must be shot.

But now, Stefani reasoned, with capitalism on the rise and relations normalized, Vietnam should experience an optometry boom. And a rush to surgical drills and pharmaceuticals and all the trappings of Western healthcare. Oliver Krane agreed: and posted the news on his corporate Web site.

From that first visit to Hué in May she traveled on to Saigon and Phnom Penh and Singapore and at last, with a feeling almost of sacrilege, to Bangkok and the Oriental Hotel.

It was there, three months after she had flown out of Courchevel, that she wrote her first letter to Max.

She said nothing of what had been between them. She never mentioned his accident. She wrote instead of river traffic on the Chao Phraya, and the whistles flying back and forth across the swollen water. She wrote of the gnarled hands of the women who sold dogs for dinner on the streets of Hanoi; of the bead maker she had met in Laos and the sweetness of a child's face turned toward her from the back of his mother's motor scooter. She wrote of life in all its variety and richness, and to the old stone house in France she sent the pages without a word of love.

Max did not reply.

Stefani kept writing. It was possible that he had never regained the use of his hands, after all; possible that he trusted no one to transcribe a letter for him; possible that he did not know, yet, what he should say or how much could be shared. But the fact that he did not return her letters heartened her immeasurably. He must read her words—and perhaps he found solace in them. She kept writing on stationery headed with the names of the most exotic commercial palaces in the world. And in the end, she knew, she was writing for herself. Forgiveness, as Oliver had said, was a personal journey.

*   *   *

Max wore thin leather gloves on his hands when he pushed the chair, thrusting hard at the wheels that propelled him forward along the mountain path. He'd refused a motorized version or Sabine's help once his hands were strong enough to work the wheels. It was an obsession with him, now, this physical training. The first two fingers of his left hand remained numb; and at first, his wrists had been as weak as a baby's. He spent every spare moment squeezing rubber balls in his palms, or flexing each foot at the ankle with one-pound weights. In the house, where the floors were level, he generally used a walker to navigate the rooms, and was able finally to complete twenty paces on his own—but he could not yet trust his balance or strength to the challenge of the ridgeline.

"You're getting too fast for me, buddy," Jeff grumbled, as they reached the head of the ridge.

"You're out of shape," Max returned. "We've only come about a hundred yards from the house."

"I know it. Too many power lunches." He flung himself down beside Max's wheelchair and stared out over the valley. A stone's throw from where they sat, the granite alp sheared off a thousand feet or more in jagged folds punctuated by sudden crevasses. A brutal landscape, even when brushed with the color of late September.

Jeff cocked his head and studied Max's face. "You've made a helluva comeback."

"Thank you," Max rejoined dryly. "I couldn't have done it without my friends. I'm starting to take an interest in everything again."

"So I gathered." Jeff looked away. "There's a guidebook on the kitchen table. For Thailand. You're not thinking of all that old crap again, are you?"

"I'm always thinking, Jeff. That's the only way I know I'm alive."

His friend plucked at a wisp of yellowed grass. "Last I heard, Stefani Fogg was in Asia."

"In Thailand, in fact." Max felt the weight of her letter against his chest, where he had tucked it into his polo. She had written from Thailand but was headed for Vietnam, and might be gone for some time.

"Max—" The expression in his friend's eyes was flat and gray as gunmetal. "You've been handed what most men dream of, and never get: a second chance. Don't blow it."

"What's that supposed to mean?"

"You're lucky to be alive. Forget her. Forget Thailand. They're both deadly."

"Jeff, how deep are you in debt?"

"What the hell has that got to do with anything?"

Max studied him, debating the question. But instead he said merely, "It's hot out here. I could use a beer."

"So could I. I'll get us some." Jeff pushed himself upright and trudged back down the path.

Jacques Renaudie sat on the stone terrace of the house, watching his daughter's dark head as she moved about Max's kitchen. She had planned this dinner obsessively, the first she would make in Max's house, dinner for his oldest friends. Max took for granted Sabine's self-appointed role as nurse; he accepted the books she brought and her bright ceaseless chatter and he patted her head as though she were a favored dog. It broke Jacques's heart to see her so blind and so unquestioning, so passionately in love with the wrong man.

"He will never care for you, *chérie*," he said to his daughter. "He is not capable."

Her head came up, and she stared at Jacques through the open door of the terrace. "He is the one man I know who is capable of *anything*. He grows stronger every day. It is only a matter of time."

"He will never love you, *ma pauvre*."

Her eyes flashed hot with malice and anger. "What do you know of love, *hein*? You could not even keep Mama happy, you drove her away with your coldness—"

"I know that Max's heart is given to another," Jacques insisted, "and that is all I need to know."

Sabine froze, her hands suspended over a dish of cassoulet. "What other?" she asked him tremulously.

Jacques moved slowly into the living room; his entire body was weary. "All those letters," he muttered. "From all over the world. He carries them everywhere. You see, *chérie*?" He turned the girl toward the view from the terrace. Max's bent head could just be glimpsed around an outcropping of rock in the distance. "He is reading one of them now."

There are two Bangkoks, one that lives in the caverns between the soaring skyscrapers, breathing smog and noise, and another that moves with the current of the water. By the river and the khlongs are the ghosts of an older Bangkok, one that remembers torches and elephants and the bodies of dancers swaying in the flickering light. I walked alone last night down an alleyway just a block from this hotel, and found the abandoned building of the old French Legation, a marvelous colonial structure of tile roofs and peeling shutters that fronts on the water. The windows are boarded up and the stone is crumbling into dust, but entire families squat in the ramshackle place, and the scents of lemongrass and fish sauce and garlic and hot oil rise from the braziers in the darkness . . .

Tomorrow I plan to see your grandfather's house . . .

Stefani Fogg stepped out of her bath in the Oriental Hotel that Tuesday afternoon in early October, and considered the lunch she had ordered.

She was still exhausted, still dreaming with half her mind of the floodwaters of Hué, of Pho's rooftop and the dead cats swirling by on the current. But the stench of the Perfume River's mud had been washed from her skin, which now smelled faintly of eucalyptus; the down comforter on her bed was sheathed in Thai silk; and she had scheduled a massage for the afternoon. It was time at last, she thought, to sleep.

The phone rang by her bedside.

"Thank God I've reached you, darling," said Oliver Krane. "You've been the very devil to track down. And you've done a wretched job, I might add, of keeping in touch."

"My cell phone got wet in Vietnam," she told him. "No batteries until Bangkok."

"*Tai-fun?*"

"At least one. I've been sleeping on the roof of a house in Hué for the past five days. Someone could make a fortune in Vietnam by funding a national weather service."

"I'll suggest as much to a woman I know. Look, heart—I've some rather dreadful news. That's why I've been so desperate to reach you. Max Roderick committed suicide six days ago."

PART TWO

JACK

1

Ceylon,
August 14, 1945

The drop plane was dark except for the moonlight streaming through the open doorway, and the roar of the engines filled the cabin like the chaos of Hell. A man could scream in terror, his mouth wide open, and his cry would still be indistinguishable from the engines and the wind; and so in mute fear and nausea they braced themselves against the fuselage, thirty men with parachutes dragging at their shoulders. The Indian Ocean fell away beneath.

Billy Lightfoot was silhouetted against the night sky, a hulking barrel of a man blotting out the stars, his head sheathed in an aviator's cap. Billy was searching for the flares that marked the drop zone, and in a few more minutes he would raise his arm and they would all stand, Jack Roderick and the rest, and hurl themselves out into the blackness simply because he asked them to.

Alec McQueen was strapped into the jump seat next to Roderick, his eyes squeezed tight and his fingers clenched on his harness. An ace reporter who'd worked the beats of New York and Chicago before Pearl Harbor was attacked and the OSS recruited him for intelligence work, Alec was twenty-six years old to Roderick's thirty-nine and he'd known a different war than Jack. He'd worked the Pacific while Roderick dropped first into North Africa and then into Italy and France, always the hurtling planes, the heart-stopping plummet through freezing altitude, the snap and jerk of the chute rising like a hangman's noose. If the chute drifted over open land instead of trees or water and Roderick survived the drop, there was always the danger of impact, a leg shattering under him, or a landing party of Hostiles waiting to cut his throat. To jump, in Jack Roderick's mind, was a wager akin to Pascal's: *If I survive the void, then there must be a God. And if the void takes me—does God matter?*

Alec had been his bunkmate in Ceylon, a poker-playing, foulmouthed kid who chain-smoked and called Roderick the Old Man when they weren't crawling through the tangled vegetation together, their knees squelching suddenly into elephant dung. Now Roderick turned his face away from McQueen; he knew that the other man was praying.

They had been flying for nearly thirty-eight minutes by the luminous dial of Roderick's watch, east from Ceylon over the Indian Ocean toward the Malay Peninsula. The drop zone was somewhere outside Bangkok; only Billy Lightfoot knew exactly where. How long, to bridge the leagues of ocean unrolling behind them in the night? How long before the order to rise, and trust himself to air?

"The Japs are packing up their shaving kits," Lightfoot had assured them at the dawn briefing. "They're peeling out of Bangkok as fast as their yellow asses can take 'em. You may meet a few stragglers in the bush before the city, but we've got Friendlies waiting near the drop zone and you should land with no trouble. Once the chutes are cut, you're free and clear. If some of you don't make the rendezvous"—he let the lonely idea of hostile terrain sink deep into each of their brains—"get north to the city under your own power. Join up once the liberation's accomplished."

The liberation. It was the first time in all the long years of knife work and encoded signals that an end might be in sight.

"What about the Siamese?" McQueen had asked. "The Unfriendlies? Pibul and his crowd?"

During the six weeks of jungle combat training in the bush of Ceylon, Lightfoot had taken care to instruct them in recent Siamese history. For most of the war there had been a military dictatorship run by Field Marshal Pibul Songgram, sympathetic to the occupying

Japanese. In 1939 Pibul had renamed the country Thailand: by 1941, he had snatched the opportunity of worldwide warfare to attack the French Protectorates of Laos and Cambodia. He'd seized a chunk of border territory in the name of the Thais, then sat back to pay a fat tribute to Tokyo for the rest of the war.

"Pibul's no threat now," Lightfoot had replied. "He's been arrested by our old friend Ruth, who runs the Free Thai."

Roderick knew Ruth as a tapping in the night, a crackling wireless operator who relayed OSS orders to the Free Thai and throughout the Malay Peninsula. Ruth was a strange *nom de guerre*, feminine and Biblical, but Roderick understood that Pridi Banomyong was an unusual man. He had trained as a lawyer and a constitutional scholar. He was cultivated, Europeanized, a charismatic fighter with nerves of iron. *Ruth* for fidelity, for wandering and sacrifice. He had been working with the Thai Resistance and Allied intelligence for the past three years.

"We're coordinating our liberation drop with Ruth's forces," Lightfoot had told them. "If all goes well . . ."

If all goes well, Jack Roderick thought, *I'll be on a boat home to New York tomorrow.*

He had actually enjoyed the weeks of training in the jungles of Ceylon, enjoyed the Sinhalese tribesmen who beat back the undergrowth with huge sticks and led the Allied soldiers around watering holes that sank without warning in the heart of the tea plantations. He liked the sudden fogs of the highlands and the aging sahibs who persisted in British customs despite the ravages of war, with their freshly ironed damask tablecloths and their packs of hounds and their tiger skins scattered over marble floors. But mostly, he loved Billy Lightfoot and the men he led.

Lightfoot was a soldier's soldier, a polo-playing lieutenant colonel who trained spies for Wild Bill Donovan. Wild Bill was the backbone and gristle of the clandestine service; the OSS was entirely Donovan's baby. In the summer of 1940, as Nazi Germany prepared to invade Britain, Franklin Roosevelt had sent William Donovan to London as his personal representative, to observe Churchill's war preparations. By September, when Britain's survival hung in the balance and the German bombing raids over the English Channel were both disastrous and commonplace, Donovan had returned to Washington with British-inspired plans for the United States' first clandestine agency: the Office of Strategic Services. Donovan drew a cadre of raw recruits from among the Old Boys of Yale and Princeton and Harvard, young men desperate to trade Wall Street for occupied territory. He'd given them a purpose for their dusty French and their effortless social skills and their knowledge of the world. He'd given them Billy Lightfoot, detailed from General George Patton's personal staff, as Head Boy and Eagle Scout.

Lightfoot was an engineer by education. Nobody's fool, he'd cut his teeth as a volunteer in the Spanish Civil War, where he'd learned that fanatics were death, whether Fascist or Communist in their persuasion. Lightfoot had been a champion of democracy ever since. He'd caught shrapnel in his left foot in Spain and afterward was good for nothing but teaching calculus at West Point, until Pearl Harbor declared him fit for action. Then Lightfoot blew up bridges and mined roads and led convoys all over Europe.

He had a talent for making the OSS feel like a passage through summer camp, and his men the most vibrant and exhilarating tribe ever assembled under one tent. However many girls might type letters and serve cocktails and tap signals from OSS headquarters in New York, the OSS in the field was first and foremost a men's club: it was a place where the American male could thrive in his natural habitat.

Jack Roderick loved men's clubs, loved the unquestioned acceptance and the wordless camaraderie and the utter lack of explanation that prevailed in such places. Princeton in the twenties—and before that, St. Paul's—had each been men's clubs; even Manhattan, in the first days of courting Joan, when every man Roderick met was a member of the Right Set.

Later, at the end of the thirties, with the love and the hatred and the jealousy at his throat, the men's clubs had become a gallery of ridicule and none of his assumptions was safe anymore. Before Pearl Harbor and the Japanese had released them both, Roderick had felt as though he were adrift on an ice floe, with Joan and the punctured Manhattan skyline receding at increasing speed.

Roderick had learned to jump with Billy Lightfoot, to use a one-time cipher pad for his midnight radio signals, to string networks of subagents in hostile terrain, to blend effortlessly with the natives of Fez and Corsica and Arles.

Lightfoot had been ecstatic on the sixth of August, nearly a month before, when the first atomic bomb dropped on Hiroshima.

"We've shown those yellow bastards how a tough people fights!" he'd yelled in the officers mess at Trincomalee.

Most of the men had shouted and raised their glasses with Billy in a toast to the firepower of Allied forces. But Roderick had set down his gin and walked out alone into the monsoon. For the first time in all his war, he was uncertain whether Right had prevailed.

And if I returned to New York tomorrow, he thought as he waited for Lightfoot's arm to rise in the moonlit airplane doorway, *would I find it stranger and more alien than Siam dreaming below?*

A crackle of radio noise filled the cabin. The plane ducked and yawed in the turbulent sky. A burst of words as rapid as machine-gun fire. The improbable sound of cheering. Roderick braced himself against the thin wall of the fuselage and strained to catch the transmission. He glanced at Alec McQueen, and saw that the younger man's eyes were wide open.

Lightfoot thrust himself away from the door and lurched toward the cockpit.

"Do you think it's Japs?" McQueen asked. "Do you think we're blown?"

But Roderick's eyes were locked on Billy as he careened drunkenly back through the darkened cabin, slapping shoulders as he came.

"Surrender!" he bellowed. "The Japs have surrendered! Tonight we land as heroes, men! The Allies have won the war!"

2

He rolled his wheelchair off the ridge above his house," Oliver Krane said matter-of-factly, "and fell a thousand feet. I'm dashed sorry, old thing. I know it's miserable for you."

Stefani could not speak.

"I suppose he couldn't bear life as a cripple," Oliver went on awkwardly. "Not that anyone could blame him. A man like that, whose whole life depended upon his body—"

"I don't believe it," she said flatly. "It's a lie."

"Stef, darling—"

"Harry Leeds, Oliver. *Harry Leeds* under the wheels of a Kowloon taxi. It didn't fit then and it doesn't fit now."

He hesitated—murder was the obvious suggestion, after all, given Max's recent history—then said, "He was seen alone on the ridgeline. And then his chair was at the bottom of it, smashed to bits."

"Who found him?"

"The alpine rescue people are still searching for the body. They believe it's wedged in a particular crevasse—but there was debris, of course. The chair, and one of his shoes. A scrap of fabric from the shirt he wore."

"But who saw the chair, Oliver? Who alerted alpine rescue?"

"Sabine Renaudie."

"Good God! She could have done it herself!"

"I think not. They'd grown quite chummy of late, she and Max."

"You believe she just *strolled* along the ridge, the day Max killed himself?" Stefani demanded. "Like her father, Jacques, conveniently surfacing at the mouth of the couloir?"

"Evidently she was at the house that evening to prepare dinner. Renaudie was with her, and the lawyer, Knetsch. It was to be a small celebration."

"More like a gathering of thieves."

"Max pushed himself to the top of the ridge—he'd become adept at such excursions—while his lawyer trotted alongside."

He had regained the use of his hands, then. And never written a word.

"Max sent Knetsch back to the house for a bottle of beer; Knetsch passed the girl on his way down the ridge. Five minutes later he heard her scream."

"Did she actually *see* the chair go over?"

"I don't think so. She went to the spot where Max was supposed to be, and found the pages of a letter scattered on the ground." Oliver paused. "One of yours, I'm afraid. So she went and peered over the edge of the cliff in the direction the pages led her."

Stefani closed her eyes. Had she written anything in that last letter which might drive a man to suicide? "Knetsch could have pushed Max off before he went back to the house. Before he even passed Sabine."

"He could," Oliver conceded bluntly. "But remember how *depressed* Max was—how he gave you those marching orders. Even old Strangholm noticed it. A man at war with his body, wasn't that what Strangholm said? He might have done anything."

"Oliver, did anyone *look* at the wheelchair?"

"I did, as a matter of fact. I'm in France, you see. In the interest of client relations."

Although the client was now dead. "And?"

"The brake mechanism was set in the locked position."

"Jesus—"

"He might have had second thoughts. After he rolled toward the cliff."

She saw Max clutching hard at the brakes in desperation—Max with his weak hands, clutching too late—and said, "The brakes were locked because he was shoved, Oliver."

"But consider the will, ducks."

"The will to die? Or to live?"

"The *last will* and testament. Max drafted his about five weeks ago. He was clearly contemplating death."

"Did he have Knetsch draw it up?"

"No. Knetsch was quite shocked to learn of the will's existence. Apparently Max called in a firm from Geneva."

"So he didn't trust Knetsch, in the end."

"Not with this. Max could expect disapproval." Oliver's voice had taken on the idle, distant tone she knew he used to disguise emotion. "Because he left everything to *you*. The house in Courchevel—the bank accounts in Zurich—and the entire Bangkok legacy of Jack Roderick, should that claim ever be proved."

Damn you, Max. His obsession outlived even the grave.

"Mr. Knetsch will never be counted among your friends," Oliver added implacably. "He's citing the will as evidence that Max was out of his mind."

She poured herself three inches of Bombay Sapphire neat and sat in the middle of the silk duvet to drink it. She was one week and half a world away from a dead man she should never have left. They had got to him somehow—murder or suicide, they had got to his very heart.

She imagined him soaring off the ridgeline as he had done a thousand times before, the wind ripping through the tousled hair, his eyes searching for landfall. And suddenly she hoped to God that he had deliberately chosen such an end. Better than the brutal push, the sickening realization of what was happening, the inability to stop it or save himself—

The gin glass shattered against the bedroom wall.

The man who had paid for the murder of Max Roderick placed a call that afternoon to Krane & Associates' New York headquarters. He was connected quite rapidly to Oliver Krane, whom he might be forgiven for assuming was also in New York.

"Sompong." Oliver's greeting was genial. "It has been months since I heard your voice. Everything grand in Bangkok and Phuket? Wife keeping well? Mistress also?"

The man named Sompong glanced down at the pair of sixteen-year-olds sleeping in the darkened room and his lip curled. He demanded so much in these daily sessions that they often slept as though dead. He placed a thousand-baht note on the dressing table and moved toward the door.

"I require the services of your firm," he said abruptly, "on the matter we once spoke of."

"Matter concluded," Oliver replied breezily. "File closed."

"Roderick is dead, yes. But he left a will. I want to know everything about the woman who inherits. This Stefani Fogg."

"Been chatting with your attorney, I see."

"Everything," Sompong repeated curtly. "By six A.M. Bangkok time."

"Oh, very well," Oliver said impatiently, "but you'd damn well better make it worth my time."

She walked into the Bamboo Bar that afternoon in search of an old man named Thanom—just Thanom, the name by which he had been known at the Oriental for over fifty years. He was polishing the gleaming surface of the counter with methodical sweeps of one wizened hand. At this hour, the bar—an updated version of the oldest expatriate watering hole in Thailand—was empty. The drinkers were sitting outside, under the wide umbrellas that ringed the pool. At the sight of Stefani, the old man tucked his bar towel out of sight and bowed.

"May I help you?"

"I hope so. My name is Stefani Fogg. I'm looking for a man named Thanom. Mr. Rewadee said I might find him here."

"I am he."

Stefani slid onto a seat and placed her pointed chin in her hands. She studied the man's face—mottled by sun, scarred with time, the eyes set like dashed pebbles in the hollows of the skull. "Mr. Rewadee tells me you have been here a long time."

"I have indeed. Would you like something to drink, Miss Fogg?"

"Tonic with two limes. How long, exactly?"

Thanom smiled, but the expression was not entirely friendly. "If you have bothered to talk to Mr. Rewadee, you know already that I have worked at the Oriental since 1946, when I first came to Bangkok from the southern provinces. I was a boy of fourteen then. I carried baggage, and ran errands for Mlle. Krull—"

Germaine Krull. The Frenchwoman who had bought the hotel with a handful of investors, one of them Jack Roderick, early in 1946.

"—and now I tend bar."

"Nineteen forty-six," she mused. "Then you must have known Jack Roderick. He was part owner in Mlle. Krull's time, wasn't he?"

Thanom set a glass of ice carefully on the counter and raised a siphon. "Mr. Roderick put some money into the place, yes. Then he quarreled with the rest of the owners and he pulled his money out; but he continued to live here like a thorn in Mademoiselle's side. And later when Mademoiselle was forced to sell and the big money came to Thailand and changed the Oriental forever, Roderick laughed the loudest. He put his silk shop in the lobby and he decorated the Royal Suite free of charge and he made money on the corpse of Mademoiselle's dream. We watched him do it."

"Tell me about Roderick." Stefani's eyes were fixed on the man's face. "Rewadee says you knew him well."

Thanom regarded her impassively. Then he reached for a knife and a lime and with ruthless motions sliced the flesh of the fruit and slid the wet, transparent green into the depths of her glass. "Why you wish to know about Mr. Roderick?"

She took a sip of tonic and shrugged.

"Always the tourists they want to know about Mr. Roderick." He said it with soft contempt. "But he was a quiet man. He did not say much to his friends and certainly not to Thanom who carried bags and tended bar. Not even when he was drinking."

"Did he drink here?"

Thanom's agate eyes flicked along the ceiling, the animal-print cushions and the glass-topped tables. They came to rest on the chemical-blue waters of the pool that glittered beyond the windows. "Not here. In Mr. Roderick's day the *farangs* crawled up from the river dock straight into the lobby with the mud and sweat of the jungle still on their skin, and they drank and boasted and lied here till dawn. Roderick always listened. He stood rounds of drinks for his new friends and he laughed at their jokes but he did not drink deeply and he said nothing about his own affairs. Is such a man to be trusted?"

"He sounds discreet enough."

Thanom pulled out his towel and began polishing the counter again, his eyes averted. "Roderick listened so that he might own his friends. One drinks betrayal who drinks with such a man."

"You believe the rumors, then. That he was a spy."

"A spy must have a master. What Jack Roderick did, he did only for himself. Perhaps that is why he died."

Her fingers tightened on the chill glass. "What do you mean, Thanom?"

"Roderick had eyes that could see a mosquito fly through the dark and ears that could hear the river current; he was strong with all he knew and he believed that nothing could destroy him. He grew powerful and had great wealth and they called him King behind his back when he wandered among the khlongs. But he forgot, Miss Fogg, that he was not a Thai himself in this land of the Smiling Thai. You have heard that expression—the Smiling Thai?"

"Yes," she replied. The tour guide's description of the friendliest people in Southeast Asia.

The old man leaned across the bar, his eyes burning with an old hatred. "There are a hundred ways to smile, Miss Fogg, and one of them says *I'm going to kill you.*"

If I'm right and you were murdered, Stefani wrote to Max on a sheet of the Oriental's stationery, *then it was one of those three all along. Sabine, Jacques or Knetsch. Each of them could have triggered any one of the attacks. The avalanche. The sabotaged binding. The final push. Each of them had access to the house, access to information about your movements. But which of them could be bought? Which of them hated you enough?*

She stared over the Oriental's pool, toward the orchids waving like butterflies in the breeze; over the tanned skin of the privileged and the well-tended who frequented the place, over her untouched glass of rum with its paper umbrella rakish at the rim.

She had considered drinking herself into a coma. The Stefani of three years ago—of even a year since—would have done it. She would have picked up a stranger by sundown, toured Bangkok with a group of new best friends and remembered nothing of Max by morning.

But she was not the same woman she had been a few months ago.

She allowed her eyes to rest at last upon a black-haired, powerfully built Asian who lounged opposite her. He held a newspaper close to his face, but from the indolent sprawl of his tanned knees, she doubted that he was very engaged.

Sabine: in love with you for years, making dinner now in your house. Invested, perhaps, in your helplessness. Your gratitude. Did you anger her by rejecting her one time too many?

Jacques: worried about his daughter's future. Or still pissed at his wife's affair. Did he hate you because of what destroyed his marriage?

Knetsch: You didn't trust him with your will. Why did you call in a Geneva lawyer? You guessed Jeff was drowning in debt. You despised his friends. Why does he insist that you were insane?

She stopped short, the pen hovering over the question. If Jeff pushed the wheelchair off that cliff, he'd need the death to look like suicide. And if he called Max mad, suicide made more sense.

She crumpled the letter into a tight ball, shoved it into her tote bag and thrust herself off the deck chair.

The Asian opposite rose and stretched. As she gathered up her sunscreen and paperback novel, he careened clumsily against her thigh, knocking the bag from her shoulder. Then, with a muttered word of what might be apology, he strode toward the glass doors that led to the lobby.

Stefani stared after him, frowning. Her book had landed in a puddle of pool water, and her pen was lying on the tile. His careless foot had squashed her tube of sunscreen.

It was only later, back in her room, that she realized the crumpled sheet of paper was gone.

3

Bangkok,
1945–1947

They diverted the drop plane to Rangoon, Burma, and for three days
Jack Roderick talked to British officers drunk with victory and bartered
precious cigarettes for goods that had seemed irrelevant when the mission was liberation. The OSS men who landed in Rangoon had their
jumpsuits and boots, a kit containing iodine tablets, rations of beef
jerky, extra rounds of ammunition and an Army-issue knife. Some carried crucifixes or rabbits' feet or pictures of their kids. Roderick had a
Polaroid of Rory taken with Santa the previous Christmas and ten dollars' worth of Siamese baht. He kept hidden in his breast pocket the final letter to Joan in which he overlooked her sins and confessed eternal
love.

With mordant humor he called this his *drop-dead letter,* in the event
he tangled in his chute or the chute never opened or he jumped onto
the point of a hostile bayonet. If he survived the war—as it seemed,
now, that he might—he would throw the thing in the first available
trash can.

Alec McQueen reverted, in those feverish Rangoon days, to the
journalist he had been before war broke out. If he wasn't drinking
whiskey or playing poker he interviewed every Burmese national who
understood a word of English and filed endless reports for United
Press International. He was giddy with survival, he talked of booking

passage on the first boat to the Philippines and demanding his discharge. He posed for photographs with Roderick, a cigar in his mouth.

On the morning of September 6, 1945, they flew at last into Thailand and found the airport clogged with thousands of fleeing Japanese troops, desperate to avoid the Allied forces and get home. A harried group of Thais—resistance fighters, all of them, with red armbands sewn onto their sleeves—tried unsuccessfully to maintain order. The control tower had been torched the week before; communications were reduced to a megaphone. Three desperate Thais, all lethally sleep-deprived, straddled the roof of an army truck with binoculars in their hands. The aircraft, circling.

The pilots joked about strafing the field in order to make room, or tipping the passengers out the side door, but in the end they managed to land as they had done a thousand times in worse conditions during the course of the bloody Pacific combat. Roderick waited his turn to disembark and, peering over McQueen's shoulder, took his first look at Bangkok.

Jungle vegetation. Buildings of stucco and wood. The heart of the city was too distant from the airfield to glimpse, but the countryside seemed little different from Rangoon. Except for the lack of British sahibs.

We are the sahibs here, he thought with a spark of surprise.

A cluster of men in olive drab, bereft of insignia, stood waiting on the tarmac in silence. Roderick could not have said whether they were Thai or Japanese, Friendlies or Hostiles, until one of them saluted Billy Lightfoot as the colonel stepped down from the plane.

"That's Ruth, God damn it," McQueen whispered over Roderick's shoulder. "Pridi Banomyong himself. Short little bastard, ain't he?"

The man standing at Ruth's right stepped forward and bowed, his palms raised high as though in prayer. "Captain Roderick, I believe. I am Commander Ruth's chief lieutenant. You may call me Carlos. Everyone does."

It was Carlos who hot-wired a Jeep abandoned by the Japanese High Command and drove Roderick and McQueen at breakneck pace through the few streets of the city still passable by anything on four wheels. Firecrackers and guns spat, and women with shining black hair and tears on their cheeks surged into the body of the Jeep at every opportunity, flinging ropes of jasmine into Roderick's lap. He felt bewildered by it all, by the babble of strange tongues and the assault of foreign smells and the sight of canals on every side with their extraordinary wooden boats and gaily colored streamers. McQueen perched on the Jeep's spare tire, waving his arms and shrieking like a Plains Indian mounting an attack. He kissed the women and slapped the men's shoulders and seemed unfazed by the lack of verbal communication. Victory, it seemed, was a universal language.

"You will like Suan Kularb," Carlos shouted over the din. Ruth's second-in-command drove with breathless skill, dogs and children scattering before him. "It is a palace set amid gardens, airy and quite clean. You will be most comfortable there. The Japanese were."

"You didn't burn the place down?"

Carlos shook his head. "We only torched what was worthless. The palaces, we kept in readiness for our friends."

A dark-haired boy with a magnificent white bird perched on his shoulder led Roderick to a high-ceilinged bedroom lined in carved teak. The windows were tall and shuttered and gave out onto a veranda overlooking the grounds. At the far end of the lawn, water gleamed in a thicket of green. An old man walked back and forth across the grass with a scythe. Roderick glanced at the bed and felt bone-weary. It had been years since he had slept on anything better than an Army cot.

The boy poured water into a brass basin and then muttered a word in Thai. His palm was extended. Roderick dropped a coin into it—part of his dwindling fund of baht—and the boy grinned hugely.

Was he ten years old? Or fifteen? The son Roderick had left behind in New York was barely eight. Would Rory look like this one day, a skinny bag of bones on the precipice of manhood, dark hollows under his eyes?

"What is your name?" Jack asked. But his gaze was fixed on the white bird. A cockatoo, he thought. A feathered crest, jet black eyes. It tugged insistently at the boy's ear. Roderick tapped his own chest. "I am Jack. *Jack.* Can you say that?"

"Meestah Jack."

Roderick nodded.

"Boonreung," the boy returned, one hand pressing his heart. He tucked the coin into his pants and darted out of the room.

At Suan Kularb it was possible to believe the war had never existed. Roderick awoke to birdsong and after a breakfast of mangosteen would bathe in a marble tub and set about learning the names of the flowers that choked the gardens. Boonreung was his companion in this, as in so many things during those weeks; as the boy's knowledge of English grew, so did Roderick's of Bangkok life. He employed the boy as guide and interpreter on his forays into the city, Boonreung perched on the seat of the jeep with his storklike legs drawn up beneath him, pointing excitedly at river boats and noodle vendors and the sellers of amulets who peddled trash and gems in the markets near Bangkok's Field of Kings.

By November, however, Roderick had tired of the luxurious isolation of Suan Kularb. He followed Alec McQueen to the Oriental Hotel, and took Boonreung with him.

The Oriental at the end of 1945 was a ramshackle hive of expatriate Allies sliding perceptibly into the brown river. It was hot and damp. The rooms had no doors, only swinging louvered shutters; the sway-backed mattresses were swathed in mosquito netting. Alec had a room above the lobby, which was also the Bamboo Bar, amid the floating pool of junior officers that shipped in and out during those chaotic postwar days. McQueen had calmed down a bit since his discharge, but he was still the perpetual cub reporter: given to colorful profanity, rumpled suiting, shirts that wilted instantly in the monsoon heat. He had expected to spend a month in Bangkok when they landed that September. By January he'd started a newspaper out of his hotel room that he called the *Bangkok Post*. He never went back to his desk job in the States.

McQueen was always in the process of seducing a woman, British or French or occasionally Thai, but Roderick was faithful to some memory of Joan and to the picture of the boy he kept propped on the window ledge in his room next to Alec's. Near Rory sat a photo of Billy Lightfoot, who had vanished back to West Point and the vagaries of Peace.

Without a war or an enemy to fight in those first aimless months,

Roderick felt at loose ends. He had no desire to return to New York, but he didn't know why he stayed. He mounted hiking expeditions to the jungle coast and took orders from Harold Patterson, the OSS station chief in Bangkok, who had spent part of his missionary childhood in Thailand and spoke the language haltingly. Patterson was a silent man whose fingers were stained yellow from the cheap cigarettes he chain-smoked. His war had been one long undercover operation with the Free Thai, and it was clear that he was ready to go home. Since his time in Bangkok was short, Patterson chose Roderick as apprentice. To him he imparted what sense he could of the city and its ways.

"The key to Southeast Asia, Jack, is the men who learned their letters at the feet of the French and now are turning to bite the hands that fed them," the station chief advised. "Penetrate the brotherhood of Frog Haters on Thailand's flanks, and you'll have the coming revolution by the balls."

Patterson took Roderick to meet exiled Cambodians with the manners of aristocrats and Laotians who had served as diplomats in Paris before the war and ideologues who espoused free love and Communism with equal ardor. First among these was the man named Tao Oum, Patterson's chief subagent and a gentle Laotian with a brilliant mind. Tao Oum was rumored to be Minister of War in the Laotian shadow government, the democratic opposition that lived in perpetual fear of French reprisal, and he loved to argue the finer points of constitutional law with Roderick, who knew next to nothing about law. The Laotians and the Cambodians and even some of the Burmese regarded Bangkok as a haven and all Americans as saviors, because America had thrown off colonial domination two centuries before and forged a path to freedom with their British oppressors' guns. Roderick listened to revolutionary dreams and bought rounds of drinks and tried to memorize the names of movements and partisans, tried to distinguish his friends from future foes.

Harold Patterson knew every monk and every whore and every dealer of Asian antiquities in the labyrinthine khlongs. With the fatality of a man who would never return he fretted at loosening his hold on the city. For Roderick he ordered food so hot it destroyed the bowels, for Roderick he commandeered boats and Jeeps and spent entire days traversing the countryside; for Roderick he journeyed three hours north over broken roads to the ancient capital of Ayutthaya and walked among the ruins. In the Nakorn Kasem—the Thieves Market of Bangkok—where every manner of plunder was sold, Patterson found pieces of handwoven silk and delicate vases of celadon and richly brocaded Burmese tapestries. Roderick bought them all and sent them back to Manhattan, where his wife Joan unpacked them in amusement and disgust.

When she wrote asking for the divorce late in 1946, he returned to New York immediately, traveling by tramp steamer around the horn of India and then overland through Paris. He arrived haggard and desperate and two months too late. He fought her because it seemed the only possible thing to do, fought for the boy and that look in Rory's eyes he could not bear to lose. But Jack Roderick lost, as he had known even in Bangkok he would lose. He handed Joan his power of attorney and returned to Thailand in early 1947.

He found the city the same, and utterly changed. Before, it had seemed exotic; now it was as though he held the khlongs and hovels in the palm of his hand.

Bangkok was his baby, in a manner of speaking: he had been appointed chief of intelligence for the OSO, the Office of Special Operations, the postwar remnant of the OSS. Whether the OSO would find a use for Roderick remained to be seen. It was an uncertain organization at best, in search of a mission, and governed by a new body called the Central Intelligence Agency, set up by Harry Truman that same year. But Roderick had found the OSO peopled with old friends—from Manhattan, and Princeton, and the half-forgotten drop zones all over Europe. Another Men's Club, this one staffed and primed for intrigue.

"Are you back for good, Jack?" Alec McQueen asked when Roderick returned and once more propped Rory's solemn-eyed photo on his window ledge.

"That depends."

"On what? A job? You can have one from me, any time. You listen, and you watch. That's all it takes to be a journalist."

Roderick smiled. "Thanks, Alec. But I've got something else in mind. Open that packet."

McQueen picked up the brown paper parcel that sat on the dresser, and tore at the wrapping. A shimmering length of rose-colored fabric spilled through his hands.

"What is it?" he asked stupidly. The stuff was like a bloodstain on the old wooden floor.

"Silk," Roderick replied. "Raw Thai silk. They grow mulberry trees in the northeast, Alec, in the countryside of Khorat. Boonreung showed me the trees and the silk thread last week. He's from that part of Thailand, you know—the kid was born in a mulberry grove. His entire family picks cocoons after breakfast."

"Boonreung," McQueen repeated. "Jack, you can't be serious."

"I found a family of weavers on a khlong not far from here. In an area called Ban Khrua. I hired them all. Piecework, for a share of the profits."

"Nobody goes to the northeast. It's a goddamn wasteland."

"A wasteland with a border," Roderick countered, "and across that border, Alec, a whole lot of unhappiness. Unhappiness is my job."

McQueen reached for the silk. He held it up to the light. "Of course," he muttered. "The war's never really ended. Is that what this is about? Protective cover?"

"I'll send the first hundred yards back to New York," Roderick mused, taking the silk from him and running it between his fingers. "A publicity stunt. I'll give them to the editor of *Vogue*. If she promotes Siamese silk—I'll have investors."

"In what? Civil disobedience?"

"Shares of my company." Roderick stared through the window of the Oriental, past Rory's photograph, his attention caught by something McQueen couldn't see. "I'll call it Jack Roderick Silk."

4

Ms. Fogg!" cried the Oriental's assistant manager delightedly as she appeared in the doorway of the Authors Lounge that Tuesday evening. "Welcome back to the Oriental!"

The weekly cocktail party for special guests—a group culled by invitation only—was in full swing. Tiers of delectable tidbits sailed by on the arms of waiters. A table festooned with flowers and exquisitely carved fruit held an assortment of sushi. White-haired men in blue blazers murmured confidentially to women with dowager's humps. Ascots were actually worn. One young man with a luxuriant black mustache had chosen to appear in wildly patterned harem pants that ballooned around his ankles, but few had such poor taste. Stefani wore a sleeveless dress of lime-green Thai silk and black Majorcan pearls.

"Hello, Paolo," she said to the assistant manager. "This is quite a crowd."

Paolo was originally from Milan and he had spent the better part of fifteen years in the most select hotels in the world. He was earnest, blond and unfailingly polite; and he never forgot a name, whether the guest had stayed at the Oriental five weeks ago or the Cipriani thirteen years before.

"Stefani." He took her hand. "It's good to see you. I understand you were caught in a typhoon."

She had almost forgot Vietnam.

Over the rim of her glass she noticed a vaguely familiar face—a middle-aged woman of the stage or screen. Beside her was a man in evening dress who attempted, and failed, to disguise his role as bodyguard. And beyond them, leaning against the wall behind the sushi station, was the powerful Asian who'd bumped into her that afternoon at the pool.

"Does that guy work here?" she murmured to Paolo. "Or is he a guest?"

The assistant manager studied him impassively. "Neither. Why?"

"I think he picked my pocket a few hours ago."

"He's talking to Rush Halliwell." Paolo's eyes flicked toward hers. "You know him? One of your embassy officers."

Halliwell was tall and graceful in a tropical-weight suit that looked like Italy and had probably been made by one of the local tailors. He seemed to be on excellent terms with the powerful thug in the dark jacket.

"He's Eurasian," Stefani observed.

"Half-Thai. The only native speaker in your diplomatic corps, I understand. And one of the California Halliwells."

"*Is* he." She had handled Halliwell money in her days at Fund-Market. The family wealth was derived from bauxite holdings, South African chrome, sugar production in the Everglades—probably a cigarette factory or chemical plant somewhere. "I'd like to meet him."

Paolo led the way without hesitation through the shifting current of guests. The thug in the black suit cast an indolent glance at Stefani as she approached, muttered a word to Halliwell and dove for the arched doors that opened onto the garden.

"Stefani Fogg," Paolo said reverently, "allow me to introduce Rush Halliwell. Rush, a fellow American."

"A pleasure," Halliwell said, and extended his hand.

He had prominent cheekbones, a square chin, sloe eyes that tended toward green. And a smile that was too caressing, too presumptuous, too damn self-assured. "Have you been in Bangkok long?" he asked.

"Several times over the past few months," she replied. "I've made the Oriental my home."

"Then you're here on business?"

"Not exactly." She accepted the drink Paolo offered and kept her expression deliberately vague. It was probable, she thought, that Halliwell knew a great deal about her already. He had been talking, after all, to the thug who'd stolen her notes.

"*Personal* business? Let me guess. You want to adopt a baby—or start an export company."

"Neither."

"Then it's a friend unfairly jailed on trumped-up drug charges." He waved off a waiter bearing a tray of puff pastry. "I should say at the outset that the U.S. government can do nothing in most cases. A life sentence is a life sentence. And I would warn you not to bribe."

"Are those the top three reasons people contact the embassy?" she inquired lightly.

"Of course. Everybody wants *something*, Ms. Fogg. This is a place where you grab what you can get." He spoke pleasantly enough; but the green eyes remained calculating.

"You can relax, Rush," Paolo interjected. "Ms. Fogg is a world traveler without an agenda of any kind. And now, if you'll both forgive me—"

Paolo nodded in Stefani's direction and glided back to the doorway. Someone with cheekbones and very little in the way of clothes—German supermodel? Russian actress?—held out her hand. The assistant manager bent over it immediately.

Stefani cocked her head at Halliwell.

"So which was the guy you were just talking to: baby, business or bust?"

"I beg your pardon?"

"The Asian. Dark jacket. Built like a wrestler. He dashed for his life when we came up."

Halliwell smiled. "I must look like an employee. He wanted directions to the nearest bathroom."

"Ah."

"It's my Thai features. Happens all the time. So where's home, Stefani? When it's not the Oriental?"

He had edged closer and filled the gap left by the departed Paolo—a move intended to suggest that his attention was entirely hers, but that succeeded in blocking her view of the rest of the room. She remembered Thanom's words. *He listened and he stood rounds of drinks for his new friends and he laughed at their jokes. But he did not drink himself and he never talked of his own affairs. Is such a man to be trusted?*

"New York," she answered abruptly. "And you?"

"Wherever I'm posted. Hong Kong last, Kuala Lumpur before that. In the dark ages, it was Ghana."

A careful omission of California money, and of his duties in Bangkok. Was he really with the State Department? Or was he reporting to State's kissing cousin, the CIA?

"A world traveler, eh?" He snatched a canapé off a passing tray. "Where have you been lately?"

"Burma. Then Vietnam."

One eyebrow rose. "You must have gotten very wet."

"I swam back to Bangkok. What exactly do you do at the embassy, Mr. Halliwell? Besides hitting cocktail parties?"

"I'm Third Political Officer. What took you to Vietnam?"

"The beaches. What does a Third Political Officer do?"

"Attend cocktail parties." His eyes, above the perfect smile, were hard as flint.

"So we're back where we started. I'd hoped you'd be able to help me—but I already know how to work a crowd."

"Now it comes out. What exactly do you need, lady?"

"Directions."

He gestured ingenuously. "I think the bathroom is—"

"—on how to sue the Thai government."

"Then you want a lawyer, not a diplomat. What's Thailand done to annoy you?"

"The government stole something that belongs to me. I want it back."

Halliwell waited impassively.

"Jack Roderick's House." Stefani watched him fail to react. "I know you've heard of it. The museum. The art collection. The teak structure on the banks of the khlong. I've just inherited it from Roderick's heir. So perhaps you could tell me, Mr. Halliwell—how does an American start, in Thailand, to claim what's hers?"

5

The Western Coast of Thailand,
December 1945

It was Tao Oum, the refugee from Laos, who drove them south that day, south and west in Jack Roderick's shining Packard. They were armed with the old military maps, much creased, that Roderick had been given in Ceylon; some dried fish and papaya; and the OSS service revolver hidden in the glove box. Five of them sharing a water canteen in the heat, a damp-fingered wind off the coast flooding through the open windows.

Boonreung sat in the middle because he was young and slight, a bundle of northeast bones. Roderick had hired the boy away from the Suan Kularb Palace where he had worked as a waiter, and kept him to run errands and valet his clothing and drive his car. He liked Boonreung's quickness and his easy laughter; he was teaching him to speak English.

Beside the boy was Vukrit and on the other side the man everyone still called Carlos because it was the name he'd earned during the war. Vukrit and Carlos were married to sisters and they should have been like brothers themselves—but the war and its hatreds divided them. Vukrit had backed the pro-Japanese dictator, Field Marshal Pibul Songgram, while Carlos had thrown his lot in with the hero of the Thai Resistance, Pridi Banomyong. The Japanese had surrendered four months ago, but neither man could forgive the other's choices. Vukrit was an Army officer and he suffered when the collaborationists fell. The army was in disgrace and Vukrit's friends were wary of him. Carlos worked for Pridi Banomyong in the new Prime Minister's office and took his beautiful wife, Chao, to glittering victory parties in the *farang* quarter.

Boonreung sat between the brothers-in-law in the back of the car and was sometimes their buffer and sometimes their only link.

Roderick sat in front, next to Tao Oum, listening to the words the others tossed back and forth in Thai. He spoke French to Tao Oum, who despised the French, and English with the others, and all three assumed that the *farang* would never understand the taunts they traded like outgrown clothes. He was Roderick and they feared him and loved him in equal measure; but in the end he was *farang*.

They had spent the night in Phetchaburi, one hundred and twenty-three kilometers south of Bangkok, where for a thousand years the royal palaces and temples were raised in the pleasant hills above the coast. Boonreung had never been so near the sea in his life and they abused him for his wonder and forced fried urchins into his mouth, staying up late over their beer to study the maps. Roderick loved to hear the old tales of conquest, told in halting English and French, and so they obliged him by inventing what they could not translate and inadvertently managed a fractured poetry. They spoke of elephants and of armies and of cities enslaved; of hermits in the hills and the sacred shrines they hid there; of women more beautiful than gems in the secret passages of the king's palace, where it was death for a common man to enter. They talked far into the night, slept on hard cots in a ramshackle rooming house and then woke to the scent of hot noodles. The cook had added seaweed to the broth and Boonreung would not eat it. The boy was ravenous now as he drank from the canteen, begging pieces of dried papaya like a favored dog. Roderick tossed him scraps over his shoulder and laughed whenever the boy caught them between his teeth.

The narrow road was pocked with old mortar shells; the train line that ran alongside it was still broken in places, with gangs of workmen slaving over rush baskets and picks. They traveled slowly and the talk surged and died depending upon the difficulty of the road. Boonreung exclaimed over the color of the water on their left hand—a translucent azure with the look of polished jade. Carlos, however, cut off the boy's words in a voice as sharp as a knife. Carlos was an educated man and in his heart a kind one, but he had been born on the Western Seaboard and would never forget how the Japanese bayoneted the men and boys of the fishing villages four years before, during the bloody December invasion of 1941. The coast around Singora and Patani had been trapped between two colliding forces: the Japanese ground troops heading south toward the Malay Peninsula, and the British advance pushing north. Five days of butchery, before Field Marshal Pibul declared defeat.

Roderick was unmoved by blood feuds or war memories. He stared instead through the open window, at the mountains rising in dense green. "There are tigers in that jungle, or were," he said, "and leopards and gibbons and two types of Asiatic bear. Gray elephants. Lemurs and birds." The four men heard the longing in his voice and when they did not understand his *farang* names for things, they thought of Burma, the land that fell just beyond those mountains, and the burning embers of rubies clutched at its heart.

And when at last they reached the marshes of Khao Sam Roi Yot where thousands of migratory birds sheltered in the grasses, and abandoned the Packard in the shade of a banana tree, the long journey had left them aching as old men. Boonreung ran joyously toward the shallows, startling a heron into the air, while the others stretched and yawned and eyed the women mending shrimp nets among the rocks. Roderick was already shifting canvas packs from the car's trunk and muttering orders in fluent French to Tao Oum, who mopped his forehead with a damp handkerchief. Carlos offered bars of chocolate to the boys who lingered near the fishwives. The boys would have preferred real *farang* cigarettes they could have sold for money, but took the chocolate and answered Carlos's questions. Vukrit leaned against the car's hood and followed Roderick with inscrutable eyes.

They had come nearly two hundred kilometers south from Bangkok with the hope of finding riches in the hills: not leopards or rubies but the hidden mouths of caves. In the old stories it was said that the great limestone outcroppings that rose sheer from the lapping sands were sacred to Buddha, and that men had long ago set up secret altars that were beautiful to gaze upon. It was for this that Roderick had dragged them here, despite their hatreds and their jealousies and their private wars; he wanted to take a walk in the jungle, and he wanted company. They had come, all four of them, because they did without question as Roderick asked. For Tao Oum it was a matter of loyalty; for Carlos, a debt between friends. For Vukrit the trip was a test. He came out of need and a thwarted desire to be loved. Only Boonreung came freely.

They walked into the jungle a few minutes after one o'clock in the afternoon, with the knowledge that they would not come down from the mountain again before nightfall. They took two local boys as guides, because the boys had told Carlos that they knew of sacred caves hidden high in the mountains and had often played near them. The boys sang strains of a nonsense song as they surged barefoot along the paths. They seemed unafraid of the rumor of tigers.

The men walked silently at first, Roderick in front. He remembered the faces of his OSS brothers as they pressed shoulder to shoulder under the cover of green leaves, while carpenter ants ran through their fingers. He remembered the tortured maze of paths that had confused and trapped them, the constant moisture, the snakes that looked like branches and the sudden surprise of a flower. In Ceylon there had been no loneliness, only the fine sandstone grind of tension and fatigue.

The day wore on and the paths rose ever higher. The canteens were emptied and then refilled from the streams that rushed among the rocks. The two boys stopped singing and talked instead in a dialect no one understood—the words of their village or perhaps their childhood. And then at last, when Vukrit had begun to complain of blisters from his hard city shoes and Roderick's pale skin was red from exertion, the children hooted and called as though in prearranged signal, and the chasm opened at their feet.

It was an astonishing plunge downward one hundred meters or more, unexpected in that hilly place. A curtain of mist boiled at its mouth, sent skyward by a waterfall that spurted from the rock, and orchids blossomed in limestone clefts. Roderick stopped short and gazed toward the heart of the earth with a look of naked wonder; behind him, the others fell silent. A white bird, disturbed, took wing. Somewhere a gibbon shrieked.

The sound broke the net that snared them all. Roderick finally spoke. "The cave is here? In the chasm?"

The two boys began to chatter excitedly. Carlos listened and nodded once. "The opening is difficult to find. It is there, a dark space behind the falling water."

They craned to see, and felt the cool mist staining their faces. Tao Oum could pick nothing out of the curtained rocks but Roderick narrowed his pale blue eyes and thought he glimpsed the cavern's mouth. Boonreung laughed out loud as though he had been given a present, and began to unload the ropes and picks from all their packs. He was an agile climber, that string of northeast bones, and would be sent first down the chasm's face.

Vukrit took off his shoes. He would not risk losing them in the torrent and he would not remain alone, in shame, at the cliff edge. Roderick set the order in which they descended, placing Tao Oum between Vukrit and Carlos, so that neither brother-in-law would owe the other his life. Roderick himself went last, as anchor for them all.

Nearly forty minutes later, Boonreung's spider foot touched down on the chasm's floor. He glanced upward, at the others so much older than he, puffing and groaning as their shaking fingers sought the rock, and grinned at heaven. Then he danced across the streambed, sunlight firing on his black hair, and placed his toes in the farther wall.

It was another hour, the men strung out like ants on the rock face, before Boonreung hauled himself lightly into the cave's mouth. Beyond the falling curtain of water he caught the image of the two children, their guides, crouched in play on the opposite side of the cliff. The image wavered and dissolved. Roderick had reached the cave before the rest, his sleek blond head, dark with water, rising like a cobra's. Boonreung reached for his hand, slick and cold with the mountain stream, and felt the shock of the *farang*'s touch. It was always thus, the boy thought: a thrill of fear and exultation, as though he had touched the sun . . .

They rested until the heat of the climb deserted them and the damp weight of their clothes raised gooseflesh on Boonreung's arm. First Carlos and then Tao Oum and finally Vukrit appeared on the rock ledge, silent and shuddering. By that time Roderick had coiled the ropes and lit the torches he carried in his pack. He raised the flaring light and turned circles in the fine dust of the cave floor: a narrow space, more like a tunnel than a cavern, with sides that sloped inward and unplumbed shadows. Boonreung found the second torch and Carlos helped him light it.

"I will not go last this time," Vukrit said sulkily. "You favor the boy, Roderick, when others are more deserving."

"Honor is won, Vukrit, not bribed," Carlos chided.

The man scuttled furiously to his feet and gripped the torch but Carlos did not release it; and so they stood, enraged, straining over the sputtering light. Roderick ignored them. He raised his torch and stepped farther into the tunnel. Vukrit clawed at Carlos's face with his free hand, his breath coming fast and shallow. After an instant, Tao Oum and Boonreung followed Roderick.

The floor sloped gently downward. At first they walked upright but after some minutes were forced to stoop, and for the space of several heartbeats it seemed that the cave was merely a pocket in the hills, a cul-de-sac rather than a sacred pathway. They could have grazed the walls with their fingertips merely by extending their hands; but they hugged themselves inward and kept their eyes trained on Roderick's back. In the distance behind they heard the noise of shuffling feet and grunting; Vukrit and Carlos had dropped the torch and were wrestling on the cave floor.

"Leave it," Roderick said when Boonreung would have turned back. "Perhaps they'll settle the goddamn future of Siam between them."

There were stairs cut into the rock, sloping downward. Roderick raised his torch high, and found no limit to its light—the cavern's height and depth a soaring vertigo. Tao Oum began to mutter words of Lao, an imprecation to the gods; Boonreung placed his hand upon the older man's shoulder.

The cavern floor. The three of them, looking upward, straining to probe the darkness. And then the light falling upon a face—a face set high into the rock wall, three stories above their heads: the sublime and lovely image of a Reclining Buddha, slumbering forgotten, perhaps for centuries. His limestone body carved in relief, his head perfect and noble. A cabochon ruby glittered in his brow.

Boonreung gasped.

"Go back and get the others," Roderick said tersely.

The boy stared an instant, motionless; then he wheeled and scrambled up the stone steps.

*   *   *

Rivalry and hatred were set aside in the flicker of torchlight. Roderick swore them to secrecy and then they debated what must be done: the child guides paid off, the cavern mouth closed until help was brought.

"What we need is a scholar," Roderick said. "Someone from the museum or the university."

"What we need is a monk," Carlos objected, "and offerings to the spirits that guard the sacred image. This place should be known and venerated."

"What we need," Vukrit muttered, "is a hammer and chisel. There are those who would pay much for so old a thing—"

In the end they left the dreaming Buddha where it had been found, and made their way back to the surface. They descended the mountain in the tropic dark, with stars pricking overhead, and because Vukrit alone still carried a knife it was he who marked the trail for Roderick, slashing at the trunks of the rainforest trees. They ate fish roasted black over a charcoal fire and slept on the marshy beach, and in the morning they headed north and east in the sweltering car.

Roderick seemed transfixed. He spoke of preservation, of salvage, of the heritage of Siam; he vowed to return in a few weeks' time, with his scholar from the university or the museum. Carlos pledged Prime Minister Pridi's help and fingered an amulet he wore at his neck. Vukrit touched the blade of his knife and stared out at the sea.

And Boonreung watched them all with a chill in his young heart. Like all Thais of sense and cunning, he feared the retribution of the gods.

6

The small alley off Chakkrawat Road snaked down to Khlong Ong Ang, a fetid ditch almost too narrow for a boat's passage. On either side were the iron doors of warehouses locked against the night, and chain-link barriers rolled to the sidewalk; green plastic awnings bucked crazily out of concrete doorways, and braziers burned there, with chicken roasting and noodles on the boil. A sweating cook hovered anxiously, while along the sidewalk hungry people waited in plastic chairs: a motorcycle mechanic, a mother shepherding twin boys. During the day the sidewalk was jammed with bodies, some buying and others selling; the old Thieves Market, the Nakorn Kasem, was only three blocks away. Even now, in relative darkness, the street was hardly menacing. But Jeff Knetsch was nervous as he made his way toward the open sewer of the khlong. He smelled the noodles and the burning flesh, and his stomach tightened.

He had flown out the previous night from Geneva, across Russia and India and then south toward the China Sea. Three days before, he had stood on the cliff edge where Max had died and endured a memorial service attended by nearly seven hundred of Courchevel's year-round residents. No body had been recovered from the jagged crevasses below Max's house; but Knetsch had chosen readings from Robert

Frost and hired a tenor to sing "Danny Boy." He'd fielded questions from reporters and cordoned off the old stone house to prevent its destruction by souvenir-seekers. He delivered a eulogy that rang with love and pride and grief. His voice broke only once during the seventeen minutes required for the speech.

And he had tried to comfort Sabine Renaudie and Yvette Margolan and Max's old girlfriend Suzanne Muldoon—who had flown in unexpectedly from Oregon to pay her final respects. She wore Prada black and a hat with a veil and she was rumored to have sold the rights to her memoirs. Max dead was far more profitable than Max alive.

Even Sabine's estranged mother, Claudine, had returned for the memorial. But there was not a single member of the Roderick family alive to bear witness; and Stefani Fogg never showed.

Through it all, Knetsch crossed his gambler's fingers and prayed for his luck to hold. He walked the ridgeline with Max in spirit: a crevasse on one side, fathomless air on the other. He put one foot in front of the next and kept going, ignoring the impulse to glance over his shoulder. It was in moments like this that Jeff's iron self-control proved its worth. He listened courteously and made adroit conversation to virtual strangers. He put his arm around Yvette Margolan and drank schnapps with Jacques Renaudie and even spoke with admirable restraint to Oliver Krane. Krane appeared without warning at the ceremony that consigned Max to oblivion, standing in an absurd wool felt fedora and black cashmere coat beside a sobbing Sabine. Krane intended, Knetsch supposed, to make sure his invoices were paid. But Jeff had a bone to pick with Oliver Krane—the man had no business running a risk-management agency as he did, sending rapacious women as his emissaries, women who annihilated men's lives. Krane would not receive a nickel for his trouble if Jeff Knetsch had anything to say about it.

"But you *don't*, old thing," Oliver had murmured gently, one hand on Jeff's shoulder in deepest sympathy. "You're not the executor of Roderick's will, are you? I'll submit my claim to his Geneva firm, of course. Now, if you'd be so good as to show me the way to the alpine-rescue chappies, I'd be no end grateful."

Jeff had shaken off the man's hand without a word of reply and gone in search of a strong drink. The terror he'd held at bay for days welled up and nearly throttled him. *Krane intended to talk to the rescue team.* The men who had gathered the pieces of Max's shattered wheelchair off the rock ledge a thousand feet below his house.

His steps slowed as he reached the middle of the Bangkok alley. A block farther on was the door he must enter, but something moved in the distance—near the faint gleam of Khlong Ong Ang—and he raised his hand to his eyes. The figure of a boy in ski-racing gear: eleven or twelve years old, tall for his age, with a piercing green gaze. The swing of his stride was athletic and confident. The boy walked up to him and held out his hand. Anguish seared through Knetsch.

They're timing us today. I thought I ought to say Good Luck. It's icy out there.

Knetsch felt the sidewalk lurch and dip. He thrust out his briefcase to ward off the demon—not young Max, immortal and blessed, but a figment of hell. His knees buckled and he almost sat down on the stinking stone curb. What he needed was rest. He had skipped too many time zones in quick succession. He had not been home in three weeks. He had not talked to his wife in days. She thought he was still in Geneva. She thought he was coming home.

One of the twin boys eating dinner with his mother hooted with laughter and skittered between the plastic chairs. He pointed an accusing finger at Knetsch, shrieked a word of Thai and fled back toward the charcoal brazier.

Jeff's fists clenched. What had the kid called him? He met the eyes of the boy's mother—black, implacable eyes with judgment in their depths. The cook was staring at him, too, and the mechanic with the greasy hands. The smell of noodles and garlic and frying oil—

He wrenched abruptly toward the street and vomited in the gutter.

"That's exceptionally fine," the man named Sompong murmured as he studied the terra cotta statue of Buddha he held in his hand. The halogen lamp was trained on the statue's hooded gaze. So was his jeweler's magnifying glass. "Seventh century, you say?"

"Possibly eighth. In such a case, it's difficult to judge with certainty."

"Yes," Sompong agreed, pursing his lips in consideration; "quite difficult." He reached for a chisel and with the utmost delicacy worked a flake of clay from the Buddha's base. Fine red dust sifted to the plastic matting on the tabletop. Sompong began to whistle under his breath, and the man hovering beside him swallowed anxiously. The chisel ground deeper. The red dust turned gradually pink, then white. Sompong sighed; he removed his jeweler's lens.

"I'm disappointed, Khuang," he said distantly. "Very disappointed. I told you expressly that the ceramic must have the delicacy of a rare antique, but the durability of a common pot." Sharply, with the stem of his chisel, he struck the clay figure. A crack knifed through the statue's face from nose to hairline. "This will never do. We'll leave a trail from here to the Metropolitan Museum. Do you want me killed?"

"Excellency—"

"Don't call me that."

"Mr. Suwannathat—"

"Do you *want* us to fail? Because I assure you that it will be your neck on the block if the shipment is traced. Not mine."

"I know that. Sir." Khuang swallowed again—like a fish, Sompong thought, plucked straight from the tank and gulping for air. "But what you ask is impossible. If the artifact is not to be judged as a fake, the clay must be extremely thin—"

A buzzer sounded from the front of the warehouse. Khuang nearly jumped out of his skin.

"Get the door," Sompong told him in disgust. "I haven't much time."

Jeff Knetsch had been in this warehouse only once, two years ago when the talk of Jack Roderick first began and Max had sealed his own death warrant. It had been daylight then, and the dust that lay so heavily upon the collection of artifacts had swum in the few bars of sunlight allowed through the stifling shutters. Tonight a single halogen lamp was trained on a bare worktable and a man sat behind it—a man with features as classically serene as an ancient figure from Angkor Wat. There was Khmer in his brow and a touch of Laos about the eyes and more than a little of the broad cheekbones of China; but this was Sompong's face, and thus a thing to be feared.

Knetsch brought his palms high to his forehead, his shoulders sloping into submission and humility, and hoped that his hands did not shake.

"Leave us, Khuang," Sompong said tonelessly.

The man scurried toward the recesses of the warehouse without a backward glance. Knetsch waited, the silence unbroken.

"The lawyer," Sompong said finally. There was a world of contempt in his voice. "The lawyer from New York who is no better than any lawyer I have ever known, in Bangkok or Singapore or Hong Kong or Zurich. You have failed me, Mr. Knetsch, and I am enraged."

"Haven't you heard?" Jeff lowered his hands and stared at the man in disbelief. "Max Roderick is dead."

Sompong traced a chisel idly through the dust on the worktable's surface. "But his woman is alive, and in Bangkok asking questions."

"That's not my fault."

"Fault!" Sompong stabbed the chisel deep into the table, and Jeff flinched. "I do not care about fault! I want to know what you intend to do to solve the problem."

"What *I* intend to do?" Jeff's stomach was churning again. "I—I hadn't realized . . . I thought . . . you would just . . . handle it."

"The way I handled the whore in Geneva?"

"Something like that."

"You know far too much about my life, Mr. Knetsch," Sompong said. "Far too much. And you came here for money, didn't you? That's why you flew across two continents. For money."

"I did what you asked me to do. Now I'm finished. A deal's a deal."

"But we differ in our assessment of your performance," the other man objected, softly. "I asked you to put an end to the questions about Jack Roderick. And still the questions are asked."

Anger flared through Knetsch's gut—his gambler's luck spun out like a roulette wheel, the ball dropping in red when he'd counted on black. "I'm *finished*, Sompong. I want my money and I want to go home."

"That is very unwise." Sompong stood and moved around the table. He was a head shorter than Knetsch but he appeared far more powerful. "I know where you live. And I know every sordid thing about your complicated life, Mr. Knetsch. Both facts could be dangerous to people you love."

Jeff felt the tic above his right eye begin to twitch. He opened his mouth as if to speak, but no words came.

"I want the woman's questions to stop," Sompong repeated gently. "You will not leave Thailand until they do."

7

Bangkok,
1946

Roderick would remember for years afterward that the June morning was clear and bright, unusual for the first weeks of the rainy season in Bangkok. June 9, 1946. All over the country, boys of eighteen were entering the traditional period of monastic retreat for the first time since the Japanese surrendered to the Allies on September 2, 1945. Ordination ceremonies were held throughout the city, at once raucous and profoundly religious. Alec McQueen was drunk and singing off-key, something in Thai. McQueen spoke the language better than any foreigner Roderick knew, even when he was drunk.

He stumbled as they mounted the steps of the Chakri Throne Hall and clutched at Roderick's arm.

"Shorry, Jack."

Roderick placed a hand under his elbow and helped him to stand.

These days, it was not unusual to find McQueen in his cups. He was struggling: with the end of a love affair, with his decision to turn his back on home, with his fledgling newspaper's increasingly desperate need for funds. Roderick felt a surge of anger with Alec. He was lonely, too—and he was heartily sick of mopping up after other people's problems. He was tired of conversations he didn't understand in a language too difficult to learn. Tired, mostly, of rain and the flooded streets, of shoes welling with water and bedsheets that stank of mold.

"Pull yourself together, Alec," he said irritably. "I'm depending on you."

The Prime Minister—Pridi Banomyong—had summoned them to the Grand Palace for an audience with the young King Ananda, Rama the Eighth. There was to be an announcement of economic and political cooperation between the Kingdom of Thailand and the United States, Roderick thought—a necessary prelude to the Thai bid for membership in the United Nations that Pridi was ardently pursuing. The wording of the note delivered to Roderick's hotel room at the Oriental that morning had been vague, and the messenger who conveyed it spoke no English. Roderick had pulled McQueen from his bed down the hall, stinking with the Bamboo Bar's rye whiskey, and threw him headfirst into one of the great ceramic water jars that served as washbasins. Alec spluttered and howled and called Jack expletives in three languages; he still reeked of whiskey an hour later.

"Why'sh the kid staying in this old barn anyway?" he demanded as they reached the carved and gilded doorway. "Thought the royal family hated the center of town. Nobody's been in reshidence here since old Rama the Fifth. We're up to Eight now, right?"

"Right."

There had been no king in Thailand since 1935, when Rama the Seventh had been thrust into exile. The present monarch was a mere boy, summoned from his home in Switzerland in the burst of postwar royalist fervor after Thailand's capitulation in September 1945. Ananda had ruled his Grand Palace barely ten months.

Roderick nodded to the palace guard who stood, frozen, at one side of the massive portal. A small door cut into the carved face opened as if by unseen hands, and Roderick guided Alec over the threshold. "The real question is why the Prime Minister asked for *you*. He ought to know by now that you're not reliable."

"You hurt me, Jack," McQueen sulked. "You really do. And after all we've been through—"

The interior was dimly lit, soaring of ceiling, and empty. Not even the doorman had stayed to give them welcome. Roderick spun around, searching for a face in the vast emptiness of the hall, the skin on the back of his neck prickling. He seized McQueen's arm.

"What?"

"Don't you smell it?"

"Smell what?"

"Death. I smell *death,* damn you."

He began to run, pelting down a corridor toward the sound of voices: a babble of words in Thai, a woman's shriek. A terrified girl brushed past them in the corridor, like a silk-clad bird blundering against a windowpane. Her hand was pressed to her mouth. Roderick reached for her but she was already gone. The two men sped on, through empty salons and down hallways, until suddenly they rounded upon a burst of light, and everything became still.

He lay with his arms flung wide and his eyes fixed on the open window. The bullet hole was surprisingly neat—and McQueen, too, would notice that detail, Roderick thought; they had both seen enough head wounds to last a lifetime. Some men shot their ears off, some blasted through pieces of skull, leaving a trench from ear to ear; but this wound was round and acutely precise, as though painted on the young king's temple. He was dead, all the same.

Three people stood huddled at the foot of the king's bed: an elderly woman, one hand clutching at her breast; a man in the livery of the royal household; and the third, a face they recognized. A man they knew.

"*Carlos,*" McQueen said sharply. "What the fuck are you doing here?"

He turned, and they saw the gun he clutched in his hand. Before Carlos could speak or raise the weapon, Jack Roderick was at his side, his fingers like a vise on his friend's wrist. The pistol clattered to the floor.

"He must have killed him," Carlos told them blankly. "Did you catch him? Did he get away?"

Roderick kicked the revolver carefully out of reach before replying. It spun like a lethal top on the marble tiles. "Catch who? *Who,* Carlos?"

"He was masked. Threw the gun at my feet as I entered the room. I should have followed—but I went instead to the king—"

At this, his face twisted with a spasm of grief.

There was another screech from the old woman and without warning the harpy was upon them, her nails clawing a bloody trail across Carlos's cheek. McQueen seized her arms. She spat out the words, a hail of Thai.

"She says they saw him. *Carlos.* When they heard the shot," McQueen translated swiftly. "That Carlos did this. He was bending over the king, the gun in his hand, when she got here."

Before Roderick could stop him, the manservant turned and ran from the room. "What are you doing in the palace?" Roderick asked Carlos tensely. "You've got no business in the king's bedroom."

"A note. From the Prime Minister. I was told to wait for papers—"

A note delivered by an errand boy, one who knew nothing.

"Did you talk to Pridi yourself?"

Carlos shook his head.

The sound of running feet echoed in the corridor; Roderick turned, an intent expression on his face. "We've been set up, my friend. When I release your wrist, head for the window. Try to get to your old meeting place. Lie low. I'll find you when it's dark. Now—GO!"

Carlos shoved the old woman out of the way and leapt to the windowsill without a backward glance. He jumped—a blur of jet-black hair, khaki suiting the color of mud—and was gone. Only then did Roderick wonder how far the drop from the sill was.

The old woman, on her knees, began to sob wrenchingly. What was she? A princess? A nurse? Roderick placed his hand tentatively on her shoulder. She spat at him.

The first of the palace guards pounded into the room. Strange, Roderick thought, that it had taken them so long to respond to gunfire in the royal household. "Tell them," he urged McQueen. "Tell them the killer went out the way they came. And get that woman to shut up."

The real question, Roderick thought later, was not why the young king had to be murdered. That, he almost understood. Ananda had grown up in exile, a child educated in boarding schools and surrounded by doting family; the boy knew nothing of government, nothing of Thailand, but he had taken to the notion of rule like a duck to water. Ananda had descended on his capital ten months before with the sorry notion that he possessed absolute power; and he'd been itching to use it. He'd quarreled with his Prime Minister, Pridi Banomyong, who thought kings should remain figureheads while elected officials ran the government. Pridi could not control the king any more than he could destroy the machine that had governed Thailand in Ananda's absence—the military faction that had cast its lot with Hirohito's

Japan, seized a large chunk of disputed territory beyond Thailand's borders, and then retired in disgrace. The military hated Pridi and the king with equal force.

No, Roderick thought: the question had never been *why* the king was shot; the question would always be *who*. Who among the floating crap game of sedition politics in the soggy, rain-swept capital wanted to destroy Carlos—the Prime Minister's most trusted aide—and through him, Pridi Banomyong? Who would want the regicide to be discovered by Jack Roderick, head of U.S. intelligence in Thailand, and Alec McQueen—who commanded the power of the English-language press corps?

Prime Minister Pridi's chief enemies: Field Marshal Pibul and his cadre. The men Jack Roderick had helped to defeat and disgrace.

He sent Boonreung that night to find Carlos, among the maze of canals and houseboats that made up the far reaches of Thon Buri. There was a place they always used for meetings—one of Carlos's safe houses during the war. A sampan with a roof over its head, a widow who peddled vegetables on the water. Her husband another dead hero of the resistance, her children too gaunt and terrified in the wavering lantern-light. Carlos crouched like a dog in the boat's shelter, the woman going about her evening business as though frying oil were all she dreamed of. In the chaotic hours that followed Ananda's murder, Roderick wondered if the hiding place was wise. It might have been betrayed long ago. It might be the first place the enemy would look. But there had been no time to regroup. First there was the necessary explanation to the palace guards. The shouted testimony of the two witnesses—the king's Swiss valet and his ancient nurse—who insisted that Roderick and McQueen were in league with the assassin. Only after an endless period, were they allowed to place calls to U.S. Ambassador Edwin Stanton and the Prime Minister, who had never summoned them to the palace in the first place. At last, when they had been grudgingly released, there was the dressing-down in the ambassador's office—the final blow that rankled in Roderick's soul.

"Did you orchestrate this fiasco, Jack?" Stanton had demanded querulously. "Did you act on orders from Washington of which I was never informed?"

"You think I'm a kingmaker, Ed?" Roderick retorted acidly. "You figure I paid the assassin myself?"

"That's what they're saying in the street," Stanton replied, "so it doesn't much matter whether you did or didn't. The air is thick with coups and plots wherever you walk, Roderick. This time you've gone too far."

"This time I'm innocent," he muttered sourly; but nothing he could have said would have mattered. From that day forward, Prime Minister Pridi's hours were numbered, regardless of how many times Roderick attempted to explain how brilliantly they had all been set up—that the real villains were those who were ruthlessly determined to regain power. A single act of bloodshed and calumny—the turning tide of public opinion—was worth more than an armored division in the streets any day.

King Ananda's death was declared an accident. No one in Southeast Asia believed it.

"Carlos gave me this," Boonreung told Roderick before dawn the next morning. "He said you would know where it came from."

Puzzled, Roderick turned over the smooth, dark red gemstone the boy handed him. It was polished but uncut, and looked quite old. A garnet? A ruby. "He told you nothing else?"

"Only that he found it on the floor of the palace, by the king's bedside. Perhaps it was Ananda's."

Roderick pocketed the stone. "Did all go well?"

Boonreung had collected Carlos from Thon Buri in a borrowed long-tail boat and poled him downstream to the city's edge. Roderick had arranged for transport—a truck packed with fish and bound for market in the interior. Carlos had clutched at Boonreung's shirt and begged him to take care of his children. The boy promised what he could and refused to say goodbye.

"I saw Vukrit Suwannathat hunting through every sampan and houseboat on the Thon Buri side with three soldiers in army uniforms, just as I poled the boat out of the khlong," he told Roderick.

"Did Vukrit see you?"

"I do not know. Maybe. He certainly did not see Carlos in the bottom of my boat." The boy shrugged. "We got away."

Unless, Roderick thought, *Vukrit had you followed*—but he said nothing of his suspicion to Boonreung. Carlos would be safe soon in the hill country of Chiang Rai. He intended to pass into Laos at the first opportunity. If Vukrit knew more than Boonreung guessed, Roderick could wait for the man's attempt at blackmail.

It was only years later that Jack Roderick understood that blackmail was not the point. It was Boonreung he should have saved.

8

That Tuesday night, Stefani made her way back to her room around ten o'clock, leaving Rush Halliwell standing on the river terrace. Halfway down the Garden Wing corridor, the strains of a viola skittered through her brain. She stopped dead, borne back immediately to the moonlit bedroom in the old stone house above Courchevel.

"Max," she said aloud in the empty hall. "Max, are you there?"

The faint strains died away into silence. She brushed one hand over her eyes, which were suddenly damp, and fumbled for her key.

Of course Rush Halliwell had invited her to dinner. Her barefaced claim to Jack Roderick's House was designed to snare his interest, and he'd risen instantly to the bait, as she'd assumed he would. He wanted to know more. Because everything to do with Jack Roderick's Bangkok life was universally irresistible? Or because the U.S. embassy's Third Political Officer was in league with Max's enemies—whoever they might be?

"I don't know a great deal about the Roderick story," he'd offered as he pulled out her chair. "Just the stuff that's in all the guidebooks."

Liar, she'd thought, and said: "That's what most people know. I was fortunate enough to be a friend of the family."

"Obviously, if you inherit under a will. But I thought even the family had no idea how Jack Roderick died."

"Oh, as to that—" she said airily, "there are probably as many theories as there are people to form them. Ideas are everywhere. It's the truth that's in short supply, Rush."

"And is that what you're looking for? Truth?" His smile was roguish, as though she should hardly take him seriously; but it was precisely *this,* Stefani decided, that he really wanted to know: the depth of the unquiet graves, and whether she carried a shovel.

"I just want my house." Max's house. And all its resident ghosts.

"That could be difficult." Halliwell unfurled his napkin with care. "I *had heard* that Roderick left his house and collection to Thailand. An altruistic gesture. That's why the place was turned into a museum, isn't it?"

"If you say so."

"What other reason is there?"

"Greed. On the part of those who manage the collection."

"Greed cuts both ways," he pointed out. "Is it greed to preserve the nation's artistic heritage—or greed to claim it for yourself?"

"That depends upon how the collection was acquired," Stefani returned tartly. "In this case, wholesale theft seems an apt description."

Halliwell shrugged, untouched. "That's probably how old Roderick came by the stuff in the first place—raiding parties on ancient temples, lost for centuries in the wilderness. The man was a connoisseur, sure— but most swear he was also a pirate."

"I've never known a connoisseur who wasn't."

"That doesn't justify piracy. Look, Stefani—the Thai government maintains Roderick's hoard and makes it available to the public. Absent that, the collection would have been broken up and sold long ago. Statues of Buddha, figures in limestone and bronze, carved heads—the treasures in that house span fourteen centuries. Roderick owned the finest example of a Thai Buddha sculpture in existence. Add to that the fact that it's almost a crime in this country to display sacred images in private homes, and by any argument those pieces *belong* in a museum."

"And yet—that's not what Roderick wanted. Not what he stipulated in his will."

"Which will?"

"The one that governs. The one that postdates the 1960 document."

Rush's fork arrested in midair. "You've seen it?"

"Of course. Roderick probably intended to destroy the 1960 testament. He drew up the final will a few weeks before he disappeared in '67. Unfortunately, that document was misplaced. It was only recently found in the home of Roderick's sister, after her death."

"Along with the Hitler diaries and an unknown play by Shakespeare."

"It's been authenticated, Rush."

He eyed her shrewdly. "Try getting a Thai court to accept that. Jack left everything to his heirs?"

"—And they, to *me*."

He smiled. "What a fortunate girl you are, Stefani."

I might say the same about you, she thought, remembering the ample assets of the California Halliwells. "So tell me. How do I get what's mine?"

He sipped from his water glass. Buying time before answering? "You'll need a lawyer who understands the Thai justice system. But possession, as they say, is usually nine-tenths of the law. As a foreigner, you'll have a difficult time winning property rights in this country. Your best bet is some sort of compromise. An out-of-court settlement."

"I abhor compromise. Particularly when I'm in the right."

"Then you'll never thrive in Thailand. Here you must be like the bamboo tree. Bend in a typhoon, lest you break. Do you know how the museum's managed?"

"By a private board—the Thai Heritage Board. It's funded in part from donations, but mainly through a trust fund managed by Dickie Spencer, the chairman of Jack Roderick Silk. Dickie's father, Charles, worked for Jack during the sixties. Charles took over the firm after Jack's disappearance. The Spencers are something of a local dynasty."

"You've done your homework. What exactly was your profession, back in the States?"

"I managed a mutual fund for a while." She threw him her impish smile; if Halliwell believed she was susceptible to flattery, she'd better look like flattery was working. "I suppose I should tackle Spencer first. He's the man with the most obvious stake in the house."

"But the power brokers behind the scenes are the ones who really control it. I know Dickie Spencer rather well. He's a good front man for the Thai Heritage Board, and he'd hate to lose the house—he's put a chunk of change into it and it's a focal point for the silk company—but he's not emotionally invested."

"The others are?"

"The others might kill to keep their hands on the place."

He said it very quietly, but the menace was real. People didn't joke about Jack Roderick's legacy. Stefani sat back in her chair and gazed at Halliwell. "Is that a warning? Hands off?"

"I don't expect you to take it." He shrugged again. "But you did say you were looking for the truth."

"Then tell me whom I should be afraid of," she challenged softly. "The power brokers *behind* the scenes."

His eyes flicked away from hers. She could almost feel him deciding how many cards to show, and which to conceal. "You understand that all of this is off the record."

"Of course."

"A gesture. Not a professional commitment. Not the official statement of the U.S. embassy. I've got to talk to my superiors before I can offer you help."

Have you got any superiors, I wonder? Or do you simply invent them when it's convenient? "We're two acquaintances having a conversation over dinner," she replied evenly.

"Right." He raised his glass again, revealing a tanned wrist beneath his elegant cuff. "Positions on the Thai Heritage Board are granted by appointment. They're considered quite prestigious and are in fact virtually controlled by certain families or interests. Something you should understand about the Thais, Stefani, is that this is a collectivist society. Not as strongly conformist as, say, the Japanese—most Thais talk a lot about individuality and personal freedom—but group-oriented all the same."

"You mean, the whole country operates on patronage."

"On clientelism," he corrected. "Patron-client relationships. Thai society is knit vertically and horizontally by bonds of personal obligation. Favors. Debts. Call them what you will."

"And so appointments to the board are won by influence?"

"Basically."

"Who controls the power of appointment?"

Rush smiled. "You must know his name."

She frowned. "Why would I?"

"You seem to know everything else."

"If I did, I wouldn't be having dinner with you."

"How frank." He looked rueful. "The man you want is Sompong Suwannathat. He's Minister of Culture in the current government. He'll probably be Minister of Defense in the next. Culture and crowd control go hand-in-hand in Thailand."

Sompong Suwannathat. "You think this guy is emotionally invested in my house?"

"I think Suwannathat would argue that it's his house," Halliwell rejoined mildly. "Sompong's run the Heritage Board for over ten years. His father was a member before him. If Jack Roderick's legacy belongs to anyone—"

"Then it's Sompong, and not the Thai public," Stefani cut in. "You've just made me feel infinitely better, Rush. I'm delighted to rob a fellow power broker."

"Don't take this lightly." The easy charm that had lingered around his eyes had vanished. "Sompong is someone to respect."

"What does that mean? That he employs thugs?"

"Undoubtedly. But he also employs half of Bangkok. Which means he owns half of Bangkok. If you cross Sompong you'll get hurt. That's not a threat. But it is the truth."

"I'll call and make an appointment with the man. That's one way to manage a threat."

"Like you managed funds. Did you meet Max Roderick trading assets?"

Stefani's fork slipped through her fingers. Rush bent instantly to retrieve it.

"He's the only Roderick left," he added reasonably. "Besides, I skied Tahoe as a kid. Max is a local hero there. And I still follow the World Cup. Didn't he have a nasty accident last year?"

"He died six days ago." She said it carefully. "Suicide."

"I'm sorry." Halliwell's somber expression suggested a proper degree of empathy; but the news was not *news* to him, Stefani was certain. "If, as I take it, your inheritance is only six days old, then I wouldn't topple the Suwannathat throne just yet. You'll have months to wait before you can justify a claim. Probate is never quick, particularly when it's done on three continents."

Three continents. In that single phrase, he'd just betrayed himself: he knew a bit more about Max than was usual for a Third Political Officer in Southeast Asia, even one who followed the World Cup. She thought of the powerful man in the dark suit and the perfectly groomed hair, the man who had taken so long to request directions to the bathroom from Rush that evening. She thought of the crumpled paper stolen from her bag, and the names and suspicions written on it. She thought of accidents that were not accidents. Of murder dressed up as suicide. Of Max, sailing out into thin air with his hands locked on the brakes—

"You've been so helpful, Rush." She smiled up into his green eyes. "I'm planning to visit Jack Roderick's House tomorrow afternoon— won't you meet me there?"

She thrust her key into the bedroom door. Turn-down service, the stereo softly playing, and beyond the windows, river traffic like a festival of lights. Someone had left her lychee fruit in a porcelain dish. She allowed herself thirty seconds to soak in the peace before she picked up her phone.

"Feeling better, ducks?" Oliver asked.

"Exhausted to the damn bone."

"That must be why you called from your room. I'd prefer, in future, that you try the street."

"Sloppy," she agreed, stung by the note of reprimand in his voice. "Sorry."

"I suppose you need something." Again, she heard annoyance.

"I need a good lawyer. Somebody who practices in Bangkok. An American, if possible."

"Civil or criminal? Corporate? Or litigation?"

"Trusts and Estates, as I think you can guess. Someone who can tell me how to prove a will in the Thai courts."

Oliver sighed. "You only want the earth, and of course you want it yesterday. Very well. I shall put in a call to the home of a man who owes me a favor, and disturb his sleep unforgivably. You may expect Matthew French on your hotel terrace by breakfast. The back terrace, mind. Don't be late. Matthew's time is exorbitant."

"Thank you, Oliver."

"That's not the end of it, surely?" He affected astonishment. "You must have a few odd fires that require putting out."

"I'd like you to run some names. They could be important."

"For your inheritance?"

"For resolving a series of troubling deaths," she returned sharply.

He sighed again. "Then do us a favor, love, and send them over the black box."

Her encrypted laptop e-mail system. Oliver was battening down the hatches. "Has something happened?"

"Something is always happening. Just do as I ask."

"Right," she replied. But the line was dead.

She sank into a chair and stared out at the river, feeling unloved. Oliver hadn't even waited to hear about the stolen sheet of paper. Was he simply short on sleep? Angry? Or was he worried?

That phrase of music in a minor key fluttered at the edge of her brain. Whatever Oliver's problem, it couldn't be fixed from a distance of six thousand miles. She closed her eyes, and said Max's name aloud.

9

Gunfire rang sporadically now from the wide oval field known as the Pramane Ground, a few hundred yards from the riverbank; had he been able to stand up in the floor of the sampan and stare intently through the darkness, he might have glimpsed flames rising in the sky over the Grand Palace. The tanks were positioned like a noose around the government buildings and the Temple of the Emerald Buddha. They would fire on anyone who dared to hurl a rock or a Molotov cocktail at the leaders of the coup—but no one, he felt certain, would dare. It was one thing to fight against the Japanese as so many had done only a few years before—to creep with a knife through the dreaming gardens and reach under mosquito netting for the flesh of a throat—and quite another to oppose tanks. A coup was nothing more than a squabble among potentates.

The boatman Roderick had sent to carry him off the quay below the Temple of the Emerald Buddha had thrown rough sacking over his head; it stank of garlic and itched. He lay facedown, his nose hovering over the stinking bilge; crates of live guinea fowl rocked perilously on his back. His suit was of silk and his shoes had been made in Bond Street; there had not been time to change. No warning but the nervous smile of Tao Oum, the Lao, who appeared abruptly in the midst of dinner: Mr. Roderick had news—he must come at once—there was no time to delay. Tao Oum's words, swift and urgent, as they ran toward the river, the boat waiting with its signal lantern doused. Tanks rumbling already in the distance.

He fought the urge to sneeze. The soft flutter of wings above his head, the musk of feathers, the surging thrust of the boatman's pole—Boonreung, Roderick's youthful friend and confidant, a child of the arid northeast who understood thirst and hardship and what it was to avenge. Boonreung was maybe seventeen, but he was already a seasoned fighter. Boonreung he could trust.

If they found him, the Army and the police would shoot him like a dog for a royal murder he had not committed. The familiar nausea and fear surged in his throat—the lies of past escapes, of night raids, of a thousand bullets dodged like raindrops. He refused to think now what he must do. He refused to think of his wife.

His name was Pridi Banomyong, though for years he had called himself "Ruth" on the clandestine radio networks that sprang up around Bangkok during the war. He had led the Free Thai in secret; he had done what the Free Thai leaders in Washington and London had ordered him to do, and many things they had never dreamed possible. His men had loved him for his easy charm, his cultivated manners, his fervent belief in democracy; they had adored him and for him they had died in sometimes shaming and excruciating ways.

When the war had ended more than two years before and the Japanese retreated from Bangkok, the Allies took over the occupation billets at the palatial villas dotted about the city and the people had carried him through the streets with brilliant streamers and burning braziers of incense. He had declared the pro-Japanese Pibul a war criminal and invited the young king-in-exile, Ananda Mahidol, to return to Thailand in triumph. Two months after the Japanese surrender, in December 1945, Pridi Banomyong—Ruth—had become Prime Minister of a democratic and devastated Thailand.

He mingled with the foreigners flooding into this Venice of the East—the *farangs* who thought they had invented Bangkok. He called the British ambassador friend, he ate with the Americans, he traded jokes and war stories with Jack Roderick himself—Roderick, who had infiltrated France and Italy with the OSS, who knew more secrets than most men still alive, who had helped Pridi run agents through all the jungles of Southeast Asia when Ruth was nothing but a voice and a promise carried on the hiss of a radio wave.

But Ananda had died only ten months into his reign and now Pridi Banomyong was a murderer of kings, an assassin on the run. Rumors flew about the city, growing large in the retelling. Pridi's quarrels with the monarch were made to look like a motive for regicide; but no one accused the Prime Minister outright, there was never a trial or the possibility of clearing his name. In public, the royal family remained silent; in secret, they cultivated Pridi's enemies. Ananda's successor, Bhumpibol, left his quiet life in a provincial monastery and ascended the throne days after the young king's murder. The new king was not the sort to argue with dictators or democrats or even the royal family. Five months after the shot rang out in the Grand Palace on June 9, 1946, Pridi Banomyong had resigned from the office of Prime Minister and vanished from public life.

He had been granted a year of relative peace while his chief enemy, Pibul, gathered support as stealthily as a rat scavenged garbage. Now the tanks were in the streets.

The river bucked under the old boat's frame like a seasoned whore; brackish water flooded his nostrils, choking him, and he lurched upward so that the guinea fowl squawked and the sacking shifted. Boonreung mouthed a caution through the darkness but it meant nothing to Pridi. The five courses of his half-consumed dinner twisted in his entrails and he vomited. A bullhorn rent the night. Tao Oum was beside him, one hand on the back of his neck, forcing him down into his own puke—*police boat*, the Laotian hissed—and then the sacking covered him.

He felt the sampan lose way; felt the jolt as the police launch came alongside. Brilliant light flooded his closed eyes; he lay motionless, in the stench of chickens and vomit, water seeping through his trousers and the soles of his leather shoes. He would be shot and his body dumped over the sampan's side to float with the dead dogs and the garbage. His wife would never know the truth of what happened to him. For how long would she believe that he still lived?

The bullhorn again, Tao Oum's strained voice answering in Laoaccented Thai. The beam rippled over the sacking and the outraged guinea fowl. The sampan rocked as a booted foot landed heavily in the bottom. Had the police joined the traitorous army? Did they know that he had fled? Were all the borders watched? In a moment the stench of vomit would hit their nostrils, they would pull back the sacking to reveal—

Tao Oum's voice was steadier now. He was offering the policeman money. The guinea fowl, he said, were for his sister—her children were sick, they required fresh eggs—not a moment to be lost—the soft chink of coins as the bribe changed hands. The sampan dipped and surged. The policeman left the boat.

Relief swept over Pridi like a scalding wind. He bit the sleeve of his jacket to keep from whimpering in the dark. The police launch moved off.

Tao Oum sighed and mopped his forehead with a dirty handkerchief. Boonreung waited an instant, took the launch's wake bow-on, then thrust his pole once more into the murky bottom.

"Where will you go?" Roderick asked.

He discarded his cigarette in a flaring arc over the edge of the Oriental's quay. It sputtered in the river and vanished.

"I don't know," Pridi muttered. He glanced over his shoulder fearfully, but they were alone at the edge of the hotel garden, the tall palms and dense foliage a screen through which the figures of dancers flickered like moths. His wife had been dressing for this ball when he fled their house. There were to be charades. The whole *farang* community was present.

"We could get you to the border of Laos by dawn," Roderick said thoughtfully. "Boonreung—take His Excellency through the khlongs to the northern end of the city. Tao Oum will meet you there with the car."

The whites of the young Thai's eyes were shining in the dappled glow of lanterns. Boonreung was a beautiful boy, Pridi thought idly; skin as smooth as a girl's, the head classically molded. He was exhilarated by darkness and subterfuge as Ruth had once been drunk with danger; but that was many years and too many deaths ago.

"It'll be dicey," Roderick added. "Army patrols. But it's your only hope. You can't stay here."

The car was Roderick's own, a prewar Packard he'd shipped from New York the previous year. Pridi remembered that it had carried the American into the northeast on several occasions. Roderick had a fondness for the northeast—he had plucked Boonreung from obscurity there, made the boy his driver and his secretary and some said his assassin. Tao Oum, too, had traveled often through the desolate hinterland with Roderick at his side; Tao Oum and all the other Lao revolutionaries plotting independence from the French in the drawing rooms of Bangkok. Pridi understood, suddenly, as he waited in the jasmine-scented darkness with the strains of Tommy Dorsey floating through the Oriental's garden, that Roderick had never stopped running agents. The end of one war was merely the prelude to another, more subtle and thus more lethal.

A cannon boomed. Miles away and from the east, by the sound of it.

"Tao Oum knows the roads," Roderick said. He stood with his back to Pridi, talking to himself or the river. He wore a white dinner jacket and black trousers with knife-edged creases and his voice suggested that coups were regrettable but not unforeseen. How long had the American embassy known of Pibul's plans before tonight's attack?

Laos. Pridi's old lieutenant, Carlos, was there. With time, they might raise an army.

He had changed into the clothes Roderick had given him—the drawstring pants and rough cotton shirt of a fisherman. Boonreung had swabbed the vomit from the sampan's bottom. Tao Oum sat a little apart, his eyes closed and his chin sunk upon his chest. It was a habit learned during the height of the resistance and not yet forgotten two years after the war: snatch sleep in odd moments, against the difficult hours to come.

The guinea fowl, Pridi supposed, would end up in the Oriental's kitchen.

He pressed his hands together and raised them high to his forehead. Roderick repeated the gesture with an air of reverence surprising in a *farang*. Then he drew from his pocket a polished stone that flickered bloodred under the Chinese lanterns and held it aloft. "Tell me one thing, Pridi," he said softly. "Did you kill him?"

"The king?"

In his mind's eye, Pridi saw His Royal Highness Rama the Eighth—just a boy named Ananda, really, fresh from a Swiss prep school—glare haughtily and motion with one finger. The dead king said nothing about the gun or the bullets or who had pulled the trigger; nothing about the blood-spattered pillow in the royal bed. There had been so much blood. Ananda's eyes were open and lost in death, his head turned toward the window. Some said his assassin had fled through it; others, that the gunman lived in the palace itself.

It was Pridi who would go down in history as a regicide.

He looked now at Jack Roderick—at the cool self-possession of the American, who would never cower in the filth of a sampan while his city went up in flames—and he wished, with a surge of anger, for the simpler rules of war.

"I thought you knew me, Jack," Pridi replied, and stepped into the boat.

Jack Roderick was the last thing he saw on the river that night, backlit by mermaids in ball dress and the strains of Dorsey and the flares of cannon and the whole fantastic enterprise of the old *farang* hotel on the banks of the Chao Phraya. Roderick was smoking again, his eyes glittering in the moonlight. Telling sad stories of the death of kings. Pridi knew he owed the man his life but he could not weigh the cost. That would come later, when they met again as equals.

Roderick followed the sampan's prow as it picked its course through the ruins of a bridge. When his cigarette had burned down to ash and Boonreung had turned without a wave into a khlong on the Thon Buri side of the river, he pocketed Carlos's ruby, and went back inside to the dance.

10

The powerful man in the dark jacket lifted his newspaper higher. Rush Halliwell knew him by sight as a paid bodyguard and by name simply as Jo-Jo. Sometimes he drove cars; sometimes he sat in the passenger seat as an obvious piece of protection; at other times he roamed the streets of Bangkok or London or L.A., a wolf tracking prey. The sight of Jo-Jo in the midst of the Oriental's private cocktail party had impressed Rush Halliwell enormously. He'd studied the man as he moved like a pickpocket through the shifting cadre of international guests, wondering what spoor Jo-Jo was following this evening. He'd chatted him up by the sushi bar in a deliberate attempt to glean information. And then, at the first sight of Stefani Fogg, he'd watched the man bolt.

If, as Rush suspected, Jo-Jo was stalking the American heiress, her level of risk had just skyrocketed.

Rush stood quietly near the protective screen of a massive ceramic ginger jar that anchored the hotel's main corridor, and surveyed the lobby beyond.

Jo-Jo was not the type to waste an entire evening in such a place. He looked perfectly at home in the soaring room—attractive, well dressed, flush with other people's money—but he preferred dimly lit holes pulsing with neon. There was petulance around his mouth tonight. Rush watched him troll uncomprehendingly through the pages of the *Financial*

Times, a cigarette dangling from his left hand. A small cairn of ash had collected on the elegant carpet below.

And then Paolo Ferretti, the hotel's assistant manager, crossed smoothly to Jo-Jo's chair and bent, with an air of concern and apology, to murmur in the man's ear.

The fluttering pages of the *Financial Times* stilled. Jo-Jo stared at Ferretti's face without a hint of amity in his own. Then he stood. Folded the newspaper precisely and handed it to Ferretti as though the latter were a bellboy. And crossed to the Oriental's revolving door.

"What did you say to him?" Rush asked as Paolo passed him seconds later.

The assistant manager stopped short. "I don't know what you mean, Mr. Halliwell. May I be of some assistance?"

"You ran that guy out of the lobby like a common backpacker. Admit it."

Paolo drew himself up. "Do you know how difficult that was for me? How repugnant?"

"Then why did you do it?"

Paolo hesitated. "He's been hanging around the hotel all day. It's a public meeting place—one can't prevent people from using it, provided they're properly dressed and well behaved—but he crashed our private cocktail party. That disturbed our guests."

Halliwell smiled. "I'll remember in future never to appear without an invitation. So what was the phrase, exactly? 'Pay for that Scotch you drank, or I'll have the law on you' ?"

"It was vodka," Paolo responded stiffly. "Straight. And I asked to see the contents of his pockets. One of our guests accused him of picking hers."

Rush clapped him on the shoulder. "It was a great party, all the same. Thanks, Paolo. And good night."

He sauntered across the hotel lobby as though he hadn't a care in the world. And was just in time, as he exited the place, to catch a final glimpse of Jo-Jo turning right at the foot of the drive. All that stood on that side of the Oriental was a convent school for girls, quite dark at this hour—and the dock for the commuter boat line, the Chao Phraya Express.

Halliwell gave him thirty seconds. Then he moved down the drive in Jo-Jo's wake.

*   *   *

He led Rush a pretty dance, although he betrayed not the slightest awareness that he was being tailed. He abandoned the water ferry four stops beyond the Oriental, at the Ratchawong dock; and for half an hour he walked the length of Charoen Krung Road into the heart of Chinatown. There Halliwell hired a *tuk-tuk,* one of the three-wheeled taxis that cluttered Bangkok's roads, and ordered the driver to move slowly. Under cover of night and the galaxy of Bangkok lights, he was virtually undetectable; but Jo-Jo never even glanced behind.

When his quarry dove into the Nakorn Kasem, Rush paid off his driver and followed on foot, his suit jacket folded under his arm and his shirtsleeves rolled high. It was late, but the market crowds were still thick, and he used them as screen and distraction, fingering the goods laid out on the pavement. Jo-Jo led him to the Chakkrawat Road, a few blocks from the old Thieves Market; and then, abruptly, he disappeared into thin air.

Halliwell's feet slowed. At the foot of the street was the dirty scar of Khlong Ong Ang. To one side, a handful of diners huddled around a glowing brazier manned by a street cook with a sweating face. To the other, blank warehouse doors. One of these must have opened for Jo-Jo. The man was either inside, or he'd pulled the oldest dodge in the book—passed through and exited on the far side of the building. Halliwell reached into his pocket and withdrew his wallet.

"The man in the dark suit," Rush said softly in Thai to the street cook. "The one who just walked past. Which door?"

The cook stared at him, then thrust a thumb in the direction of a warehouse half a block farther down the street. "The one on the end. Near the khlong." His fingers closed over Halliwell's money.

It was possible, Rush thought, that he'd been led here on purpose—that this was Jo-Jo's bolt hole, and the street cook was paid to steer the inquisitive in the wrong direction. It was possible, even, that a thug with steel knuckles waited beyond the warehouse door. He had not survived a decade of tours in Southeast Asia without cultivating a healthy caution. He ducked into the crawl space between two shuttered buildings and crossed to the next block, approaching the warehouse from the opposite side.

A sliver of light framed the main door. Rush Halliwell sauntered up the paving with an air of indifference, the echo of his footsteps drowned in the clamor of the city. He slid noiselessly into the entryway and fixed one eye on the scene just visible through the door's narrow opening.

Four people were grouped under a floodlight suspended from the ceiling: A tall, thin Westerner Rush didn't recognize, in a rumpled business suit. A Thai woman in high-heeled patent-leather boots and a miniskirt, whose long black hair was bleached orange. A third man stood behind a desk in an attitude of respectful misery. And at the desk itself, with a jeweler's monocle fixed to his eye—surely that was none other than—

Footsteps behind. Before Halliwell could turn, a bomb exploded at the base of his skull. *Jo-Jo,* he thought as he fell over into the street; and then he knew nothing more.

11

**Bangkok,
March 1949**

Jack Roderick stood near the French windows that lined the ambassador's office, one hand parting the heavy drapery, the other nursing a cigarette, his body canted away from the sights of a possible sniper's gun. Once he had believed that the Thai police would never fire upon the embassy of the United States—the police chief, after all, was on Roderick's payroll. But that was before the summary executions of his Thai friends during the first week in March, before the pretty little dance pavilion in Amphorn Gardens had been abruptly converted to an official interrogation chamber, before Tao Oum had fled back to Laos three nights ago.

"How many are out there today?" Alec McQueen was slumped in a Moroccan leather chair that Ambassador Stanton had shipped from Washington along with a '47 Ford and a pair of aged poodles. His long legs were sprawled lazily across the Turkish carpet and his socks had slid down to meet his shoes, exposing a strip of white skin. He was eating kumquats now, noisily, as another man might chew peanuts at a prizefight.

"Groups of three, every second corner, all the way down New Road," Roderick reported.

"Damned hot work in the noon hour," Stanton muttered from his desk. "Hope the bastards are well paid."

"They're allowed to live," Roderick replied absently, "and these days that's enough."

They had all danced together under the pavilion in Amphorn Gardens on the night of Pridi's failed coup. The penultimate night of February, 1949. When Roderick thought of the interrogations held in the pavilion now, he saw the glow of Chinese lanterns, the faces of the accused grotesquely framed in fancy dress. The Bangkok police stationed in the street below were in costume, too, he thought—their uniforms vaguely British, although Siam had never been part of the empire. They turned as precisely on their chaotic corners as if the horde of vendors that lined New Road was hired specifically for this performance.

"They watch me all the time," the ambassador barked. "Do they watch you, Alec?"

McQueen laughed. "Remember the article? That damned noble article I had to go and *print*?"

There was only one article, now, that mattered.

Pridi Banomyong had reappeared in Bangkok on February 27 in a hail of bullets that failed to change history or even impress anyone much. Four men—former ministers in the old Pridi government, friends of Jack Roderick's—were arrested that night. They had been friends of Pridi's, too, it seemed. Seven days after the coup all four were murdered in what the police called a "mysterious ambush" and what Alec McQueen bluntly suggested, in the pages of the *Bangkok Post* that same day, was in fact an execution conducted by the police themselves. McQueen had viewed the bodies. The corpses were riddled with more than eighty bullets. Two of the men had been tortured. Not a single member of the police "escort" was wounded in the "attack."

Later, Roderick slipped out of his shoes and knelt beside the hushed and frightened widows in the temple. Four bronze urns filled with ashes, four large photographs of unsmiling men. Joss sticks and lamentation. Roderick bowed his head and begged forgiveness from any god that might listen. The taste of ashes in his mouth.

"Paper's been clapped under official censorship," Alec said, "and I'm not chump enough to walk home alone. Tried to bed a willing woman three nights in a row and caught some jerk spying in my windows. My houseboy's quit and my cook's balls shriveled out of sheer fright. I'm seriously considering skipping town."

"Don't." Roderick's eyes remained focused on the noonday street. "We need you."

"We?" McQueen tossed another kumquat in his mouth. "Who's 'we'? You and Truman and the dumb-fuck chief of whatever they call the OSS, now?"

"The Central Intelligence Agency." Roderick said it patiently. He was not surprised Alec found it hard to track the acronyms of intelligence; they changed almost monthly. Roderick's Office of Special Operations—the OSO—had given way in 1948 to the OPC—the Office of Policy Coordination. Roderick's conception of his job underwent a similar reorganization every few weeks. He had expected to be Washington's point man on the future of Thailand: collecting what information he could about political movements, persuading right-minded intellectuals to support democracy instead of Communism, setting an example of the worth and superiority of the American Way. But he soon saw he was simply Washington's bagman. The Soviets were flooding the Third World with funds to foment the proletariat revolution. Roderick was flooding Bangkok with cash to avert disaster.

"I'm not worried about the States," he told Alec, "but Siam needs you."

McQueen snorted. "What Siam needs is to be left in goddamn peace. You and the rest of Truman's friggin' boy scouts have thrown this country right into Marshal Pibul's lap, and he's got his thighs clamped tight as a virgin's. Have you heard from that horse's ass Ruth lately? Or is he too busy raising another army?"

"Heard from your willing woman, Alec? Or is she too busy telling the cops about the size of your dick?"

"Jack," Stanton chided quietly.

It had always been like this between Roderick and McQueen. When the fever pitch of combat training had been too much to take, four years before, McQueen broke the tension by spouting profanity, and Roderick, by snapping his head off.

"Ruth is in China." He turned away from the window and the drapery swung closed, obliterating the sunlight. "He's recruiting men from the Chinese National Army—the Kuomintang."

"I thought the KMT was running south," McQueen objected. "Chiang Kai-shek's losing his shorts to that peasant Hitler, Mao Tse-tung."

"Exactly. Chinese Nationalist troops are flooding into Laos and Burma and Thailand's northern provinces. Armed men desperate for a leader and a cause. It's a balls-up and a fucking rout and it's perfect for Ruth. Freedom fighters and resistance all over again."

"Good Christ!" Stanton burst out. "He could have gone to New York or London merely for the asking! He's still got friends in Washington."

"Ruth won't raise another army in London or New York," McQueen interjected petulantly, "and that's all the prick can think of."

Roderick saw again in his mind's eye the masquerade ball in Amphorn Gardens and the terrified face of the young Thai girl under her *kinnari* headress—a mythical figure, half-bird, half-woman—whom he had driven home at dawn. He saw the boiling smoke and the desperate exchange of gunfire and heard the shouts and pleading from the captured radio station over the crackling night air. Saw the hero they still called Ruth, cornered by the Thai army that had *not* gone over to his cause, break away from his comrades and race toward the river, leaving the men who had followed him to certain death. It had not been Roderick who'd saved Pridi this time.

"If he tries it again," the ambassador declared, "he may expect the full force of American disapproval. We shall not lift a fucking *finger* to protect his ass in future."

"We didn't lift a fucking finger in the past," Roderick retorted. "We dumped him over the side like garbage and recognized the government of a man who collaborated with the Japs. As far as Pibul's concerned, the Allied victory was just a brief vacation."

"Tell that to the Pentagon, Jack. I'm sure the Top Brass would love to hear they fought the last war in vain."

"The Pentagon?" Roderick scowled. "What the hell are you talking about?"

"A delegation of military observers." Stanton glared at him from under his brows. "They're due to arrive in Bangkok any day, and your briefing is high on their dance card. Can't think why. Somebody named Lightfoot asked for you by name."

Lightfoot. Roderick glanced at McQueen. The mere mention of the name, and the two of them were back in the darkened cabin of an OSS drop plane. Billy Lightfoot's arm rising in the moonlit doorway.

"Since when did the Pentagon give a rat's ass about Thailand?" McQueen demanded.

"Washington is quite concerned about the state of affairs in Southeast Asia," Stanton said reprovingly. "We have my cogent cables to thank, no doubt. Unrest on all sides, colonials in revolt, the Red Menace flourishing in the north—compared to Mao Tse-tung, Jack my boy, our friendly Field Marshal Pibul looks like the second coming of Christ. And don't you forget it."

"I can't forget it, Ed," he shot back. "I'm paying Pibul a thousand bucks a month to make nice to the United States. What are you giving him? A few cookies when he comes for tea? I'm the biggest employer in Bangkok, Mr. Ambassador. I pay kids of nineteen to hand out leaflets in support of democracy at Thammasat U. I pay radio announcers to broadcast the truth to illiterates who can't read Alec's newspaper. I pay the leaders of the Democratic Opposition to run for office, I pay the thugs in power to behave themselves, I pay the local Communist underground to stay there, and I'm sending the police chief's kid to college in Philadelphia, for Christ's sake. I bought the top-ranking general in the Thai army a brand-new Ford. All in the name of stability and democracy and death to Red China. So don't tell me about your asswipe brown-nose jackshit cables, all right?"

"Jack." McQueen rose, eager to get out the door. But Roderick was still staring at the ambassador. Stanton's face was purple, his eyes snapping. He opened his mouth, then closed it again. The pencil he held between his fingers snapped abruptly in two.

He was not, Roderick thought, a bad man. One to respect, even, in certain places and certain times. But Stanton was confused right now— bewildered by the lack of rules, by the wild fluctuation of the playing field and the arbitrary composition of these foreign teams. He took orders from Harry Truman and advice from Roderick and he pretended to represent some sort of inviolable standard that had perished in the trenches of Europe a generation ago. He believed he was an authority at the embassy, when the Thais knew he was just a figurehead. Roderick might have pitied the man if he had not despised him so much.

"Your secretary," Stanton spat out. "Your young assistant."

"Boonreung." A vise twisted in Roderick's bowels. "What have you heard?"

"More than you. What did you do, forget to pay the chief torturer?" Stanton fingered his shirt collar. "Your young friend was shot last night while trying to escape."

Roderick braced himself against the window frame, heedless for once of all snipers. He'd lost Boonreung on the fourth of March, six days after Pridi's failed coup, in a deserted northeastern hotel run by a tired war widow. Five men in Army uniforms and an official black car, Boonreung dragged from the dinner table while Roderick stood helpless with a rifle at his back. Shouting. In English no one understood.

"Tell the truth, Stanton," he said through his teeth. "You don't escape Pibul's goons. They put Boonreung through hell. Then they blew his brains out."

"I'm sorry, Jack." Alec's hand was on Roderick's shoulder. "He was a good man."

"He was a boy."

"He was a traitor to the present government," Stanton corrected, "and we all know it. Jack, you've been running Boonreung in and out of Laos for months. The boy was your liaison with *Ruth*, for God's sake. If it weren't for that American passport of yours, you'd be lying dead in the khlong beside him."

"Think he talked before the end?" McQueen asked.

One of the fancy-dress cops in the street below was staring straight up at the embassy. Roderick thought of Boonreung as he had been the day they found the Buddha cave, more than three years ago, his skin shining in the torchlight. He thought of the careless honesty in the black northeastern eyes and all the blood and loss those young eyes had seen. He shook his head. "Boonreung would die before he'd screw his friends."

All the same, Jack," McQueen said as they walked swiftly down the embassy's back stairs and through the gate that led to an old, disused khlong long since drained—Roderick's preferred method of retreat, through the overgrown gardens and refuse piles of the people who lived near the waterway—"you ought to lie low. Go to Europe. Finger Italian silks. Finger Italian broads."

"And miss Billy Lightfoot? Not a chance."

"That old fucker Lightfoot." McQueen basked in a moment of nostalgia. "We've got a night of hard drinking ahead of us. Like old times."

"Who's the woman?"

"What?" Alec glanced at him sidelong.

"The willing woman. The one you're seducing."

"Nobody, really."

"Someone's wife? Stanton's, for instance?"

"She's Thai." He said it flatly, a closed door. The men Roderick knew might admit to lovers among the native population, but they never introduced these women around the *farang* community and they were rarely seen together in public. "And not as willing as I make out. She's scared to death of her father. He could slit her throat just for meeting me."

"She should be scared of you."

"But nobody listens to warnings, and we all give death the finger. Look, Jack—" McQueen gripped his arm. "I'm serious. If Boonreung talked, and they know, now, that he was working for *you* when he helped Ruth escape the first time, last year—"

"They'll come after me, day or night, and fuck the U.S. passport. You don't have to say it."

Roderick stopped abruptly under the leaves of a longan tree and pulled out his cigarettes. He shook one into his palm, offered the pack to McQueen and waited while the other man produced a lighter. Smoke drifted upward in a blue haze.

"Alistair Farnham's shipping home," McQueen observed.

Farnham was Roderick's opposite number at the British embassy. Secret Intelligence Service, Bern, during the last war. Suspected by the Pibul government of transporting his old chum Ruth to China the night after the failed coup, through an SIS pipeline.

"I stood drinks for him yesterday," Roderick replied. "He's gotten death threats. He doesn't want to leave, but he's thinking of Marjorie."

"We've all thought of Marjorie," Alec sighed. Farnham's wife was a legend in the expatriate community: clever, charming, blue-blooded and disappointingly faithful. Roderick considered her aquiline nose and her brilliant eyes and then thought of Boonreung, crucified under a bare lightbulb. He inhaled sharply.

"Are you in love with her?" he asked McQueen.

"Marjorie?"

"Your Thai girl."

Alec shrugged. "Call it that if you like. Go to Paris, for God's sake, Jack. I don't want to print your obit in tomorrow's paper."

"I wanted Joan that way," Roderick said through the cigarette haze. "I wanted her with a violence I'd never known and that I thought would consume me. I'd watch her talk to another man across the room at one of those damn parties and want to crush her throat in my hands."

"But you walked away," Alec said brutally.

Roderick shrugged and tossed his butt into the drained khlong. "It's no kind of life, with murder in your heart. Besides, I was hurting the boy."

The boy. Rory with his pale face and his gnawed fingernails, peering through the crack in the doorway at his father's rage. Joan languid in the satin dress that hugged her curves, diamonds choking her neck. A glass of whiskey shattered on the parquet floor. The rich and lovely apartment thirty stories above Park Avenue, a cage they prowled together. Roderick had not seen his son in two years. Not since the divorce.

"Is your buddy Carlos with him?"

"With whom?"

"*Ruth.* The KMT."

Roderick shrugged. "Alec, if Boonreung talked, then a month in Italy won't help. I could never come back."

"Does that matter?"

"I don't see you leaving Bangkok."

"I'm not trading potshots with the dictator, pal. Given a choice between death and Europe, I'd take Europe any day."

"A hunted man has nothing to lose," Roderick muttered, "except the hunters."

"What the hell is that supposed to mean?"

Roderick walked on beside the stinking khlong, while the high-pitched screech of an angry woman drifted across the back gardens and the sagging water gates. The scent of fish sauce and fried mangos and garbage spiked his nostrils. The smell of something rotten.

He never answered McQueen.

12

Stefani Fogg, in a large straw hat and a silk sarong, picked her way through the orchids and rustling palms of the Oriental Hotel's back garden. At seven on a humid Wednesday morning in early November, the grounds were almost deserted. The hotel barge ferried a few early risers from the main dock to the spa and gym, a peak-roofed structure on the Chao Phraya's opposite bank; but in general she had the world to herself. Except for the shadows that hung just beyond the range of vision: Jack Roderick and his pals, smoking a last cigarette under the waving fronds.

The river terrace blazed with refracted sunlight. She detected Matthew French within seconds. French was every inch the sort of man Oliver Krane would deem appropriate to the occasion: silver-haired, superbly suited despite the promised heat, with a grave line between his eyebrows. His gaze seemed fixed on the churning river water; a copy of the *Bangkok Post* lay disregarded on the table before him. A black leather briefcase was propped correctly at the foot of his chair.

"Mr. French?" she inquired, and was gratified to see his eyes narrow with interest as he turned toward her.

"Ms. Fogg?"

She extended her hand. "I hope Oliver didn't ruin your sleep last night. I'm very grateful that you were able to meet on such short notice."

"Not at all." He rose and grasped her palm firmly.

She slid into the opposite chair. "Were you waiting long?"

"A matter of three minutes."

"Oliver will be proud of me. May I have coffee, please, and a fruit plate, croissants and some oatmeal?" she asked of the waiter who hovered at her shoulder. "I believe in a solid breakfast, Mr. French. So often it's the only meal I'm sure of getting."

"Just coffee, for me. Ms. Fogg—"

She considered inviting him to call her Stefani; she decided against it. She needed the formality of the gray suit far more than she needed a friend.

"Oliver Krane was brief in his instructions when we spoke last night," French began, "but he faxed me copies of several documents this morning—and I've spent the better part of two hours examining them, in anticipation of this meeting."

No chitchat, no disarming preamble; just a cold dive into the facts. Oliver got what he paid for.

"You've seen the will?"

"*All* the wills," French corrected. "The 1960 document, the second one dated February 1967, which Krane assures me has been declared legitimate by your counsel in the United States; and Max Roderick's final testament, in which he left everything to you."

Stefani's insouciance faded. "You have a copy of Max's will?"

"Would you like to see it?" The decision was made for her; French was already extracting a sheaf of paper from his briefcase. She waited, numbly.

"Most of this is irrelevant. The crux of the bequest is right here." He slid a single sheet in front of her.

. . . To my friend, Jeffrey Knetsch, I leave my Olympic medals and trophies won on the World Cup Circuit. To Jacques Renaudie, the sum of 100,000 francs, with the intent that he should spend several months in Paris with his estranged wife. To Sabine Renaudie I leave my drafting equipment and the contents of my studio, in recognition of her gift for drawing and the hope that she will pursue a career in design as ardently as she once pursued the Austrian Ski Team.

To Yvette Margolan, I leave my copper pots, my wine cellar and my viola, with the condition that she throw a party in Courchevel in my memory after I am gone.

Stefani felt her throat constrict; but the sound that emerged was a laugh, not a sob.

> *... and to Stefani Fogg, citizen of the world, I leave the remainder of my estate: to include my house in Courchevel and the entire legacy that has haunted the Roderick family, not excepting the group of assets belonging to my grandfather, John Pierpont Roderick, at present illegally held by the government of Thailand and enumerated under the Last Will and Testament of John Pierpont Roderick dated February 27, 1967. Any resolution of the case involving John Pierpont Roderick's estate should be awarded to Stefani Fogg as my direct heir.*

She looked up from the document, and met French's assessing eyes. "Interesting reading."

"Quite. In this town, one might call it explosive. But there is a problem, Ms. Fogg."

"Only one?"

Coffee materialized at Stefani's right hand. Matthew French stirred some cream into his.

"Jack Roderick has always been more than just another legend," he said thoughtfully. "Roderick's a symbol of an entire era in Thai history—a figure that has entered the public domain, if you will. And practically everything that belonged to the man is regarded as sacred."

"Oh, *crap*." Stefani settled back against her chair, one hand on the crown of her hat and the other wrapped around her coffee cup. "I'm not terribly interested in sacred cows, Mr. French."

"No. I didn't think you were." His gaze swept the length of her saronged figure. "What do you intend to do with the house, anyway?"

"Live in it. That's what houses are for."

"It might help," he suggested delicately, "if you could guarantee that the art collection would remain available to the public. Such an assurance might smooth your path considerably."

"In the courts? Or among the networks that really run Thailand?"

"Any Thai court worth its salt would throw out this suit on the grounds that Max Roderick never possessed his grandfather's legacy before he died," French retorted, not bothering to conceal his impatience. "Max's attempt to pass his vague inheritance on to you is—in a word—invalid. Your best hope is to strike some sort of bargain. Accept an out-of-court settlement."

"That's one interpretation."

"It's the interpretation that will probably govern." French spoke sharply. "Consider the facts, Ms. Fogg. Jack Roderick's estate—the house, the art—has been ably administered by the Thai Heritage Board established for that purpose. The assets have never passed out of the Board's hands since Jack Roderick was declared legally dead in 1974. Max Roderick's claim to his grandfather's estate was unproved at his death. The weight of convention—the status quo, if you will—dictates that the courts do nothing."

Stefani stabbed a piece of mango with her fork. "But what about the penumbra, Mr. French?"

"I beg your pardon?"

"The penumbra. That gray area surrounding the facts. Jack Roderick made a will awarding his estate to his heirs. The Thai government systematically violated that will. If the man remains a legend in Thailand—a source of national pride, a sacred cow—this heist of his legacy should be a major embarrassment. How will my claim play in the realm of public opinion?"

Matthew French regarded her steadily. "Do you anticipate engaging the realm of public opinion?"

"Naturally. A PR campaign is all I've got. Mere law, as you've pointed out, isn't enough. I need to take this case to the streets."

French thrust his cup aside. "You run the risk, Ms. Fogg, of alienating exactly those people whose support you'd most need to win. You're *farang*—a foreigner—and you're a woman. You would appear . . . insensitive."

"And too ballsy by half." Stefani smiled dazzlingly. "But that's where *you* come in, Mr. French. You can advise me. I'm sure you'll know just how I should proceed. How long have you lived in Bangkok?"

"Nearly twenty-two years."

"Then the informal networks that govern this place must be child's play for you. Tell me something." She leaned toward him. "Sompong Suwannathat. Head of the Thai Heritage Board—"

"And the Minister of Culture. Not a man to cross. Sompong owns half of Bangkok."

"I'm so *tired* of hearing how many people Sompong owns. Nobody ever talks about the people he's *sold*. The bastard must have enemies."

"Indeed he does."

"In the course of your long residence in Thailand, Mr. French, have you perhaps formed acquaintance with any of them?"

Matthew French sipped judiciously at his coffee.

"—Enemies of Sompong's," she went on, "who work in the broadcast media . . . or at the *Bangkok Post?*"

Rush Halliwell was accustomed to getting too little sleep. No matter how late the previous evening, he awoke at five o'clock precisely, coming out of his dreams as though doused with icy water. He meditated for half an hour in the semidarkness, then ran three miles around the waking city, before the pollution and the strident noise of *tuk-tuk* engines were too thick for comfort. By six he was drinking orange juice in the shower, and by six-thirty on the dot he was crossing Wireless Road, where the U.S. embassy dominated an entire block.

This morning, however, he winced at the crack of light filtering through the shade, felt the dull pounding at the base of his skull and fell back upon the pillows, cursing. His pride hurt as fiercely as his head. He had never seen the man or weapon that bludgeoned him in Chinatown; but he awoke a few minutes after one A.M. to find a light glaring in his eyes and a Bangkok policeman prodding his rib cage with his boot. He was probably lucky to be alive.

The essence of tradecraft, Rush believed, was strict attention to detail. He followed his internal schedules religiously except when he varied them on purpose, so that what was predictable did not get him killed. The death toll for espionage was lower than for UN peacekeeping work, and indistinguishable from its cousin, diplomacy. But some neighborhoods of the world carried peculiar threats. Rush liked threat— or rather, if asked, he might have said that he relished outwitting the dangerous of the world. He was one of the CIA case officers who worked the hard targets for Bangkok station: armed insurgents, drug runners, the men (and women) who bartered illegal arms. And he was extremely good at what he did. Headquarters had left him in Thailand for nearly five years—an unusual period in a world of two-year tours. They admired his language skills and his effortless networks; they asked few questions about his personal life; and they awarded him medals as proof of national esteem.

This morning, he decided, he would avoid all mention of last night's stupidity.

By nine o'clock Rush was sitting at a government-issue desk with coffee cooling at his elbow and a pair of headphones over his ears, listening to tapes of conversations held in the Ministry of Culture—an annoying collection of chitchat and innuendo punctuated by the sporadic gold nugget. Sixteen months before, the chairman of a joint U.S.-Thai delegation on antiquities had presented Sompong Suwannathat with a rare Khmer statue carved from limestone. Four feet high and three across, the statue now rested on a credenza in the minister's office.

Sompong loved antiquities; he coveted them as another man might long for precious gems. Embedded in the statue's limestone, and masterfully disguised with an application of gold leaf, was a voice-activated microphone. Sound was relayed remotely to the station's recorder.

The statue might be moved eventually or donated to a museum; and at that point, the bug would be deactivated. But right now, every word Sompong Suwannathat spoke in the confines of his office was overheard by Bangkok station. U.S. Intelligence could gauge the pulse of Thai governmental power from the depth of silence in a room; track the bloodless succession of Sompong's varied mistresses; anticipate coups within the ministry and practically download the minister's personal calendar.

It was the last that mattered most. Sompong performed the bare minimum of his official duties. But he used the power of his office—the public domain of Culture—to delve into an astonishing array of activities beyond his portfolio. He was jockeying, now, for the Ministry of Defense in the next government; from the agency's perspective, his appointment could be disastrous.

Rush's headphones were on his ears, his expression impassive. The conversation was in Thai—and the tape too delicate for Foreign Service nationals to translate. So complete was his concentration that he never looked up when Marty Robbins walked into the vault.

"Anything interesting?" Marty leaned over and thrust his face into his case officer's. The exalted Chief of Station, Bangkok. Another early riser. Marty was a veteran of Vientiane, Kuala Lumpur, Hong Kong and most recently, Phnom Penh. Pugnacious and sartorially challenged; grotesquely flamboyant of tie, balding of pate. The second generation of CIA operators in the post–Vietnam War era, canny and tough and unscrupulous and kind-hearted in surprising ways. Competitive with Rush, his junior by a hairsbreadth, in this blood sport of nations.

Marty thrust out a broad finger and stopped the tape.

"He quit early last night." Rush eased the headphones to the desk and rubbed tentatively at the back of his head. "He's booked solid today. Public appearances. Tomorrow he's planning to fly to Chiang Rai."

"Of course, Chiang Rai," Marty muttered in disgust. "Sompong's personal kingdom in the fabled north. Is he entertaining clients, or flying up alone?"

"Alone. In the ministry plane."

"Shit." Marty spun around, a vein in his forehead pulsing. "Another delivery to the boys in the bush. What I wouldn't give to recruit somebody on Sompong's staff. A mechanic who services the plane. Anyone who could give us a clue as to what the bastard's swapping."

"What we need is one of the troops on the ground," Rush added pensively. "Find out why they're training."

Marty did not reply. They had already lost one recruit—a developmental asset among the farmer population of Sok Ruap, found with his throat slit one balmy morning—and the CIA staff at the base in neighboring Chiang Mai was growing restive. The Chiang Mai base had too much on its plate already to bother with Bangkok's conspiracy theories. There had always been roving bands of armed men in the borderlands of the far north, and there always would be.

But Rush and Marty had been tracking Sompong Suwannathat's flights to the Golden Triangle for the past seven months. They had overhead reconnaissance and infrared photography that suggested a sizable population of men living and training in the jungle area Sompong liked to visit, but even the CIA had trouble making the case that the Minister of Culture was plotting to march on the capital and seize power. Sompong was not the official liaison for a secret government security force. So why the army?

"Personal protection," Marty had suggested during one late-night survey of intelligence. "He's got a sideline. Something high-risk. These guys are insurance."

"They're pretty far away from Bangkok," Rush had replied doubtfully.

"So's the sideline. Drugs?"

The Minister of Culture might be cultivating heroin with the aid of his troops—opium poppies, after all, had been the major crop of the Golden Triangle for time out of mind—but Bangkok station could find absolutely no evidence that Sompong was brokering drug sales back home. When in Bangkok, he led a venal but hardly criminal life in the company of his peers. His customary routine was beyond legal reproach. The impenetrability of the minister's motives—and the frustrating loyalty of his personal staff, which had thus far proved impervious to bribery, threats or seduction—had Marty Robbins foaming at the mouth.

Rush considered telling his boss that he had seen Suwannathat the previous night, in a warehouse near the Thieves Market, examining what appeared to be antique pottery—but Marty's questions would lead inevitably to the admission that he had spent the better part of the evening insensible in a Bangkok gutter. Rush kept silent.

"What about this Fogg chick?" Marty's interests roved; as a case officer, his skill lay in connecting parallel lines of investigation. He valued coincidence far more than established patterns. "Is she one of the world's nasties?"

"I don't know. She's not what she says she is. I watched her fabricate one story last night while she told me another. I'm still figuring out which pieces were true."

"Probably none of 'em. You heard the tape." Marty stabbed at the recorder once more. "Sompong Shithead Suwannathat ordered a background file on Fogg yesterday, from his private investigative hack. He's got Jo-Jo staked out at the Oriental. Something's going down, Rush. What's the broad doing in Bangkok?"

"Pleasure trip."

"My ass. No affiliation?"

"None but a series of bank accounts."

"This has black market written all over it. She's financing. Or receiving."

"She was last seen in Vietnam. And Laos."

"What, no interest in Burma?"

"There, too," Rush admitted ruefully.

"And you *bought* it? Jesus H. Christ, Halliwell—this woman sells you a crock of shit and you're lappin' it up. She must be pretty hot."

"She inherited Jack Roderick's place. The museum on the khlong."

Marty stared at him. "That name just won't die, will it?"

Rush shrugged. "I'm invited to meet her there this afternoon. She says she wants the embassy's help with the Thai Heritage Board."

"Meaning, Sompong Suwannathat. This is too fucking good. Fogg pretends to be hostile to the minister and all his works, and co-opts *you* into the bargain. The lady's got *cojones*. Think she knew you were Agency?"

"Absolutely."

"Make that meeting at Roderick's," Marty ordered, "and stay on Fogg—in a purely friendly capacity, of course. I want Avril to run her name. See if that story about the house is true."

Avril Blair was the embassy's legal attaché—the Federal Bureau of Investigation's representative in Bangkok. It was illegal for a CIA officer to run background checks on a U.S. citizen. But the FBI was *encouraged* to do it.

Rush watched Marty pour himself a cup of coffee. Then he picked up the phone and held it two inches from his aching skull.

"Avril," he said softly into the receiver, "I need to find out who's storing ceramics in a warehouse off Khlong Ong Ang. Here's the address."

13

Bangkok,
March 1949

The morning after he received the news of Boonreung's death, Jack Roderick appeared at the central police station in the Dusit quarter of Bangkok and demanded the release of the boy's body. He bore an official document from the United States embassy and one from the Thai Ministry of the Interior, stamped with seals, and he was prepared to wait while the papers were examined. He spoke few words of Thai but understood many more; and as he waited, shrouded in a false air of calm, he listened to the phrases tossed among the men.

A special case.

I know nothing.

One of Gyapay's boys.

Nothing, I tell you.

The political section.

Don't speak of it, fool; better to stop your mouth than utter such things.

The farang *is waiting. His papers—*

Send him to the morgue. That's where Gyapay's boys all end.

Roderick's Packard crawled through a swarm of *tuk-tuks* down the length of Chulalongkorn Boulevard to the city morgue, where the bodies of the poor and the politically untouchable lay stacked on field stretchers abandoned four years earlier by the Japanese. He walked among the dead, a silk handkerchief covering his mouth and nose, and lifted the rough sacking that covered the corpses.

Old men, their mouths slack and toothless. The obscene nakedness of elderly women. A little girl, dead of dysentery or fever, her rib cage sharp beneath the unformed breasts. A teenager with his throat cut.

Roderick walked the aisles while the dizzying stench of bloated flesh curled in his hair and his nostrils. Flies buzzed around him like an enemy squadron.

When he found Boonreung, Roderick wiped the boy's face gently with his square of silk. He took careful note of the obvious things—toenails torn from the thin feet; bruises where electrodes had seared the scrotum. Then he lifted the frail body—that bundle of northeast bones—and turned it tenderly on the sagging stretcher. The corpse was slack and Roderick was clumsy with grief, but he saw the wound immediately: no bullet in a fleeing back, no shot fired at random, but a precise hole at the base of the skull. Boonreung's glossy hair was matted stiff with blood.

He wrapped the boy in a freshly ironed sheet borrowed from the Oriental, and carried him out to the car. Crude, this mismatched *pietà,* and a grown man weeping.

That night Roderick sat alone in the babble of the Bamboo Bar. Thanom, the young bartender, kept Roderick's Kentucky bourbon on a shelf next to McQueen's single malts. Both were procured from Europe through infinite patience and expense; marked with their owners' names, they were off-limits to the rest of the hotel. Roderick turned the whiskey in his hands, Boonreung's cockatoo on his shoulder.

"You want a peanut for that bird?" Thanom asked.

"Why not? Somebody ought to eat."

The bartender dropped a nut on the counter and watched the cockatoo tear into the shell with its sharp beak. Thanom was roughly Boonreung's age, Roderick thought; certainly the two boys had been friends. Boonreung used to hang around the bar in his free time, laughing and talking in Thai too rapid for Roderick to catch. Thanom knew a lot about everyone at the Oriental—what they liked to eat and drink; how much they gambled and lost; if they preferred boys to girls, and exactly how often. What had Boonreung told Thanom, during those idle half hours? Had he boasted of mad escapes through a maze of khlongs, of car rides to the Laos border? Of a trip to the northeast in a *farang* car, four days after Pridi's failed coup?

"You waiting for somebody, Mister Jack?"

"Yes," Roderick replied. "A man named Gyapay. Know him?"

Thanom swept the counter with a damp cloth, the strokes unfaltering. "I have heard the name, I think. An Army man. My uncle would know."

"Is your uncle in the Army?"

"Not anymore. What he does now is so secret, he dares not speak of it."

"I would like to meet your uncle."

"He is a busy man." No hesitation in Thanom's voice; at seventeen, he drove a hard bargain.

Roderick pulled his wallet from his trouser pocket and found a thousand-baht note. Thanom's monthly salary. He slid the cash across the shining counter and watched the boy's palm close over it.

"My uncle works at night," Thanom murmured. "By day you will find him in Thon Buri, near the Chakkawat Market. Ask for Maha. It is the name he goes by."

The cockatoo screeched and thrust its beak at Thanom. He tossed it a peanut. "A bird like that, she cares for nobody. Where is Boonreung today?"

"Consigned to flames."

The color drained from the bartender's face.

"Someone betrayed him, Thanom," Roderick said softly. "I intend for someone to pay."

A water taxi ferried him upriver to the bend in the Chao Phraya, and left him on the landing below the Chakkawat Market. If he was hunted by the men who hated and feared Pridi Banomyong, as Alec McQueen believed, he was more likely to be caught in his room at the Oriental than in the maze of canals on the city's edge. Increasingly uneasy, Roderick listened to the whistles of those who lived on the water, ringing from bank to bank like the calls of nightbirds.

His old friend Carlos had known the Thon Buri side of Bangkok intimately, but Carlos was three years gone into the hill country of Laos. Glad that the water was low with the dry season, Roderick felt his way by instinct along the muddy banks, toward the huddle of sampans and stilted houses near the marketplace. There was a widow named Dunadee who lived in a boat on a dead-end khlong—a widow with several children. She had harbored Carlos once, when escape was all that mattered. It was possible, Roderick thought, that she would know how to find the man named Maha.

Two days later Colonel Billy Lightfoot breezed into Bangkok at the head of a delegation of U.S. military brass. The colonel laughed out loud at the difference four years could make, at the neat new airfield and the prosperous mood of the people. He slapped McQueen on the back and drank sherry with Stanton in the ambassador's office, he introduced his colleagues and made sure they knew the name of Jack Roderick.

"All those reports you've read on Laos, fellas?" the colonel barked. "About the revolution to come? The end of Indochina? This is the guy who's got the goods."

Later, when the stag dinner was done and the delegation had toddled off under McQueen's aegis to see the glittering underbelly of Bangkok life, Roderick took his old trainer for an unofficial tour.

"Never thought Pridi Banomyong would turn out to be such an unholy fuck-up," Lightfoot mused, as the Packard nosed through the traffic on New Road. "Remember how we admired him, Jack, in the OSS days? The way he refused to lie down while the Japs rolled over him? Ruth stood for something then. Now he's just a lousy sideshow. Disrupting traffic every time he reenters the country."

"And the guy we kicked out of town is back in office. Makes you wonder why we bothered."

Lightfoot sighed. "At least Pibul's a soldier. Duty and honor before personal gain, right? And he's no Communist."

"Neither was Hitler."

"Hitler's dead. Stalin's alive and kicking. You know what Truman's facing in Korea? A whole Red army, hellbent on revolution. The Commies are agitating in Vietnam, too, and it's Mao who's bankrolling the fuckers. Communism's the next great war, Jack. At least Field Marshal Pibul's on *our* side this time."

"It's not a goddamn football game, Billy." Roderick pulled up before a shuttered storefront on Silom Road, empty of life at this hour. Chinese characters advertised a laundry, but Lightfoot couldn't read them.

"You got a woman shacked up here?"

"A man. Name of Gyapay. Minister of Torture in the Pibul government, and head of the secret police."

Lightfoot whistled softly under his breath.

"Five men operate inside that building, Billy. Two work electric shock, one does the punching and kicking, another patches up the victim for as long as they need him and the last one—Gyapay—asks the questions. I know the names and faces of all five."

"Jesus. Nothin' gets by you, old buddy." Billy Lightfoot squinted through the darkness as though it were a gun sight.

"I followed a man named Maha—whose personal specialty is castration—from his home two nights ago. I waited here in the street until dawn, to watch Maha and his friends come out. Over the past thirty-eight hours I've learned where each man lives and exactly what he does. Gyapay's the criminal in the bunch. The rest just do as he asks."

"What's the point, Jack?"

"This is how your good soldier Pibul handles duty and honor, Billy. He tortures the opposition into silence. He tortured a friend of mine to death."

"Was your friend Communist?"

"My friend was just a kid."

"Makes you think, doesn't it?" Lightfoot muttered. "Thank God we live in the good old U.S. of A."

When the first body appeared in Thon Buri the next morning, none of the boat people gave it much thought. It was true that Old Man Maha's throat was viciously cut, and that by the time his corpse was dragged from the khlong, the rats had gnawed out his eyes. But as Widow Dunadee judiciously said, Old Man Maha was an evil soul; it was the end he deserved. The boat people burned joss sticks and fingered amulets and averted their eyes until Maha's relatives came to dispose of their dead.

In the days that followed, three more bodies were found, each in a different part of the city. One had a knife wound straight to the heart, one a bullet hole in the temple. The third had been garotted to death. The murders made no ripple in the Thai-language press: the victims were known to be members of the secret police, and thus were hated. But by the time the fourth corpse surfaced, Alec McQueen at the *Bangkok Post* caught wind of something.

"Ex-Army men, all of 'em," he mused as he read the police homicide records. "Knives in the dark. Christ. It smells of resistance, all over again."

But when he dropped by Jack Roderick's room at the Oriental Hotel, Roderick showed no interest in the story. Jack had been hard to reach, McQueen thought, ever since that boy's murder.

On the final night of Billy Lightfoot's stay, Roderick and McQueen stood several rounds of drinks for everyone in the Bamboo Bar. Thanom wore a black armband and watched through heavy-lidded eyes while the *farangs* swapped war stories and got each other drunk. Then Roderick gathered his friends into the aging Packard and went to dine in the Thai manner. He and McQueen talked while Lightfoot choked on Kaffir lime leaves and *galangal*, washing down the pineapple curries and fried catfish with copious amounts of beer. Three golden-limbed women danced for their pleasure in the stylized, hypnotic fashion of traditional Thai *lakhon*, and when McQueen announced he was horny enough to fuck a goat, Roderick suggested they pay a visit to Miss Lucy's Hall of Girls.

The Hall of Girls was famous in the *farang* quarter as the one place a Western man could get a slice of Thai ass without fear of entanglement or murder. Roderick sailed into Miss Lucy's in time for the nightly revue, when the girls shed what little clothing they still wore. He consigned Billy Lightfoot to a tall, rangy Russian émigré who went by the name of Lola. McQueen had too many favorites among the Asian girls; Roderick chose for him, and followed him upstairs with Miss Lucy herself.

She was a canny woman with sharp eyes, a ready smile and fabulous legs; legs that, according to local legend, had once graced the Paris stage. Roderick admired Lucy's charms in company with every man in Bangkok, but what he valued most was her discretion. Lucy was an old friend and confidante of Harold Patterson—Roderick's predecessor as Bangkok intelligence chief—and it was Patterson who'd told Jack to trust Lucy implicitly. She'd never proved him wrong.

He watched her kick off her shoes, shimmy out of her dress and present her overflowing brassiere to his ready hands. He stuffed a wad of currency into her cleavage and pecked her on the cheek.

"Jack, Jack," Lucy mourned. "Always it is business? Never pleasure?"

"Pleasure increases, sweetheart, the more it's delayed. Cover for me. I need three hours."

He let himself down as quietly as a cat from the bedroom window, into the lush depths of the whorehouse garden. The sound of laughter and Western jazz, tinny with distance, floated out on the perfumed air.

Chacrit Gyapay was a compact man of fifty-three with a bland face and brown eyes reminiscent of a basset hound's. He was neatly dressed this evening in a formal Army uniform, and though his mistress had spent nearly an hour disarranging his pomaded black hair, it was now slick and shining beneath his military visor. Each night at three minutes after eleven, he strode from the apartment house where he kept his woman to the chauffeured car that waited at the curb. Tonight was no different. Gyapay adjusted his cuffs and glanced up and down the deserted pavement. Like many side streets in Bangkok, this one was without lights. The dim glow from the apartment house outlined his idling car, the driver behind the wheel. All as it should be. Why, then, did a finger of uneasiness stir at the base of his spine? Why did the brutal deaths of four men—seasoned professionals, it is true, but nothing to match the terror of Gyapay's name—disturb his peace?

He paced briskly toward the backseat. His chauffeur slid from behind the wheel to open his passenger door. He heard the satisfying *thunk!* of heavy steel as the door swung closed. The car pulled away from the curb and he glanced idly over his shoulder at the lights of his mistress's building. It was twelve minutes past eleven before he realized that his car was headed in the wrong direction.

Why did you torture and kill the boy named Boonreung?

"I torture nobody—I do not know what you mean."

Liar. Tell me. Before I execute you as I executed the men you made.

Gyapay had shrugged wearily, as though he had no patience with the foreplay of death.

Did he die for me? Or for one of my friends?

"He died because the minister ordered it."

Which minister?

"There is only one who matters."

I want his name.

"Why should I tell you, Roderick? You'll still blow my head off."

He was right, of course: Roderick would never stoop to torture, as Gyapay would, just to get information. Roderick had killed him, finally, because there was nothing else to do.

Miss Lucy was waiting for him, sunk deep in the bed cushions, filing her nails. Roderick left her at dawn and got Lightfoot a shower and some eggs before the colonel flew out of Bangkok. Then, alone, he turned the Packard north and drove deep into Khorat, with the small iron box that contained Boonreung's ashes.

"I avenged your son's murder," he told the tiny woman who waited among the wizened mulberry trees. "His spirit is at peace."

"But yours is not, *farang*. I do not think it ever will be." She placed a wreath of jasmine around his neck and bowed deep in the ceremonial *wei*.

Roderick opened the car to the wind as he drove back to the city. The smell of death remained.

14

The television cameras—at least three different networks, including a unit from CNN's Asia bureau—were waiting patiently in the main courtyard of Jack Roderick's House that Wednesday afternoon, despite the raincloud that had burst minutes before. The docents in traditional Thai dress and the coolly efficient, Donna Karan–suited women who worked in the offices above the retail store attached to the museum had attempted, at first, to turn the reporters away. They had been overwhelmed, however, when the straggle of radio and print journalists was bolstered by the arrival of satellite vans and klieg lights. The docents had settled for roping off the press in a tight bunch in the far corner of the courtyard, to distinguish them from the tour groups in seven languages that waited patiently in the adjoining café. The cool women in business suits stood aimlessly near the front entry of the museum, with clipboards and microphones clutched to their breasts.

"What exactly is going on?" Dickie Spencer inquired, as he shook the rain from his umbrella at a quarter to one. The Managing Director of Jack Roderick Silk had received a message from the Thai Heritage Board's dismayed secretary that afternoon, informing him that he was wanted at the museum. Spencer had driven to Jack Roderick's House without delay.

"Some sort of press conference," one of the women with clipboards told him. "We thought you knew."

By one o'clock there was quite a crowd assembled in the courtyard. The peaked roofs of Jack Roderick's House, with their deep red tiles, and the jungle foliage of the garden made a striking backdrop for the television cameras; the technicians were already focusing their lenses and barking orders about lighting. The cloudburst ceased as if on cue. The tourists were gawking openly at the spectacle, ignoring the docents who pleaded with them to check their cameras and remove their shoes in order to preserve the polished teak floors. Someone whispered that royalty was paying a call, but whether British or Thai, no one could say. Dickie Spencer ran blunt fingers through his salt-and-pepper hair and called his assistant on his cell phone.

A cream-colored Mercedes sedan driven by a uniformed chauffeur was admitted to the courtyard at seven minutes after one, and Spencer immediately paid his respects to the figure seated in its shadowed interior. He thrust his head through the open window and chatted for several seconds, but was not invited to sit in the car itself. Then Spencer darted across the courtyard to the retail store and the gaggle of well-suited women. He disappeared inside.

At one-fifteen precisely, a long black car nosed down Soi Kasemsan, the narrow lane that terminated in Roderick's compound. Three reporters vaulted over the cordon that separated the press pool from the courtyard proper, and raced to better positions by the entrance gates. Lights flashed. The car halted near the front door, and a silver-haired *farang* emerged from the backseat with such aplomb that for an instant, the watching crowd was completely fooled and believed it was Jack Roderick himself, sleek head and elegant form untouched by thirty-five years of age and absence.

Someone shouted, "He's returned! Roderick has returned!"

The gray-suited figure held up his hand and smiled. The waiting crowd saw then that this was no Silk King, no Legendary American. He reached into the depths of the black car and drew forth a woman: slim, correct and clothed entirely in black. A figure of mourning.

The reporters and the tourists fell silent.

Rush Halliwell, from his post at a second-floor window inside the museum, stared down at the scene with a faint smile of amusement.

Stefani Fogg, he thought, was a ringmaster. She'd turned the whole of Bangkok into a circus.

"... **given the clear** indication of Mr. Roderick's governing testament," Matthew French intoned, "we would like to challenge the Thai Heritage Board and the Ministry of Culture to review the 1967 will, as well as the Board's policy regarding administration of Jack Roderick's House, in order to fairly address Ms. Fogg's claims."

He raised his eyes serenely from his notes. "Thank you very much. Ms. Fogg would be willing to take a few questions."

A clamor of shouting broke out. Across the courtyard, the rear window of the cream-colored Mercedes slid down silently, and Stefani glimpsed a man's head within, his attention concentrated entirely on her. There was malevolence, cold as a viper's, in the man's look.

"Ms. Fogg! Ms. Fogg!"

The reporters were baying for attention. A Thai woman was wedged painfully between two burly men, her arm extended in supplication. Stefani pointed at her.

"Why did the family suppress Jack Roderick's second will for so many years?" the woman cried, and thrust out a microphone.

"It appears that Jack Roderick misplaced the will by accident," Stefani replied, "and that when it was discovered eighteen months ago, the document was contested by the Thai Heritage Board and the Minister of Culture. The Roderick family lawyers have authenticated Jack Roderick's signature, however, and there can be no doubt that the testament reflects Mr. Roderick's final wishes. I'm standing before you today in an effort to see justice done."

"Do you think Roderick was killed so that the Thai government could seize his art collection?" a man shouted.

"No one can say what happened to Jack Roderick. We can all see, however, that the Thai government benefited far more from Roderick's estate than did his heirs."

Stefani's eyes roved over the surging mass of reporters and came to rest on one who held no microphone, no tape recorder or pen. A powerful Asian with expressionless eyes and gleaming black hair, his arms crossed protectively over his chest. The thug from the Oriental. Her shadow. Rush Halliwell must have told him where and when to find her. She had invited Rush to the museum that afternoon as a sort of test: now she had her answer.

"What do you plan to do with the house?"

The question came from a mild-faced man with a shock of white hair and bright blue eyes, a Westerner who held a pad of paper in his hand.

"I have no plans as yet," she replied. "My object is to honor Jack Roderick's memory and win restitution for his family, whose rights have been disregarded for decades."

"But the family's gone," the reporter countered. "Admit it, Ms. Fogg. You're fortune-hunting at the expense of the Thai people. You're hijacking our national treasures."

Our treasures? she thought. "I have no wish to deprive the public of access to the collection. If the Thai Minister of Culture, Mr. Suwannathat, is willing to meet me halfway, perhaps we could arrive at a compromise regarding the museum's future."

Across the courtyard, the window of the cream-colored Mercedes slid closed. The engine throbbed to life.

At the far end of Soi Kasemsan, a siren wailed. Dickie Spencer had called the police.

"Nice show," Rush Halliwell breathed in her ear. He had slipped down the museum's main stairs and out the front door, so that he was standing just behind Stefani when the police arrived. "You look like a woman in need of consular support. Want me to run interference?"

"Call off your dog," she said tersely.

"My dog?"

She nodded in the direction of a broad-shouldered man with dark hair who was forcing a path toward them. Journalists bobbed like bowling pins in his wake. The lump at the base of Rush's skull throbbed sharply.

"The man's name is Jo-Jo and he belongs to the guy in the beige Mercedes," Rush muttered. "Sompong Suwannathat, if I'm not mistaken. I know his license plate."

She stiffened. "Introduce me?"

"To the minister? No thank you." He grasped her wrist tightly and half-pulled, half-propelled her toward the waiting black limo.

But Jo-Jo had reached it first; he'd propped himself firmly against the passenger door, an immovable wall. There was no way out by the front gate: the police were using bullhorns, herding the journalists like cattle toward the sole exit. Camera crews were avidly filming the scene as they went.

"Shit," Rush muttered to himself.

Stefani wrested her hand from his grasp and darted back toward the house. She was making for the garden—for the khlong gate, and the water beyond.

The khlong. It might work.

He turned abruptly and came up hard against Matthew French's chest. The lawyer was staring after his fleeing client.

"Hold the guy who's blocking the car," Rush said urgently. "Do anything you can. She's not safe."

She had dragged a bench against the garden wall's ornamental stone-work, and was attempting to swing her leg over the vicious barbed wire that spooled along the ledge.

"Did you have to wear that skirt today?" Rush asked. "*Jesus*—how tight is that thing?"

He jumped up beside her and began cutting the wire with a Swiss army knife.

"I don't need you—"

"Yes, you do. Hold this."

He handed her his suit jacket and dove without hesitation into the khlong.

The water was colder than he expected, colder than in the days when he'd jumped off the lock gantries for the sheer joy of doing it with the other tanned and bare-chested Thai boys. How old had he been? Eight? Ten? Rush came up sputtering, and swam toward the Ban Khrua side of the khlong and the dock thrust out into the water. The weaving families were long gone, now, and what faced him was a series of industrial sheds. He did not like to think about what swirled around him in the brown current.

He heaved himself onto the dock, which bounced and swayed on its pylons. Two boats lay overturned on the muddy bank. He righted the smallest of them and found oars tucked beneath.

There was a splash, and he glanced hastily around to see Stefani's dark head rising out of the turgid water. Jo-Jo stood on the garden side of the khlong gate, his hands grasping the wall.

She pulled herself up beside him; Rush thrust the small craft into the water and she quickly stepped into it. People were shouting at them from both sides of the khlong, now.

She gave Jo-Jo the finger as they rowed away.

"That guy reported to you at the Oriental's cocktail party last night," Stefani said, as she squeezed the khlong out of her hair. "Explain."

"Jo-Jo is a piece of paid protection whose weapon of choice is an Uzi." Rush leaned into the oars and feathered the brown water. The smell of garbage and decaying water plants was fetid: Stefani wrinkled her nose as she surveyed her ruined suit.

"I've watched Jo-Jo for years," Rush went on, "but I've never run into him at the Oriental before. I blocked his path at the party, and he told me in exquisite Malay to go fuck myself."

"He was sitting in the hotel lobby when I arrived Tuesday morning. He took something from my tote bag that afternoon. And if I'm not mistaken, he intended just now to haul me off by force. In the course of twenty-four hours he's gone from surveillance to kidnapping."

"He's working on Sompong's orders."

"The minister wanted to chat?"

"Don't joke about it," Rush said brusquely. "Jo-Jo's methods aren't pretty. I'm more worried about your safety now than I was last night— and last night I was worried sick." He winced at the memory of the blow to his head. "What did he steal from your bag, anyway?"

"A piece of paper. I'd made . . . notes . . . on it."

"Then assume Sompong's read them."

She pursed her lips, but volunteered no more information.

"Stefani, you've got to tell me why the minister's trained his paid gun on you."

"I want Sompong's house."

"It isn't that simple. He saw you coming."

"You expect me to believe that Sompong Suwannathat knew my name—knew what I intended in Bangkok—before this afternoon? That's bullshit."

"You're willing to believe the same of me," he observed quietly.

"You're U.S. government," she shot back. "You know far more than is healthy for anybody. Yesterday I'd have said you put Jo-Jo on my tail. But since you failed to hand me over this afternoon—"

"Let me make one thing clear, Ms. Fogg," Rush said brusquely. "I don't make contact with my own surveillance in the target's direct line of sight. I don't have an intimate dinner with somebody I'm following. And I could be fired—or worse—for surveilling a U.S. citizen. I didn't unleash the dog."

Her dark eyes regarded him steadily. "I was warned about you. Or rather, the people you work for."

"By whom?"

"Max Roderick. He told me the CIA knew the truth about his grandfather's death. And that they'd make sure it stayed . . . buried."

"Who says I'm CIA?"

She snorted and held his gaze.

Halliwell sighed in exasperation. "You think Max was murdered, don't you? So do I. But I didn't push his wheelchair off that cliff. And neither did anybody I work for."

He saw from the slight movement of her head that he had surprised her. He shipped his oars.

"Max told me the same fairy tale about his grandfather eighteen months ago. He'd found the second will just weeks before, and made a quick trip to Thailand. It was the beginning of all his troubles."

"You *met* him?" She broke in quickly, as though the very idea were painful. "Why the hell didn't you tell me?"

"I spent about three days in his company. He hit town the same week as our Secretary of Defense, and most of the embassy staff paid homage to Washington. I stayed behind to do some real work. I got to talk to Max."

Her eyes had filled with a hunger that disturbed him. The boat rocked gently in the sluggish current.

"What did he want?"

"Anything we might have concerning his family. He thought there'd be file drawers with Jack's name on them, I guess. I couldn't help him."

She laughed with bitterness. "He expected you to shut him down. And you did."

"Jack Roderick was rumored to have been a spy for most of his life.

Who knows how close his ties were to the United States after he started his silk company? For a man who was supposed to be plotting coups in the fifties and sixties, he spent an awful lot of time supervising weavers and buying art. Max seemed convinced that his grandfather opposed the Vietnam War—and was eliminated by his own intelligence service because of it."

"Is that so shocking?"

"Grow up, Stefani," Rush snapped. "It's the classic cynicism of the conspiracy theorist. It's ignorance masquerading as privileged information. I told him as much. But then I realized: *Max is a Roderick.* Two generations of Roderick men died in brutal and unexplained ways. What else is the third generation going to believe?"

"It wasn't just a theory," Stefani persisted. "He saw things, as a kid—"

"The man in uniform, running downstairs," Rush mocked. "Roderick shouting, with blood on his face. What the hell does that prove? Nothing but that a kid of four, awakened from a sound sleep, will always see nightmares."

"Did you ever check the details?"

"I didn't have to." He dipped the oars once more into the khlong. "If you'd studied the history of the Vietnam War, you'd know that the CIA fought pitched battles with the Pentagon for years over what constituted truth in intelligence. North Vietnamese troop strength assessments, for instance: the Agency projected far greater enemy numbers than Army Headquarters would report to LBJ. The Army rewrote the Agency's numbers and got their asses kicked when too many Viet Cong crept out of the rice paddies. Heads rolled and good men fell on their swords over that one. But nobody was blown away. Not even Jack Roderick."

"The fact remains that Roderick disappeared. And no one—in Thailand or the United States—has been willing to say why."

"Maybe he killed himself," Rush retorted. "Twenty years of buying people's souls can be hard to live with."

15

**Bangkok,
1951**

In the months after Boonreung's murder, Jack Roderick gave himself
up entirely to the business of selling silk. He devoted hours to what he
loved instead of to Edwin Stanton or Stanton's successors in the am-
bassadorial post. As the years of Truman gave way to those of Eisenhower,
and Mao Tse-tung straddled China with iron knees, Roderick avoided the
embassy and lived on his own terms, a figurehead in the expatriate
community, a fulcrum of every rumor among the Thais.

There was good cause for the whispers behind Roderick's back.
Although he had brokered a deal with the CIA that allowed him to
work as he chose—an export merchant unattached to the embassy, with
no diplomatic status—he continued to serve as eyes and ears for the
spymasters in Washington, and too many Thais knew it. His numerous
and influential friends came from every strata of Bangkok life: police-
men on the beat, noodle vendors, courtesans and barbers, the assistant
chiefs of police. Assistant chiefs were ambitious, and thus more open
to persuasion. They sat down to dinner and shared their heartaches,
muttered their opinions, confessed their lovers' secrets. If, after one of
these evenings, a modest sum of money exchanged hands . . . the payment was only a sign of esteem and affection. It hardly constituted a
binding contract. The essence of Roderick's power lay not in what he

bought, but the charm with which he bought it. It was clear to his friends that Roderick loved them all—understood them all—and cherished their dreams of an expansive future.

And yet there were moments, when his clear, light eyes saw through a man to his very soul, and the memory of Gyapay the Torturer's fate surfaced in the unquiet mind, and the sum of cash was spent quickly and heedlessly and not without a shudder.

Roderick was Washington's clearinghouse for every covert operation undertaken in Thailand. Covert operations, in that Cold War decade, were the CIA's reason for being. The Agency did what no president or Congress was prepared to admit: influenced voters, propped up democratic candidates, threw elections, leaned on newspaper editors, made or broke careers. Covert operators managed all this with the ample funds provided under the yearly defense appropriations authorized by Congress, and they did it in the name of defeating the Soviets, who—along with Mao's China—were hellbent on ruling the world. It was a dirty game, but it succeeded in part because of American prestige. The United States had saved the world from tyranny in the last war. The United States stood for freedom. It was the sole shining beacon capable of countering the immense Russian darkness; and Roderick never questioned its ultimate purpose. He was an American by privilege, by birth and by conviction; he knew that he was the envy of the world.

Washington was content to maintain Field Marshal Pibul in power. Pibul was no democrat, but he was the farthest thing from Communist that Thailand could offer. Now that Pridi Banomyong had traveled to Beijing, and thrown himself under the protection of Mao, the CIA was leery of wartime resistance fighters and their dubious ambitions. For the moment, the Field Marshal was comfortingly sound. Pibul had learned the lesson of his torturer's gruesome end, and kept his secret police on a tighter leash.

The people of Bangkok had long ago decided that Jack Roderick was responsible for Gyapay's murder and those of his staff, and they were by and large grateful—the exception being Thanom, the young bartender at the Oriental. Thanom had circulated his suspicion readily among the staff; and though he could not prove Roderick had slit his uncle's throat, any more than he would discuss Old Man Maha's duties as a torturer, his words carried conviction. It was well known that

Roderick was in the arms of Miss Lucy when the chief of the secret police, Chacrit Gyapay, was shot dead in his own car. But Thanom could imply great knowledge of sinister deeds—he could speak darkly of the *farang* who pretended to be one of them. Thanom could make the sign against evil behind Roderick's back. And eventually fearful powers were accorded the American. He was treated with care and respect.

Roderick moved out of the Oriental and hired rooms not far from Ban Khrua, where his silk weavers lived.

He found, to his surprise, that the management of his business connected him to the life of Siam in a way he had not expected. He began to know the weavers' habits, the dictates of their Muslim faith, the names and ages of their children. He sat cross-legged on their wooden porches in the early morning, Boonreung's orphaned cockatoo nibbling at his ear, and uttered halting words of the Thai none of his Western friends thought he spoke. He studied antiquities and Siam's history and the chemistry of Swiss aniline dyes, and he experimented with the khlong's waters, lifting silk skeins high on wooden racks, cerise and aquamarine and viridian. He hiked with his friends from the Siam Society—a local group of antiquities enthusiasts—into the dense jungles of the interior, and brought back treasures of lost empires. Never again would he leave something as priceless as the Buddha cave to the chance knives of scavengers. He had returned to the Western Seaboard only once since that first trip in 1945, and found the cave plundered, the head of the Buddha hacked from the living rock.

And he went back, again and again, to the ancient capital of Ayutthaya.

The city had been built in the fourteenth century as a refuge from smallpox, on a group of islands trapped in the confluence of three rivers. Ayutthaya grew in wealth and power until by the end of the seventeenth century it had subjugated all Siam. And then, in 1767, the Burmese sacked the city and enslaved all those they did not put to the sword.

Now the ruins poked disconsolately through the modern town's sprawl—snarling *singhas*, mythic lions as massive as horses, still standing guard around the crumbling *wats;* astronomical observatories set in the heights of towers; crumbling palaces, their fountains dry. The tombs of withered princes were smothered beneath clinging vines. Even the hallowed temple that held the footprint of the Lord Buddha was submerged in green.

Roderick wandered and gazed not at *wats* or palaces but at the commoners' houses, which were built of wood ornately carved: houses three centuries old, whose teak sides were pegged together and capped with steep roofs. From their corners flew the *cho fa,* the cobralike gable ornament Siam had borrowed from the Khmer. Roderick loved the teak houses and their carving. He tracked them in the ancient capital itself, and in the villages north of Ayutthaya; he found them even in the tangled web of Bangkok's humblest quarters. He had been trained as an architect in those far-off days before the war and before Joan: something of the draftsman still lurked in his fingers. In March of 1951, he bought six of the old teak houses from owners eager to sell, and disassembled them where they stood.

The land was a half acre snatched from the bank of Khlong Mahanak. He knew the waterway well, because the silk-weavers' quarter of Ban Khrua bordered it, and he walked among the weavers each morning of his life, now, inspecting the lengths of silk as they unfurled from the looms. He imagined a house, commodious and winged, formed from the six jumbled frames on the swatch of tended garden; he saw a terrace of soft Ayutthaya brick, three hundred years old, that faced the khlong. He saw torches and people and he heard laughter in the night. He would hire barges and float his six houses down the Chao Phraya and bring them directly to the site on Khlong Mahanak, he would turn the houses' walls inward so that he might run his fingers over the carved teak. He would hire craftsmen from the ancient capital who still remembered the old ways of building. He would pave his floors with royal marble scavenged from abandoned palaces.

The Buddhist priests came three times during the long months of building the house on the khlong. The first ceremony was held at a precise hour early in the morning on the day when astrologers foretold auspicious spirits, so that the workmen could raise the first teak column of the house. Roderick threw a sort of party for his friends and the Brahmin priest and the nine ordinary monks from Ayutthaya, who chanted prayers while the column was raised. Bowls of food were left at appointed spots about the compound to encourage the earth spirits to keep Roderick and his builders safe. The food was consumed by rats from the khlong but as this was expected, it was deemed a favorable sign; construction commenced with a vengeance and went on for months, until the second ceremony was due.

This was the placing of the spirit house in Roderick's garden. It is necessary in Thailand to provide a lodging for the spirit one disrupts from its place in the earth—and the spirits that governed Ban Khrua and Khlong Mahanak had always been deemed powerful. The spirit house must never be touched by the shadow of a building, and in the crowded quarters of the city this became a singular problem. All manner of ills—burglaries, poor sewage, squabbles with servants and bad luck in business—could be traced to the mismanagement of a spirit house. The priest spent the better part of a morning concluding that the house might be placed exactly where Roderick preferred; and then the old man consulted his astrologic charts and mapped the genealogy of the resident spirits.

The day for moving house required that the charts be consulted again, and further calculations performed. In Roderick's case, the ideal time for luck and appeasing Fate proved to be several weeks before his house was finished—but he brought back the nine monks to sit in the lotus position on his rough drawing-room floor, their faces turned toward the khlong, and they chanted and blessed the house. Gold leaf and sandalwood powder were placed above the lintels of each door and daubed on Roderick's brow. He slept alone that night on the floor of his bedroom, and rose to the sound of his weavers singing across the khlong.

And finally, on a day of sun and rain, he set off for the Nakorn Kasem, the old Thieves Market, with a lark rising in his breast and his palms tingling. Something was waiting for him in the warren of alleys and shop fronts where all the treasures of Asia ended; something was singing through the weavers' voices and the ripple of the khlong. He could do no wrong on such a day—he was on the hunt, and the hunt was all he lived for.

He handled vessels of worked silver and Bencharong cups; dirtied his fingers with the dust of manuscripts; cleaned them again for a lunch of shrimp and beer. He traced the beads and embroidery on a pair of silk shoes, and held a ruby brooch to the light, before he re-called with a sinking heart that he had no wife anymore to send such things. And still the call of that singing lark went unanswered.

It was as he made his way home through the markets of the Chakkrawat Road that he stumbled upon it.

A carved poetry of stone; the limestone eyes half lidded in sublime repose; the brow resting lightly against one hand. And where he re-membered the head curving into the neck and then the massive weight of the trunk—nothing but a chiseled hole.

The Buddha of the Hidden Cave. *His* Buddha.

Where there had once been a ruby set into the forehead, there was now only a ragged wound. He crouched and traced the edge of the hole with his fingertip. Thinking of the dull red stone he had kept safe for five years in his bedroom. The ruby his old friend Carlos had found be-side the corpse of a murdered king.

"Where did you get this piece?"

The dealer smiled. "It is quite fine. Very precious. Very old—"

"I know what it is." Roderick stood and faced him. "I found it my-self, six years ago, in a cave on the Western Coast. It had a body, then. I ask you again: Where did you get it?"

The dealer's smile soured and he backed into his shop. "The gentle-man is mistaken. The gentleman has never seen this piece. I have had it in my warehouse thirteen years. I have had it from a very old customer, very old, from Vientiane—"

Roderick gripped the wooden door that would have closed in his face. "Let us roll dice for the truth." He drew a money clip from his trouser pocket and thrust it beneath the dealer's nose. "Two thousand baht. If the luck favors you, you tell me nothing and the two thousand is yours. If the luck favors me, I pay two thousand for the head and the name of the man who sold it to you. Agreed?"

The thief of Nakorn Kasem considered the deal, and then he con-sidered the implacable eyes of the man who offered it. His fingers closed over the money.

16

Stefani Fogg frowned as she peeled a clementine by her breakfast-room window Thursday morning. It was not that the view of the river was any less enchanting than it had been the night before. She had slept well and had ventured across the Chao Phraya before breakfast for a workout and a massage at the spa. What troubled her now was the coverage of the previous day's spectacular press conference in the *Bangkok Post*.

The local television news had devoted six minutes to the story, complete with footage of Stefani, her lawyer and the police decked out in riot gear. One Bangkok television station had presented the story neutrally, another with obvious sympathy for her claim. CNN used the piece as a springboard to review the sinister history of Jack Roderick's disappearance and espionage connections; the footage closed with a tour of the house and its treasures. Stefani watched this final segment with interest from the comfort of her sofa, swathed in one of the Oriental's cotton robes and a glow of self-righteous satisfaction.

But the *Bangkok Post* had ignored the press conference as a news item, and had buried the story in a column written by one of their oldest hands.

Fortune-Seeker Lays Claim to Bangkok's Pride, the headline shrieked.

There was no photograph of Stefani in her mourning garb, no attractive backdrop of Roderick's famed house. Just a mug shot of the column's author: white-haired and mild-faced, his eyes ingenuous and true. The middle-aged reporter who'd fired the tough questions, yesterday. She glanced at the byline. Joe Halliwell.

Joe *Halliwell*? Surely he couldn't be related to Rush. It must be coincidence.

Stefani read on.

The reporter's tone was indignant. Stefani Fogg was exploiting the legendary memory of Bangkok's Silk King, Jack Pierpont Roderick, for personal promotion and private gain. A foreigner, a woman from New York without a blood connection to the Roderick family, she had shamelessly capitalized on the death of Roderick's grandson to attack a respected museum and its board of directors with a preposterous claim she could barely prove. Halliwell closed his piece with the injunction that the people of Bangkok should rally behind Dickie Spencer, who had managed Roderick's legacy superbly, and demand that the Legendary American's gift to the Thai people—his home and priceless collections—be left undisturbed. This was the only fitting tribute to Jack Roderick, and all that he had done for Thailand.

"Another sacred fucking cow," Stefani muttered, and tossed the newspaper across the room.

Halliwell. *Halliwell*. It wasn't a common name like Jones or Smith. So Rush must have called in the family chips at the dominant English-language newspaper in all of Southeast Asia, and the *Bangkok Post* had obediently shut Stefani down.

Rush had been so *nice*, too, last evening—waiting patiently in the Bamboo Bar while she showered and changed her clothes, although his own were a mess and he frankly stank of the khlong. She should have expected betrayal; she should have seen the shaft behind the smile. But she had been tired out and off her guard. They had clicked glasses of Scotch—for medicinal purposes, Stefani said, though the smoky palate reminded her wistfully of Oliver Krane. Rush had promised to arrange a meeting with Sompong Suwannathat as soon as possible, and to escort her to the ministry himself. He'd left her feeling grateful after one drink, with a warning ringing in her ears.

Jo-Jo isn't a subtle kind of guy, Stefani. If Sompong's put him on your trail,

Sompong wants you scared. Next time, Jo-Jo will do more than pick your pocket. Watch your back.

Last night she had even thought it possible that Max had been wrong—that Rush Halliwell, the U.S. embassy, the CIA, even—were not arrayed against her. But the headlines this morning changed everything.

It was time, she decided, to ask Oliver to investigate Rush. What Oliver couldn't find was not worth knowing.

Tenacious and not unintelligent, the Krane & Associates' report noted, *but prone to a surfeit of confidence. Her chief weakness is a tendency to believe too much in herself and too little in the existence of evil.*

"In other words," Sompong Suwannathat said to himself, "she's just a woman."

He thrust the sheaf of paper into a leather case and glanced out the jet's window. The sun was rising over Chiang Rai, striking the airport runway and the sprawl of trekkers' hotels; but shadow still lay thick and jagged on the terraced hills of cabbage and tea and coffee plants on the outskirts of the city.

Sompong knew the streets of Chiang Rai and the *wats* and the immense statue of a fat Buddha, sitting with its hand raised in a gesture of peace, as intimately as he knew his own roof garden in Bangkok. He had dedicated the Hill Tribe Museum himself, years before, when he was just a ministry functionary. He had even spent a sweltering afternoon on a boat trip down the Kok River, smiling and bowing distantly to the Akha and Hmong and Karen and Lisu tribal chiefs, brought in as dogs and ponies in the traveling show the Ministry of Culture mounted each year for the Foreign Aid people from the United States. The Foreign Aid people wanted to protect the subtle and varied cultures of the Golden Triangle before they completely died out. They encouraged the growth of cabbage and tea and coffee plants in the hills, preferring them to the opium poppies for which the Hmong and Lisu had fought and died during most of the past century.

Travel agents the world over talked glibly of the beauties of Chiang Rai province—about the soaring vistas of Burma and Laos, about the tribal crafts and the pristine rivers meandering among the monsoon forests. But Sompong knew the villages of Fang and Mae Salong and Tha Ton better than the tour operators. He knew the hill paths and the riverbanks with the sure-footed certainty of the boy he had once been, a child of seven loosed like a wolf in the woods; and he knew, too, that the Golden Triangle was—and would always be—a crucible of illegal trade and war.

It was a saddle of terrain ringed by hills and the borders of three nations: Burma, Thailand and Laos. China loomed like a goiter to the north, and from China the usual evils came: war and addiction and the violence both spawned. In 1949 it had been Chiang Kai-shek's Nationalist troops, the Kuomintang defeated for the last time by Mao Tse-tung. The Kuomintang settled in Mae Salong and squabbled over the Lisu women and worked the poppy fields under mounted guard; they gave the streets new names in a different tongue and called their children after broken warlords. By 1959 the king of Thailand had outlawed opium production, but the ban only made trade more lucrative. In the early sixties—the years of Sompong's childhood—the Shan United Army, led by the Burmese warlord Khun Sa, had fought its way into the rich border country and preyed on the Chinese. They partitioned the hills and bought missiles from the Soviets and shed blood for the right to sow poppy fields.

The American war with Vietnam had merely sanctioned the Triangle's lawlessness. It convinced the people who worked the fields that the only salvation possible was from the muzzle of a gun. The Communists and the Nationalists who had slaughtered each other in Beijing brought their quarrel south, and now civil war infected all the ancient kingdoms of Southeast Asia.

Khun Sa had retreated to Burma in the 1980s, but the men with guns remained. No less a personage than Vukrit Suwannathat, Field Marshal and Minister of Defense at the time of his death, had been found dead by the road leading to Mae Salong, his body riddled with bullets and his ministry car burned to a blackened steel frame. Vukrit had been murdered in 1986, and in the wake of the outrage, government troops had been deployed to stamp out the last of the drug farmers. Sompong himself had supervised the scorched-earth campaign, and watched the chemical defoliants wither the fields in which he'd played as a boy. Opium production in the Golden Triangle had fallen by nearly eighty percent in the past decade, to Sompong's satisfaction.

He had managed, by government fiat, to destroy the supplies of his chief competitors.

The tea and the cabbages and the cash crops encouraged by the king flourished now in the terraced hills, but illegal trade still coursed down the rivers and along the more secret paths: endangered ivory or forbidden teak, the rubies sliced from the heart of Myanmar.

The tribesmen, as always, were pawns who gained nothing, their numbers fewer each year.

What the tribesman wants is simple, my son, Sompong's father had told him thirty years before. *Not glory or justice or world dominion. Just rice for his table. Just safety from war.*

"That's right, Father," Sompong told himself softly. "The world and glory belong to men like me."

Two and a half hours later, the sun full in the sky, he abandoned his rental car and set out for the hill station by foot.

He had brought no driver and no bodyguard. It was the first of Sompong's rules: *In deadly business, trust no one but yourself.* He had picked out the pattern to existence long ago, crouching in the serrated shadows of the jungle undergrowth, watching his father and the men the General commanded. Loyalty was cheap. It was lifeblood that came dearly.

There was a whistling akin to birdsong above him in the trees; he recognized the signal and ignored it. The whistles would turn to radio transmissions muttered into microphones, and by the time he emerged from the last branching of the path, the committee would be waiting. He walked straighter under the gaze of the unknown scouts, trying not to gasp with exertion as the path climbed, though he was past forty now and could never again run with a boy's fleetness. Something of the old nobility, nonetheless, descended upon his shoulders. He stood alone and powerful against a rabble army. He was the General's son.

For an instant, the American woman in Bangkok tramped heavily through his brain.

She has courage at the bone and does not scare easily. Does this reflect a belief in her own immortality? Or worse yet, a disdain for her own life? Whatever the reason, she relishes a good fight.

"Then she has never been beaten as she ought," he said grimly, and chose the final turning in the path.

He had disliked the American from the moment he saw her in the courtyard of Jack Roderick's House the previous afternoon. He had watched her pose and preen for the photographers, her *farang* body too thin and hard, her voice too shrill. This woman was naïve, and stupid because of it; she would fatally misjudge her enemies. For all their guns, Americans had not the slightest comprehension of the way violence established order in society. They thought of violence as an urban blight, a horrific toll engendered by untrammeled capitalism. Whereas Sompong Suwannathat had learned at his father's knee that the chief gift of violence was power. Violence alone established hierarchies. Violence made kings.

He had driven directly to the Peninsula Hotel after the farce of the press conference, in a high rage because Jo-Jo had failed to muscle the woman into his car as he had ordered. He had persuaded the Peninsula management—who were beholden to Sompong as so much of Bangkok was—to admit him to Knetsch's room. Sompong waited in the semi-darkness nearly two hours before the lawyer stumbled through the door. Knetsch still suffered from jet lag and from something worse—the ravaging erosion of mortal fear.

It had not taken Sompong long to say what he wanted.

He reached the crest of the path and emerged onto a ridgeline that offered a view of three countries, flung out like a carpet on every side: Burma, Laos and Thailand. His personal kingdom. His paradise on earth.

His duty and honor to the father taken so brutally from life, so long ago.

They escorted Sompong under armed guard to the small hut where the business was usually concluded.

It was windowless and damp, five meters square. He knew the distance to within a fraction; he had measured it repeatedly during one bout of imprisonment as a boy. The floor was unpaved dirt but someone had thrown dried grass underfoot to make the place sweet smelling. In Sompong's mind, however, this would always be a place of execution.

Tell me again about the night Jack Roderick died.

Himself, much younger, his right hand wrapped decisively around the pistol butt. The muzzle against the old man's ear. A ring of soldiers outside the hut, standing at attention as they had for hours, in honor of their fallen comrades. The smell of sweat from his own armpits and urine from the old man's bladder. The other two, already shot but not yet dead, staring dully at what remained of their knees. The old man beginning to tremble.

Tell me again.

Today there were burlap sacks piled on the spot where the corpses had lain fifteen years before, and Wu Fat now sat in the old man's seat. Sompong thought of the rocket-propelled grenade launchers and the surface-to-air missiles crated in the belly of his ministry plane at Chiang Rai, and felt a piercing relief for the art of the deal. Today there would be no shouting or pistol shots, no brains spattering the dried grass of the floor. Just a handshake and the exchange of priceless commodities.

Today it hardly mattered how Jack Roderick died.

Wu Fat pushed back his chair and saluted the General's son.

17

Bangkok, 1952

The night of the first full moon of the dry season in 1952, Jack Roderick opened the doors of his home to all of Bangkok, and they came by car and by boat, up the gravel drive and down the waterways, through the lanterns that flickered amid the jungle palms like jeweled fireflies.

He placed torches along the drive and up the staircase of his soaring entrance hall, luminous with women in silk. There was a Western orchestra and champagne and caviar, and the men were dressed in white tie and they smoked Dunhill cigarettes and wore their hair clipped very short. Most of the Thais were people Roderick knew from the years of the war or his hunting expeditions among the old caves of the West; they were doctors and lawyers or men who had no love for Pibul and never talked politics in public at all. Some of them were agents that Roderick handled, but tonight was not a night for business. Alec McQueen had sent reporters and photographers with enormous lamps, and they bathed the most spectacular of the new arrivals with phosphorescence.

Tonight the *farang* community was out in force: wives of French-legation members, who spoke of *l'Indochine* in guttural tones; British envoys, plotting the ruin of victorious Mao; American businessmen whose breezy laughs suggested that the world was a damn big oyster, and they had the tools to open it. Alec McQueen wore a white ascot and brandished a cigar, his black hair unkempt over his flushed brow. One very blond and languid beauty, a divorcée come to Bangkok for the fun of it, competed for Roderick's attention with a black-eyed Chinese woman dressed in a skin-tight *cheongsam*. Several men grew drunk on Roderick's Scotch and began tossing champagne corks from the terrace wall, in an effort to reach the waters of the khlong; and across the khlong itself, rocking gently on their floating doorsteps, sat the silk-weaving families of Ban Khrua.

The weavers stared at Roderick's lights and listened to the foreign music that prevented their children from sleeping, and one boy dove suddenly into the water and surfaced with a handful of corks, laughing uproariously at the foolishness of *farangs*.

The Minister of Culture, Vukrit Suwannathat, came without his wife, Li-ang, whom he had abandoned recently for an exotic mistress. Vukrit came in the shining glow of confident power, and his body-guards hugged the walls with drinks untouched in their hands. He came, and where he passed, the party shifted like a rice paddy swept by a fitful breeze. Roderick laughed just as loudly as the rest of the Americans, but his eyes followed Vukrit as though the man might steal him blind. McQueen's reporters gathered dutifully around the minis-ter and jotted his comments in their notebooks while the cameras seared his image in their brains.

At eleven o'clock, when the brilliant hum of the spinning party threatened to slow and jangle, Roderick ordered the lights doused and left the room dusky with coconut-oil torches. He gazed out over the wilted crowd of sweating men and women, assembled willy-nilly among his bright silk cushions and his priceless salvage of ancient em-pire, and he clapped his hands twice. The terrace doors swung open. The *lakhon* dancers filed in.

There were eight of them dressed in silk and jewels, their head-dresses elaborately worked, their masks and painted faces like figures cut down from the walls of the Grand Palace. A hush fell over the crowd; most had seen Thai dancers before, but never like this, with the torchlit shadows and the khlong waters moving ceaselessly behind them. It was as though for an instant they were all returned to the days when dance was a court ritual, and the movements of sinuous women the privilege of kings alone. *Tonight,* Roderick seemed to declare, *I am royal, too. Roderick in his palace. Roderick the king.*

The music was made of wind instruments and strings, the movements were studied and controlled. There was impossible grace in the curve of a fingertip, the turn of a cheek; grace in the principal dancer, a woman dressed in the guise of Taksin, the warrior king of Ayutthaya. The dancer's eyes were expressionless when they roved the crowd, but once—and only once—they widened slightly, as though in shock or fear. That was the moment they fell on Roderick, standing spare and elegant in his dinner jacket. His pale hair was swept back from the high forehead, a cigarette burned forgotten in his fingers. It seemed the dancer's wrist trembled slightly as she extended her palm in a choreographed gesture of denial; then it steadied, and she moved on.

"What is her name?" Roderick muttered to Alec McQueen. Alec alone in all that room was certain to know.

"Thongchai Pithuvanuk," he said slowly. "Trained in the Royal Palace. Her friends call her Fleur."

"Fleur," Roderick repeated. "It suits her."

Later, when the last of the guests had left, Roderick strolled through his garden in search of Alec and the woman named Fleur and instead, in the breezeway amid the stilts of his house, found His Excellency the Minister of Culture leaning against a massive limestone head of a reclining Buddha. The head was sunk in a square of gravel like a meteor fallen from the sky.

"And this is what comes of your fine words, Jack." Vukrit spoke with distaste. "You wanted experts and priests, someone from the museum—you put us all off with talk of what is sacred—and then you returned alone and cut the thing from the wall."

Roderick stopped short, his hands slouched in his trouser pockets. "You know the story better than that, Vukrit. You know all the stories, don't you? You collect them, I think. You spin them out of thin air. You even sell them to the highest bidder. Like you sold your friends. Carlos. And Boonreung."

"I could have you arrested," the minister replied evenly, "for the theft of precious national artifacts. What else do you have hidden away? I could bring my troops here tomorrow. Examine your papers. Confiscate your house—"

" 'There is only one minister who matters.' A dying man told me that. Was he talking about you?"

Vukrit threw back his head and laughed. "I certainly hope so. May I ask his name?"

"Chacrit Gyapay. It was almost the last thing he said." From his pocket, Roderick drew something—a dull red stone. He fitted it tenderly into the hollow in the Buddha's brow, then returned it to his pocket. "How much did you get for your brother-in-law, Vukrit? Tell me that."

"Carlos was never found." The laughter stopped abruptly, and Roderick saw that the minister perspired in the torchlight, his eyes shifting from Roderick's pocket to the hole where the gem had rested. "Carlos's life is forfeit if he returns. He killed our king."

"No," Roderick replied. "Not Carlos. That's another story you've sold."

"You dare to call me *liar*?"

"I could call you *murderer* instead."

Something pulsed between them like the strobe of a camera bulb: hatred, blood lust. Roderick stepped closer to this man he despised as he might a viper lying underfoot, and Vukrit moved instinctively backward, his spine against the ancient stone head.

"I know some stories of my own, minister. I know the trails you blazed through the jungle, I know the treasures you've sold in the Thieves Market and the man who paid your price. You cut Carlos out of his life, just as you cut this head from the wall of the cave we found together." Roderick held up the stone as though it were a sacred bond. "I will see Carlos avenged. As I avenged the boy."

"Boonreung was a traitor," Vukrit spat contemptuously, "and you're a *farang*. You backed the wrong horse. Pridi! My God, how it makes me laugh!"

"I back *all* the horses, Vukrit." Roderick's voice remained low and ruthless. "I back your boss, Field Marshal Pibul, and I back his chief rival, Sarit Thanarat. I've got money on the favorites, money on the long shots, I've got the bookies in my pocket and I'm even setting the odds.

You see, I'm the guy who's staging the race. The only horse not entered is yours."

"There you are, Jack," McQueen drawled through the darkness. His hair was in his eyes, his white scarf dangling over one shoulder, and on his arm was a woman. *Fleur.* Roderick's heartbeat quickened.

She had shed the martial uniform and the startling makeup and now wore a long, slim skirt made of silk he recognized immediately as having come from his own shop. She looked quite young—eighteen?— and the bones of her face were as delicate as porcelain. She raised her palms to him in reverence but he returned the gesture immediately, as though unworthy, his hands far higher.

"Yours is a beautiful home," she murmured.

Her voice was plangent and dark, the voice of a goddess and not a child.

"And yours, a beautiful dance."

Her eyes slid away in humility, but he saw that she was pleased. Vukrit seized her by the arm and muttered something swift and brutal in Thai. Roderick's expression changed as he understood the slur. He took a step forward and came up hard against Alec's restraining hand.

"What's your hurry, Minister?" McQueen asked Vukrit. "We're all old friends here. Or were you and Jack plotting coups together?"

"I plot nothing with this man." Vukrit spat deliberately into the gravel at Roderick's feet.

Alec's right hand tightened implacably against his chest and the left came up around Roderick's neck, as though he'd cheerfully strangle Jack rather than allow him to brawl in his own courtyard. "Steady," McQueen muttered. "Steady. There are reporters here."

Vukrit gripped the girl by the wrist and dragged her furiously toward the khlong gate. Fleur stumbled in the narrow skirt and high Western heels, and gasped a beseeching word of Thai. Vukrit did not turn his head.

"Poor kid'll pay for her kindness to *you* tonight," Alec told Jack quietly. "And she was a virgin when he bought her. Bastard brags about it."

A spurt of anguish tore through Roderick's gut. "How long?"

"—Has she been his mistress? Three months. Maybe less."

Shoulders nearly touching, they stood together in the fragrant shadows. McQueen offered him a cigar but Roderick refused it. The smell of khlongs in the dry season and burning tobacco mingled in a way that might almost be confused with incense. *Roderick the king.*

He had threatened a man and made him look foolish, then presumed to flirt with his toy. He'd given Vukrit an excuse for rape.

Cotton-mouthed and ashamed, he doused the torches.

18

Have you seen the papers?" Matthew French demanded over the phone on Thursday morning. "The press has been calling my office all morning. It has been *most* disruptive."

"Anything interesting?" Stefani retorted. "Exclusive interviews? Talk-show appearances?"

"I'm afraid the media spin is highly negative, Ms. Fogg." The lawyer sounded disapproving. "Your public display at the museum yesterday is regarded as a deliberate attempt to humiliate both the Minister of Culture and the Thai Heritage Board."

"Poor them," Stefani cooed.

There was the rustle of newsprint over the line.

"Sompong Suwannathat states unequivocally, in one of the Thai-language papers I wouldn't expect you to have seen, that your claim is 'a *farang* woman's brazen effort to exploit a national legend, and strip the Thai people of their priceless heritage.' "

"So Sompong owns more people in the press than he's sold out. Bravo for the minister. How do we save the situation? Publicly request a meeting with the museum's Board?"

"I would urge you to abandon the public assault and employ back channels."

"Such as?"

"Any that are available to you," French concluded. "For my part, I must refuse to act further on your behalf. Several clients informed me this morning that they are taking their business elsewhere. I can no longer afford to link my name to yours."

"I see why you're in Trusts and Estates, Mattie—a nice, comfortable branch of the law that'll never get your hands dirty." Acid words, but she felt an undeniable thrust of panic in the pit of her stomach.

"Trusts and Estates is what you said you needed," he shot back. "I have never claimed to be a celebrity publicist."

"Does Oliver know you're dumping me?"

"Mr. Krane was kind enough to support me wholeheartedly."

"When?" Stefani demanded. Oliver had dropped off the face of the earth. His private number—the discreet voice at Carlton Gardens—was disconnected. And he'd sent no reply to her e-mail inquiries.

"I received a severance wire from his account this morning."

Stefani swore under her breath. "Matthew—I need to reach Oliver. Can you put me in touch with him?"

"Unfortunately, no." French was smug. "He requested that I say nothing of his whereabouts—a simple request, as I never know where Oliver is."

The woman seated alone at the rickety table outside Jimmy Kwai's Guest Café was drinking a Michelob and toying with a tired plate of *pad thai*. They were always toying with *pad thai*, Jeff Knetsch thought; it was a backpacker staple on Khao San Road, like the cheese steaks and the soba noodles and the Oreo cookies imported and sold in the thousands to homesick Americans. But usually the women moved in twos or threes, if they weren't hooked up with a guy; women preferred the protection of numbers. It was a defense against muggings and pick-up lines and the sudden surrender of loneliness; and so Jeff decided the sole female next to him had left someone sleeping off a hangover in one of the seven-dollar-a-night guesthouses nearby.

She wore the woman backpacker's garb of choice: a featherweight sarong that limned her tanned legs, and a spaghetti-strapped camisole she could wash out in a basin. She was very blond, in the sun-damaged way that comes with excessive exposure; her cheekbones were raw and hungry and she'd spread glitter provocatively along her brow. A Californian on self-imposed exile? Or an Aussie touring the Pacific-rim world? As Jeff watched, she shoved the plate of noodles and the plastic fork to one side and leaned protectively over the paperback in her lap. He realized, with a faint buzz of anticipation, that she was conscious of him watching her.

"Food's pretty bad, isn't it?" he asked.

She glanced up. "Least it's cheap."

New Zealand, probably. Or south Australian. He wondered if the person she'd left behind was male or female, and whether she practiced massage or aromatherapy. Everyone who drifted through Khao San Road did one or the other. They also did Ecstasy and pot and psychedelic drugs, when they weren't toying with heroin; they traveled overland in the back of pickup trucks to Tibet and Bhutan; they danced to techno-rave for three days straight on the beaches of Ko Pha Ngan; and they all believed in a Universal Experience of Love and Peace, at least until their parents' money ran out.

After his chilling discussion with Sompong Suwannathat at the Peninsula Hotel the previous night, Knetsch had immediately checked out of his room and hopped a *tuk-tuk* to the warren of bars and cafés and Internet outlets on Khao San Road. He had been a gambler long enough to know when his luck had turned. His blood money was out of reach. He couldn't go home; he couldn't pay off the debts that were about to bury him alive. Sompong owned the city: Sompong would track him down.

Knetsch had landed on Khao San in the suit and tie he'd worn for the past two days, and booked a bed for ten bucks in a guesthouse whose name and location he promptly forgot. Somewhere around midnight he traded the suit for tie-dyed drawstring pants and a T-shirt with the words *Hard Rock Café, Reykjavik* emblazoned across the chest. He'd lost his loafers after a three A.M. rerun of *MI:2* and gave up his briefcase for a pair of Taiwanese Tevas. Khao San Road was lined with the refuse of lost backpackers' lives, all of it for barter or sale. Travel agencies offered cheap tickets on unknown airlines to obscure destinations. Tiny shops sandwiched between street vendors and tattoo parlors sold bedrolls and iodine tablets and pocketknives and Sony Walkmans. One of the shops bought his cell phone for a song. After that, he felt absurdly free, as though his last bond to life had been cut in two.

Amid the noise and neon it was harder to see the shadowy silhouette of the boy-specter who'd been following him through Bangkok. Knetsch still heard Max's voice, babbling inconsequentially about snowpack, time trials and the new race wax he could lend Jeff—but once Knetsch started singing Gilbert & Sullivan tunes, desperate and badly off-key, he hardly heard Max anymore.

The knowledge that he was hunted—by Sompong's people, by the boy-ghost—drove him relentlessly through the shops and arcades, as though he would not be found if he did not stop moving.

In the hours between five A.M. and noon, he ordered eggs and bacon, eggs and sausage, eggs and noodles. He talked to Israeli soldiers taking a break between compulsory service before hitting college in Tel Aviv; to Germans and Danes who thought they'd found paradise; to American Peace Corps volunteers returning to the United States from posts in Africa and New Guinea and Bucharest. And he drank a raft of beer. Beer was plentiful and cheap, like everything sold on Khao San Road. What started as a necessary sedative became, with time, a pleasant background buzz of befuddlement, but he could not screen out the thoughts of what he'd done and what might happen, the thoughts of what he meant to do.

The aromatherapist from New Zealand slapped her guide book closed and stood abruptly. She wore some kind of hill tribe fanny pack instead of a purse, and her bare arms were lean and muscled. Jeff stared at the woman—all rangy legs and sharp angles, the damaged ends of her hair—and felt a desperate impulse to save her.

"Come with me," he said urgently. "I'll get us a room at a nice hotel. We'll have dinner. Somewhere great. The Peninsula, maybe. Down by the waterfront. Have you even seen the river?"

The girl glanced at his tie-dyed pants and hopelessly dated T-shirt, his pale white toes in the knock-off Tevas. "Bother me again and I'll call the cops," she said.

By three in the afternoon he had drunk his final beer, paid his tab at Jimmy Kwai's and woven his way through the foreign tourists to the address he'd learned by heart.

It was a closet of a place, with a beaded curtain across the door and a sign written in five languages, offering Tarot card readings. Jeff slid through the swinging strings of beads and paused on the threshold as his eyes adjusted to the lack of light. A joss stick smoldered on a Buddhist altar in the far corner. The air was thick and warm as though someone, somewhere, was showering.

In such quiet, Max was sure to surface. Knetsch squeezed his eyes shut and began to sing. *Three little maids from school are we/Pert as a schoolgirl well can be . . .*

"May I help you?"

The Thai woman emerged from the gloom, thin and cramped in a long-sleeved shirt and cargo pants.

"I'm looking for Chanin."

Her expression of hostility deepened.

"Sompong sent me."

"You're drunk. I can smell the beer on you from here."

"I just ate lunch."

"Drank it, probably. I do not deal with *farang* drunkards. Neither does Chanin."

Jeff reached a hand to his brow; it was cold and clammy. What *was* the name of his guesthouse? He'd left his luggage there. His ticket home. Panic surged in his throat. *Filled to the brim with girlish glee . . .*

"I've got to see him. It's important. Sompong—"

"You use that name too freely." The woman's lips had tightened with anger. Behind her, a man's voice barked out a word of Thai. She glanced over her shoulder, then looked grudgingly back at Jeff.

"Chanin will see you now," she told him.

Dickie Spencer usually spent his days in the executive office of Jack Roderick Silk, which occupied the rear of the main store on Surawong Road. The building was only as old as Roderick's disappearance; Jack had opened the shop weeks before his fateful Easter holiday in March 1967, when the jungle highlands of Malaysia had swallowed him whole. But Spencer's realm was calculated to suggest the elegance of antiquity: paneled in carved teak, it was furnished with planters' chairs and vivid silks and clay urns tucked into niches in the walls.

When Stefani was shown into the room that afternoon, Spencer was bent over a drafting table—a tall, spare man with sandy hair and the mottled skin of an Englishman displaced to the tropics. He wore ivory flannel trousers, a silk shirt of the same shade and a cashmere jacket the hue of sandalwood. She expected his hand, when he offered it, to feel papery and dry, like the leaves of an old book; surprisingly, it was supple as doeskin. On the drafting table, under a light, were colored drawings of textile designs.

Spencer offered her one of the planters' chairs, which were backed with enormous silk cushions in carmine and chartreuse. She sank into it, feeling instantly disarmed by its slope and comfort and thus at a tactical disadvantage. This was a chair for drinking rum, not for negotiation. Spencer leaned against the drafting table and stared down at her, completely at ease.

"You're very kind to see me on such short notice," she said.

"I am," he agreed judiciously. "I'm usually far too busy to make room for heiresses, particularly pushy American ones. I understand you'd like to snatch the entire business out from under me—the factory, the silks, the old khlong house—lock, stock and priceless barrel. But you arrive without a black limo or a phalanx of lawyers. I am encouraged. More to the point, my next meeting is unaccountably delayed and my schedule, at loose ends. So here we are."

She smiled. "I haven't come for the keys to your empire. Nor to slap down an ultimatum. I want some information."

"About Jack Roderick? I never say a word. A legend deserves to be left . . . legendary."

"To be frank, I'm more interested in Sompong Suwannathat."

Wariness flickered across Spencer's features, and was immediately replaced by the blandest inquiry. "You mean the Minister of Culture?"

"The man who controls the Thai Heritage Board that governs the disposition of my house. I imagine he puts more than a finger into your business as well."

"My dear, I run a company that employs over one hundred thousand silk weavers and thirty textile designers. I export my goods worldwide. Sompong may like to offer advice from time to time, but he represents the public sector and I the private."

"Nothing's that clear-cut in Thailand. You grew up in Bangkok.

Your father worked for Jack Roderick, when Sompong Suwannathat was just a boy. You're embedded in this culture and your company couldn't survive without favors won, and favors bestowed. You must have a thousand reasons to respect—or hate—the minister."

Spencer quirked an eyebrow. "You're never subtle, are you, Ms. Fogg? I admit that personal and professional histories can become a bit tangled in Bangkok. But I'm too old a *farang* to be caught in my own snare."

"Mr. Spencer," she retorted bluntly, "I intend to win title to Jack Roderick's House. The process may require months. Or it may take decades. I may spend a fortune in legal costs. None of that matters. A man I loved died violently because he wanted that house. His grandfather had left it to him in his will. I intend to see that legacy placed in the proper hands."

Spencer's lips twitched. "You don't know Thailand at all, do you? Proper hands don't exist. They're all too busy grabbing what they can."

"I came here today to make a deal," she rejoined implacably. "*When* I am awarded the rights to Jack Roderick's House, I may do any number of things. I could auction the art collection at Sotheby's. I could use the place as a weekend retreat. Or I could turn it into a luxury inn and charge a fortune for a single night's stay."

"All of which would be a tragic waste," Spencer replied softly, "of a very great national treasure."

"I agree." She sat back and gazed up at him. "I might be prepared to consider, however, turning over the house, and the management of its collections, to a hand-picked team of curators and trustees. I'd prefer to see them handled by the same people who've safeguarded the Jack Roderick Silk Company all these years. People like you—and those you employ—have kept Roderick's legend alive. Not politicians or bureaucrats. Not Sompong Suwannathat."

"I see." Spencer met her eyes steadily. "May I thank you, Ms. Fogg, for that testimonial of faith. What you want is help in toppling Sompong's personal empire?"

"Got it in one."

For the space of heartbeats, he studied the dust motes trapped in a band of sunlight that divided the room between them. He said finally, "I only heard about the will a few months ago. The second will, I mean. I had often wondered where it was. I was asked to witness it, you see, along with my father, five or six weeks before Jack disappeared. And then no mention of it was ever made again."

"I saw your signature on the document. Roderick placed the will between the pages of some blueprints and sent them off to his sister. The will went undiscovered for over thirty years."

"How terribly sad to think that no one bothered to study those blueprints. Jack was such a superb draftsman. These are some of his designs, you know. He had a flawless sense of color."

Spencer handed her the sketches of fabric she had glimpsed on the drafting table. An intricate damask of blue and green, fluid as the sky where it meets spring grass; a plaid of cherry red and mango yellow that sprang off the page. A strong, light hand had penned one word in the lower corner: *Roderick*. She traced the name with her fingertip, and longed for Max.

"You realize the risks in what you ask of me, Ms. Fogg? Or are you just terribly naïve?"

"Both. But no one speaks of Sompong Suwannathat without adding that he's dangerous—*a man to respect,* they say. That kind of man always has enemies, Mr. Spencer. I intend to befriend Sompong's enemies."

"How very Thai of you. I think you should call me Dickie."

Surprised, Stefani laughed out loud. "Very well. Tell me, Dickie— why did Jack write a new will five weeks before he disappeared?"

"Because Jack was an old man. He was worried about his son and he wanted, at the end, to give him all the things he'd failed to offer during the boy's life. You know about Rory?"

"—And the Hanoi Hilton? A little. My friend Max—from whom I inherit the house—was Rory's only child."

"Ah." Spencer rubbed at his eyes as though they pained him. "The Vietnam War did terrible things to Jack Roderick. It seemed to place in question the value of his whole life in Asia."

Stefani waited in silence for him to explain.

"Jack had this vision of what Thailand could be, when he arrived here after the Second World War. But the years Jack spent here— perhaps even the work he did?—resulted in a different sort of country than he'd hoped." Spencer shrugged. "He hated the new roads and the filled khlongs and the sex workers and the ugly, slapdash concrete skyscrapers. By the time he disappeared, he no longer seemed to enjoy the things he'd always loved—the silk weavers' homes in Ban Khrua, the dealers in the Thieves Market. Perhaps he was merely tired."

"You blame the war. Did Jack?"

"I don't know," Spencer mused. "My father told me that Jack didn't support the American engagement in Southeast Asia. For the first time in his life, Jack Roderick was at odds with the country he'd always served."

"Meaning the United States? Or Thailand?"

"Hard to separate the two. They were hand-in-glove during the Vietnam War. It was one of the best periods in history for Thai-U.S. relations. Washington needed a friendly staging ground for troops; Thailand needed support in the region—everyone else in Southeast Asia was battling Communist insurgencies or revolution or both. It was a marriage of convenience between two strangers marooned on an island."

"How old were you in 1967?" she asked impulsively.

"I had my sixteenth birthday three weeks after Jack disappeared."

"And people knew that Jack was a spy?"

"We preferred, in our family, to call him an intelligence operative," Spencer answered. "A spy might be anything—a man without honor, telling tales to the highest bidder. Jack Roderick had integrity. Perhaps that's why he said: *No more.*"

"Max was convinced that his grandfather died because he opposed the Vietnam War."

"Eliminated by right-thinkers on one side or the other?" Spencer shook his head. "I don't believe anyone killed Jack. I suspect he set about quite purposefully to drop off the face of the earth—and from the look of things, he succeeded."

Stefani stared at him wordlessly.

"No one believes me, Ms. Fogg." His smile was disarming. "No one agrees. It's far too simple a solution, you see. But consider the money. Consider Fleur."

"Fleur?" she repeated, bewildered.

"Fleur Pithuvanuk. Jack's once-and-forever mistress, an exquisite dancer of *lakhon*. She was decades younger than he and they'd drifted apart toward the end of his life, but she reappeared a few weeks before Jack left for Malaysia. I think Fleur's the reason Jack went."

"I've never heard her name before."

"Fleur is the key to everything." Spencer said it softly. "She was another man's mistress before she was Jack's. Jack lured her away from Vukrit Suwannathat, Sompong's father. Blood was bad between Roderick and Vukrit, from that time forward."

Stefani remembered something Rush Halliwell had said. "Sompong's father was Minister of Culture once, too."

"It's a family sinecure."

"Dickie—do you think Vukrit hated Roderick enough, because of Fleur, to kill him in the Cameron Highlands?"

"I think Vukrit hated Jack so much he could have killed him with his bare hands. But Vukrit was investigated thoroughly—if not by his pals in the Thai government, then by the U.S. team that tracked the Roderick case. Jack's family was persistent. Vukrit was never accused."

"But why should Jack just . . . vanish? Without explaining where he went?"

"Perhaps he didn't want to be found," Spencer suggested. "Look— two days before Jack left for Malaysia, he took me aside in this very room. He put a sealed envelope and a briefcase in my hand. *Dickie,* he said, *I need you to run an errand. Go to the bank and give that letter to the manager. Then do as he tells you. Come straight back here and don't talk to anyone along the way.*"

"What was in the briefcase?" she asked.

"Nothing at all. I could tell by the weight that it was empty. I didn't question the fact, or read the sealed letter. I ran errands for Jack quite often—it was one way to learn the business. I went to the bank in a hired *tuk-tuk* and I remember every meter of the journey. It was beastly hot and the fumes from the traffic were stifling. I thought I should never arrive."

He paused, and peered at her soberly. "I can recall almost nothing of the trip back. I was in shock. I had never held so much money in a black bag in my life. That letter I gave the manager must have cleaned out the entire Roderick account."

"Jack used the funds to start a new life?"

"He'd written his will, leaving everything else to his heirs. He couldn't help his son Rory, trapped in the Hanoi Hilton. And he'd grown mortally tired of Bangkok. Jack cut his losses and got out."

"Did this Fleur woman disappear, too?"

"On Good Friday, Jack took Fleur and that briefcase full of cash to the Cameron Highlands. On Sunday night, he disappeared. But for some reason, Fleur stayed behind. She never explained why."

"You spoke to her?"

"The entire world spoke to her." Spencer sounded amused. "She'd been privy to one of the most spectacular vanishing acts in history. *The New York Times* sent their Bangkok stringer, the Agence France-Press, UPI, even the *Bangkok Post*."

"What did she say?"

"She insisted that Jack had got lost in the jungle. And in a sense, of course, he had—with over a million dollars in U.S. currency. We should all be so lucky."

There was a knock at the office door. "Sorry, Dickie," Spencer's assistant said, "but the woman from the museum has finally arrived. She's brought a rather large portfolio, so I've put her in the conference room."

"Very well," Spencer replied. "I've enjoyed our discussion, Ms. Fogg. But I'm afraid—"

Stefani's farewell was drowned in a gushing British voice.

"Dickie, *darling*, it's so *fabulous* to see you again! I couldn't *wait* to get out of London—you know how dreary it always is in October. How is your delicious place in the suburbs? Is the houseboy still pining for me? Shall I come to dinner tonight?"

There could be only one woman with that peculiar combination of familiarity and affront.

"Ankana." Stefani turned toward the door. "Ankana Lee-Harris. What are you doing in Bangkok?"

"I might ask the same of you—if I hadn't seen the morning papers!" The woman held her arms wide. "*Dearest* Stefani. So tragic about Max. I cried *buckets* when I heard. Of course, his life was over—no skiing, no sex, no fun in a wheelchair, one could hardly expect him to put up with it. We must accept that he died as he lived—mustn't we? And move on?"

Spencer looked from Stefani to Ankana. "You two know each other."

Ankana slid her manicured fingers along Spencer's sleeve. "Ummm. That cashmere's perfectly yummy, Dickie, but then so's the arm beneath it. Ready to talk? Or should we relax a bit, first?"

"Talk," he said firmly. "In the conference room. You were expected an hour ago."

Roguishly, she laughed. "I'm worth the wait! You'll love the things I've brought—I had to sell my very soul to get them."

"Ankana and I are coordinating on the big Met show that opens in a month," Spencer explained to Stefani. "Two Thousand Years of Southeast Asian Art. A fortune in sculpture and ceramics will soon be winging its way to New York."

"From Roderick's House?" Stefani turned to Ankana. "And the Hughes Museum?"

"Of course," she replied. "Nothing *we've* got can touch Jack Roderick's treasures. You're so right to want the collection for your greedy little self—God knows *I* would. Have you any idea what it's *worth*?" Malice gleamed in the woman's sloe eyes. "I couldn't *believe* Max left you a fortune like that. 'Must be a pretty fabulous lay,' I told Jeff, 'if he turned over the kit and caboodle for a mere week of her life! He might have left *me* his wine cellar, at least.'"

"I'll send you a bottle," Stefani said smoothly. "So you've talked to Knetsch recently?"

"Yesterday. Jeff's in Bangkok, too."

And Oliver Krane had dropped out of sight. What had she called her precarious position? A highwire act, with no safety net? "I thought Knetsch was in France."

"That was *last* week. As a trustee of the Met, Jeff's got to meet with the Ministry of Culture. It's a busy time for them, between our show and your grab for Jack Roderick's House—but they seem to manage. They've got a crackerjack chief, you know. Sompong's hand is in every pie."

Ankana smiled broadly, and in that moment a series of pennies dropped somewhere in Stefani's mind.

Jeff Knetsch was acquainted with Sompong. Jeff Knetsch, Max's personal attorney and closest friend. According to Oliver, Knetsch had serious financial problems—and Suwannathat could help.

"Jeff informed on Max," she said aloud. "He kept tabs on Max's private life, his movements, his legal problems, his dreams—and sold what he knew to Max's worst enemy."

Ankana shrugged. "Darling, we've all got to survive. We prostitute ourselves in various ways. I wouldn't throw stones, if I were you."

19

**Bangkok,
1954**

No one in Bangkok—not even Alec McQueen—understood how much of a slave Roderick was to dance.

He guarded the secret as one might a sexual perversion; but this man of cunning and solitude could trace the growth of his obsession through the high-water marks of his past life, knew the wrack it had left in heaps on his personal shore. It had begun when he was a boy, on a trip to Paris with his wealthy and cultured family—Jack at eight, all knees and knickerbockers, as his indulgent papa might have said. *L'Après-midi d'un Faune,* perhaps, or *Rite of Spring*—something pulsing and savage by Diaghilev. He'd sat on the edge of his Louis XVI chair, chin perched on his hands as he peered over the edge of the theater box, and after three hours of tumult and color, he was never the same.

It was the sets, mostly—blocks of vivid paint, abandoned in feeling and beyond the bounds of classic restraint—that moved him as a boy. Later he understood that the shifting screens and monumental objects were mere expressions of something deeper: the violence of a dancer's heart. He begged his mother to take him to the ballet during his vacations from St. Paul's. He never spoke of these visits once he returned to school.

At Princeton he scanned the papers for notices of traveling troupes, and bought furtive tickets as another man might visit a bordello. And at last, a thirty-year-old Manhattan bachelor, he took what funds he had and threw them into the Monte Carlo Ballet, George Balanchine's experiment in the grand tradition of Diaghilev.

It was there that Roderick met Joan—on her hands and knees with a paintbrush between her teeth.

She was thirteen years younger than he, a *debutante manqué* with a piquant face and prominent collarbones. Her father had lost his fortune in the Crash of '29; her mother was delicately described as "indisposed," and resided in an institution somewhere in Poughkeepsie. Joan was an only child, headstrong and outrageously indulged; a product of serial governesses and despairing finishing schools and protracted transatlantic tours. She possessed one talent—the ability to cover large surfaces with brilliant color—an eye for form, and the desire to provoke.

Her outfits were pastiches of old treasures and designer castoffs. Her body was careless and perfect and could bring a man to his knees. She laughed a great deal, at her own jokes and sometimes at others'. She could talk earnestly and drunkenly in smoky rooms until three in the morning, on behalf of social justice; and when Roderick met her he thought that they were driven by the same things: a repugnance for frivolity, a respect for art and truth. For Joan he abandoned Republicanism and took up with Democrats. As Roosevelt was then in power, a Brahmin like himself, this was no very great leap; but the conversion made him feel dangerously independent. He brought Joan home to meet his family in Delaware, and though he reveled in her cheeky looks and untamed views, he was vaguely reassured that she understood the use of fish knives and iced teaspoons.

They were married four months later.

He wanted to give her everything: clothes as bright as plumage, a studio that faced north. He sold his interest in the Monte Carlo Ballet and dedicated himself to architecture. Joan abandoned her set-painting job and dabbled in oils. The two of them sailed firmly out into the sea of Society in which they had both been launched, years before, and found the water not nearly so cold as they remembered.

It was only in the midst of his son Rory's third birthday, in 1939—a chance expression intercepted, a hand lingering too long—that Roderick understood. Joan required a full house for each of her performances, and she was cultivating a new leading man. Roderick was surrounded by props and scrims and bit players he hadn't hired, a character always on the point of exiting. He found it a relief when the Japanese finally bombed Pearl Harbor.

Another high-water mark in Roderick's life, etched in torchlight on the back terrace: the night he first saw Fleur Pithuvanuk dance.

There was nothing in the movements of *lakhon* to suggest Diaghilev; no echo of drums that conjured Debussy. A feral pulse, all the same. Roderick watched with his back to the wall and his cigarette burning between his fingers. Fleur turned, her arms outstretched in an attitude of war. The branching flames flickered. Fleur shuddered, her eyes lost and swooning; and his heart rose wildly in his chest.

He employed all the tradecraft he had ever learned, by art or instinct, in stalking her.

There were the casual comments to friends and acquaintances, when they chanced to thank him for the evening's entertainment: *Yes, those Thai girls are really quite good. They should get more support from the foreign community than they do. I'm thinking of speaking to the ambassador about it.* There were the subtle hints to one of Alec's reporters that he might consider donating silk to the *lakhon* production company. And when he chanced to learn that the latest American ambassador had a daughter who loved ballet, there was the utterly spontaneous proposal of a cross-cultural festival of dance, under the auspices of the embassy and Jack Roderick Silk.

Philanthropy gave him cover. Philanthropy allowed him to observe Fleur's *lakhon* troupe, in its severe rehearsals, for six weeks; and to shower the dancers with attention and flowers. Philanthropy gave him access to Fleur herself, and hours in which to memorize the line of her back, the tilt of her chin, the precise length of her smallest finger as it curled upward toward her wrist. She was lovely, ethereal and heartbreakingly sad, like a bird dying for lack of flight. With his palm clutched in the hand of the ambassador's little girl, Roderick watched Fleur sway. And contemplated the ruin of Vukrit Suwannathat.

*   *   *

She came to him on a night of torrential rain, two days before the cross-cultural festival was scheduled to close, and stood under the shelter of his house with her feet in the floodwaters of the khlong.

"Fleur," he said, from the pool of light at the top of the stairs. "What is it?"

Her black hair streamed and her eyes were blank with terror; her lip torn where Vukrit had struck her. She had taken a bus and then walked through the flooded streets.

"His wife. A terrible scene. I could not bear to stay, but when I tried to go he struck me in the face. I hate him, Jack."

It was the first time she had ever said his name. He went slowly down the steps, careful not to touch her. But she reached out a hand and placed it on his shoulder, as if they might waltz together beneath the soaring house; and though the monsoon air was heavy and warm, she trembled uncontrollably. He should have been warned.

"Your lip," he said. "It's bleeding."

"I do not feel it."

He fetched her towels and a robe and as she changed her clothes he warmed sake over an open flame. The rain beat upon his red-tiled roof as though it were a boat battened down at harbor; the floor beneath his feet rocked and swam. He set down the sake and drew a steadying breath. He was forty-nine years old. He assumed she was not yet twenty.

When he looked up, Fleur sat with her face toward the old brick terrace, watching the palm fronds whip in the storm. He crossed the room and proffered the sake.

"Is there somewhere I could take you? A friend's house, perhaps?"

Her head turned in alarm.

"Urana—what about Urana?" he asked.

Urana was the mistress of *lakhon*, a tight-lipped and exacting woman.

"She will call Vukrit," Fleur whispered, "and make me go back. Our troupe depends upon the Ministry of Culture."

He understood, then—the practiced abuse of power. Vukrit held one string of his government's purse. The minister chose where to place the funds at his disposal. And in return, Urana was willing to act as pimp. There were other *lakhon* troupes for Vukrit to support; but as long as Fleur was available to the minister, Vukrit would support

Urana's. It was a classic business exchange in a land where everyone—
everyone, Roderick thought—had something to sell.

"He would never come here. It is the one house he fears to enter. He
told me so himself. He hates you, Jack, as much as I hate him."

He should have been warned.

But instead he touched her lip where the blood had dried. She
closed her eyes and curled her cheek into his palm.

"You'll have to go back."

"Not for hours and hours," she said dreamily. "Perhaps never."

It was a lie, of course. At the time, he believed lies would be enough.

20

Sompong Suwannathat intended to wait for darkness before he returned to the airport and his ministry plane.

In the hours of sunlight that remained, Wu Fat put the men through their drills and set up target practice and offered Sompong a young Akha girl after their lunch of roasted kid.

As night fell he visited the General's shrine. It sat on a slight rise near a trickling stream, and prayer scarves hung from the nearby trees, saffron and scarlet. Sompong thought of the ashes melting deep into the alkaline soil. He thought of a gun butt, warm in his hand on that night fifteen years before. Then he tossed his cigarette aside and whistled for Wu Fat.

The six men wore Royal Thai Army uniforms Sompong had borrowed from a friend at Defense. Wu Fat had a colonel's stripes. The uniformed men fell into correct military line near the baggage hold, swinging the heroin sacks hand over hand from the Jeep into the plane. Wu Fat directed them and inspected each wooden crate of missiles and grenade launchers himself. The whole operation required only eighteen minutes, which was five minutes less than the first time they had done it.

"I will return soon," Sompong told Wu Fat. "Tomorrow night or perhaps Saturday morning. Prepare the hut for trial."

He saluted on the tarmac. Wu Fat raised his right hand and offered a blessing in Chinese. The plane's engines roared and the men dropped backward into darkness.

Twenty-three minutes after takeoff, Sompong drew a report out of his briefcase and found the page where he'd stopped reading that morning.

Her hallmark is a short attention span. She's intrigued with Max Roderick's legacy in about the same measure as she was intrigued with Roderick himself. Give her a few weeks. She'll move on.

"You're slipping, Mr. Krane," he said softly into the shadows. "I never give a woman more time."

The hollow-eyed man in the Hard Rock T-shirt and the drawstring pants was staggering slightly as night began to fall on Khao San Road. He had not slept in thirty-six hours, he was jet-lagged and giddy on cheap beer, but his singing head kept terror at bay as long as the daylight remained.

There's a fascination frantic, in a ruin that's romantic; do you think you are sufficiently decayed? Lines from *The Mikado*, executed in falsetto. There was another phrase Jeff Knetsch was searching for—the name of the operetta he could not remember: something about black dogs howling at the moon, and the ghosts' high noon.

The ghosts' high noon.

He came to rest by a public telephone kiosk, and fished aimlessly in his trouser pockets for a coin that might work in the machine. He could not find one.

Was it envy, he wondered, of a life whose high points he'd never quite equaled? No, envy was too petty an emotion to warrant the absolute destruction of a man he'd loved. As he leaned against the booth in the fading heat of a tropic day, he remembered himself, suddenly, at the age of thirteen, teeth chattering with fear as he stared down the racecourse from the starting gate. The ice, perhaps, had shaken him— or was it the brutal falls of three previous competitors, one of them carried screaming off the course? Max at his elbow, impatient, incredulous. "The clock's running! The buzzer sounded! *Get off your ass, Knetsch!*" He was still not sure whether Max pushed him, in the end.

Max lived without hesitation. He never second-guessed. Knetsch controlled for every possible variable and only then moved forward. And he had risked too little. Until the final gamble: Sompong's money on the table, his dearest friend's life on the line.

There was a shadow lurking beyond the corner of his eye, a shadow that vanished the instant he turned to stare. *Go away,* he pleaded, and heard a child's shrill voice. Accusing him of something.

What he needed was a drink. His hands were shaking and darkness was falling. Darkness cut both ways—it hid the predators as well as their prey.

As he worked his way among the plastic chairs and metal tables of Joe's Fish & Chip, it happened: a burly Asian with sleek black hair and dark glasses clipped his shoulder clumsily. The lawyer fell backward against a table, caught in the grip of claustrophobia so intense it bordered on panic. The Asian steadied himself with a hand at Jeff's hip, and muttered some words in Thai. A second later he was gone.

Jeff sucked in a shallow breath, sweat beading his forehead. The crush of bodies, the constant noise of *tuk-tuk* engines—he groped for a vacant seat at a table already occupied by two boys and sank into it.

He was nursing his ninth beer of the day when the shadow at the corner of his eye materialized.

Solid, immovable, blocking his view of the street. The boys sitting opposite—two Germans on holiday—looked alarmed.

"Are you Jeffrey Knetsch?"

"I used to be."

A gloved hand descended upon his arm. The police officer should have smiled at him, Jeff thought—he was, after all, an American. The two Germans pushed back their chairs. Jeff stumbled to his feet.

"Is there something wrong?"

"You're under arrest."

"For having a drink?"

Like a conjurer, the officer pulled a small plastic bag of white powder from Jeff's hip pocket. "Heroin possession. Please—come with me."

The main corridor of the Garden Wing was always empty, despite the fact that at least twenty guest rooms lined the hallway and each had a butler dancing attendance. They danced, Stefani presumed, well out of sight; and the guests themselves were too busy to spend much time in transit from elevator to luxury suite.

It was the dinner hour at the Oriental, but Stefani intended to order room service. She needed quiet and privacy. Her visit to Spencer's office that afternoon had given her too much to consider. She knew, now, that Sompong Suwannathat had run two agents in Courchevel the previous March: Jeff Knetsch and Ankana Lee-Harris. Either might easily have sabotaged Max's skis and caused his crippling fall. Knetsch had been in France again when Max died. And now both Ankana and Knetsch had arrived in Bangkok—to watch her claim Max's inheritance?

The battle lines had shifted. Yesterday she'd assumed she was in charge of this campaign—but Sompong had anticipated and outmaneuvered her. She could feel him at work in Jo-Jo's shadow, behind Ankana's shrewd eyes; she could sense his malevolence as she had once glimpsed, fleetingly, the man's profile in the depths of his limousine. She would have to step lightly if his net was not to close upon her.

Where the hell is Oliver Krane? Rush Halliwell had been right to warn her. She needed to watch her back.

She thrust her key into the door. As it swung open, a hand closed around her neck like a vise. The room was plunged into complete darkness.

The iron hand at her neck dragged her across the threshold; the door slammed shut. Wildly, she swung out as a second hand gripped her hair, forcing her head back. There was no sound but the tearing gasp of her breath. From the power of the gloved hand and the thickness of the fingers, she guessed her attacker was male. She scrabbled at the wrist nearest her throat, nails clawing.

Useless. She couldn't breathe. There was a soft metallic click—a sound she recognized sickeningly—and she knew instantly how it would be: the switchblade unerring through the darkness, the spurt of blood bubbling at her neck. Over in a matter of seconds.

She reached back with both hands, gripped the man's shoulders, then bent double with such sudden force that her assailant was thrown off balance. He flipped over her head, landing heavily on his back. Something skittered over the carpet—the switchblade, with any luck. Stefani lunged for the man's chest, her hands driving for his throat. The

C-clamp Oliver had taught her: shove inward, upward against the Adam's apple. The black-clad Ken doll shrieked. She had to silence the alarm. *She had to turn it off—*

His windpipe moved beneath her fingers, then collapsed like a soft-boiled egg. The man gave one choking sigh and lay lifeless on the floor.

Gulping air, Stefani scrambled to her feet. Her hand jabbed at the lights.

He lay face upward, a woman's stocking grotesquely flattening his features. In that instant she knew.

She had expected Jo-Jo. This man was a stranger.

21

Chiang Rai Province,
1955

Jack Roderick had been on the road for the first three weeks of June 1955. He'd lurched in a borrowed Jeep over the dirt tracks of Khorat and up into the mountains of Laos. Everywhere he saw the poverty and hardscrabble existence of the Asian countryside, but on this trip—his first in months—there was a new and more sinister presence: guns. Boys as young as ten carried rifles jauntily on their backs; they fired bullets at makeshift targets the way they had once lobbed stones at the river. When Roderick tried to learn where the weapons came from, he got vague or mendacious answers. The boys clutched at his hands, pleading for coins, but they told him lies.

He guessed the guns filtered down from China—the cast-off treasures of Mao's victorious troops, bartered for bread. Why did the hill-country boys want weapons? Who was the enemy, and who the friend? Disquiet soured in him like an ulcer as the Jeep lurched on.

He broke his trip in Vientiane, talking to laconic men assembled in the back rooms of shops that had closed for the night. There was his old friend Tao Oum and others like him, their ageless hostility toward the French overlords of l'Indochine fueled now by a new religion—Mao's Communist text had spread like the guns. The Laotians, too, had revolvers they wore near their hearts and concealed under their bamboo mats at night. He promised the friendship of President Eisenhower and the prosperity of free trade; promises as old as Roosevelt and Truman, promises that were as arid as the borderlands of Khorat.

"We need antiaircraft guns," Tao Oum told him. "We need Washington's assurance that America will not intervene in our fight for independence from France."

Roderick listened uneasily and remembered Eisenhower's command of the Allied landings on French beaches in '44. He could not say the words Tao Oum hoped to hear.

He began to have the sort of nightmares he'd suffered only once before in his life, during July and August 1945, in Ceylon. Roderick, walking alone through the densest jungle, snipers training their sights from the trees. But a decade had passed since his OSS days and the conflict in Korea had ended in stalemate and Ike was now playing golf on the greenest fairways in the free world. What could possibly go wrong?

One night in Laos, he woke in the grip of a scream, dressed hurriedly in the dark and turned his car toward the Thai border.

He could have gone on into Burma and taken soundings in Rangoon. He could have prolonged the moment of reckoning. But he had grown bone weary of guns and death and pointless conversations. He felt heartsick and old. He missed his home and the weavers who bowed to Mecca across the khlong and the way the wind tossed handfuls of rain on the old brick terrace. It was time to make his final call.

The road into Thailand was unguarded. No one in Bangkok cared very much about the Far North, the Golden Triangle, where the hill tribes mingled freely with wild bands of Chinese soldiers who had once fought against Mao. The Far North was a place of exile, ungoverned and crude, and yet almost a kind of Eden. There were teaks with massive trunks, and higher against the backbone of the hills, rainforest conifers rose black and silent. The lush growth was alive with insects and vermin. Snakes and glorious birds tangled along the riverbanks. The soil was little good for farming—but opium poppies had thrived there for nearly a century, and they danced like butterflies over the terraced fields. Along the flower beds, more men with guns patrolled.

He entered Sop Ruak just as the sun rose. The town was a collection of hovels that had existed from time immemorial. The people were a blend of Lao and Burmese and Thai Lue hill tribe; lately something of the Chinese lurked in the children's faces. As the Jeep creaked to a halt on the settlement's edge, Roderick saw the doors of the houses were already flung open, and a clutch of women half-knelt, half-lay in the dust of the main street, keening hopelessly over the fallen bodies of their men. Flames seared through the roof of one hut. A baby girl toddled unsteadily down the street, screaming in terror. Her hair was on fire.

Roderick seized his suit jacket, leapt out of the car and beat at the flames with the fabric. He was panting with fear and horror and bitterness, the child rolling at his feet, no longer screaming. A woman clutched his arm, shrieking pleas he did not understand, and when he stepped back she curled over her baby, wailing.

The steel orb of the rifle's mouth nipped at the skin below his skull, where the cords of his neck met the spine. He stiffened, gulped for air, then raised his arms.

"You cannot walk like a prince into the hills of Chiang Rai," a voice said softly in English, "whatever you may risk in Bangkok, my friend."

Roderick closed his eyes and said: *"Carlos."*

"They come across the river from Burma near the town of Fang, or perhaps Mae Sai. Bandits and renegades, ruled by one leader. The point of entry varies, depending upon the season; but it seems that whichever fording place we patrol, they find another."

"What's their reason?" Roderick asked. "Plunder?"

Carlos shrugged. "They want the poppy fields that belong to my men. I refuse to give them up. And so the fields burn at night and the scent of opium drifts across the hills on the smoke, and good men die for bad reasons."

"Burmese?"

"National borders mean nothing in this part of the world." Carlos studied him grimly. "The opium wars between Burma and the Chinese—and my men are nearly all Chinese—are of ancient origin. You might credit the British, who fostered the trade and farmed it out all over their empire, if you were prone to blame only white men for Asian troubles; or you might credit instead the overlords of Burma and Thailand, who starve their peasants. Whatever the cause, we live with fire and bloodshed in the night. Guns and vigilance are a fact of northern existence."

"But you, Carlos?"

He shrugged again, his canny eyes half-lidded. They had hunkered down near the river two miles out of town, in the shade of a teakwood tree, to trade stories and eat longan fruit. "My fate turned on a gun, Jack, as you may recall."

As if the murder of King Ananda had been yesterday, Roderick saw a younger Carlos standing dazed, a pistol in his hand. The elderly nurse screaming. Ananda's face turned toward the open window. The neat round hole, and the welter of blood. Nearly ten years ago.

"You were never just a victim of circumstance, Carlos."

"No?" He reached for one of Roderick's cigarettes. "What do you hear of Ruth? Does he carry on the fight?"

"I hear that Pridi Banomyong has traded his soul for a Mao jacket. He sits in a place of honor in Peking."

"Then you hear lies." Carlos spat into the dust. "It is good to see you, *farang*. I had forgot that men dressed like that, in places like these."

Roderick smiled, the first grin he'd managed in days. Carlos was dressed in the faded garb of a Kuomintang soldier, distinguished by a general's stripes. Roderick's silk suit jacket was burnt in several places and stank to high heaven. He rolled it in a ball and handed it to Carlos. "Be my guest."

"With thanks," he said gravely, and placed it in his pack. "My wife can do anything with a needle. And the boy is always growing."

"How is Chao?" Roderick asked. *Chao*. The Thai word for *river*. She had been a charming woman when he'd last seen her, in 1948—as fragile as blown glass, with a cunning mind that had made her indispensable to the Free Thai during the war. Boonreung's final journey in Roderick's service—the last before the failed '49 coup and the boy's execution—had been to smuggle Carlos's family into the north.

"Chao endures, like the waters after which she is named."

"You were always a poet."

"But no longer." The General buckled the straps of his pack and rose. "We shall have to build funeral pyres for those men before nightfall. It is required of our honor."

"You run this village, Carlos."

"Much worse, *farang*. The peasants think I'm a god."

*   *   *

It had been no exaggeration, Roderick thought ten minutes later as he watched Carlos enter his camp. A crowd of men, some grizzled and some mere boys, came to attention as the General approached. Three Burmese raiders had been captured during the night; the trio were gagged and tied to posts thrust into the dirt a hundred feet from the door of Carlos's bungalow. Chao stood in the doorway, her arm resting on the shoulders of a young boy; at the sight of Roderick her once beautiful face lit up with joy. Then she glanced at the three captives, and all expression was extinguished. She turned back into the house, her son herded in front of her.

Carlos barked a question in what Roderick guessed was pidgin Chinese. A soldier on guard near the prison posts shouted a reply.

"They've been tried and found guilty of murder," Carlos told him casually. "We'll carry out the sentence in due course. But first, a real breakfast! You will eat with us, of course."

Roderick felt his skin prickle where Carlos's rifle had rested earlier, inches below his brain. A hearty meal before the execution. And the boy within earshot. He thought of his own son—of the Rory who was nearly eighteen. Then he followed Carlos into the bungalow without a word.

Chao sank to her knees before him, her palms lifted high in the ceremonial *wei*. There were tears on her sunken cheeks. He bowed in return. She dissolved in a deep and painful coughing.

"We have rice and fruit and a fish done over charcoal," Carlos said. "And while we eat, you will tell us all the news, Roderick."

"You know the news before I do."

"Informants, Jack. They will save us both, one day."

"Or murder us in our sleep."

Carlos did not reply. He motioned him to a chair, then sat in one himself; the boy had disappeared into the loft above, and could be heard singing to himself as he played. But Chao, before she turned back to the brazier and the earthenware bowls, said, "Jack—"

"Yes, oh river goddess?"

She bowed her head. "I wondered . . . You must know the minister, Vukrit Suwannathat."

"The only minister who matters."

"He is married to my sister, Li-ang. I have had no word from her in more than two years, and I thought—"

"Your sister has forgotten you," the General broke in harshly. "Her husband makes sure of that. You are dead to Li-ang, Chao. She should be dead to you also."

"I believe," Roderick interposed quietly, "that Madame Suwannathat has lost her husband's favor. She has left Bangkok, and lives in a family villa on the coast near Pattaya."

"My parents' house," Chao murmured, "where we stayed as girls. Li-ang must be happy if she has returned to that place! Did Vukrit shame her?"

"Vukrit shames himself."

Chao glanced around the hut. "There are some who would find my present life an embarrassment. But I have been happy here. Carlos is a good man."

"I know that, Chao. I will learn what I can of your sister, and send you news."

She bowed again, and busied herself over her fire.

"I do glean some information about Bangkok now and again." Carlos pried the cap from a beer bottle with the blade of his knife. "I hear that Vukrit is more entrenched than ever. That the Pibul government will never fall. That the powers of the West shall feel the anger of Indochina, and die upon their swords."

"That is Communist propaganda."

"It is also truth. This part of the world is like a paddy that is drained and baking in the sun. It is ready to burn at the slightest spark." He drank deep of the warm beer and brushed his hand across his mouth. Carlos's hand, Roderick thought, had changed as much as his uniform. It was brown and hard and had the permanent stain of gun-barrel grease embedded under each fingernail. "But I remain loyal to the West, Jack, and so do my men. They are Chinese Nationalists who hate Mao and all his works. They have sworn a blood vengeance. When the time comes, they will know how to fight—and upon which side."

"I believe you."

Carlos offered him the bottle. Roderick sipped and felt the bitter aftertaste. Chao placed a platter of fruit and seared fish upon the table, and his appetite unexpectedly surged, despite the three Burmese prisoners strapped like sides of beef to the posts outside the threshold.

"I also hear," Carlos continued, "that Roderick no longer sleeps alone. A dancer, they say, as lovely as jasmine flowers that bloom in the night. Are you happy?"

"A man who loves is never happy, Carlos."

"No. Love blinds our reason. It brings death into the house. You are rarely stupid, Jack—only once that I can think of, when you gave your hand to Vukrit Suwannathat long ago, on the Western Coast."

"He sank in his fangs, my friend."

"And yet you take his Flower into your bed. Are you insane? Have you not considered what use he finds for her there? Do you choose this wound so willingly, Jack, that you thrust in the knife yourself?"

Roderick flinched and closed his eyes. Immediately she was there: black hair gleaming in the moonlight, dressing gown trailing. With his sleepy gaze he followed the curve of her back, outlined in silk, and the movements of her hands. She was a dancer in this, as in everything. They had made love and fallen together into sleep: he had awakened before dawn to find her sifting through his private papers. What risks she had taken—

What was she searching for? What did she need? The price of her freedom from both of them—Vukrit and Jack alike?

"I am a fool, my friend." He said it wearily.

"You must be indeed, to ignore so fine a breakfast," Carlos returned. "Now it is time for the execution. Come, Jack!"

When it was done, and the Burmese pirates lay like crumpled clothes in the dust of the camp, Roderick made his farewells.

"You did not meet my son," Chao said, as he bowed to her. She coughed into her hand and turned away. "I am sick, Roderick. I have not much time left."

He looked at the faded woman who had been named for a river, and said, "You will live as long as the Chao Phraya itself."

"Do not lie," she replied brusquely. "You saved my husband's life— and saved me an eternity of loneliness. But I must ask one more favor."

Her dark eyes burned fiercely in her wasted face. Nine years ago they had danced in Amphorn Gardens. Exile had cut away Chao's grace as water will erode a streambed, leaving rock-hard strength exposed.

"Anything," he replied, and meant it.

"When I am gone, take my son to my sister, Li-ang. He will forget this place, with time."

"He will never forget you. Or Carlos."

"Carlos wants for Sompong the life that has been denied him. But it is death for Carlos to take our son to Bangkok."

"You have my word," Roderick said; and saluted the General's wife.

22

Mr. Halliwell," Paolo Ferretti said into the phone Thursday evening, "I'm afraid we have a problem here at the Oriental. You remember Ms. Fogg? The American woman you met at the cocktail party Tuesday?"

Rush leaned against his secretary's desk in the half-empty station. "I remember," he answered.

"She's just killed a man."

Halliwell cursed silently.

"I have to call the police," the assistant manager continued. "We would appreciate it if you could come over right away. To explain to Ms. Fogg her rights, before the police arrive."

"Of course. Is she okay?"

"Unharmed." Paolo hesitated. "But she is perhaps too much in command of herself. She was attacked, you see. A very curious incident. Quite beyond our usual experience. How the man ever got in—"

"Are you saying this guy was in her room?"

"Exactly."

"I'll be right over," Rush said, and hung up the phone.

*   *   *

Paolo moved all the guests from Stefani's corridor to a different wing of the hotel, with complimentary champagne and no explanation. They left the corpse where it lay.

She sat in a chair to one side of his desk, cradling a glass of brandy in her hands. Someone had put a blanket around her shoulders, as though she had survived disaster, and offered her a cigarette. It burned unnoticed in Paolo's ashtray.

"How did you . . . do it?" the assistant manager asked her once.

"You should be wondering how he got into my room."

"He used the key."

She glanced up swiftly from her brandy.

"Your butler was found dead in the service elevator."

"I crushed the bastard's windpipe," she offered. "Instinct, I guess."

"Instinct," Paolo repeated, and looked away.

In Bangkok there are two kinds of traffic: rush hour and worse. Tonight the streets were snarled in ways that even a native could not penetrate. Halfway to the hotel Rush abandoned his taxi and walked. The police employed sirens. He beat them by three minutes.

"What happened?" he demanded as he strode into Paolo's office.

Stefani looked up. "Rush, he was going to cut my throat—"

"But you got to him first."

"What does it cost to whack a stranger in this town? A hundred bucks?"

"Try forty."

The Bangkok police spent five hours and forty-two minutes in the Oriental Hotel. They sealed the elevator where the murdered butler lay, they sealed Stefani's suite, they sent in forensics teams to manage evidence collection and they muttered into walkie-talkies the length of the Garden Wing corridor. They found no identification on the dead man.

What they did find was a pack of clove cigarettes and a matchbook imprinted with the name of a tattoo parlor on Khao San Road. They took Polaroids of the corpse's face and sent an eager young officer to sweep the backpacker district.

Rush followed Paolo Ferretti up a service elevator and into the deserted corridor. He took in the details: Stefani's laptop on the coffee table, a bottle of Bombay Sapphire three-quarters full. She liked a Bulgari scent that smelled like green tea and she had very little in the way of luggage. The room had not been ransacked. But he had never thought burglary was the motive.

A police medic had slit open the stocking that shrouded the dead man's features. He was Asian, neither young nor old, with a head of spiky hennaed hair. He stared at the ceiling, amazed. Rush bent to study the crushed throat.

"How is it possible?" Paolo whispered anxiously. "She's such a small woman—"

Halliwell shook his head. "This is a Green Beret's move. And it wasn't done by accident. Have the cops mentioned it yet?"

"No."

"They will. Stall." He straightened and said in Thai to the medic, "We've never seen this man before."

The most senior of the floating pool of uniforms, a detective named Itchayanan, sat down to talk to Ms. Fogg. He was studying English and wanted to practice. The experience proved unhelpful.

I don't know the man and I don't know how he got into my room. He had a knife and he tried to use it.

I'm not sure how I killed him. He had his hands on my neck and I just shoved at him in the dark. Suddenly he was on the floor.

I have no idea why anyone would attack me.

I'm in Bangkok for pleasure. My permanent address is New York City. I have no place of employment.

"Stefani Fogg," Itchayanan repeated, tasting the strange name on his tongue. "You're the *farang*—the American lady—who wants to steal Jack Roderick's House."

Stefani did not reply.

"I saw you on TV. You've got a pretty big mouth, huh?" Itchayanan waved his pen under her nose. "This guy you killed probably wanted to teach you a lesson."

*   *   *

They searched her room for drugs and large sums of currency and black-market ivory or artifacts. They examined the purpled bruise where three fingers had gripped her slender neck and tagged the pocket switchblade they found under her coffee table. They considered the possibility of attempted rape. They asked where Miss Fogg had traveled last, where she intended to go next, and why. Then they told her to remain in Bangkok, pending further developments.

An hour and forty minutes later, Detective Itchayanan informed the U.S. embassy's Third Political Secretary that they would not charge Miss Fogg for the crime of murder. Still sitting in her chair beside Paolo's desk, she rolled her eyes in disdain.

Americans, Itchayanan thought bitterly, took the most amazing things for granted.

Rush signaled one of the ivory-colored Mercedes sedans that sat in front of the hotel, day and night. When the driver pulled over he put a question to the man in Thai. The answer must not have pleased him, because he slapped the car roof and motioned to the next in line. It, too, was rejected. So was a third. When the fourth pulled up, Stefani snapped, "If you send this one away, I'm walking."

Rush slid in beside her and slammed the door. A fusillade of Thai.

"What's going on?"

"I'd prefer a driver who doesn't speak English," Rush muttered.

"Then you want a city cab, not one of the hotel's."

"Please," he told the man at the wheel, "play some music. Something loud. We're trying to stay awake."

The driver reached obediently for a knob and the Beatles—"Penny Lane"—filled the backseat. The car pulled away from the Oriental. Stefani thought it unlikely that she would ever return.

"Have you eaten lately?" Rush asked.

"Not since breakfast."

"It's nearly two A.M. Never kill a man on an empty stomach."

He cast a glance toward the rearview mirror, but the driver seemed oblivious. Stefani curled herself into a corner of the seat, arms wrapped tightly under her chest. She was suddenly overwhelmingly tired of death and her intimacy with it.

"I have a penchant for gallows humor," Halliwell said unexpectedly. "Forgive me. The police located your attacker's wife in a fortune-teller's den on Khao San Road. They're questioning her now. Why would a guy who reads tea leaves for a living want to kill you?"

"Because he works two jobs," she retorted. "Why wasn't that Jo-Jo lying on my floor?"

"Be glad it wasn't. Jo-Jo's too strong and too cunning to be flipped on his back by a girl."

She kept her eyes on the flow of lights. There was little traffic on the streets now. "Where are you taking me?"

"My father's house, in Nonthaburi. No one will look for you there."

"Is your father Joe Halliwell—of the *Bangkok Post*?"

"He is."

Just what she needed: a hostile journalist over the breakfast table. She considered putting up a fight. But a hotel would be difficult at this hour of the morning. And a hotel would be watched. She shuddered at the thought of another empty room.

"I read his column," Rush was saying awkwardly. "You should ignore it. He's touchy on the subject of Jack Roderick."

"And your mother?" Stefani asked. "She's Thai, if I recall?"

"She died when I was ten. That's when I came to live with Joe." He said these words so carefully that she knew not to probe further.

Had his parents never married? She imagined Rush as a kid: half-Thai, illegitimate and cut loose with too much money in southern California. A Eurasian was often the butt of both his cultures. Had Rush grown up determined to join neither of them? Had he wandered the world, watching and listening, behind his mask of easy charm? For the first time since she'd learned that Max was dead, Stefani felt pity for someone besides herself.

Joe Halliwell lived in a small house with a dense garden on the outskirts of Nonthaburi. A single light blazed through the dark. "That's the guest-room window," Rush whispered as they stood on the doorstep. The hired Mercedes was idling; the Beatles had given way to jazz. "Dad's probably in bed. You'll be okay?"

"I'll be fine."

"Do you carry a gun?"

She smiled faintly. "Of course not. I'm a tourist."

"You're not a tourist," he retorted, and she heard his irritation. "I'll call you in the morning."

23

Bangkok,
1957

In February of 1957, Field Marshal Pibul was an old man of sixty who had ruled Thailand, with the exception of a two-year hiatus in prison, for nearly twenty years. Washington was worried about Thailand—about the increasing fractiousness of the governing elites, the unrest of student groups, the cries for democratic process and the growing attraction of Communist insurgency. Indochina was in armed revolt against the colonial power of France: men with guns were stalking the hills of Laos, the rice paddies of Vietnam and even the wide and leafy boulevards of Phnom Penh. In the domino game of Southeast Asia, Thailand could not be next.

Washington worried about the guns; and Washington believed that Field Marshal Pibul was too indolent, now, in his advancing years, to stem the flood of cheap Soviet and Chinese rifles into his country. It was time to effect a change.

Please advise fault lines of current government clique, Langley cabled the Bangkok embassy. *Also likely candidates for covert support in upcoming elections.*

Elections in Thailand had never meant much. They were lip service to the public, allowing it to believe it chose the members of its national assembly, who were actually in thrall to the cabinet members who'd bought their seats.

"Shouldn't we be supporting free and fair elections?" asked the young case officer who sat over roasted pork and mangosteen, in Jack Roderick's house one evening in late January. "Isn't that the reason we're all here? To promote democracy?"

He was maybe twenty-four years old, Roderick thought; a former quarterback from Yale. His name was Chip. The current station chief at the U.S. embassy had sent him over to meet Jack Roderick in a ritual, repeated every year, that was known within the ranks as "sitting at the feet of the Great White Case Officer." Roderick was supposed to slap some sense into the kid.

He was growing increasingly tired of the role. The new recruits reminded him of the man he had once been: idealistic, engaged, unquestioning. Less tired, purer. Certain of his goals and the motives behind them. Now he collected his thoughts and focused on the bewildered young face opposite.

"Free and fair elections are a farce. Every son of a bitch in Thailand will be scalping votes in front of the polling places like tickets to the Army-Navy Game. Next month's election will be no different. In fact, it'll be worse. The Coup Group smells blood. They're ready to cut Pibul off at the knees. They'll be at each other's throats for every last seat in the House."

The Coup Group was Pibul's cabinet, so-named in recognition of their ascent to power on the back of Pibul's 1947 coup. The cabinet ministers were military officers, drawn from the Army, the Navy and even the new body of Marines set up with Washington's help and ruled by Pibul's son, Rear Admiral Prasong. None of them was loyal to Pibul.

Chip looked mulish.

Roderick tried again. "You can't stop the flood of cash. And so you might as well put some bills in the kitty. In support of the right people. Understand?"

The most likely man to grab power was Field Marshal Sarit Thanarat, a horse Jack Roderick backed. Roderick had taken Sarit's measure years before, when the Field Marshal was a mere Colonel, and considered him intelligent, ruthless and no friend to Mao. Sarit had threatened the Pibul government in 1951, and been placated with rapid promotions: from lieutenant general to commander in chief of the Army and, by this time, Minister of Defense. Sarit controlled the Finance Section of the State Lottery Bureau, and skimmed huge sums of cash to buy political support. But the real reason Jack Roderick watched Sarit's progress was because he hated and undermined the power base of another cabinet minister: Vukrit Suwannathat. Any enemy of Vukrit's was worth keeping on Roderick's payroll.

But his immediate problem was Chip. "Look," he attempted, "think of it in terms of football. You can run yourself ragged trying to score against a dirty defense. Or you can size up the opposing team—in this case, the Soviet Union—and undermine each one of their rotten plays. You may not reach the end zone every quarter, but you're bound to spike the other side's chances of getting a touchdown. Make sense?"

Chip nodded tentatively. "It just seems so . . . un-American. I can't believe that Ike would admit to these kind of tactics."

"You're here," Roderick concluded bluntly, "so that he never has to."

Months later, in the rainy season of August, he took Fleur by boat upriver to Ayutthaya with a picnic hamper at her feet. Fleur's feet were a subject he was supposed to ignore—it is bad manners in Thailand even to glance at the feet, which are the lowliest of objects—but he loved them for their strength and suppleness and for the extraordinary flexibility of the toes. It was his habit to spend an absurd amount of time caressing those feet, which had stamped out the tragedies of Thailand on a hundred stages. They were born to be carried aloft on a silken cushion, to command from an elephant's back; but the feet and Roderick's obsession with them caused Fleur acute embarrassment. He restrained himself now, content to admire her poise in the boat's prow, the gay flags that rippled from stem to stern all about her.

They had often gone to the old capital, bumping along the dusty roads in the Buick he had imported as successor to the Packard, a monstrous shining thing the dark green of a crocodile. He had bought her a very fine Bencharong tea set at a dusty shop in the modern city, and had walked with her through the islands at the confluence of three rivers, marveling at the sounds her lips could form as they parsed out the words engraved in ancient stone. Roderick had never quite mastered the subtleties of tone—mid, high, low, rising, falling, like the stages of earthly love—and he had completely despaired of the elegant script with its eighty sinuous characters. On these trips he and Fleur retold the kingdom's oldest stories, of betrayal and passion and mortal loss. That was why he had chosen Ayutthaya today.

"You are very serious, Jack," she commented, scooping up a handful of river water and sprinkling him with the drops. "I think we grow fat and dull in our old age."

" 'Age cannot wither her, nor custom stale/Her infinite variety,' " he said, with all the longing of a man who will not see fifty again. She was unfamiliar with Shakespeare; and yet there was something very like Cleopatra about her, as she perched in the bow with her head lifted and bare ankles crossed. She was not yet twenty-five. Time had worn away the lost look of her youth; but her eyes were as dark and deep and changeable in their expression as they'd been when he'd first glimpsed her.

"Serious," she repeated, "and gloomy. What's troubling you, Jack? The silk trade? Politics?"

It was a judicious question. February's general election had been the dirtiest contest in memory. Students had marched in the streets, and Pibul sent out his riot police. When scores were injured, Field Marshal Sarit Thanarat sided with the students and protestors, and resigned his cabinet post. He was maneuvering, most Thais thought, for the right moment to seize power. Pibul had just cut off Sarit's main source of income: he'd been stripped of the State Lottery post.

"I'm worried about my house," Roderick said abruptly. "Your friend the minister—Vukrit Suwannathat—sent two men yesterday. They came while I was out and took four of my small bronze Buddhas away with them, despite the protests of my cook and houseboy. I shall never see those figures again; and I shall be very lucky if worse is not to follow."

"Petty. Vukrit's like a bad child shooting peas across the dinner table, don't you think?"

"I loved my Buddhas—loved them enough, Fleur, that I haven't displayed them for nearly two years. They were packed away in a storage cupboard. Vukrit's men knew exactly where to find them."

She was staring into the water, her profile etched against the gilded roof of a distant wat. "I remember," she said vaguely. "You showed them to me once, I think. There is a royal barge!"

He glanced in the direction she pointed and saw the prow of a great boat, some forty oarsmen chanting time as their blades slid through the water. A single figure swung high in the stern, plying the massive oar that served as tiller. The passenger amidships—royal or no—was indistinct at such a distance, dwarfed by pageantry.

"That's where you belong," he told her. "Cleopatra."

"The motion of the river is making me sick," she retorted, "and I don't want to be treated like a princess."

"Good. I'm fond of the present queen—particularly when she wears my silk—but I don't care much for royals in general."

"Because of King Ananda," she said quietly. "Because the palace insists his death was an accident. But you know the truth, don't you? Alec McQueen says so."

He glanced at her piercingly. "Surely that was before your time, child."

"I know all the best stories."

Cruelty prompted him to ask, "Did you learn them at your minister's knee?"

"Don't talk about him. That's *twice* today. You're jealous and you're determined to spoil everything."

"I know that you still see him." *I know you tell him everything. You are his ears in my house.*

"We've been over and over that," she returned wearily. "Sometimes I wish—"

"That you'd never met me?"

"That I was free of you both," she said.

Roderick's face hardened. "You can always go back to the south, Fleur. No one's keeping you. In the strictest sense."

She rose up in the boat's stern as though she had been struck. "You know that I would sooner die than leave you. It is just that my stomach is sick and I have a headache and I was a fool to say it. *Jack*—"

"You would sooner die than return to the south, yes," he cut in with reckless brutality, "but not for love of me. It's the dancing that matters. Your art. I understand that, Fleur—I understand it so well that I'm able to forgive you almost everything. *Almost.* For your art I put up with the Ministry of Culture rifling my home, and the petty boy shooting peas. I put up with having only a fingerhold on your heart. Because without your art, Fleur, you would be half the woman you seem."

He reached out his hand.

"You said *almost*," she whispered. "What is it you cannot forgive, Jack?"

My bronze Buddhas, he was tempted to say; but it was too much like an accusation, and he could not bear to utter it while the bright flags fluttered around her.

Fleur did not eat much and Roderick questioned her about her sudden illness; but she gave him half-answers or silence and eventually he dropped the subject. She seemed to improve once they left the boat and he promised to hire a car for the return to Bangkok.

They drowsed on the grass amid the remains of their lunch, and the afternoon was so pleasant that he almost forgot to plant his betrayal in her ear.

"I have to go away in three days' time," he told her. "For a week, maybe longer. You could stay at the house while I'm gone."

She propped herself up on one elbow and stared down at him. "Where are you going?"

"Khorat. Then into Vientiane. I may come back by way of Chiang Rai."

"There is no silk in Chiang Rai. Only hill people and men with guns. I wonder what you find to take you there."

He smiled faintly. "Old debts."

"The kind that money can't repay," she said acutely. "Spy business."

"I haven't been a spy since 1947, Fleur."

"I don't believe you. You were born with a hunger to know everything, and a heart that shares nothing."

He plucked at the grass before replying. "I have a meeting in Chiang Rai. An old friend from the resistance. Your minister's brother-in-law. They hate each other."

"I am sick of my minister. Who is this old friend, that you prefer to spend a week with him instead of me? A lady friend, perhaps?"

"He is a brave and tired man who has lost everything he loves, including his wife. And now I must take his son from him as well."

She spread her hands on his chest; even at rest, her fingertips curved upward like the petals of an opening flower. "What kind of man would give up his own son?"

He thought of Rory and answered: "A man who had no choice. Promise me you'll stay at the house."

"To keep your bed warm?"

"I like to think of you there."

A sidelong glance. "And where must I think of you?"

"On the outskirts of Sop Ruak, where the river path meets the jungle," he said deliberately. "I shall be there in a week's time, to see my old friend."

She sighed and fell back in the grass. "You must bring me a present from Vientiane."

"Promise me you'll stay at the house. There may be violence in Bangkok while I am gone. You'll be safe in Ban Khrua."

"Violence! What kind of violence?"

"A man with a gun and an army at his back. Your minister knows all about it. But even knowledge will not save him, this time. Will you stay at the house?"

"I'm so tired of armies," she said plaintively. "They disrupt the electrical service. Bring me back a Lisu headdress, Jack—something colorful from the hills. Then perhaps I shall forgive you."

He set out the next morning, two days early, and did not go to Khorat at all.

Instead, he drove due north from the city, past Ayutthaya where he had lain for the last time in the grass with his beloved; past Lop Buri where he bought a small statue of a snarling *singha* to give to Fleur; past the jungle of Thung Yai Naresuan where tigers lurked in the shifting green; and after many hours, through the ancient ruins of Sukkothai, the most distant outpost of the old Khmer empire. There he paused to eat some mangosteens in the cool of the evening and to watch three small boys wrestling in the riverbank mud. He was sad and yet hopeful, as one who has survived a death.

Two days later he reached Sop Ruak and found his way through the paths that meandered and led to the General's stronghold in the hills. He was conscious of the watchers in the trees above, and of the whistles and calls that preceded his passage. He moved with the prickling knowledge of being tracked by a gun's sights, and resisted the impulse to run.

"Carlos, my friend, it is time to break camp," he said as he entered the hut, "lest Vukrit and all his soldiers find you here."

"Let Vukrit come," the General replied without hesitation. "I will break him like a twig."

"You did not live in the hills for eleven years, guarding your men like children, to throw them to the dogs. Vukrit is fighting for political survival. He will have a new master soon, and needs an easy victory—like the capture of a king's assassin. You must be gone before nightfall."

Carlos stood with his hands on his hips and stared out over the fields toward Burma. "Vukrit would kill me, you say. And I believe you. Why, then, should I send him my son?"

"Because Chao wished it. Because Vukrit has no child and will treat your boy as his own. Because Vukrit has the power to give Sompong a life beyond poppy fields and bullets."

When the other man did not answer him, Roderick added, "Your son will come back to you, Carlos."

The General spat. "I curse the day I gave my word to Chao!"

He had changed since her death, Roderick realized. Every softening element in his nature had been sheared from his soul by a diamond knife.

"Has your Flower betrayed us?" the General asked Roderick.

"I don't know. But it's better not to wait."

Carlos rubbed at his hair with a hand stained by gun grease. "I have no money to send with the boy."

"I will take care of that."

"The rearing of a son is a fearful obligation. It places me in my enemy's debt."

"Then at last the balance is struck," Roderick replied. He held up the cabochon ruby that Boonreung had given him on the night of Carlos's flight from Bangkok—June 9, 1946. "How long have you held Vukrit's life in your hands? Since the day of the king's death—or earlier?"

The General's eyes were on the ruby. "I found that on the floor of the Grand Palace. The murderer of King Ananda dropped it."

"This ruby was pried from the head of the Buddha we discovered together in the hidden cave. Vukrit cut the head from the rock and sold it. The ruby he kept, until the morning he murdered the king."

"Then Vukrit wore a mask in the palace," Carlos said stubbornly. "I did not see his face."

"But you have always known," Roderick persisted.

"There are obligations, Jack—debts that one owes. My wife loved her sister. I could not betray my brother-in-law."

"Although he leapt at the chance to betray you?"

"So I possess more honor than Vukrit. I have always known that."

Roderick gazed out from the ridge where they stood at the dense canopy of green. A brilliant bird rose up from the treetops. "Let me take you back to Bangkok with your son. Or if not Bangkok, then north to Vientiane."

"I believed in Pridi Banomyong, when he fought the Japanese and snakes like Vukrit and Field Marshal Pibul. If a man cannot believe in something, Jack—what does he live for?"

"I don't know," Roderick returned quietly. "But at some point, my friend, belief costs too much."

The General shook his head. "I have only the troops who follow me, now. I cannot destroy their pride. They are all I have left."

"Pibul the Dictator is about to fall from power. Vukrit might fall with him. You could still come home."

"I have no home but this."

"I tell you it is betrayed," Roderick said brutally. "Break camp, and call your son."

Seven nights after he had told Fleur his plans in the grass of Ayutthaya, Roderick lay sleepless in his cot at Sop Ruak. Carlos had torched the huts of his encampment and led his men on a long and twisting journey south, through the borderlands of Burma. The General intended, after several days, to reach the Cameron Highlands of Malaysia. Ever since the battles of the Malay Peninsula in the Second World War, the Highlands had sheltered bands of armed men. And the hills were beyond even Vukrit Suwannathat's reach.

A beetle crawled purposefully along the boards of the roof, where the jungle vines had forced an entry; Roderick counted off the seconds of the minutes and hours while the moonlight shifted across the dirt floor of the room. He imagined the river path where it met the jungle, and the poppy fields blossoming with flames. He thought of Vukrit, and the soldiers he must have brought, creeping through the mud. He liked to think of the minister's rage, when he discovered that Carlos had eluded him.

The boy slept soundly in the opposite bunk. He was seven years old, Roderick thought, with Chao's cheekbones and Carlos's nose; Sompong was thin and tough from running wild along the mountain paths. When the crackle of gunfire sprang up like rain from the hills to the northwest, he sighed in his sleep and curled into a tight ball. It was a sound he had known from birth.

Roderick left him sleeping. Before dawn, he walked with the rising sun to Chao's funeral shrine and knelt among the teakwood trees. He told her what he had done; he asked for her blessing. Then he collected her boy and turned the Buick south.

Fleur was gone from the house on the khlong when Roderick returned. He did not go in search of her.

He sent the carved *singha* and the Lisu headdress to Urana, the mistress of *lakhon*.

The boy he delivered to Chao's sister, Li-ang, at the villa on the coast near Pattaya.

And on September 16, 1957, Sarit Thanarat seized supreme power in Thailand.

24

Joe Halliwell's house in Nonthaburi was a peaceful place, and Stefani dreamed neither of murderers nor hands throttling her neck. She slept until almost ten o'clock and awoke to the sound of a bird screeching.

Someone tried to kill me. Oliver would like to know, she thought, that the C-clamp he'd taught her had saved her life.

She found Rush's father seated before his computer, typing madly. There was nothing remotely of his son in his manner or face. A white bird perched on his shoulder, and for an instant she was certain she had imagined it. The cockatoo lifted one viridian claw as she approached.

"Welcome." He kept his eyes fixed on his screen. "There's coffee and fruit in the kitchen. Make yourself at home. I don't have guests that often."

"Thank you," she replied. "I won't trouble you for long."

"I understand there was a problem at the Oriental."

"You could call it that."

"Crazy damn town. That press conference of yours might not have been the best idea."

By way of answer she asked, "Where did you get that bird?"

Halliwell smoothed the cockatoo's feathers with a stubby finger. "They're all over Thailand. She's not a bad old girl. Just loud."

"Jack Roderick had one."

"So he did. Ever eaten a durian?" Halliwell rose, set the bird on its perch and led her toward his kitchen. "They grow 'em around here. Look like dinosaur eggs and they stink to high heaven. Have a slice."

The fruit was tough skinned, with sharply flavored, mustard-yellow flesh.

"It's an acquired taste," Joe told her. "Took me years. Now I can't get enough of it. Some need in the blood."

"Like Thailand?" she asked.

"For some people, maybe. The ones who want to escape. If you stay here long enough, you choose Thailand—or it chooses you."

"When did you make your choice?"

"Forty years ago. I took Rush back to school in California for a while. I wanted him to know what the States were like. You planning to stay?"

"It depends upon the house. What was Jack Roderick escaping? When he first chose Bangkok, in 1945?"

"Himself, probably. Caught up with him in the end."

"Did it?" She eyed him curiously. "Do you know how he died?"

"Everyone's got a theory."

"But no one wants to tell."

"I'd like to live in Thailand for the rest of my life," Joe said flatly, "and I intend to live a long time. I don't talk much about Jack Roderick."

"Because he was your friend?"

"Jack was news," Halliwell corrected icily. "I just followed him around for the paper."

He grabbed the slices of durian and led her to a terrace, glass-walled and shaded with bamboo blinds. There was no breeze; an insect whirred from the jungle garden. Photographs of his son stood on every surface. But none of Rush's Thai mother. Another story with an unhappy ending?

"So," he said briskly. "You were nearly killed and your attacker died instead. Trouble follows Jack Roderick's name like a shark follows blood. I should tell you to forget Bangkok and catch the first plane back to wherever you're from."

"I wouldn't go. You don't approve of me, do you?"

His eyes slid away. "The old stories are better left buried. When people start digging, innocent folks always get hurt."

"I got hurt last night," Stefani said bluntly. "And I didn't demand the truth about Jack's death. I just asked for my inheritance."

"It comes down to the same thing. Let sleeping dogs lie, Ms. Fogg. You won't solve the mystery by stirring up trouble. And maybe there's no mystery at all. Jack could have been killed by a tiger. Or a truck that ran off the road. Ever seen how those Malay truckers drive? High on amphetamines, all of them."

"I just want the house."

"But it was never Jack's to give," Halliwell replied unexpectedly. "The Ministry of Culture took it by fiat, the day he left for the Highlands. Nobody told you?"

"Told me what?"

"That Jack was a criminal. Branded one by the Thai government. 'Dealing in stolen artifacts' was the exact phrase, I think; his house was confiscated along with everything in it. Quite a sensation at the time."

She frowned. "By the Ministry of Culture, you must mean Vukrit Suwannathat—Sompong's father."

"Vukrit was at Defense by '67. He'd been sidelined for a few years when his buddy Field Marshal Pibul was sent off at gunpoint, and everybody figured he was washed up—but Vukrit clawed his way back. He was never down for long."

"I'm told that he and Jack were enemies."

"They were." Halliwell shifted in his seat. "Vukrit had been threatening for years to clean Roderick out. It enraged him to see Asian artifacts—religious, at that—in a *farang*'s home. In the end Jack vanished, and Vukrit's successor at Culture got to grab the goods."

"How convenient."

"The government set up the Thai Heritage Board, which ran the place as a museum for seven years, until Jack was declared legally dead. At that point, a Thai court ruled that the property belonged to the state. But you know that."

"Do you think someone had Roderick killed just to get his house?"

"No." Halliwell shifted again. "Everybody knew Vukrit was behind the seizure, regardless of which ministry he was supposed to be running at the time. Getting Roderick's goods was a symbol of Vukrit's power—though much good it did Vukrit. He was shot to death in '86, you know—on a road in the middle of Chiang Rai. Car burned to

cinders. Body riddled with bullets. The government claimed drug runners did it—but Vukrit had a lot of enemies. Who's to say what really
happened?"

"Who were Jack's enemies, Mr. Halliwell?"

His glance grew shrewd. "If you'd asked me the day before Jack
went to the Highlands whether he was a marked man, Ms. Fogg—I'd
have laughed in your face."

"You thought he was invulnerable?"

Halliwell's expression altered slightly, as though he were listening
to a voice she couldn't hear. "Politics is a vicious game and plans sometimes go wrong, but Jack believed in making the world a better place."

"Sounds naïve."

"We were all naïve after World War II. We'd fought the Good Fight;
we'd made the world safe for democracy. Vietnam woke us up. Napalm-
ing the kiddies turns you real cynical, real fast. But Jack lived and died
an idealist. That's why his failures tore him up inside."

"I didn't know he'd had any failures."

Halliwell sighed. "Jack saw *people* when he looked at Thailand, not
politics or the U.S. interest. That got him into trouble—here and at
home. He never quite belonged in one place or the other. By the time he
disappeared, he was remote as Everest. My boss—Alec McQueen—was
Jack's closest friend, but even McQueen didn't understand him. Just
caught the pieces when they fell at his feet."

"What was it? The napalm? The spying? Being *farang* in the land of
the Smiling Thai?"

"Jack Roderick loved spying. Loved the Smiling Thai. Some men
love drink, but it still rots their guts."

"What exactly was Roderick doing for the United States in this
town?"

"Watching the men with guns. There were a lot of 'em in the old
days. You people who were born after 1950 forget what it was like back
then. The Red Menace was everywhere. We'd lost China to Mao in '49.
The next year, we fought a war on the Korean Peninsula. In the late
fifties, the French were whipped out of Indochina and Communist insurgencies were springing up like weeds, all of them armed to the teeth.
Jack's job was to stem the tide."

"What about Vukrit? Was he a Communist?"

Halliwell snorted. "He was a strongman's bag carrier, nothing more. If Jack saw only people, Vukrit saw only Vukrit. He was the ultimate opportunist."

"You didn't like him."

"He was a nasty little thug."

"And his son?"

"Is worse."

They were both silent for a moment. Then Stefani asked, "Joe, what made it worthwhile? What did Jack Roderick live and die for?"

"To be king," Halliwell answered softly. "That's what they called him, remember. And he had moments of happiness, Ms. Fogg. When Jack walked past the weavers' looms or watched them dye the silk. When he found a rare piece of Bencharong pottery in the Nakorn Kasem."

"Did Fleur make him happy? Or was she just another piece in his collection?"

Joe's eyes flickered. "Fleur was one of the most beautiful of the classical *lakhon* dancers, in her prime."

"But she belonged to Vukrit before Jack Roderick."

"Fleur did what she had to do in order to survive. Jack didn't understand that; he liked to be sure of his possessions. Fleur was always on loan."

"What happened to her?"

"She drowned herself in the khlong." Halliwell said it brusquely. "Not long after Jack disappeared. I don't want to talk about it."

"Bad luck dogs that family. You know that Jack left a son?"

The old reporter's hand clenched involuntarily, and she watched the knuckles whiten. "Did you ever meet Rory Roderick?" she persisted.

"Only once. Rory came to Bangkok sometime in the sixties. Nice kid. Nothing like Jack."

"Rory was executed in the Hanoi Hilton a few weeks after Jack disappeared that Easter Sunday. On the face of it, there's no connection between the two deaths."

"None whatsoever. Boys were dying all over Vietnam."

"Did you folks at the *Bangkok Post* hear about Rory Roderick's execution?"

"If he was killed a few weeks after Easter, I would have been in the Cameron Highlands. I flew there the night Jack's disappearance broke."

She went quite still. "You went to look for Jack?"

"Who didn't? That patch of Malaysian jungle was like Grand Central Station for a while." He barked out a mirthless laugh. "Two hundred-odd people combing the damn rain forest. No footprints, no witnesses and no corpse."

"Jack supposedly carried a million dollars U.S. into the Highlands in a black briefcase."

"Dickie Spencer has told a lot of people that fairy tale."

"That doesn't make it untrue. What was Jack buying in the Highlands?"

The phone rang.

"Rush," Halliwell said with relief into the receiver. "She's just fine. We've been chatting about the old days. I warned her they're better left buried."

He held out the phone to Stefani.

"Detective Itchayanan just called the embassy," Rush told her without preamble. "An American named Jeff Knetsch was arrested on drug charges last night. He's claiming to have killed you."

25

Before dawn Jeff Knetsch had finally dozed, his head lolling on the shoulder of his grimy T-shirt. There was little light in the group cell—the glare of a naked bulb from the corridor—and the mutter of conversation all around him in the fetid darkness. His body trembled from exhaustion. Every once in a while the fingers of another man fluttered over his face; he flinched when the grip settled on his jaw.

It was possible, he thought, that he might yet be saved. He had looked honest enough, hadn't he? He had posed his arguments in the best legal manner. He was an American. He had an embassy.

He had been framed.

Sompong.

The minister owned everybody in Bangkok. Ankana and Jeff and the man named Chanin, who must have squealed about the contract murder. The minister even owned the police.

He thought of his wife, Shelley. By now she would have called the managing partner of his firm in a desperate bid to find him. The firm might have reported him missing to the police or the FBI—but then again, when Jeff considered the discretion habitual among lawyers, he figured they probably hadn't. *Calm down, Shelley. Wait for Jeff to call. Maybe he's spending a bit of time, hiking in the Alps. Grief can affect people in strange ways.* He had, after all, suffered a loss in Courchevel ten days ago. He had eulogized his best friend.

What should I have done differently? Max taunted him from beyond the cell. He was older today, more like the man Jeff had last seen in a wheelchair. *Asked better questions? Taken more time? Paid you higher fees?*

"I just wanted to win," Jeff answered fretfully. "I was sick to death of running second to you all my life."

As he watched, Max rose and shoved the wheelchair away. And without another look, he walked easily through the prison wall.

Jeff felt a flare of panic and loss. He surged to his feet, thrusting stray bodies aside. Gripping the bars of his cell, sticky with other men's sweat, he screamed a name aloud.

The murmurs behind him fell abruptly silent.

And then, like the growing beat of coming rain, the laughter began.

He swung around to face them. Twelve, maybe fifteen men of every class and description, all reeking of alcohol and filth and days-old urine. Their eyes were mocking and ruthless. And they were advancing upon him.

"**You say this** Ankana woman told you yesterday that Knetsch was in Bangkok," Rush repeated for clarity's sake as he and Stefani waited in the conference room that the police, after a brief but heated squabble in Thai, had grudgingly turned over to him. A pad of paper and two pens, caps mangled by other people's teeth, rested on the table before them. "He was already in custody when you talked to her. Raving about murder."

It was almost noon on Friday by Stefani's watch. She was drinking Thai iced coffee and lusting for a cigarette. She doubted Rush carried one. During the drive from his father's house, she had told him everything she knew about Jeffrey Knetsch: that he had been Max's attorney and best friend. That he was friendly with Ankana Lee-Harris, a British woman of Thai birth whom Max loathed. That Knetsch was heavily in debt and had probably sold information to Sompong Suwannathat. The last, she admitted, she could not prove.

She said nothing whatsoever about Oliver Krane.

"Ankana told me that Jeff was meeting with the minister to discuss the loan of artifacts to the Metropolitan Museum of Art," she added. "There's a show going up in a few weeks that both Ankana and Knetsch are involved in. He serves on the Met Board, she's a curator at a British museum."

Rush's expression of interest sharpened. "You mean—they're borrowing paintings?"

"Dickie Spencer said sculpture and ceramics. He's loaning pieces from Jack Roderick's collection."

"Ceramics," Rush mused. "I caught a glimpse of a few clay pots Tuesday night, at a warehouse near the Thieves Market. What does Ankana look like?"

"She's Thai. Her hair's bleached orange."

Rush drummed his fingers restlessly on the table. "I've seen her—with the minister and a guy who might even be Knetsch. But we can talk about it later." He glanced significantly at the opposite wall.

A large framed mirror hung there. One-way glass, with the Bangkok police arranged on the other side. Microphones were suspended from the ceiling. The police hadn't bothered to disguise them.

The door swung open and three men shuffled inside. A burly cop in the close-fitting dark khaki uniform of the Bangkok police, a man in the blue jumpsuit of the prison guards, and Jeff Knetsch. The latter's hands were cuffed.

For a moment, Stefani did not recognize him.

Rush Halliwell stood. "Mr. Knetsch? Rush Halliwell, from the U.S. embassy. Please sit down. We haven't much time."

"You've got to get me out of here." Knetsch shrugged off the hand of the prison warden and was thrust, stumbling, toward the table where Stefani sat. His eyes were bleary, his skin ashen beneath a growth of beard. What looked like a human bite was purpling on his neck.

"What *happened* to you, Jeff?" Stefani asked.

At the sound of her voice, his gaze drifted vaguely toward her face. "You're dead," he said firmly. "So shut up."

Rush shot her a warning glance. She sat very still.

"Mr. Knetsch. Please—have a seat."

"Just get me the fuck out of here!"

"It's not that simple, I'm afraid." Rush came around the table and helped Jeff to sit.

He sagged into the hard wooden chair and laid his cheek on the table like a child. "They searched me, you know. Without a warrant! My clothes. My . . . my . . . *body cavities*." His shoulders began to heave. Dry, racking sobs. "He framed me. He set me up."

"Who?"

Jeff reared like a jack-in-the-box. "I'm not talking to you," he countered craftily. "I want a lawyer. An American lawyer."

"There is no legal organization in Thailand that specifically represents foreigners. I can try to find you local counsel, but it will have to be a Thai who understands the criminal justice system. Until then, it might help if you simply told me what happened."

"Make the monkeys leave," Jeff insisted.

Rush said a few words in Thai to the impassive policeman and his warder. The two men left the room.

"Lot of good that'll do," Stefani murmured, with an eye to the mirror.

"I told you to shut up," Jeff snapped querulously. "You're *dead*."

Stefani felt Rush's hand squeeze hers under the table, in warning. "Did you kill her, Jeff?" he asked.

"I don't get my hands dirty." Contempt soured the words. "I paid the kid to do it. He came cheap enough. And look where it got me! The fucking rat squealed to Sompong. He *set me up*." Knetsch lunged suddenly across the table, seizing Rush's jacket. "I was *framed*, do you hear me? They put that friggin' bag in my pocket."

"I hear you," Rush said calmly. "Let's sit down, shall we? And start at the beginning."

"It was a guy in dark glasses and a tropical shirt. At a fish & chip place in Khao San Road. He bumped into me. Next thing I know, the cops are pulling heroin out of their hats. A full ounce."

"Was this *after* you paid the kid—that would be Chanin, I suppose—to kill Stefani?"

"Two thousand baht," Jeff muttered. "All the cash I had on me. I can't even make cab fare home. Oh, God, I want to go home . . ." He crumpled again, weeping into his hands.

Two thousand baht, Stefani thought. *I almost got my throat slit for a lousy fifty bucks.*

"Why did you want to kill her?" Rush's voice sounded almost bemused.

"Because she asks too many questions. Sompong says so. She's going to ruin everything—the shipments, the *show*. Sompong is fucking out of his mind, he's so pissed."

"At you?"

"I've failed him. First Max, and now this . . . She should never have been allowed near him."

"Near Sompong?" Rush pressed sharply.

"Near *Max*." The weeping man's voice rose hysterically. "If Oliver hadn't sent her to France, none of this would have happened!"

Oliver. The name jolted through her like an electrical current. Knetsch was on a first-name basis with Oliver Krane.

Rush glanced at her, then wrote on the pad: *Is Oliver somebody from FundMarket?*

Later, she slashed back.

"Max has been driving me nuts," Knetsch muttered. "Following me around. Talking, talking. Now she will, too."

"You pushed him off the edge, didn't you?" Stefani demanded, her pulse racing with rage. "In his wheelchair. He left the brakes jammed on."

"No!" Jeff reared upward, his cuffed wrists straining. "I triggered the avalanche and Ankana trashed his binding—but he had those coming. You know he did. He left me alone in that chute with a broken leg, years ago, when *I* tried to save him. Dragged himself out and they called him a goddamn hero. *I was supposed to be the hero.* I never skied again. Not so it counts."

Rush gripped the man's shoulders and eased him back into the chair.

"Make her stop," the lawyer implored. He refused to look at Stefani. "She always hated me. Jealous."

In that instant, she barely restrained herself from smashing his head down onto the table. *"Who killed Max, Jeff?"*

"Someone else. Sompong's man. Oliver, perhaps."

"Oliver *Krane*?"

"He was in Courchevel," Knetsch confided. "He's always where you least expect. He's a snake in the grass, Oliver. Been in Sompong's pocket for years. Working both ends of the stick."

The unknown client. The vague referrals. The high-wire act with no safety net and enough rope to hang herself, several times over. What had he said? *The beauty of it is that I can deny you, ducks.*

"When Max decided to hire Krane's, of course I agreed. Couldn't be safer than old Ollie. The right hand would tell the left exactly what it was doing, right? But then Oliver sent *her*. I knew something was wrong. Playing us all false. Tried to tell Sompong."

Stefani went cold. "Sompong *knows*? That Krane is playing both sides?"

"Thought we'd all be safe. Oliver's cuckoo in Sompong's nest! Now he's sold the bitch down the river, too. Doesn't know she's dead."

"What are you saying?" Rush demanded.

"Oliver *gave* her to Sompong. Lock, stock and nine-millimeter barrel. He faxed his report to Bangkok Wednesday. Sompong won't need it, though, now that I've killed her."

Knetsch rubbed fretfully at his ears as though he heard something that pained him.

Her mind darted frantically down a darkened corridor, snatching blindly for a door. There must be a way out. *Not Oliver, with his hand on Max's chair.* Jesus, what had she been thinking, last March in New York? She had practically begged to be screwed.

"Why kill Stefani, Jeff? What threat does she pose?" Rush's eyes were narrowed as a snake's before it strikes.

"Sompong wanted her dead. Happy to oblige, of course."

Stefani reached for the pad and pen. *Ask him,* she wrote, *to tell us everything he knows. About a man named Harry Leeds.*

PART THREE

RORY

1

Hanoi,
January 1967

When the dreams came, as they always did a few hours before dawn, he thought that he was back on the flight deck of the USS *Coral Sea,* sitting in the cockpit of the A-4, pulling his helmet and then his canopy down while his parachute rigger gave the thumbs-up sign. The plane in front was Jimmy Serrano's, except that Jimmy was dead and not taking off in a surge of sound and flame at the cliff edge where the tilting carrier became the South China Sea.

In that moment of dozing hallucination it was all possible again: the ordnance clutched like a lethal goose egg under the wing and wild hope still beating in his veins. He might slip through the boiling black cloud of antiaircraft flak that streamed upward from the wide boulevards of Hanoi and buzz the opera house or perhaps the tree-lined park of the old French governor's mansion. The Walleye smart bomb might actually hit the thermal plant he was supposed to target and not the apartment house next door. The goose egg would slide harmlessly toward a forest of industrial stacks, he and Jimmy would both pull up and out into the sunlight, with no thump of Jimmy's fuselage crumpling suddenly like a Christmas cracker.

If the dream were true he would not have turned back, to circle eight times over the antiaircraft guns with his eyes straining for the white surrender of Jimmy's chute, until the surface-to-air missile sliced his own wing in half and he was spiraling toward the lake at the heart of Hanoi, scrabbling for the ejection-seat handle. His leg would not have shattered against the cockpit mouth as he hurtled from the plane, his left wrist would still be whole.

In the seconds before he shook off the dream, it was one version of events—more real than the nightmare of waking.

His dangling legs twitched now as he dozed, and the movement sent a spear of pain from his broken femur up along his spinal column, screamed across his numb shoulder blades where they had been drawn back tightly like a chicken's, to end in a whimper at his biceps. The ropes were tied just below each muscle to cut off his circulation, then drawn back behind the head and slung from the ceiling. He had been suspended at dusk the previous evening; it was now, he thought, nearly dawn. Each night they trussed him like a bird and every morning they cut him down. He was supposed to confess to something.

I am an American, fighting in the forces which guard my country and our way of life. I am prepared to give my life in their defense.

The Code of Conduct for American Prisoners of War. It chattered like a radio jingle around and around his brain, a fragment of doggerel he had memorized at the Academy years ago.

When questioned, should I become a prisoner of war, I am required to give name, rank, service number, and date of birth. I will evade answering further questions to the utmost of my ability.

After the first four days of interrogation at the Maison Centrale, the former French prison, he had told them he was Richard Pierce Roderick, a lieutenant commander in the United States Navy. When they beat him and stamped on his fractured leg, swollen and black from the blood pooling beneath the surface of the skin, he shouted the numbers on his dog tags and the fact that he was thirty years old. Seven days later, lying in his own vomit and shit on a dank cement floor, he offered the starting lineup of the '43 Yankees as members of his squadron. By the time the prison doctor arrived sometime that night, he was delirious and could say nothing at all.

If I am captured, I will continue to resist by all means available. I will make every effort to escape and aid others to escape. I will accept neither parole nor special favors from the enemy.

There was nothing special about beatings and solitary confinement: all the pilots interned in the Hanoi Hilton got them.

"Too late," the Vietnamese doctor muttered in disgust as he probed the splintered femur. Medical care was not wasted on the badly wounded.

Jimmy Serrano, dead in three pulses of flaring light, waggled his wings at Rory and soared off into the blue. Rory raised his right hand and managed a salute.

At dawn three prison guards had arrived to carry him from the room. He had known, in the part of his brain that remained clear despite the fever and the pain, that he was being taken away to die. They would want to work him over once more in the hope of extracting something—a list of bombing targets, a filmed confession denouncing the United States. He had heard confessions in the ten days he'd been lying on the prison floor—voices broadcast loudly over the prison's speaker system, so that every downed pilot would comprehend that resistance was futile.

He would not, Rory decided, confess to anything. Before he died, he would raise the middle finger of his right hand and thrust it full at the camera's lens. Maybe little Max would see a broadcast of it someday, and understand.

They had carried him to an unventilated cell, six feet by three feet, and left him to die of dehydration and shock. Except that he had not died. He lay listening to the rasp of his own breathing while a Beach Boys song circled maddeningly in his head. Forty-nine hours later, the guards opened the door and peered inside.

Something had changed. He was too weak to bother wondering what it was; he knew only that the guards were agitated, they were barking orders and abuse at one another, and he was hauled painfully out of the hole in which he had been supposed to die and carried at a run toward a different block of the prison. He caught sight of American faces peering through narrow bars and slatted windows and he'd tried to shout his name and rank and carrier group. But his lips were swollen shut. They left the prison yard behind and entered the cool depths of the central block, where the guards ate and the commandant had his offices. He was shunted down a hall and into a bare room with a great stone tub. There his filthy clothes were cut away from his body.

As water sluiced over his head he tried desperately to drink, the bile choking in his throat. One of the guards forced warm tea between his lips. They threw a set of prison pajamas over his chest and legs and carried him hurriedly toward a gurney with a bare lightbulb swinging overhead.

Rory had thought that he was beyond the reach of fear, but the sight of medical equipment in the hands of the Vietnamese brought a flood of adrenaline coursing through his system. He battled upright. Two guards forced him down while a medic attempted to set his fractured leg without benefit of anesthesia. He opened his mouth wide at the agony of it and bit hard on the forearm of the nearest guard, who leapt backward, howling and cursing, while the other guard punched him in the face. Rory passed out.

A great while or perhaps only a few minutes later he found that he was lying in an actual bed made up with clean linen. His leg had never been set—he knew enough of injuries to understand it required surgery—but there was a cast about his left wrist. A cool breeze was blowing through an open window. In one corner of the room was a camera mounted on a tripod. Three men stood at the foot of his cot. Two wore the uniform of the North Vietnamese. A fourth man stood behind the camera, rolling film.

"Lieutenant Commander." It was the civilian who spoke—a short, aged man in a Mao jacket. He inclined his head in what might be a salute, although that seemed impossible.

"Who the hell are you?"

"It is I who should ask that question. What is your name?"

"Richard Pierce Roderick."

"Also known as Rory?"

Rory did not reply. *When questioned, should I become a prisoner of war, I am required to give name, rank, service number and date of birth.* Not sexual preference, favorite foods, specifics of warheads. And never my private name.

"You will answer!" barked one of the soldiers.

I will evade answering further questions to the utmost of my ability. He doubted they'd stamp on his fracture in front of the camera. He shifted his head fretfully on the pillow. That seemed to satisfy them.

"Your father, I think, is Mr. Jack Roderick of New York and Bangkok?"

"Your English is damn good, pal," Rory told the small man in the Mao jacket. "Where'd you learn it?"

"I taught it to myself. Please answer my question."

"Go to hell." He slumped back onto his pillow.

"You were born in New York, I believe?"

"So was half the world."

"Tell me your father's name."

"Or what? You'll have me killed?" Mirthlessly, Rory began to laugh. "My dad checked out when I was a kid. It doesn't matter what his name was."

"Do not speak that way." The Mao jacket came closer. He reached for a chair, and sat down close to Rory's head. "The name of Roderick is one to honor. These fools in the uniforms know little English but all the same I shall speak softly, and for your ears alone, Rory Roderick."

Rory stared fixedly at the ceiling.

"Your father's name is Jack. I know this, because Jack spoke often of you in the days when the world and I were young. He called me Ruth. Does that name mean anything to you?"

Rory collected what spittle he could and hawked derisively at the placid face.

"He showed me your picture," the Mao jacket went on. "You were a little boy crouching beside a terrier dog and the dog's name was Joss— an Asian name for luck. Your father loved Asia and abandoned his son and for that you cannot forgive him. But Jack Roderick gave me his faith and he saved my life. I am prepared now to repay my debt. Would you like to go free? Have your wounds treated by an American doctor? See your wife and your boy? I have the power to send you home, Rory Roderick."

He understood it, then. In exchange for his release, the man named Ruth would force Rory to dishonor his name. *I will accept neither parole nor special favors from the enemy. And that includes any friend of Jack's, buddy.*

"American prisoners of war may only accept release in the order they were taken prisoner," he said through his teeth. "Call me in a few years."

"You would be wise to admit that you are Jack Roderick's son."

For an instant Rory saw the curved nose and the pale eyes, the intense *stillness* of his father. Deep in thought as he smoked a cigarette on the terrace by the khlong, the white bird always on his shoulder.

"I never had a dog. I have no father by any name."

The man stood up. "In the *Bangkok Post* they say that you are missing.

The Americans believe you are dead. I still read the *Bangkok Post,* you see, although it is unfortunately several weeks old by the time it arrives. I will send word to Jack Roderick that his son is alive."

Rory had a deep and bitter horror of cowardice, of collaboration, of leaning away from torment into the nameless temptation offered him. Ruth had some bargain in mind, a *quid pro quo;* and Rory knew that if he accepted, he was lost. He would be unable to face the other men whose tortured screams filled the warren of cells, men whose fathers had never had the ear of ambassadors or been a sinister legend that struck fear in people's hearts. When the man named Ruth returned a few days later, and asked him to write to Jack Roderick, he refused. He refused the surgery they offered for his damaged leg. He kept his eyes fixed on the flies that buzzed about the ceiling of his cell while Ruth whispered in his ear.

"I have sent word to Roderick through a mutual friend. Your father knows you are alive. He knows you are here, Rory. He knows that I struggle to win your release. Will you not honor your father, and do as I ask?"

"Leave me alone, old man."

"*Rory.* You are not a dutiful son."

His arms were slung back behind his head and his weight suspended at night. He marked the days of solitary confinement in a series of scratches on his prison wall. There were thirty-nine days of fever and dysentery, thirty-nine nights of dangling in the air.

When he dreamed, now, it was Annie he saw and sometimes Max, tanned and clear-eyed from a summer spent by the lake. Max was hunkered down as he examined something—a tortoise ponderously crossing the dirt road, Annie impatient to continue the walk and a dog barking farther in the distance. Annie's hair was fluttering gold in the breeze off the water and he longed to touch it, but she kept her eyes averted from him, fixed on their son, still hunkered in the dust. Max would be nearly eight now but Rory could not remember his birthday. It was disturbing the way these things—dates, a few names, the faces of his flight mates on the *Coral Sea*—were slipping from his grasp. He had not seen Max since September. Did the boy believe he was dead?

Rory's left toe jerked in a spasm and again the firestorm of pain ripped through his nerve endings.

He's dead, he heard his own childish voice say accusingly. *He's dead and you never told me, Mama.*

It was the only explanation for Jack Roderick's absence when Rory was seven years old. Why else would a father abandon his boy to the desert of divorce? His mother packed up her paintbrushes and her clothes and they left Manhattan along with Joss, the terrier, in the entourage of one of her men, to a new life in Chicago. Rory was supposed to call this man Uncle Pete, except that he hated the farce of fictitious uncles and called him nothing at all. They lived in a great house on Lakeshore Drive and Joss ran barking after fat squirrels as though he had never been king of the city streets. Rory invented wild stories in the emptiness of the backyard, stories of assassins with pistols and cunning hands, and his father was the hero of all of them.

Boxes arrived from time to time, thick with foreign stamps, full of bejeweled monsters and silk jackets embroidered with dragons. There were photographs, too, and short sentences in his father's hard-to-read hand. When his mother asked Rory if he wanted the letters, he turned away. She tucked the photographs in his bureau drawer, where he would look for them in the middle of the night and study them under the bedclothes.

Jack in his shirtsleeves, eyes crinkled against the sun, a cigarette dangling from one corner of his mouth. His toes were bare, his hand stretched toward the gray water. A panama hat on his head.

Uncle Pete left one day and they moved again, this time to an apartment in the heart of Chicago. Later it was a house she rented in Evanston so that he could attend a good school, and for a while the letters stopped coming from Bangkok because she had forgotten to forward their address. When his mother spent money lavishly, Rory understood that his father was writing again, and that he'd sent her money. The knowledge shamed and sickened him worse than if a stranger were keeping her.

He was fiercely protective of his mother. At fifteen he knew that he must choose allegiance in this private war, the agonizing battle between what he wanted and what he had been left. He chose the woman no one needed any longer, with her high brittle laugh and her greasepaint makeup; he became Joan's protector, a supporting hand when the gin flowed too freely. He gathered the letters that had accumulated in her drawers and burned them in the basement furnace.

The photographs he kept.

His father at the prow of a great boat, teeth bared in his tanned face. His father in the skeleton of a peak-roofed house, with lizards at his feet and a white bird on his shoulder. His father with a length of silk in his hands, eyes direct and piercing for the camera.

"Your father is renowned throughout Southeast Asia," Ruth insisted during one dark eternity of interrogation. "They call him Legend and King and Man of Many Faces. You should be proud to be Jack's son."

"That is why I will not dishonor him," Rory said clearly, "by begging for your mercy."

2

It's time you came clean," Rush told her as they threaded their way through Bangkok's Friday afternoon traffic. "You're not a tourist or an asset manager or even Max Roderick's heiress. You're working for Oliver Krane, who flips off crooks and cops alike, the world over. Krane got you in deep with the wrong sort of people, and now the wrong people want you dead. Fair summary?"

"I don't have to tell you anything," Stefani said curtly.

Rush stabbed at his horn and swerved viciously into the right-hand lane. "As long as you're in my car, honey—and I'm all that stands between you and a bullet in the brain—you'll answer my goddamn questions."

"Then let me out here."

Jeff Knetsch had known nothing—or nothing he was willing to share—about Harry Leeds. He claimed he'd never heard the name, and when Rush cut the interview short and sent Jeff back to his group cell, the lawyer lost his last fingerhold on sanity. He brayed an unintelligible snatch of verse as the police hauled him back to the cell.

Stefani got no more information, no free passage from the labyrinth she'd entered that Friday morning. *Oliver's sold the girl to Sompong.*

Rush slid onto the highway's shoulder and slammed on the brakes. As she reached for the door handle, however, he seized her wrist.

"Where the hell are you going? Where do you think is even remotely safe from Sompong and his thugs? He got to you at the Oriental. He got to a whore in Geneva and to Max in Courchevel. He'll find you, wherever you are. Flight is not an option."

She glared at him—at the golden-skinned, half-Thai face with the eyes that weren't calculating, now, or veiled with facile charm—and saw that he was furious and prepared to be as ruthless as necessary. She let go of the door handle. He released her arm and turned off the engine.

"You've heard of Oliver?" she said. It was a rhetorical question.

"His name has come up in the course of my work. You can't run an operation like Krane's—selling information to corporate entities or countries or individuals with dubious or no loyalties—without brushing the margins of the law."

"Was Knetsch telling the truth? About Sompong being one of Oliver's clients?"

"I've known that for over a year," Rush declared baldly. "How long since Krane hired you?"

"Eight months."

"Do the math. You flew to Courchevel in March to represent Max Roderick? What did Krane tell you to do?"

"Explain to Max that the murdered prostitute was just the opening round in a campaign to destroy him. Figure out if the lost Roderick fortune could be traced. Decide whether Max was serious about challenging the Thai government—and what exactly that effort might cost."

"You were Krane's spy. He needed a pair of eyes in Max's camp, so he could monitor events for Sompong."

"Knetsch was *already* in Max's camp, reporting to Sompong! What would Oliver need me for?"

"To report on Knetsch. Oliver was taking fees from Max *and* Sompong, but working solely for himself. He played his clients against each other: he dictated every move. What a game! How could Oliver Krane resist?"

"*You and I will be working both ends of the problem, ducks,*" she quoted bitterly. "Only one of us got royally screwed."

"And Max died. You have to consider the possibility that your boss pushed that chair off the cliff."

"He's not my boss anymore."

Rush smiled grimly. "You helped Krane engage in what might be called a flaming conflict of interest. What in Christ's name were you thinking?"

"I trusted him," she shot back. "I fell for the oldest male traps in the world: flattery and fine wine. He offered me the world on a silver platter and I condescended to take it. I never saw the setup."

"Then Krane must be damn good—because you're not a stupid woman."

"He was so obviously torn apart by the death—murder, he called it—of his partner in Kowloon."

Oliver in his worn leather chair in the Scottish Highlands, submitting to the sacrament of penance. She hadn't imagined that pain on his face, or the hair shirt of culpability. Had she?

"Kowloon?" Beside her, Rush stiffened. "What do you know about Kowloon?"

"Harry Leeds," she said. "Harry fucking Leeds. He was run down by a taxi on a Kowloon street and Oliver couldn't accept it. I thought he wanted to nail Harry's killers, and that I could help him do it."

"Explain." Behind their backs, the clogged street traffic inched by.

"Harry Leeds was Oliver's Asian partner, operating out of Hong Kong—also his oldest friend, if we can believe anything Oliver says."

"Does Krane have a Bangkok office?"

"No. Just Hong Kong and Shanghai, in this part of the world. Oliver's primarily focused on the Chinese market."

"Is he?" Rush's eyes glinted. "Go on."

"When the strangled girl showed up in Max's bed last January, Piste Ski—the French firm for which Max designed equipment—called in Krane's to investigate."

"Covering its corporate back."

She nodded. "Oliver used his networks to research the girl's murder. The Swiss police knew nothing of Max's Thai inheritance or his trip to Bangkok or Jack Roderick's disappearance thirty-five years ago. They didn't realize that the dead prostitute was a warning. *But Oliver knew.* The whole hit was Thai. And Oliver thought he knew who'd ordered it."

"Sompong?"

"He didn't tell me. But whatever report he sent to Harry, requesting help or information from Krane's Asian division, got Harry killed. Four hours after receiving Oliver's secure fax, Leeds was dead."

"Let me get this straight: You trusted Oliver Krane *because* he'd gotten his oldest friend killed?"

"I thought he was emotionally invested." She looked away from Rush, toward the lush jungle growth that bordered the snarled highway. "Why are you so interested in Kowloon?"

"I lived there once." Abruptly, Rush turned his key in the ignition. "Oliver Krane set the rules of this game, up until Wednesday night—when Jeff Knetsch told Sompong who you really are."

"The cuckoo in the nest. Oliver's fucked, isn't he?"

"Question is—will Sompong go after Krane? Or Krane's pawn—you?"

Rush settled her in his living room with a glass of Thai iced tea and a copy of *I Was Amelia Earhart* to entertain her. He solicited a promise that she wouldn't move from the condo, wouldn't open the front door to anyone but himself, and left her alone.

When he reached the pavement, he walked purposefully in the direction of the U.S. embassy until he knew, from experience, that he was beyond the sight of someone watching from his living-room window. Then he turned left along a side street and doubled back to Wireless Road. There he took up a sheltered position near a news kiosk that offered an excellent view of his building's front entrance.

It was possible, of course, that she had told him everything she knew about Krane and Sompong Suwannathat. She might actually be a victim of circumstance—a puppet whose strings had been tangled against her will. But Rush believed that she was smarter than that—too smart to be played the way she insisted Oliver Krane had played her.

Is it a coin toss for control of Sompong's empire? Rush thought, as he surveyed a rack of magazines. *Is she pretending to be at odds with Krane, because Knetsch said too much this morning?* It was possible that Krane intended to take over Sompong's operation—and Stefani intended to take out Oliver first. Might she actually be shooting for all the marbles? Winning, Rush knew, was fundamental to Stefani Fogg. Almost more fundamental than survival.

He would pretend to be a credulous chump. He would leave her to her own devices for a while, and if she bolted—follow where she led.

"Marty," he said quietly into his cell phone, "I'm waiting for our friend. I don't know how long I'll be."

"Keep me posted."

Rush shut off his phone. Marty Robbins, his station chief, knew all about Kowloon. Marty didn't have to be told what Krane & Associates could do. He wanted Sompong Suwannathat by the balls and he was convinced Stefani Fogg would carry Rush to the end of all the questions the station had asked about the minister for years.

Why are you so damn interested in Kowloon?

He flipped through a sports magazine, his attention focused on his front door.

Once upon a time Rush Halliwell had been a junior case officer in Hong Kong, with responsibility for the internal Chinese triads that controlled commerce and crime. Triads were an accepted part of the fabric of the colony's life, and they made dull work for a CIA case officer—or had, until Rush took over the job. He landed in Hong Kong in 1995, when the fantasy of the island's reversion to mainland China was about to come true. The greatest capitalist enclave in Asia would soon be handed to the greatest Communist power left in the world, and everyone who read tea leaves for a living was jumpy as hell about the consequences.

The U.S. embassy muttered darkly that the British were almost certainly fomenting Chinese rebellion, just to make the handover painful. The British countered hotly that the CIA must be funding triad violence to make the colonial administration look bad. In the midst of all the backbiting a cache of guns nobody could explain or account for was actually discovered in the ceiling joists of a condemned house in Kowloon. And the problem became Rush's to solve.

Guns were banned from the Crown Colony of Hong Kong; possession of them was a capital offense. No one, however, would claim the Kowloon guns; thus, who could be prosecuted? Two men who loitered near the condemned house—triad scouts, in the hysterical language of the Hong Kong press—were arrested and questioned, but the trail was cold: interrogation led nowhere. Rush fruitlessly trolled the station's best fishing grounds. He gauged the quality of the street silence and assessed the level of official no-comment and decided that the arms were intended not for triads or Commie haters among the Chinese population, but for a powerful man's private militia. Somebody with massive amounts of money and no British passport—somebody who couldn't get out of Hong Kong with his fortune intact—had decided to do a little gun-running as insurance against the Communist takeover.

The matter, as far as Rush and the Hong Kong police were concerned, would never be solved.

Except that Rush was intrigued by an item he found while scrolling through files on gun-running, worldwide. A series of arms shipments intended for mainland China that same year had never arrived at their appointed destination. The guns had originated in Slovakia—part of that country's Soviet legacy being liquidated in the name of democracy. A Chinese broker in Bangkok had arranged and insured the sales. The entire transaction was legal and above-board. Except that thirty million dollars' worth of guns had never arrived.

Pirates hijacked one load from a commercial vessel in the Gulf of Thailand. Another disappeared when a transport plane crashed in western Burma. A third, traveling overland through Laos, was seized at gunpoint by masked guerillas. By the end of five unfortunate months in 1995, nearly ninety thousand weapons—street sweepers, AK-47s, nine-millimeter handguns—had vanished into thin air.

Rush called up an old friend in Bangkok who served as legal attaché, and requested background.

"The gun broker's name was Chiang Wu Fat," Avril Blair had said. "He rented a warehouse in the Nakorn Kasem—the Bangkok Thieves Market—but the warehouse is shut down now and Chiang can't be found. He probably doesn't exist."

"He paid the insurance?"

"A hefty sum. Nothing compared to the street value of those guns, of course. Call it Chiang's modest investment in his own future."

"How did the FBI get involved?"

Avril had paused, no doubt debating Rush's need to know. "We were approached by a man named Oliver Krane. You've heard of him?"

Rush had.

"Krane was hired by the insurance company that got stiffed for the full value of the guns, roughly thirty million dollars, all told. They'd like to recover a few of them. Krane figured the bureau was the only organization capable of handling this big a mess. And he suggested delicately that we wouldn't want those guns to land in L.A. or Newark."

"Any progress?" Rush asked.

"None," she replied cheerfully.

He'd laughed out loud. "Krane picked the wrong agency, Avril. But the CIA is delighted to help."

By 1997, when the handover of Hong Kong seemed to be progressing smoothly, Rush traded the colony for Bangkok and, during his first week in the embassy, visited the warehouse in the Thieves Market. It was empty.

"Who owns that place?" he asked Avril later.

"The Minister of Culture—Suwannathat. You'll find Sompong's name behind a lot of local real estate, if you search hard enough."

"He uses proxies to buy up land?"

"Extended networks of them."

"Could we pin the minister for those Chinese arms heists?"

"Not a chance," she'd retorted.

Had Sompong arranged the weapons thefts to supply his private army in Chiang Rai? Had he done the 30-million-dollar deal simply for kicks? Neither the LegAtt nor the station could say. The minister's motives for his shadow life were obscure. Sompong possessed more than enough political power to protect himself; he had inherited millions from his father. "So what," Marty had demanded in futile frustration, "is the asshole's *point*?

"He's growing poppies up there in the hills," the station chief complained, "and he's got the Army to protect his drugs. The guns he stole from the Chinese *pay* for the drugs—and the drugs sustain Sompong's offshore bank accounts. Which in turn support his Army. It's one big circle-jerk. What the hell's he doing it for? And where is all that poppy dust *going?*"

The station had never, in the five years of Rush's tour, fingered Sompong's distribution network. The failure was acutely embarrassing. They got no help, of course, from Thailand's panoply of security forces. Sompong remained untouchable.

As Rush stood before the kiosk on the pavement opposite his

condo building, he thought of all that Stefani Fogg had told him that day. One fragment of information—so casually dropped she probably thought he'd overlooked it—was the key to everything.

There's a show going up in a few weeks that both Ankana and Jeff are involved in. Rush knew all about the art exhibition intended for the Met. For months, the embassy had worked closely with the Ministry of Culture on the project, approving the duty-free shipment of artifacts and oiling the delicate wheels of international exchange.

What Rush hadn't understood was the significance of Jeff Knetsch—whom Halliwell had glimpsed studying ceramics with Sompong Suwannathat in the Nakorn Kasem Tuesday night. Knetsch, the distinguished member of the Metropolitan Museum of Art's Board, who'd been arrested Thursday for heroin possession.

Rush returned the magazine he'd been scanning and pulled out his cell phone a second time.

"Marty, we need a favor from Liaison. Find a Bangkok police detective named Itchayanan. Tell him you've got a lead in a murder case he's tracking. He should visit a warehouse in the Nakorn Kasem—"

Rush would have told Marty about the ceramics Sompong was using to ship drugs to the Metropolitan Museum of Art, but he broke off in midsentence, his eyes fixed on the entry of his building.

Stefani Fogg had just walked out the door.

3

Bangkok,
1963

The three of them sat in a corner of the Bamboo Bar until nearly two A.M., not drinking much but enjoying the protective cover of other *farang* conversation. Amid the English and French and occasional spurt of Italian it was possible to converse without drawing attention. Joe Halliwell was in his shirtsleeves and his tie was loosened. Roderick wore a pair of light cotton pants and an open-collared shirt; three hours earlier he'd worn an elegant suit fashioned of his own Thai silk, but had handed it to the host of their dinner party merely because the man admired it.

Self-promotion, Roderick explained airily as he ducked into a taxi in a borrowed dressing gown. *Grand gestures. Market sense.* Halliwell refrained from snapping a photo or quoting him for the morning edition. It required all his strength.

Alec McQueen was his usual disheveled self. In the course of nearly two decades in Thailand he had acquired a bit of weight to his frame, a rounding of his garish edges. He blew smoke rings to torment Jack, who had been advised for his health to forgo tobacco. Roderick followed the rings' flight through the huddle of heads in the shadowy room, his eyes narrowed and his thoughts quite far away.

"They're saying a few more months," McQueen murmured around

the stem of his pipe. "Months!—When Kennedy's facing a stiff reelection campaign, and needs to look like a winner? Call it a few more weeks."

"You think JFK escalates," Halliwell countered, "and wipes up the mess in an afternoon? Or does he keep the boys at home and save lives? Which strategy wins the most votes?"

"They'll never kick Jackie out of the White House," Roderick said absently, "so Kennedy should stop worrying about the election and get the hell out of Southeast Asia. Every local boy between the ages of nine and eighty-three, from Vientiane to Rangoon to Phnom Penh, has an AK-47 under his pillow courtesy of Chairman Mao. We're outgunned and in this terrain we're bound to be outmaneuvered. I told the President so, myself."

"Kennedy? You talked to the President?"

"I sent some fabric to the First Lady. Kennedy phoned in his thanks."

The newspapermen stared at Roderick, who shrugged. "She'd seen *The King and I* on Broadway. All the costumes were made of Jack Roderick Silk. She liked them."

Halliwell fidgeted with his lighter, snapping the flame on and off. Then McQueen said, with a barking laugh, "You never urged retreat in the jungles of Ceylon, Jack."

"We were fighting the Japanese then. They had ships and planes and an organized attack. There was predictability, Alec—something we could target, an enemy we could find. This bunch in Vietnam is nothing but a lot of armed zealots firing knockoffs of Soviet missiles."

"Exactly. We'll roll over 'em. Give us a real army! The hell with military advisors!"

"Roll over them—just like the French did?"

"The French are a bunch of pussies. We bailed them out in '44, and we're about to do it again. Besides," McQueen added, changing tack, "it's not a real war in Vietnam. It's all about Uncle Ho. A cult of personality."

"Look what that did for the Chinese."

Roderick had silenced them again. Across the room, a girl with platinum hair and a beauty mark like Monroe's laughed in a timbre husky with smoke. The three men allowed their eyes to graze her form but none of them was moved to comment.

"Your old friend Ruth still alive, Jack?" McQueen asked idly.

"As far as I know."

"Spouting propaganda in China? Or has he moved on to Laos?"

"We aren't exactly in touch, Alec."

"Who's Ruth?" Joe Halliwell asked.

"I've been thinking about a profile for the paper," McQueen persisted. "Pridi Banomyong, fifteen years after the failed '48 counter-coup. Thailand's wartime hero, disgraced and living in exile. Where is Ruth now? Was all the blood and loss worth it? That sort of crap."

"Who's Ruth?" Halliwell repeated.

Roderick glanced at the reporter's innocent face, a good twenty years younger than his own, and reflected that experience of war made a profound difference in a man. He and Halliwell had both sprung from privileged families, on opposite sides of the United States, and they'd both had an Ivy League education; but there the commonalities ceased. Too much history filled the chasm between them.

"Ruth is an old war hero, Joe. Heroes, you'll find, never age well."

"Speaking of which," McQueen broke in, "I saw that little shit Vukrit yesterday. He didn't see me, however, so I crossed to the opposite sidewalk and ducked into a doorway. Word has it he's bought his way back into power."

"Impossible," Roderick said easily.

"This is Thailand, Jack. Nothing's impossible."

Roderick drained his glass. "Vukrit's been wandering in the wasteland of Pattaya for at least six years." Ever since Field Marshal Sarit had ousted the dictator Pibul. September 1957—the same month Roderick had delivered Carlos's son to Vukrit's wife at her villa on the coast. Six years ago. The last time Roderick had seen Fleur.

My God, she'd be thirty-one. What does she look like now? And where has she gone?

"Word has it Vukrit's got the Ministry of Culture back in his pocket," Joe Halliwell put in unexpectedly. "Paper's running a piece on the appointment tomorrow."

"We expect him to come out swinging on behalf of tradition and heritage," McQueen added. "Siam for the Siamese, that sort of thing."

"When a man is afraid of the people he leads," Roderick said, "he makes them hate the outsider instead of himself."

The two journalists were both watching Roderick now, McQueen's eyes glinting through his tobacco smoke. Roderick knew that he was pontificating in a way that was embarrassing—ideals had gone out of fashion lately—but he could not stop himself. The lateness of the hour, the effect of gin, the mention of Vukrit's name. The memory of Fleur—

"Vukrit will circle the wagons around his sacred ruins while the rest of Southeast Asia goes up in flames," he said, more loudly. "And you know what, gentlemen? He'll get funding from the United States to do it. Vukrit's our boy, now. We've put the palace thief in charge of the armory. That's where two decades of fostering democracy have got us."

"He'll start by attacking the *farang* community," Halliwell observed.

"By seizing my house, in fact. Isn't that what you're trying to tell me? Vukrit will come calling, and carry out everything I own in a wheelbarrow? At least it'll save me having to invite him to dinner."

Roderick rose from the table. He was fifty-eight years old and the weight of age was suddenly stifling. "Gentlemen, I believe I should call it a day."

"Come on, Jack," McQueen said brusquely. "Let me buy you another drink! The evening's young."

"I wasn't talking about the evening, Alec." Roderick nodded courteously to Halliwell, then turned away.

He decided to walk for a bit, although Ban Khrua was miles off and the streets at this hour were empty. Another man might have felt vulnerable, the sole *farang* in the night of an Asian city, but Roderick waved off the Oriental's taxi and set out at a brisk pace along New Road. He walked with one hand in his trouser pocket and the other swinging at his side, his shoulders hunched slightly forward. *Six years.* Fleur might even have died in so much time.

He wondered, as he walked, when it would happen to him—that instant of oblivion called death. His doctor was worried about his heart. *His heart.* He laughed mirthlessly. Perhaps he should leave Bangkok, and put behind him forever the factions and the folly and the endless cycle of warlords supplanting warlords in the name of democratic process. He had no love for Communism but he could not distinguish it from the military dictatorships in Siam that called themselves constitutional monarchies, and he could not support this new

American "engagement"—a word for a wedding party!—with Vietnam. He had dreamed a dream of Asia that sprang from silk and the bones of a boy named Boonreung, but art and the desire for justice both grew cold with the passage of years. Perhaps he should go home to die.

Mother's not well, his son Rory had said the previous afternoon as they stared at each other across the gleaming expanse of his teakwood floor. "She's got high blood pressure. There's the possibility of stroke."

He had tried to imagine Joan as she must look now, twenty years further into her gaudy gypsy life. He failed to conjure a face. Joan, with high blood pressure. A box she could not paint herself out of.

And there was Rory standing in his living room—a tall stranger in a naval uniform, his hair clipped short and his cap tucked neatly under his arm. All the lost years like high water between them. In the absence of photographs, Roderick had conjured Rory's face a thousand times. And never imagined *this*.

The boy had sent letters, of course—at least three of them scrawled childishly on lined yellow paper, several others that were typewritten and signed. For his part, Roderick had corresponded persistently after the final break in 1946—mailing cheerful, abrupt, unrealistic letters. He shipped lengths of silk to Joan and sketches of the dresses she might make of them. Hand-carved wooden toys the boy had long outgrown. Pictures of himself with Boonreung's old bird on his shoulder. And money. Bank drafts were the surest antidote to guilt Roderick knew.

He had made four trips back to the United States during his years in Asia. He'd visited his son in Evanston and California and at the Naval Academy when Rory was a cadet, Roderick established in an elegant hotel room, the boy delivered like a package by an efficient bellman. Joan flitted in and out on these occasions, waving gloved hands, and spoke heartily of Rory's need for "man time." They visited museums together. They conferred on the finer points of baseball. They shook hands efficiently at parting.

But Rory was no longer a boy. It was September 1963, and he was twenty-seven years old, married now to the daughter of a Chicago banker he'd known since he was eleven. He'd brought to Bangkok a four-year-old named Max—Roderick's only grandchild, whom he had never before seen. They had three days until Rory joined his carrier group in Subic Bay.

"How long has it been?"

He stood, correctly gripping his son's hand, Rory's gaze on a level with his own at last.

"Since that trip to Stowe? I'd just turned sixteen."

Roderick remembered then the patchy snow of Vermont in January, shining blue with ice in places, and the way Rory's fear had hunched his body over the skis, so that the boy was rigid with the certainty of falling. Had the kid ever skied again?

"But I came to Annapolis," he protested. "For your commission."

"So you did. Five years ago, then."

The house was lashed with rain; the khlong curled above its banks in a heavy brown spume. It was the height of the monsoon season. Roderick introduced Rory to Chanat Surian, the houseboy, who took young Max under his wing and fed him rice pudding made with coconut milk. Roderick filled the silences with anecdote. He found he was bracing for some vital communication—news of a death, of emotional upheaval—that might explain his son's unexpected visitation.

"Your life's nothing like I imagined it." Rory's gaze roamed the soaring rafters of the room. "I always saw you in the jungle, surrounded by crocodiles. Like the ends of all the old maps: *Here there be dragons.*"

Roderick liked the sailor's image, though the truth of it pained him. "Your wife," he said diffidently. "She doesn't mind you being gone for months at a time?"

"Annie hates it. And I swore if I married I'd never leave like . . ."

. . . *I left you,* Roderick supplied mentally.

"But what can I do? I can't catch tailhooks in the middle of Illinois. That's why I brought Max on this trip. I've got carrier duty next week. He'll be almost five by the time I get back."

Max, with a shock of blond hair and the self-absorbed expression of a child who lives in his head, was sliding across the floorboards in his stocking feet. Murmuring to himself. The sounds were akin to birdsong.

"You never found . . . anyone else, I suppose? After Mother?" Rory asked unexpectedly.

"No," Roderick lied. "I never found her."

He'd taken off his shoes then and scooted across the floor in his grandson's wake while Rory watched them: balancing, balancing.

The breeze was halfhearted in the banana trees, the air thick with moisture. The glare of neon in the red-light district was something new in recent years, electric sketches of faceless nymphs flexing their endless legs. Howling floated down the block as he stood, repulsed and fascinated, under the arched gates; it was a compound of men, Americans mostly, off the ships that had begun to troll the China Sea.

"The girls wear numbers," Alec McQueen had told him once, "pinned to their breasts. You pick them off the shelf like candy bars. Jack, you ought to come with me sometime. It makes old Miss Lucy's look positively quaint."

The boys from Spokane and Des Moines and Raleigh had no idea that the women of Siam were among the most bashful on earth, that the display of a shoulder in public was considered licentious, or that the nude country girls working diligently under the harsh lights were amassing their dowries and only tolerated the looks and touch of these *farang* soldiers because money was money and marriage was everything.

In her years at the house on the khlong had Fleur been just another working girl? Amassing riches and secrets against some rainy day, when dancing no longer sustained her? Roderick could not say. He had believed in Fleur's love because she was necessary to his happiness. He knew nothing of what she had felt or all that she had hidden—only what she had sold.

He turned his back on Patpong.

It seemed to him that this city he loved—a place of waterways and dancers as lovely as birds, of gilded temples and jasmine bloom—was a fruit left too long to rot. The taint of war and death was upon it.

He flagged down a taxi and went home.

It was past three-thirty in the morning when at last he mounted the stairs of the house on the khlong. There was a torch burning in the entrance hall and other lights elsewhere; but he thought nothing of this because Rory was visiting, and perhaps young Max suffered from nightmares. He imagined a pot of milk warmed by the houseboy, and Max's legs kicking at the bedcovers as he drank. Rory's hands smoothing the child's hair. He had done that himself quite often in Rory's early years—a father's mute gesture of love. But as he turned toward the terrace he heard a murmur of voices through the open doors. Max's bedroom was dark.

Two people leaned against the railing—Rory and another man in uniform. Roderick's gaze swept the length of that never-to-be-forgotten figure and he felt his heart leap. "Billy Lightfoot," he said softly. "You old son of a gun."

"Where the hell you been, Jack?" his OSS trainer chortled. "A grandpa like you shoulda been in bed long ago!"

Lightfoot seized his palm and slapped his shoulder and guffawed with the grand American *bonhomie* of a man accustomed to giving orders. That quickly they were both returned to the open door of the jump plane out of Ceylon—August 14, 1945—and Roderick could have sworn he was thirty-nine years old with a drop-dead letter and seven dollars' worth of Thai baht jingling in his pocket.

"Son of a gun," he repeated. "What are you doing in Bangkok? And why didn't you tell me you were coming?"

"Wouldn't have been a surprise," Lightfoot rejoined unabashedly. "Thought I'd turn up like a bad penny and have the Legendary American show me the town. Course, you were already out wining and dining. Houseboy very nearly wouldn't let me in."

"Chanat is trained to turn the world away."

Lightfoot must be over sixty, now, but hard as iron; a ramrod soldier to the death. White hair flecked his temples. His eyes were piercing in the half-light of the terrace.

"It's damn good to see you, Billy. You've met my son?"

"*Fine* boy, though he chose the wrong service. Remember seeing his picture when he was just in diapers." He punched Rory's shoulder, a gesture Roderick could never have managed without awkwardness. *The command of men*, he thought, surveying the two faces, lit by a kindred flush of power and certainty. *Billy's always had it in the blood.*

"You made flag rank." Roderick eyed Lightfoot's uniform. "Brigadier general. That's grand. Come into the house and have a drink."

Lightfoot shook his head. "Rory here made me some java and it set me up great. Drove down from Khorat in a Jeep and the thing damn near broke my back, plowing through those ruts. Man! This country!"

"Khorat?" Roderick was arrested by the word. "Why in God's name go there? Nobody does."

"They will," Lightfoot said sagely. "You know we've been beefing up the Royal Thai Air Force over the past few years—giving 'em training and planes we don't really need—and they've been flying air recon for us since '60."

"Over Laos?"

"Of course, Laos. Place is a hellhole. They've got a three-pronged civil war sapping the bejesus out of the countryside—the Communist Pathet Lao, the centrists, the ultraright military faction—and we've had reports that North Vietnamese Army regulars are integrating with the rank-and-file Pathet Lao. You see what that means."

"An extension of the conflict from Vietnam to Laos." The war jumping like brushfire from treetop to treetop until all of Southeast Asia was ablaze.

"Damn straight. Pathet Lao have already shot down some of our planes."

"And Khorat makes a perfect staging ground for retaliation."

"It'd be illegal to fight this war on Thai soil. We're not gonna throw bombers into the sky from the northeast—though it'd make a lot of sense, I don't have to tell you. Pentagon sent me out to find a good staging ground for air recon, pilot rescue and the like. We need that goddamn wasteland they got around Khorat—no people, no rain, no livestock for the F-One-oh-Wonders to buzz."

"Just mulberry trees," Roderick murmured, "and clay pots. You may not plan to fight the war on Thai soil, Billy, but you can't avoid it. Half the Thais in the northeast are ethnic Lao and Khmer."

"Then we'd better make damn sure they know which way their loyalties lie."

"With their families. They don't understand anything else."

"We'll have to start schooling 'em," Lightfoot said stringently. "We're not just fighting little men in pajamas and lampshades, Jack. We're fighting Khrushchev himself. You know what the Russkie bastard said, coupla years back—the U.S.S.R. supports these 'national wars of liberation.' Seems to me wars are breaking out all over your neighborhood, and you're content to let the Sovs just roll on in."

"Dad—" A strange word in Rory's mouth. He was flushed with impatience. "Everyone has to choose which side they're on. Ours—or the Communist Party's. Thailand's no exception."

Since when have you been an expert on Southeast Asia? Roderick thought. But all he said was, "How can I help, Billy?"

"I'm due to be posted to Vientiane next month." Lightfoot beamed. "Military advisor, they're calling it. I can't wait to get back into the action again."

"Vientiane is a beautiful city."

"Probably spend most of my damn time checking the bottom of the Jeep for bombs. Bound to be a target. That Pathet Lao don't fool around, you know. One of your old friends is pretty high up in the organization—fella by the name of Tao Oum."

Tao Oum. Roderick understood, now, the reason for Lightfoot's sudden visit. Lightfoot had gone operational: Roderick was his best hope for a subagent with access.

"Rory," he told his son, "thanks for entertaining Billy. We'll have a late breakfast in the morning."

"I'm not tired," Rory replied.

"Kid don't need to leave on my account," Lightfoot said easily. "Hell, he'll be fighting this war in another coupla months. Deserves to know what's at stake, right? Training in A-4s, he tells me. Pentagon's got plans for *those.*"

"He's not a kid," Roderick objected, and heard the strain in his voice. "I hope to God we're out of this before he has to fly bombing runs over Hanoi."

"I think I'm the best judge of that."

"Of course you do, Rory. But you've no idea what this war will be like. I'm betting it won't match up to the diagrams in the strategy books."

"Not if we hit hard, and hit early," Rory argued.

The weariness and age Roderick had felt earlier in the evening were like coils of rope, twined about his chest, throttling his throat. He wanted to tear at them with his hands, cast their weight into the khlong. He wanted to watch the years sink from sight like dead leaves.

"Since when did you turn defeatist, Jack?" Lightfoot demanded. "Wasn't part of your OSS training, far's I can tell. Remember how the

Japs ran, that day we landed here in Bangkok? I was just telling Rory what this place was like, before his old man moved in and took over."

"I didn't take over, Billy. Nobody does, in Asia."

"Seems to me that's the crux of the problem."

"Hear, hear," Rory muttered.

Behind the brisk impatience of both of them lay a continent's worth of ignorance. Roderick's heart sank. He glanced at his son's face and saw disdain for this father who'd gone native, who was so patently out of step.

And so he'll make war, Roderick realized, *in spite of Max and the wife he loves and the future before him, to prove he owes nothing to me. To show the world we're utterly different people. Jesus, this life and everyone in it are fucked.*

"This isn't the time for false sympathy, Jack." Lightfoot sounded confused—worried, even, as though in the dark he'd blundered against a stranger. "If we don't stop the cancer in Laos and Vietnam, it'll spread to Thailand next—and your silk business will be one big Commie co-op."

"It already is, Billy. I set it up that way."

"*Shit*—you been gone from the States too long."

"Perhaps I have." Roderick reached for the packet of cigarettes he was not supposed to smoke and lit one deliberately. "And maybe you've been gone too little."

There was a tense silence as Lightfoot considered and changed tactics. "That's why I wanted to talk to you. Nobody's got this neighborhood down like the Legendary American—you know that's what they call you up in Khorat? We need your help, Jack—and I'm not afraid to ask for it."

An encircling maneuver, Roderick thought, *once the frontal assault has failed.*

"I've been reading reports," Lightfoot went on. "Rafts and reams of 'em, to get me up to speed. Reports in Washington, reports on the transport plane over here, reports that date back twenty years. Agency stuff, mostly. The covert boys are all over the hills of northern Laos. But I liked the old pieces best—the real background. You wrote most of *those* papers."

Roderick blinked as the smoke bit at his eyelids. "That was a long time ago. I sell silk now."

"Your networks," Lightfoot persisted. "The guys you used to run. Some of 'em must still be out there. You must know what happened to 'em. Like that Tao Oum, in Vientiane. Think he's open to reason? A heart-to-heart with his old pal Roderick?"

"From what I know of Agency operations in Tao Oum's neck of the woods," Roderick replied, "I'd get a bullet in the brain if I so much as contacted him."

The undeclared war in Laos had been raging, now, for three years. It was conducted through sabotage and betrayal and payoffs and throat-slitting; it involved the parachuting of trained double agents into the countryside, where they were invariably captured, killed or doubled back against the next team to be dropped at night. Roderick was famil-iar with the charming, well-mannered young men who orchestrated such operations. He had entertained the first wave of them at his home on the khlong, before he understood what they were prepared to do. He recognized in their classically molded faces and their extensive edu-cations the natural successors of the men's club he'd known in the OSS—recognized, too, that the Good Fight of 1945 had evolved into the Cold War, where ideals were secondary to expediency. He'd come to loathe the profound ignorance of region and culture these men exhib-ited; loathed their self-assurance and the offhand way they spoke of ca-sualties, as though death were a tool like any other they deployed. He had thrown elections in his day, but never entire countries into the maw of civil war. In November of 1960 he resigned his unofficial, un-mentionable espionage role—a life that had been second nature for as long as he could remember—and settled down to sell silk full-time, in-stead of secrets. He tried not to regard this as a defeat.

"I assume the CIA is still in touch with the agents I once ran," Roderick said. "They'd be happy to brief you before you head out to post. But I told you, Billy: I retired from the business a good while back. I didn't like the trend I saw in local politics."

"Then help us reverse the trend." Lightfoot gripped his shoul-der painfully, a soldier's weight in his fingers, bearing down. "What about your old buddy holed up in the hills—the guerilla commander? Code name Carlos. He worked with Pridi Banomyong during the war, and went AWOL soon after. You never gave *him* to the Agency handlers."

"I have no idea where he is." Roderick's face was rigid with suppressed rage. *Not Carlos. Never Carlos. I will be true to one thing in the end, at least.*

Lightfoot glanced at Rory. "Your Old Man doesn't get it, son. This is a war we're fighting!"

"Dad," Rory said with brittle anger, "if the General's asking for help, don't you think you should give it? You owe it to your country. To *me*, for God's sake. I'm the one whose life will be on the line."

Oh, Rory, he thought, *you burn to put it there.*

"This Carlos," Lightfoot continued. "He's got Chinese in his troops—you wrote that, in your reports."

"Nationalist Chinese," Roderick reminded him patiently. "They hate the Communists, Billy. They're not a threat to U.S. security."

"Those boys in the hills are vicious as hell," Lightfoot countered. "They're mercenaries. They know the border country, they've got jungle tactics. A gift or a curse to U.S. forces, depending how they're handled. We need to sign 'em up for our side, before Uncle Ho adds 'em to his column."

"And if they want no part of a foreign war?"

"Then we neutralize 'em, before they stab us in the back." Lightfoot's eyes had hardened. "Come on, Jack. You know the score. Remember Miss Lucy's? The broad in the whorehouse marking time, while you whacked that backroom goon?"

"You knew about that?"

"About *what*?" Rory's head swiveled from one man to the other.

"I put two and two together," Lightfoot retorted. "Didn't take a rocket scientist. One night we're touring the torture district, and the next the torture chief is dead."

"Miss Lucy sold out seven years ago, Billy, and you already know enough about Carlos. You don't need me."

"I need to know where your sympathies lie, Jack." Lightfoot stepped closer, his massive chest like a blunt wall. "You handled this joker for years. I'm giving you a choice: Take our position to Carlos and get his commitment in writing. Sign him up for our side."

"And if I refuse?"

". . . Then stand down. And don't cry at the consequences."

Roderick studied Billy Lightfoot—his cropped hair, his clear gaze, his untroubled brow. Billy fought the good fights. Billy carried certainty in his heart. Billy understood that the world was one of brute survival, a place where friendship and trust and obligation were secondary to the demands of the nation he served. Billy was fortunate in having only one country to love, only one way of life that made sense. He had never lived in the wilderness between black and white, where every secret agent ends.

"I want no part of your war," Roderick told him softly, "and I'll act as I think best."

Later, he could not have said whether it was Billy's fist or Rory's that hit him first.

He stood at the head of the stairs, watching Lightfoot descend in blunt, angry steps. It was nearly dawn. He held a white silk handkerchief to his bleeding nose and Rory—who should have thought of his career, and left with Lightfoot in a hired taxi, never to return—was crouching in the doorway of Max's bedroom.

"It's okay, Max," he told the four-year-old, over and over, stroking his hair just as Roderick had imagined he would. "It's okay. Go back to sleep. It will all be fine in the morning."

4

Awareness that one is a hunted animal will focus the mind wonderfully; but not, it seemed, upon *I Was Amelia Earhart*. Abandoned in Rush Halliwell's apartment, Stefani found the character of the doomed aviatrix uncongenial. She dropped her book a mere twelve minutes after Rush's exit, and roamed restlessly about his apartment in search of distraction.

She did not, as he suspected, watch at his window to be certain he was truly bound for the embassy. She ran one finger over a Bencharong vase he had placed squarely in the middle of his bookshelf and scanned the few photographs, mostly European landscapes—there seemed a marked absence of people in Rush's private world—that he had propped on surfaces about the room. She had no interest, as some partygoers might, in examining the bathroom medicine cabinet for clues to his weaknesses. She was leashed like a dog in the confines of her own mind, prowling the walls without discovering an escape hatch. *Flight,* Rush had said, *is not an option.*

It occurred to her that if the sum of a person's talents might be regarded as, for example, a mutual fund—then she had performed very poorly since her departure from FundMarket. She had operated on untested assumptions: that Oliver possessed integrity, and valued her as a person; that her instincts were sound; that her native intelligence would save her from mortal error. When viewed in retrospect, however, her actions of the past eight months were appalling. She had misjudged almost everyone. She had badly miscalculated the level of risk in the games she played, and fatally underestimated the depth of her own entanglement. Sompong Suwannathat had possessed greater knowledge of her movements than she had known of his; he had outmaneuvered her from the start. It was reasonable, in sum, to feel like an ignorant fool.

It was not constructive to feel terrified.

She had always believed that the rest of the world was less intelligent than she was. That arrogance had blinded her. As the lawyer Matthew French had pointed out, her style was anything but subtle. A truly devious woman would have looked obvious while operating deftly behind the scenes; but she had somehow skipped that part of the agenda.

How could she recover? How could she beat Oliver and his brutal client—outwit the odds—and *win*?

She needed an ally. Not Rush Halliwell. He obviously mistrusted her and clearly had the interests of the CIA to protect. But someone who might benefit materially if she came out on top. Someone like . . . like *Dickie Spencer*. Dickie was on air-kiss terms with Ankana Lee-Harris, it was true, but not even Jeff Knetsch had implicated him in Max's murder. Dickie seemed like a subtle thinker. He had his silk business to protect, and control of the Thai Heritage Board to wrestle from Sompong's hands; he would instantly comprehend the advantage in joining forces with a dark horse like Stefani. Dickie knew Thai politics and Thai culture backward and forward—and that knowledge would counterbalance her abysmal lack. She was stuck in the tightest possible corner—on the lam in Sompong Suwannathat's city—and Spencer looked like the sole avenue out. Besides, she liked his dry British wit. Her gut insisted that Dickie could be trusted. Used, even?

The fact that her gut had led her astray more than once was irrelevant at the moment.

She flagged down a *tuk-tuk* in Wireless Road. Crossing the street casually in her wake, his head buried in a sports magazine, Rush Halliwell did the same. He wondered, with a dismay that surprised him, why she had bolted so quickly and where she was going without her luggage.

They jostled south through the evening rush hour, past Lumphini Park with its tandem lakes for boating and its vendors peddling fresh snake bile, then turned into Surawong Road.

"Marty," Rush muttered into his cell phone as the *tuk-tuk* pulled up before Jack Roderick Silk, "our lovely friend is souvenir shopping. Did you find Detective Itchayanan?"

"He's heading to the Nakorn Kasem."

"Keep in touch," Rush said, and told his driver to wait.

Surawong Road cut through the commercial soul of Bangkok, a place of skyscrapers and choking smog that was renowned, before the Second World War, for its fruit orchards. Now, the noise of cars and motorcycles and *tuk-tuk* horns drowned out the conversations of pedestrians standing yards away from Rush, and completely masked all activity on the street. He wandered past shop windows, his eyes apparently focused on the leather purses and rattan chairs offered within, while his gaze actually studied the reflection of the silk shop's doorway opposite. It remained persistently empty. Rush killed seventeen minutes this way, before abandoning the shops for a street cart positioned at the corner. He ordered a bowl of noodles and kept his eye roving over the opposite pavement while he ate them. Rain spattered the sidewalk and he huddled under the street cart's umbrella. The idling *tuk-tuk* driver blasted his horn.

Rush tossed the empty noodle cup in a trash can and glanced at his watch. Twenty-six minutes had passed since she had entered Jack Roderick Silk. How long did a woman need to choose a scarf? Was she Christmas shopping for her family back home? Assessing upholstery fabric for her New York apartment?

Apprehension gathered in his gut. He handed the *tuk-tuk* driver a hundred-baht note and told himself that he was absurd; women lost all track of time in places like Jack Roderick Silk. He'd worked surveillance for too many years to be so easily spooked. *Thirty-three minutes.* His eyes flicked back to the empty doorway, and suddenly he snarled, "Fuck it."

He stepped into the street and tore recklessly around cars idling in the sluggish traffic. He slowed as he reached the shop itself, only long enough to glance through the glass door. The interior was empty but for a girl arranging neckties in a display case. She glanced up when he entered, and smiled.

"The woman who came in," he said hurriedly in Thai. "Black hair. American. Where'd she go?"

The girl frowned and looked helpless.

The oldest dodge in the book, he raged to himself. *In by the front door, out by the back. The bitch gave me the slip.*

"Sir," the salesgirl called in distress as he sprinted for the offices at the rear of the store. "You cannot go back there without an appointment. The offices are closed! Sir!—"

Rush pushed through the door and found himself in a corridor. The lights were on, but the space was empty. So was the conference room to the right. And the large office with the planters' chairs on the left.

At the far end of the corridor a lighted *Exit* sign glowed. The door to the loading dock.

He slammed it open, furious now at his own stupidity, and stood staring down at the empty back lot. The rain was lashing down, drumming on the concrete of the delivery bay, running in steaming rivulets toward the drains. Rush turned his face into the wet and cursed Stefani Fogg. He almost hoped Sompong found her.

Marty Robbins stared intently through the one-way mirrored panel that lined the interrogation room's door. He had a clear view of the man seated at the table; his head was in his hands and he was sobbing uncontrollably. The police officer leaning over him—a Thai detective named Itchayanan, responsible for collecting evidence in Stefani Fogg's hotel room the previous night—barked something harsh and guttural. Everyone in the room behind the mirrored panel—Itchayanan's superior, a woman seated at a tape-recording device and Marty—straightened a bit, as though correct posture might help them comprehend the hysterical words filtering from the room.

His name was Khuang, and he worked as a potter. An exquisite craftsman, by all accounts. He had been found in a warehouse in the Nakorn Kasem, filling museum-quality ceramic vessels with heroin. Detective Itchayanan was exceedingly grateful to Marty Robbins for the tip. The discovery of Khuang, in fact, placed Itchayanan in Marty's debt.

Marty had been in Thailand long enough to know how to use that obligation. Cooperation between host-country and foreign security services was not unknown; but in a routine police matter like this, the CIA had no place. Itchayanan, however, had allowed Marty to watch the interrogation.

The American paid a hefty bribe to the woman running the tape-recording device, and was promised a copy of the suspect's confession. Khuang had said little, thus far, beyond a broken plea for his wife.

The atmosphere in the Bangkok police station was quite different, had Marty known it, from five hours earlier when Jeff Knetsch sat at the same interrogation table. It was one thing for a *farang* scooped up on Khao San Road to implicate a respectable Thai minister with every kind of wild calumny, and bring shame upon the police before the eyes of their American liaison. It was quite another for a distinguished Bangkok detective to discover monumental wrongdoing through hard work and good fortune.

"Itchayanan is one of the best," boasted the police chief, whose name was Thak. He stood a few feet away from Marty, a broad man whose face gleamed perpetually with sweat. "If the khlong rat does not tell him what he wishes to hear, he will hang him by his thumbs in the men's cell until Khuang screams for mercy. And then we will see what Khuang tells us."

Itchayanan's face was thrust close to his suspect's; the detective muttered in a low and vicious tone. Marty's knowledge of Thai was only adequate, but Itchayanan was speaking slowly and the threat came through the microphone loud and clear.

Tell me who gives you the opium and where you send it, or by the king himself I'll find your wife. I'll throw her in the men's cell and leave her there all night. Is that what you want? You want to hear her screaming?

Khuang sobbed wretchedly and covered his face with his hands. Itchayanan slapped the side of his head.

We left a woman there once. She was raped fifty-three times. By morning, she couldn't stand. Don't make me do it, Khuang. Don't make me find her.

The potter screeched like a wounded animal. "All right! All right! I'll tell you. I'll tell you what you want to know."

Itchayanan sank down into a chair at the opposite side of the table.

"His Excellency," Khuang gasped. "The Minister of Culture. He brings the drugs down from Chiang Rai on the ministry plane. He flies it himself."

"Liar!" Itchayanan roared, and shoved the table hard against Khuang's chest.

"I swear it! I swear it! The minister is in charge of the whole operation—"

Itchayanan reached out and seized the man's shirt. He lifted Khuang off his chair and hurled him across the room.

"So sorry," muttered Thak. The chief's face had gone white. "The khlong rat is devious. Not worth hearing. You will wish to leave."

"We've been tracking Sompong," Marty replied softly. "He's been running guns for years. His number's up this time."

From the interrogation room behind them came the sound of a fist crashing against bone.

"The Bangkok police have always found His Excellency most benevolent." Thak looked as though he might be sick.

"When His Excellency rots in prison, his benevolence will end. The man who brings him to justice, however, can expect a promotion. And the respect and gratitude of the United States—which sends millions of dollars each year to Thailand, to fight the drug trade."

Thak's voice dropped to a whisper. "Sompong is untouchable. Untouchable! If we try, and fail—"

"Listen." Marty leaned closer. "I have a source in the minister's office. Sompong flies to Chiang Rai tonight. His plane is already on the tarmac. I know the coordinates of his camp. If we hurry—if together we bring our case to the right people—we could have troops there by morning."

The potter, Khuang, lay whimpering in a ball on the interrogation room floor. Itchayanan drove his boot viciously into the man's ribs.

Thak stared at them through the one-way glass, his mind working. Marty waited.

5

Hanoi,
February 1967

Sometimes the men talked through their drinking cups, wrapping the filthy cloth of their prison garments around the tin and pressing it like a mouthpiece to the wall of their cells; and sometimes, when a message had to be sent up the chain of command—for the discipline of military rank was one of the few things their captors could not steal from them—the words were tapped in a simple code. On a night when Rory had been left inexplicably free of interrogation and the ropes slung from the torture room's ceiling, a twenty-two-year-old named Milt Beardsley, a Navy ensign from Indiana, taught him the system in a murmur through the wall.

"Divide the letters of the alphabet in five columns," Milt whispered. "Five letters each."

"That's only twenty-five," Rory said, puzzled.

"Drop the *K*," Milt instructed patiently. "Line the rest up in your head. It's good to think about something clean, once in a while."

Clean, Rory thought. *Letters arranged in clean, vertical lines, nothing emotional or distracting about them.* A, B, C, D, E would be in the first column. F, G, H, I, J, were in the next. To form a word, Milt told him, he must first signal which column of letters he was using—one through five—and then the order of the letter in the column itself. The letter *A* would be one tap followed by another; the letter *J*, two taps followed by five.

Thus Rory joined in the conversations flying around the prison walls.

The men traded war stories and news of interrogations and offered support to the ones too weak or depressed to communicate. They boasted of old conquests and reminisced about carrier duties they'd shared; they passed on insults or jokes. They rarely talked about home or those they loved. Such topics were painful and intensely private—the only parts of their souls the Hanoi Hilton could not invade.

What I don't get, Rory tapped one night to his commanding officer— an Air Force colonel by the name of C. J. Howard—*is why they don't just force me to leave. It's not like I could resist if they hauled me out of here.*

Assholes are afraid, Colonel Howard tapped back. *If you agree to early release, you sign a statement thanking them for their kindness. You promise not to say how bad things are for POWs. But if they kick you out on your butt against your will, God knows what you'll tell the press. They can't risk bad press.*

It seemed simple enough. To keep his honor—to cling to his code— to destroy a man named Ruth—all Rory had to do was resist. Until he died.

As a boy he'd been certain he was a coward. He refused to play chicken with the freight trains in the Chicago stockyards, and was ridiculed in school for weeks as a result. His heart pounded painfully when his mother drove her car too fast or swung recklessly into oncoming traffic. He dreaded visits to the doctor and bare needles gleaming under bright lights. He once cracked his toe while dashing through a door frame, drew blood and fainted.

He kept his cowardice locked in a crevice of his mind, where it crept out in the form of nightmares his mother mistook for an overactive imagination. Joan forbade him to watch horror movies and made sure he had cookies and milk before he went to bed, but still the demons came.

His father's visits were the worst because Rory yearned to be worthy of the man in the photographs who lived in the jungle with a white bird on his shoulder. Each visit was a kind of test, the most disastrous being the ski trip to Vermont when Rory was sixteen. His mother had talked brightly about all the "man time" he'd get alone with Jack, so that he had been sick with apprehension before the trip even started.

He had hated skiing—hated the lack of control over his own legs, the fierce pitch of the trails, hated the way his father's body curved effortlessly into the fall line and obeyed his slightest movement. Rory desperately wanted Jack Roderick to crow with delight—to slap his son's shoulders in unabashed admiration and shout, *That's my boy!* like Fred MacMurray might have done if he were a real parent instead of an actor. But in Vermont, Jack had stared at him appraisingly with those cool blue eyes and said, "Are you scared, Rory?"

Later, in the final year of school at Evanston, there'd been a boy named Aubrey Smith who divined Rory's weakness. He'd lie in wait by the lockers when classes changed, and as Rory passed, Aubrey would crow the word at him like an epithet. *Yellow, yellow.* Other boys picked up the chant and it would follow Rory the length of the hall, so that he came to dread the unprotected expanse of the school corridors, a gauntlet he traversed seven times daily. He hated the lunchroom, and the wads of clenched bread hurled at his ear. Dreaded the moment he was forced to fight Aubrey Smith, and prove his schoolmate wrong.

It was inevitable, a rite of passage in most boys' lives: the deserted lot three blocks from school; the circle of bloodthirsty classmates, one of them a bookie taking bets on the fight's outcome; Aubrey stripping to his shorts and swinging his arms while Rory struggled with the knot in his tie. He had lasted three minutes and twenty-seven seconds, swinging blindly at Aubrey's head until the other boy landed a kick squarely in the groin. It was his tears, not the pain, Rory despised the most.

He had tried to hang himself that night from his bedroom light fixture. It was a source of shame to him even now, that memory of himself balancing on a chair, his necktie too short for the elaborate loops he'd thrown over the brass. He'd called frantically for his mother to save him before he toppled to the floor.

Try the Army, Jack had told Joan when she consulted him by long-distance telephone call a few hours later. *Something that'll make a man of him. He's been with women too long.*

In hatred and rage Rory had sought an appointment to the Naval Academy instead. And found, on the bucking surface of an aircraft carrier, the one thing that made boyhood fears irrelevant. To gun a plane's engines and fire himself straight off a deck demanded a different kind of courage, and Rory's fund of it was limitless.

*   *   *

He awoke each morning now to the broadcasts of Hanoi Hannah, the shrill-voiced Vietnamese who recounted the latest American losses with relish. Next he was visited by his turnkey guard, who demanded that he bow low in obeisance. When Rory refused—partly from defiance and partly because his leg was healing badly and could not support his weight—the guard punched him in the face, after which he was ordered to hobble into the courtyard and fetch his breakfast: a hunk of bread and a bowl of thin soup. His bowels were wracked with dysentery and he lost as much nourishment as he managed to consume. When he returned to his cell he scratched a mark on the wall to note another day, and waited for the rattle of a key in the lock that signaled the next bout of interrogation. Sometimes his captors let entire days lapse between his torture sessions. Sometimes it was a matter of hours. Unpredictability spawned most of the fear.

It was the dry season when his plane fell out of the sky and his cell was airless and baking. Under the single bulb that stayed perpetually lit, even while he slept, he dreamed of rain: rain and the black asphalt of Michigan Avenue dreaming in the car headlights, the swish of tires and the gutters roiling with wet. The waters of the Severn and the Chesapeake in heavy chop, rain like a spatter of bullets against his cheek. He dreamed the spring rain on leaves and the dim green light of an April morning filtering through a tent's canvas in the backyard. Max's rib cage rising and falling gently beneath his encircling fingers.

And he remembered, almost against his will, the way the Bangkok streets had been flooded that day in September '63, when he had journeyed with Max to visit the boy's grandfather—how the muddy brown water had swirled and fanned about the wheels of the *tuk-tuk* and Max had crowed with delight. Rory had wanted to hate Bangkok as he hated the whole idea of Asia—Bangkok his father's mistress, Bangkok the destroyer of happiness—but Rory had stared about him in wonder. When they arrived at last at the house on the khlong, his father had waded out into the flooded courtyard with his silk trousers rolled to the knee and clutched the child in his strong, light grasp. Max had gone to Jack Roderick without a backward glance.

In that sepia light, Jack had looked exactly like the hero of Rory's childhood photographs—a man already a legend—and Rory had sat rooted in the *tuk-tuk,* his son in his father's embrace, tears like rain on his cheek.

You are guilty of black crimes against the Vietnamese people, his interrogators shouted. *You are an air pirate of the United States, personally responsible for the murders of one thousand women and children. Admit that you bombed a school and a hospital filled with nursing mothers. Admit that we have been kinder to you than you deserve.*

For numberless days in the room reserved for interrogations, he refused to transcribe the official confessions into his own handwriting and sign them. For this he was beaten by men who shouted obscenities in broken English. They tossed him between them until a black miasma swam before his eyes and it was obvious he was of no further use to them. He would awake under the stifling light of his own cell and know from the pounding of his heart that the keys had rattled somewhere in his sleep, and the interrogators had returned.

Hang tough, tapped Milt Beardsley, the boy from Indiana. *If they want you to take early release, they're not going to kill you.*

Sometimes in his dreams—the ones without rain—he heard the taped confessions of other men who had broken, broadcast throughout the cells.

Fifty-three slashes on the wall, fifty-three days. Fifty-four slashes. Fifty-five. The marks were losing their definition, his hand trembled so badly. He had not seen the man named Ruth in ten days, and for an instant he thought that perhaps they had given up. He would die here, after all.

How long would death take?

There came an hour in the middle of a black and fevered night when the guards shattered his healing fracture a second time and the agony in his ruined leg nearly destroyed him. When they had dumped him once more on the floor of his cell he lay in his own blood and excrement, aware of the tapping that went on around him and too feeble to care what it meant. On the fifty-ninth day he summoned enough strength to rise on one leg, remove his shirt and invert the bucket intended for his waste.

Looping the ragged cloth through the louvered grill of his window he made a rough slipknot and would have worked the noose around his neck, but he toppled and fell. When the guards came they were outraged and carried him immediately to the airy, sunlit room where he had first been offered freedom.

There, his hands folded placidly in front of him, sat the old man in the Mao jacket, his black eyes quite steady as he gazed up at Rory's face.

"You would rather die than accept my gift?"

"I would rather die than accept dishonor," Rory replied.

The old man grazed Rory's cheek with the tip of his finger. "The soldiers who guard you feel the oppression of their country very deeply, you understand. They savage you, who cannot savage the United States."

The finger moved along his chin. Rory could not suppress a shudder.

"It tears at my heart to see what they have done," Ruth said softly. "One might almost call them animals."

"Fuck off," Rory muttered.

The old man did not reply. Then, leaning back in his chair, he said, "You are very proud. That is as it should be, for Jack Roderick's son."

"I am not Jack Roderick's son."

Ruth withdrew a paper packet from his sleeve. He thrust it across the table.

Rory ignored it.

"That is a letter from your little boy."

His eyes slid toward the envelope. It was crinkled and soiled, as though it had traveled many miles. The censors would have read it already. He could glimpse a faint pencil mark, the scrawl of childish writing. His breath rose like a balloon in his chest until the effort to suppress it choked him.

"I bring it to you at considerable cost," Ruth told him. "Many people have labored to send it so far."

Rory stared at the peace offering. The bribe. *Max.*

The old man thrust his face within an inch of Rory's. "He *knows*." The words were brusque and brutal. "Your father knows that you die a little, every day. Although you do not even call yourself his son, this letter is proof of all he hears and all that he can do. While Jack Roderick lives, he will move heaven and earth to save you. Do you understand, Rory?"

Would he? Would Dad give a damn if I died?

Once he'd believed Jack Roderick was the most wonderful man in the world—a hero, a true American, a warrior with a just cause. He'd needed to believe that an extraordinary father existed somewhere, a father larger than life. But now he knew that Jack Roderick had whacked backroom goons and settled scores and delivered payoffs and refused to support this war his son was making. Billy Lightfoot had told Rory everything. Jack lived for himself alone. He had no allegiances, no higher laws. He had no right to a son.

Still, Rory said nothing. He felt mesmerized by the letter, by what accepting it might mean. The first step down a long and desperate slide.

"Read it, Rory. Your son wrote it himself."

His eyes closed. Then he reached out his hand. His fingers trembled.

The man named Ruth placed the envelope tenderly in Rory's palm.

"Pride," the old man said gently, "is merely another kind of prison, my son. Your father taught me that long ago, when he gave me back my life."

6

Bangkok,
1966

Brigadier General Billy Lightfoot stayed in Thailand for eight months after his visit to Jack Roderick's House in the rainy season of 1963. He traveled by Jeep for weeks at a time through Khorat and the border country of Laos and Cambodia, carrying a machete on his hip in case he was trapped by jungle vines or tigers or militant Communists. In August 1964, three North Vietnamese gunboats fired torpedoes at the U.S. Navy destroyer *Maddox* in the Gulf of Tonkin and an aircraft carrier named *Ticonderoga* returned fire. It was tantamount to a declaration of war against Vietnam, and Lyndon Johnson—who faced a brutal reelection battle against the Republican Barry Goldwater in November—was in no mood to look soft on Communism. Lightfoot's plans for Khorat were given priority. By the second week of August, the 36th Tactical Fighting Squadron of the U.S. Air Force was transferred to northeast Thailand and F105s were flying rescue missions over Laos soon after.

"Fighter jets?" Jack Roderick said when Billy tore into Bangkok one September morning to give him the news. "This is Thailand, Billy. Not Vietnam."

"The boys are there to fly classified missions I don't like to talk about, Jack. You understand."

Roderick understood. His clearances had been stripped; he no longer had need to know.

By 1965, the air war over North Vietnam was raining fire on the villages and rice paddies; bombing runs against Hanoi were routine. Lightfoot spent much of that year in Washington, poring over blueprints and plans. He sent Roderick cheerful bulletins the Silk King read with distaste, and seemed to have forgotten the punch he'd thrown on his old friend's Bangkok terrace.

And so it was with resignation that Roderick found Lightfoot standing in his front courtyard one morning in September 1966, hands on his hips and a cigar in his mouth. Billy stared, narrow-eyed, at the dense vegetation of Roderick's garden as though it might hide any number of Hostiles. He had a PFC to drive his Jeep now. There were flags fluttering on the front end.

"What's your rank these days?" Roderick called from the doorstep.

"Major-General. Commander of U.S. Forces, Khorat."

Roderick thought of Boonreung's dusty plateau and the Mekong River, broad and red, that wound into Cambodia. He knew the place had changed profoundly since the American pilots had arrived there. He did not wish to see it again.

"Congratulations. That's quite an assignment, Billy."

"How's that kid of yours?"

"Flying A-4s off the *Coral Sea*," Roderick replied.

"Good man."

Good man. Good for you, Rory, as you carry the ordnance high over Hanoi: the wide, tree-lined boulevards, the shady stucco mansions of l'Indochine, flaring like phoenixes as you pass. There had been bombs in the Good Fight of World War II, carpet bombs over Dresden and the mushroom cloud over Hiroshima—Roderick had no claim to moral superiority. Jack loved the boy who flew the plane more than he loved the ravaged city streets. Weren't his hands as bloody as anyone's in Washington?

"Come for a little ride," Lightfoot urged. "Up to my neck of the woods. Maybe into the Triangle, if the scouts say it's safe enough. We can do some recon. Pitch camp in the rainforest. You can tell me what the place was like during the old days."

"Quieter," Roderick said. He did not want to talk strategy with Billy over four hundred miles of broken road. He could recite the phrases in his sleep.

The Pathet Lao, squatting on the border. The Khmer Rouge to the east. Probably somebody in Burma playing with matches and Uncle Ho's got everybody bound in blood to the Chinese. Jackals, all of 'em. You think the Soviets aren't looking for a way in? Give 'em half a chance, they'll fund the Malays and drive a wedge into Thailand from the south.

He thought of his Laotian friend, Tao Oum—the fine dissecting intelligence honed in a French *lycée,* the gentle manners wasted now on the Pathet Lao—and remembered the drive down the Western Seaboard they had taken together in 1945. Vukrit and Carlos, wary as dogs, with Boonreung laughing between them. The moist air tearing through the open windows of the Packard and the insults flying in Thai and English and French from backseat to front. The easy brotherhood that seemed more true than anything before or since.

He had believed he could help Asia and his friends emerge from a brutal war. They were all scattered now, twenty-one years later, some of them dead, some still fighting battles they would never win. Only he and Vukrit Suwannathat remained, opposite sides of the same coin.

"Billy," he said, "thanks for the offer but I think I'll stay home."

Lightfoot wheeled. "Those junior grunts at the CIA don't know their heads from their asses, Jack. They can talk numbers and positions and pinpoint a Communist enclave on a goddamn map—but they don't have the relationships with *people* you do. The human element is missing, old pal, know what I mean?"

"I know what you mean."

"It's the human element I need. *We* need. Hell, what've you spent all these years in Asia for—if not to put your contacts to good use?"

It wasn't the first time the Pentagon had run headlong into an Agency wall; it wouldn't be the last. The problem, Roderick guessed, was a gulf Lightfoot would never span: the chasm that fell between intelligence and tactics, between the generals with their maps and those quieter folk who sniffed the wind. The Agency believed that Uncle Ho had far more men than the Pentagon wanted to admit. The Agency and the Pentagon wrangled endlessly over troop strength and enemy numbers. The Agency wrote estimates; the Pentagon scribbled red ink in the margins before sending the reports to LBJ and his cabinet. The Agency spoke its piece, and the Pentagon said what Johnson wanted to hear. The dialogue over this war had become an escalation of mutually deniable statistics.

"Sometimes I'm amazed by the people you know," Lightfoot persisted. "Not just the ones you invite to dinner—but the guys you never

mention. Like that new Defense Minister. That fella with the unpro-
nounceable name."

"Vukrit Suwannathat. Field Marshal now."

"Yeah. He's the one. The Defense Ministry will be critical to us in
the next few months." Lightfoot slapped his thigh with his army hat,
and a cloud of dust rose in the moist air.

"Vukrit's the only minister who has ever mattered. But you'll learn
that I have no influence with him."

"He says the Thais are going after your old buddy Carlos—the rene-
gade who keeps an army in the hills. The Field Marshal thinks Carlos
has gone Communist, and he means to stamp him out."

"He'll have to find Carlos first," Roderick said.

That afternoon in September, 1966, Jack Roderick decided it was
time to put his affairs in order.

He watched Billy Lightfoot's jeep spin in the courtyard and plunge
into the narrow lane beyond his gate. He thought of Boonreung
dying in agony and of Fleur as she had been at nineteen, a frightened bird caught in a snare; thought of Carlos's wife Chao fading to
nothing in the jungle. If he wanted to he could place all those sins in
Vukrit's column, but he knew that he bore equal responsibility for the
blight and he knew, at last, that he must stop it before it destroyed
Carlos.

He thought briefly of Chacrit Gyapay and the way the gun had felt
as he placed it against the torture chief's temple and pulled the trigger.
A March night, seventeen years ago. He was still fresh with an assassin's
training then, and whipped to violence by the outrage of Boonreung's
murder. He'd drawn blood in a way that was unthinkable to him now.
His kind of war was over. Vukrit demanded subtlety and cunning, not a
knife in the dark.

Roderick went inside and made two phone calls: one to his lawyer
and another to the Ministry of Defense.

When the lawyer arrived, he gave the man his instructions: tear up
the will he had signed in 1960, leaving his home and his collections of
pottery and art to the people of Thailand; and draft a new one, leaving
everything he possessed to his son, Rory.

Then he sat down at his desk and wrote a brief letter to his old friend Alec McQueen. He signed it with the lawyer as witness and when the man had notarized it, placed it in his desk for safekeeping. Scrawled on the front were the words, in Roderick's minuscule handwriting: *To be opened in the event of my death.*

Roderick did these things with deliberation, as though he had received a diagnosis of a terminal condition that morning. Then he put on a hat in honor of the occasion, and went out into the street holding the lawyer by the arm. The man took him as far as Dusit in his car.

Dusit was the administrative center of Bangkok, the royal quarter, an oasis of calm in the chaotic city. Chulalongkorn, Thailand's most Europeanized king, had designed and built the district at the close of the nineteenth century, and the spacious boulevards and grand vistas might have been lifted from Haussmann's Paris. At this hour of the afternoon, most of the bureaucrats were dozing in their chairs.

He passed the racetrack at the Royal Turf Club and the cages of the Dusit Zoo, the National Assembly and the Prime Minister's house and the residence of the king. At the Ministry of Defense he was admitted without question and ushered up three flights of stairs to the office, large as a ballroom, where Vukrit presided.

The Defense Minister had been named to his post only six weeks before—the culmination, Roderick suspected, of a lifelong ambition. Vukrit must be in his mid-fifties now. Roderick was sixty-one.

"Your Excellency," he said with a slight nod.

"The Legendary American," the minister replied. "Isn't that what they call you?"

Vukrit remained seated as Roderick approached, like royalty, and made no move to form the ceremonial *wei*. The significance of his rudeness would not be lost on the five Thais who stood around his desk—some of them in uniform, some in civilian dress. All gazed at Roderick unsmilingly.

"I can give you very little time."

"I'm grateful. I wish to speak to you in private."

"Then you should have invited me to your home. I do business at this ministry, Roderick—to meet alone suggests an unhealthy tendency toward plotting."

"I was pressed for time. The Commander of U.S. Forces in Khorat spoke with me this morning, Your Excellency, and having seen him I came directly to you. If we could speak in private—"

Vukrit hesitated, as though it would give him pleasure to deny any of Roderick's requests; then he waved his hand, and his coterie departed.

Roderick waited until the door had closed firmly behind them. Then he drew something from his jacket pocket and held it aloft. Though uncut, the smooth surface of the dark red gem shimmered like a well of fire between his fingers. "Lightfoot tells me you have plans for Carlos, Vukrit. Don't act on them."

"Do you think that old stone frightens me, Roderick? You cannot prove I ever touched it. You cannot prove it was left in the chambers of the king."

"True," Roderick conceded. "But you of all people understand the power of rumor. You rose on rumor's back. Rumor branded Pridi Banomyong the assassin behind the king's murder, and rumor caused his government to fall."

"I'm more powerful than Pridi Banomyong ever was. More powerful than you, however many petty thugs you may once have murdered by moonlight. I hear that not even the CIA listens to Roderick anymore."

"May I inquire as to the health of Your Excellency's son?"

Vukrit's eyelids flickered. "Sompong has earned his wings in the Royal Thai Air Force. My son trains in Khorat with your General Lightfoot, and wears a uniform like his father before him."

"Which father, I wonder? And which uniform? If you care nothing for the power of rumor, consider what it can do to that boy. If you so much as *think* of hunting down Carlos again, your career—and your son's—will end in shame."

Vukrit threw back his head and laughed.

"I wrote a letter today," Roderick continued imperturbably, "instructing Alec McQueen, the publisher of the *Bangkok Post,* to print its contents should I die. Other papers will pick up the story, in the United States and around the world."

"You think your dying will be like a king's? You flatter yourself, Roderick."

"My letter summarizes the case against you. You stole a gem—a talisman of good luck—from a priceless artifact you hacked out of a cave wall. The artifact sits in my house and the dealer who sold it is prepared to bear witness against you. The talisman—a cabochon ruby I will place with my letter—was dropped by the man who murdered King Ananda on June 9, 1946. Vukrit Suwannathat."

Roderick leaned across the minister's desk. "If you hunt down Carlos, the rumors will begin. If I die, the rumors will twine around your neck until you strangle under their weight. It's the only kind of justice left, Vukrit—that you fall the same way you rose."

"You cannot prove I killed the king."

This time it was Roderick who smiled. "Your enemies would snatch at any excuse to hang you: no one in Thailand is interested in proof."

7

Does this place always empty out before six o'clock?" Rush Halliwell demanded as he strode back from the loading dock. He glanced through an open doorway, but the lights were doused. "Dickie Spencer keeps his office here. Where's he?"

"It's Friday afternoon," the salesgirl said indignantly. "Mr. Spencer quits early and goes to his country place on the weekends. Just who are you, and what do you want?"

"Did you see the American woman leave by the back door?"

The girl shook her head. "I'm supposed to stay up front. Mr. Spencer's assistant might know where your friend went, but she's gone home for the day. If you'd like, I can have her call you on Monday."

"Doesn't matter." Rush swung back into the shop, his gaze scanning the brightly colored aisles. "No other exits, right?"

"None. Is this . . . really important?"

"Not to you," he answered with one of his most charming smiles, and hurried out into the street.

He arrived home to discover that Stefani's luggage was still in his guest room. This brought him up short. She had carried nothing but a backpack when she'd left his building, but a woman of Stefani's resources could easily jettison an entire season's worth of unwanted ballast.

She was less likely, however, to leave behind her U.S. passport. As she had certainly done.

Rush stood over the contents of her luggage, tossed willy-nilly on his spare bed, and thought. Did she keep a second identity handy—passport and all? Such a thing was common practice in CIA circles; did Oliver Krane's operatives do it, too? Or was he reaching for an explanation? Had she meant to return from Jack Roderick Silk that afternoon?

"That's crazy," he said aloud. "Asinine, in fact. You just can't accept that she flipped you off and escaped."

He headed for the embassy at a run.

Before she was fully conscious, she knew that something dreadful had happened. The catlike shrieking near at hand was unbearable. She struggled awake, resisting the impulse to sleep, *sleep*, and forget the world. It was important that she open her eyes and somehow strangle the damn cat.

"The amount of trouble you've caused—you *vicious* shit." Ankana Lee-Harris's Knightsbridge croon had vanished. "I might have had the whole evening with Dickie—but here I am, carting *you* to the airport. God, it makes me wild!"

Clarity returned slowly to Stefani's mind, and with it, a ton of self-abuse.

Dickie Spencer had been supremely accommodating when she called that afternoon to request an interview. He seemed genuinely pleased to hear her voice and enthusiastic at the prospect of a meeting. Her arrival at the shop had brought his assistant hurrying to the door, a warm smile on her lips, to personally conduct Stefani past the glowing squares of silk patterned with elephants and parrot tulips, the pillowcases and bed coverings and drapes, past the bolts of fabric in every imaginable hue. The woman had offered Stefani water or coffee and when Stefani refused both, had ushered her into Dickie's office and closed the door behind her.

Stefani had advanced, her hand extended, toward the man who stood somewhat stiffly by the drafting table; but the pleasantry she meant to utter died on her lips. Spencer's face was strained, his eyes focused on someone behind her—and as she instinctively began to turn, the small, hard cylinder of a gun was pressed sharply into her spine. It was quite emphatic; impossible to confuse with anything else.

She went rigid, her eyes fixed on Spencer's face.

"I'm sorry, Ms. Fogg," he said gently, "but not all of us are capable of tilting at windmills." Then he dropped his gaze to the silk pattern that rested on his drafting table.

It had been Jo-Jo who held the gun, and even now she could not say whether Dickie had called Sompong the moment she set up the appointment, or whether Ankana Lee-Harris had done it—Ankana who had been in Dickie's pocket all day, ostensibly coordinating museum loans for the big show, *darling*, but actually insinuating herself as only Ankana could. Spencer's motives—his personal integrity versus the pressure Sompong had brought to bear—would remain open questions. For now, Stefani had stickier problems to solve.

Her arms, bound behind her, ached. The base of her skull throbbed. She tried to part her lips, and decided they were fused with electrical tape. She was slumped in one corner of a large car, Ankana in the other. Jo-Jo, predictably, driving. It was he who had knocked her out with the butt of his gun, and tossed her into the backseat.

"Left to myself, I'd have shot you dead and slipped your body into the Chao Phraya," Ankana complained. "But Sompong says no. He wants you for his own."

The U.S. embassy on Wireless Road was a massive concrete block, derisively known as an "Inman Box," after Bobby Ray Inman, the Navy admiral chiefly responsible for its design and construction during the 1980s. It was a structure intended to foil the worst sort of terrorist attack, and it was so secure that it resembled a penitentiary rather than a seat of diplomacy. Two decades ago, Inman Boxes had sprung up on U.S. installations worldwide, and as one wag observed, they could withstand assault by an entire platoon of tanks—but as they had virtually no windows, no one inside would be able to tell.

Rush was staring intently at his computer terminal within the embassy's CIA station. He and Marty Robbins were the only two working this Friday evening. It was seven-thirteen; most of the lights within the vault were extinguished.

"You think she knew she was being followed?" Marty asked Rush for the third time.

"What else can I think? She went into the silk shop by the front door. She left by the loading dock." Rush printed the screen he had been studying so acutely and shoved it at Marty. "I knew I'd heard that name before. She wasn't lying about *this*."

Marty adjusted his reading glasses and peered at the cable Rush had given him. It was a back-channel report—one sent between two regional stations without the knowledge or transmission of headquarters in Washington. He glanced at the date and time group that headed the cable coding, and noticed Rush had received it from the CIA's Hong Kong base only minutes before.

Regarding your query re: Harry Leeds, British national formerly resident in Hong Kong, we can confirm Leeds died in a pedestrian accident November 23, 2001, in Kowloon. Summary of Leeds's station file follows. Note: this file was compiled for the most part by LegAtt then residing in Hong Kong, since posted on to London, and represents Bureau interest in subject rather than active Agency development. Nothing contained herein should be construed as official Agency information regarding Leeds. End Note.

Subject first came to Bureau attention in 1997, in the course of an investigation into gun-smuggling networks then operative around the island. Subject was suspected of using highly sophisticated electronic interception equipment to surveil the Royal Coast Guard and Hong Kong Harbormaster's offices in an effort to provide early warning and escape-and-evasion assistance to ships involved in the smuggling network. Subject admitted to possessing such equipment but asserted that it had been stolen from his offices and subsequently operated by persons unknown to him. When asked why he never reported the theft, Subject stated that had he done so, his true profession in Hong Kong would be known. Subject is director of HK office of Krane & Associates, the international risk management firm, an occupation he wishes to remain secret. It would not help Krane's reputation as a security firm, moreover, if it were generally known that Leeds had been successfully burgled. Note: Subject is generally regarded as a socially prominent man of independent means, a member of the Jockey Club, and not as a security professional. End Note.

LegAtt conducted interviews of Subject's professional assistant (See file No. HK-2467-1997), who denied all knowledge of smugglers and corroborated the story of the theft. LegAtt also investigated Subject's personal financial statements and found no apparent gain in assets, such as might represent criminal profits, during the period in question. Subject participated fully with both Hong Kong police and LegAtt throughout, but was extremely anxious regarding conclusion of investigation. Subject ultimately was not charged with wrongdoing.

Final note: From 1997 to date of death in November 2001, Leeds drew no further interest from Hong Kong law enforcement.

There the cable transmission ended. Marty looked up from the sheet of paper, and growled, "What the hell?"

"Stefani told me this morning that she decided to work for Krane because he said his best friend and Asian partner, Harry Leeds, had been murdered in Kowloon and he wanted to bring Leeds's killer to justice. Krane suggested that the same people responsible for Leeds's death had it in for Max Roderick."

"We've always suspected Sompong Suwannathat was running guns in Hong Kong in '97," Marty mused, "the same year, according to this cable, that Leeds was under FBI investigation. I see the connection—but I don't see why we should care. If one crook kills another—"

"Leeds's name rang a bell this morning, but I couldn't put my finger on why. I left Hong Kong almost five years ago. I never looked at the smuggling operation itself—that was Bureau and police territory. I was charged with pinpointing which triad or terrorist group had *received* the guns, and what they intended to do with them. Harry Leeds didn't come into it."

"Rush, are you clutching at straws?" Marty glared at him from under his brows. "Trying to dig up something—*anything*—that suggests Fogg didn't snow you? If Oliver Krane actually trained this broad, then she knows *when* to use the truth. A scrap of honesty at the right time could make Satan look plausible."

"She left her passport behind. That feels wrong to me."

"She probably has ten of them, complete with visas. She's probably on a flight to Europe as we speak. Not every girl who's set up to be whacked is a victim, Rush. Speaking of which—Police Chief Thak informed me that Jeffrey Knetsch was knifed to death in his cell two hours after you left him. We'll have to arrange shipment for the body."

"Christ." Rush groaned. "Of course he was killed. That pathetic bastard—"

"You did what you could. You couldn't get him out—they don't post bail in drug cases."

"I should have learned more from him while I had the chance. He never told us who's on the receiving end of the drugs Sompong is shipping to New York."

"I've handed that problem to Avril Blair. She'll get the Bureau's Manhattan office working on it ASAP."

"And what about us? Do we use that potter's confession to go after Sompong?"

"You know goddamn well the CIA's got absolutely no jurisdiction here. We don't do law enforcement, Rush. We pinpoint the crooks. We don't snap on the cuffs."

"But we know people who do."

"Police Chief Thak passed the buck to the federal security forces—and most of their relevant bodies have already gone home for the weekend."

"We can't miss this chance," Rush muttered through his teeth. "It's the best we've had in five years—*five years,* Marty, we've been watching this asshole pull shit that'd get him castrated in public in any self-respecting country."

"What do you want me to do? Hire a gunship and buzz Sompong's compound in Chiang Rai myself?"

"Call in your chips! Get on the horn to Washington right now, and use any clout you can beg, borrow or steal. If the Thai federal police have gone home for the weekend, then fuck 'em. Let's go over their heads."

"And catch hell on Monday?"

"Look—our DEA guys have spent over a decade training Thai drug enforcement squads to sniff out opium networks and kill government corruption. But what's the Thai enforcement record?"

"A lot of small stuff, nipped in the bud."

"Because the big stuff—the kind Sompong Suwannathat breeds—is out of reach. We're in a position, you and I, to hand these poor jokers the biggest bust of their lives: one of the most powerful and hated figures in Thai government, caught with his goddamn pants down. We should be auctioning seats in the Chinook, Marty."

"Chinook?" Marty chortled. "You're dreaming, Rush. By the time we get a chopper full of commandos in the air, Sompong'll be long gone."

"Sompong won't know we're coming. Thak's too afraid of *you* this time to report what he knows—that Khuang the potter blew Sompong's network. Sompong thinks he's silenced Knetsch, and that the Bangkok police are in his pocket. He's free as a bird."

"Unless Miss Fogg told him otherwise."

Brought up short, Rush stared at his station chief. It was a vulnerable point; indeed, it was the crux of the whole dilemma. Doubt about Stefani's motives—her loyalties, if she had any—had sent him careening here to the embassy to write a priority cable. He had been searching for any sort of evidence to tip the scales in his mind. And still he could not say with certainty what she had done. Or what she was capable of doing.

"I can call in my chips," Marty said slowly. "I can get on the horn to Washington and disturb some VIP weekends. I can move heaven and earth if I have to, Rush. But I don't care to look like shit afterward."

"You won't. Provided we move fast."

"And Miss Fogg?"

Rush snapped off his computer and grabbed his suit jacket. "Is a chance we'll just have to take."

8

Bangkok,
February 1967

Fleur was standing on the terrace as the sun went down. The house-boy, Chanat Surian, moved like a faint breeze among the braziers, and as the torches flared, Roderick studied the woman he had once loved. She was still slight and elegant as a question mark, with all the life of Siam in her fingertips; but she was no longer young. He noticed the difference first in her mouth, which was hard and unyielding. Her eyes gazed flatly on a disappointing world. She wore her sleek hair in a tight knot at the crown of her head, but the attempt at discipline collapsed with her neck. The slim bones of her spine where it met the nape of dark hair were as fragile as a kitten's.

It was the only part of her that he ached to touch.

He had found her waiting in his entrance courtyard just after four o'clock that afternoon, simple sandals on her bare feet and a cotton scarf tied around her head. She looked like a peasant—one of the country women who begged rides on the back of market trucks bound for the city—and from the condition of her clothes, which were clean but shabby, Roderick understood that she lived in poverty. She stood humbly, with her hands clasped, and would not have been surprised, he thought, if he had refused to recognize her.

"Fleur," he said in bewilderment, "what are you doing here?"

"I read about your son."

The English words came haltingly after a decade of disuse. Ten years. *My God, has it been so long?*

"In the newspaper," she went on. "The Viet Cong shot down his plane. I never knew you had a son."

"I'm sorry, Fleur. I should have told you."

"But at least he died for his country. There is much honor in such a death."

"They're calling it 'Missing in Action.' Not killed," Roderick said awkwardly. "A formality. They don't know for certain Rory's dead. Won't you come in? And have a drink?"

She had demurred for a while but in the end he'd ushered her upstairs, with the careful politeness he reserved for strangers referred by mutual friends.

It was one of the few nights he had no guests to dinner, and so she sat on his couch and talked glancingly about the decade that had passed. The houseboy brought plates of satay and papaya salad for them. Roderick exerted himself to be charming—the uncomplicated polish and amusing words that had carried him through a lifetime of difficult encounters—but this was not the way he had been accustomed to talk to Fleur. Watching her unresponsive face, her thoughts so obviously elsewhere, he knew she felt the difference in him, despite all his care.

More than the knowledge of Rory's plane had brought her to the house on the khlong. Some trouble preyed on her mind. He waited for her to explain, through the food and the talk and the silences that fell between them.

"So much has changed," she said now as they stood on the terrace. "The garden has grown so wild, I cannot see the waters of the khlong. Even your cockatoo has forgotten me."

"She's just angry you neglected her for so long. Did you keep up your dancing?"

"It's a habit, like any other. But no one would choose to watch me perform now."

"That can't be true."

"I speak of art, and the loss of art, and you know nothing of either, Jack." She said it bitterly.

"I know you've been gone too long."

She traced the wood grain of the railing with her fingertip. "Did you ever look for me?"

"Relentlessly."

"I didn't want to be found."

"Why not? Because you'd betrayed me? Sooner or later, we all betray what we love."

"Cynic," she said violently.

"No. You confuse me with that other man in your life."

She opened her mouth to say something harsh, but with an effort controlled herself. "I'm sorry, Jack. It's this war. The men in uniforms and the guns everywhere. The planes flying overhead. I hate the war and it frightens me. Do you ever think of going home?"

"Home?"

"To the United States." She clutched at his shirt, her face suddenly beseeching. "Why stay in Bangkok when the world is in flames? Why stay and wait for death, Jack, when we could run away from it?"

"We? Fleur, is that why you're here? Are you—"

But she gave a startled little cry and clutched at his arm. A man was climbing over the khlong gate, which was locked against the night. *The wolf,* Roderick thought, *the wolf is at the door.* He'd been waiting for this moment ever since he'd threatened Vukrit Suwannathat in the minister's office, four months before. Vukrit would want the letter that could destroy him.

Roderick pulled Fleur behind him, shielding her with his body, and backed toward the terrace door. As he did so, a more deadly thought entered his mind: Had Fleur come tonight by purest coincidence? Or was she here as decoy, while Vukrit's assassin crept through the darkness?

The black-clad figure dropped heavily from the khlong gate to the ground and crouched low, his head turned toward them.

"Jack!"

A guttural whisper, scored with violence.

Roderick stopped dead, eyes straining through the dusk of the torches. Then he released Fleur, very gently, knowing that he had misjudged her. He went to the terrace railing and reached down into the darkness. A shadowy hand gripped his own, and Roderick hauled the man upward—filthy uniform, mud on his face, no longer young.

"*Carlos,*" he breathed. "Good God—you should be safe in the Cameron Highlands. Vukrit is hunting you."

"A man must do certain things, Jack, regardless of the risk."

Roderick glanced over his shoulder at Fleur. "I'm sorry," he told her, and meant it. "I have business. We'll finish our conversation later. I know it's important."

She bowed her head silently and turned away from them, toward the house. Roderick closed the French doors behind her and steered Carlos to the far end of the terrace. He did not wait to hear if she crossed the gleaming floor on her soundless feet, or if she remained by the door, listening. But he kept his voice low.

"I cannot stay long," the old soldier muttered, "though I'm tired to death. Bangkok has grown in twenty years! I did not know how to find you, Jack—but I learned quickly. The lowest khlong rat has heard of the Silk King."

"Why are you here, Carlos?"

"Your son. I have news of him."

"Alive? Or dead?"

"Alive," Carlos replied. "Barely. He's kept in the Maison Centrale—the old French prison. You know it?"

"The Hanoi Hilton."

"Not a hotel, Jack—" Carlos began, but Roderick interrupted him.

"I know the Maison Centrale. I saw it during the fifties, when it was still run by the French." He passed a hand over his eyes, as if to blot out the image of those thick-walled, lightless cells. The manacles soldered to the stone, like a medieval dungeon. The tongs for twisting testicles, the pincers for tearing out fingernails. The guillotine, in permanent operation in the central courtyard. The French had not been kind to the Vietnamese who hated their rule.

"How do you know Rory's there? I've had no word—"

"Ruth is with him."

"*Ruth?* Pridi Banomyong?"

"Quietly, Jack," Carlos cautioned. "I would not want that woman of yours to hear."

"What is Ruth doing in Hanoi?"

"What Ruth has always done. He writes poems. He declaims manifestoes. He makes great speeches to his friend Ho Chi Minh. He does this at the behest of his keepers in Beijing, who have preserved his life these twenty years."

"What you mean," Roderick said bitterly, "is that he's sold everything he once loved, and has convinced himself otherwise." *Why should Ruth be any different from the rest of us?*

"He found your son. Rory is wounded—his leg is badly broken. He has fevers and dysentery and is very weak. The Vietnamese guards beat him, despite what Ruth says. Ruth is urging Rory to accept his offer, Jack, because he hopes to save his life—but the boy is stubborn. He will not listen."

"Rory is no boy," Roderick replied tersely. "What is he refusing?"

"Early release. Your son could walk out of his prison tomorrow. But he will not do it."

"It can't be as simple as that. Why the favor, Carlos?"

"Because he's Roderick's son." Carlos said it simply.

Comprehension flooded his mind in a sickening tide. Ruth had asked Rory to buy freedom with shame—and had done so in Jack's name. Would Rory ever forgive him? "Rory says what every American soldier would say, confronted with this same devil's bargain. He's thinking of the men imprisoned with him. He's refusing special treatment. I can't go against that."

"The choice is not so easy," Carlos replied. "If it were only your son and his sense of honor, I would never have come these hundreds of miles. It is not only Rory. This is a matter between you and Ruth, Jack.

"You once saved a life. You gave Ruth his freedom in a way that ravaged his pride. He tried to win back his glory and his reputation—through the coup that failed in '49, and then, by turning his heart toward Mao. A new allegiance he believed would negate the old. But his debt—his debt to you, and the shame that goes with it—rankles in his mind. Ruth is old. He must discharge his debt and be freed. He can do that by saving your son."

"I understand," Roderick said. "But—"

"Ruth has new masters," Carlos said. "He can't control them or even admit how subtly they use him. The Viet Cong know Rory's name. They know the name of his father."

Roderick's eyes narrowed. "A silk merchant in Bangkok?"

"One of the greatest spies that Asia has ever known," Carlos corrected softly. "Master of networks and of secrets told in darkness.

Avenger of the innocent and killer in the night. It is *you* and the country you serve that Ruth's masters think to strike, by using your son."

"What do they want?" He thought of Rory at the mercy of such people and his throat felt parched. "Some sort of photo op? A press release, thanking them for their kindness?"

"They want to embarrass you," Carlos said impatiently. "There's nothing new in that! But they intend also to profit from the exchange. They want you to ransom your son, Jack. They ask for one million dollars—a paltry sum for the widows and orphans of North Vietnam, who lament the cost of your American bombs."

It always came down to money, in the end. Roderick smiled faintly. "How . . . *capitalist* of them. Rory can't know that part of it."

"He knows nothing. But I think he guesses. He refuses even to admit that you are his father."

"I can well believe that." Roderick stared bleakly out toward the khlong that moved unseen beyond the banana trees, and thought of another night, four years ago, when Rory and Billy Lightfoot had stood opposite him. Rory had believed then that his father was a traitor— a man who refused to support his country. The better part of Rory's stubbornness in the Hanoi Hilton was a determination to show just how different the two of them were.

"Ruth chides him with disrespect," Carlos added, "but I detect in his pride the way your son honors you. Rory has courage. He has suffered a good deal."

"And if I refuse to ransom him?"

"He will die."

Roderick reached out his hand. The old soldier gripped it.

"You have my thanks, my friend, for all you've done. You will sleep here, tonight?"

"I cannot risk it. I will come again at dawn, and have your answer."

"You may have it now," Roderick said with difficulty. But Carlos raised his hand.

"The choice brings with it all manner of kharma, my friend. Think not only of your son, but of yourself and your son's son as well. What will cause you the least misery, until the end of your days? The loss of face—or the loss of life? Use the hours of night I've given you. And consider well."

Carlos let himself down over the terrace wall, slipping like a darker shadow among the fronds of the back garden. Dawn was merely six hours off; there would be no sleep tonight. Roderick stood in the torches' glow until the houseboy came and extinguished them with sand.

When he called for Fleur through the rooms of his slumbering house, he found that she had gone.

9

There's a bug the size of a condom in my bunk," Ankana said acidly, "and no toilet paper anywhere. You might have told me what it was like before I came. I ought to have been prepared."

She could have spoken Thai to the man who stood in the doorway, but the Sloane Ranger drawl was infinitely better suited to expressing contempt, Stefani decided.

"If I did, you would never come," Sompong Suwannathat replied. "Some journeys are better made in ignorance."

A thinking person might have found the sentiment disturbing; but Ankana had never wasted much time on thought. In her lipstick-colored leather jacket and stiletto heels, she looked like Tina Turner descended upon a USO show. The men of the camp were torn between leering at her legs and avoiding her eye. She stalked out of the hut without another word.

It was true there were bugs of uncommonly large size, Stefani thought hazily, but if you chose to pretend they were a figment of drug-induced sleep, they swiftly lost their power. She had been drugged ever since the wild drive to Don Muang airport, and the hurried transfer of the contents of Ankana's car to the private jet that waited on an auxiliary runway. Jo-Jo's parting gift had been the plunge of a hypodermic in the muscle of her thigh: she had awakened, gagged and bound, to the deep velvet of jungle darkness. Someone was dumping her into the flatbed of a truck.

Much later, the whistles and calls of birds and a feral cat's howl. In the predawn gloom, a cock crowing.

She sat propped now against a wooden post that supported the roof of a dirt-floored cabin. Trussed behind her, her arms were so numb she could not feel the ropes at her wrists. A squat and muscular man, clad in faded khaki, sat in a chair by the door. When she stirred and moaned, he crossed the space between them and yanked up her head by the hair. He stared an instant into her eyes—judging the size of her pupils, she guessed—then tore the gag from between her teeth. He tilted a little water into her parched mouth.

So much for breakfast.

Sompong stood in the doorway with his arms folded. The first light of morning must be flooding his face, but as his back was turned Stefani could not see his features. He was short, like many Thais, with a broad back and sloping shoulders. He looked fit and alert and without fear of any kind.

"How long you want to wait, boss?"

"We have some time, Wu Fat." He glanced at the sky and then turned. "Good morning, Ms. Fogg."

She allowed herself to study his face—the broad nose, the eyes as black as olives, the gleaming thatch of close-cropped hair and the high, flat cheekbones—but she did not return his greeting. Neither did she rant or scream or break down in tears. In a world where Ankana Lee-Harris was the model for women, she was determined to look as alien as possible.

He made a pretense of adjusting the rope that secured her to the wooden post. "You are in Chiang Rai province, Ms. Fogg. You have seen many strange and beautiful places in the world—but never the heart of the monsoon forest, where the General's men stand guard."

She kept her eyes fixed on the dirt floor.

"No questions?" he demanded; and she felt delight at having provoked him enough to ask. There were so many questions: *Why am I here? Why haven't you killed me? What were you waiting for, in that sunlit doorway?*

But instead she said only: "Where do I pee?"

He snorted with laughter. "Ankana will take you. It will give her something to do."

There was a crackle of static from one corner of the hut, and Sompong's head swung around. Wu Fat leapt to the radio. They all listened to a spate of words—incomprehensible to Stefani—and then the voice went dead.

Wu Fat glanced at Sompong. He nodded once. The two men ducked through the open doorway and left her alone.

For a while she strained her ears to catch what she could of the sounds beyond the hut. There was the thwack of wood splitting under an axe, the murmur of conversation rising and falling. A screech of complaint in high-pitched Thai. How many people were out there, anyway? And what exactly had Sompong meant by *the General's men*?

Ankana never came to conduct her to the latrine.

She tried, for a time, to force herself upright by bringing her knees to her chest and thrusting downward with her heels; but the rope was tied too efficiently to the post. She felt weak and sick and utterly helpless—a condition so unlike her usual one that she burned with rage: rage at Sompong and the way he had outpaced her; rage at Oliver Krane, who had sold her life without remorse; rage at herself, for believing she controlled her fate. She had entered into Oliver's service as though it were a lark, a fantasy turn on the set of some action movie. She had deceived herself far more than Oliver could. He had counted on that.

She worked futilely at her bonds, their stiffness another insult, and loathed the tears of frustration that gathered under her lids. Her heels scored raw wounds in the packed earth and she cursed aloud.

At least an hour passed before she heard whistles and calls in the distance: Sompong must be returning. Her breath came quickly in her dry mouth. She closed her eyes and tried to think of Max—of the old stone house in Courchevel and the coldness of the stars at night—but there was the sudden thunder of many feet, the call and response of military orders. Her eyes flew open and she stared, intently, at the hut's door.

Had Sompong brought her executioner? Or a local dignitary—some lord of the poppy fields—invited to view her killing?

"Don't put yourself out, Sompong old son," said a languorous voice just within earshot. "A glass of orange juice, perhaps, but nothing more. That little jaunt through the plantain has me positively chuffed. Couldn't ask for a finer morning, what?"

Oliver was laying it on thick, she thought with a surge of outrage and despair. Graham Greene on his morning stroll. Never mind that mass of trained mercenaries standing at attention, their automatic rifles in hand.

How many were there? A hundred? A thousand?

His shadow edged over the doorstep, and then the ginger head with the foppish fall of hair. He was dressed like an Abercrombie & Kent safari guide, although his shoes were probably more expensive. Even now, when she knew he had deceived her in every possible way—when she knew that his hands had shoved Max's wheelchair from the cliff— she was struck by the innocence of his face. He blinked once, allowing those elusive eyes to adjust behind his spectacles, and when his gaze fell on Stefani she was surprised to catch the faintest lifting of his brows.

Whatever Oliver had expected to find at the end of his chuffing trail, it had not been her.

Sompong entered with Ankana at his heels. Wu Fat closed the door and thrust his back against it, one finger looped casually around the trigger housing of his rifle. Oliver stood alone in the center of the room, looking bored. Stefani heard the rush of feet through the dried jungle grass as *the General's men* hurried to form a ring around the hut. Sompong's snare had closed on her neck.

Rush would assume she had simply cut her losses and gone back to New York. He would decide that she had never been someone to trust. The knowledge filled her with anguish.

"I believe you know Ms. Fogg," Sompong said formally.

Oliver glanced in her direction. "We've met once or twice. On the last occasion she threw a glass of Scotch in my face."

The minister smiled. "Was that in the Central Highlands, where you trained her to kill? She's impressive, Oliver, I'll give you that. A friend of mine was choked to death in her hotel room two nights ago."

"Sompong, heart, I've been flying for the past twenty-two hours," Oliver responded wearily. "I ate wretched food, surrounded by wilted orchids. I'm utterly done in. Where's that orange juice?"

Sompong reached for Wu Fat's chair by the closed hut door, and presented it to Oliver. "Sit down."

"Happy to." Oliver settled himself on the hard wooden seat as though it looked nothing like a place of interrogation.

"Do you expect me to hunker in the dirt?" Ankana asked the Chinese soldier indignantly. "You're enjoying this, you sod—I smell like a zoo and I've got chicken shit on my shoes. This whole bloody trip's been one huge laugh. Well, *I've* had enough. I'm going home. Get out of the way, you oily-mouthed son of a whore, or I'll cut off your secret sack and stuff it down your throat."

"Ankana, darling," Oliver drawled, "Wu Fat would rather die than move without Sompong's orders. The poor man yearns for martyrdom. Don't make him happy."

She bared her teeth in a snarl and leaned against the hut's bare wall, arms crossed beneath her breasts.

"The past few days have been terrible," Sompong said slowly. "People dying like flies. First poor Chanin—the one Ms. Fogg crushed in her bare hands—and then Mr. Knetsch, knifed by a pack of jackals in a Bangkok jail—"

"*Jeff?*" Stefani choked on the word. And she hadn't even liked the man.

"My condolences, old son," murmured Oliver Krane. "*Dulce et decorum est,* and all that. But what's one less lawyer in the world, after all?"

"Knetsch was a complete liability, as everyone in this room knows," Sompong observed. "But he did me one service before he died. He told me exactly how you used Ms. Fogg, Oliver. You never mentioned she worked for you."

"Knetsch lied," Oliver said stonily. "He spun a crock. You've been had—coming and going, Minister."

"Certainly. But not by Knetsch. You sent Fogg to Max Roderick without telling me. You sent her to Bangkok to make that public and quite infantile claim on Jack Roderick's House. You believed she'd distract me, while you moved in and took over my entire network. It must have looked easy—Knetsch was so vulnerable, he was scared and he needed money. Ankana never cares where the cash comes from, so long as she gets it. But you forgot the General's men, Oliver, who are impervious to bribes. Did you really believe you could take me down?"

"It was a question of survival: yours, or mine." Oliver studied Sompong coolly. "I'm not in the business of risk management for nothing, ducks. I see the handwriting when it's scrawled in blood on my door. You wanted Max Roderick dead—and I did my best to give client satisfaction. Would it be possible to get on with the business that brought us here?"

"It all began with Harry Leeds," Sompong mused. "Harry, who lived a blameless life in Hong Kong, with his classic Jag and his sharp-tongued wife and his clandestine occupation on behalf of Krane's. Harry had a weakness for pretty girls, particularly Asian ones. He liked them gold-digging and hard as nails."

"I set up old Harry like a house of cards," Ankana crooned with satis-faction. "Poor old gent—I shagged Harry thirty different ways and then I blackmailed the hell out of him. I told Harry I'd squeal to his wife—I'd send the bitch pictures. After that Harry did whatever I told him."

Oliver's indolent form stiffened slightly; and Stefani knew that for all his air of boredom, he was alert as a cat. "Harry's dead, old thing," he said to Sompong. "He explained all about those guns he helped you run into Hong Kong. That was the start of a beautiful friendship, Sompong. Your guns, my electronic surveillance . . . *Think* of the weap-ons we've placed in deserving hands!"

"Harry died," Sompong observed, "because you sent him out to learn anything he could about a hit man named Jo-Jo, who'd worked as a bodyguard in Harry's part of the world. You knew Jo-Jo dropped a dead girl in Max Roderick's hotel room. What you didn't know then was that Jo-Jo worked for *me*. But Harry did. He'd seen Jo-Jo before, with Ankana."

"Was it *you* he went to meet, that day in Kowloon?" Oliver asked Ankana. "Dear, dear—it *is* a small world."

"Why should it matter what Harry knew?" Stefani burst out. "Why did Max have to be killed? You're going to kill me—so tell me the truth. Why did Max Roderick die?"

"For this." Sompong swept his hand around the hut. "To pro-tect the General's men. They are my sacred charge, Ms. Fogg. The sol-diers who stand outside these walls depend upon me for their survival. Everything I've done—the guns I've sold, the risks I've taken to send opium to market, even the people I've killed—*Duty*. A son's duty to his dead father."

"You took Max Roderick's life for that little thug Vukrit? A man murdered by drug runners fifteen years ago?"

Sompong's expression changed, and he spat into the dirt.

"Oh, no, ducks," Oliver told her softly. "That's the tale you've been sold. Max died because he wanted the *truth*."

"I don't understand—"

"The man you call my father, Vukrit Suwannathat, was no blood relation of mine," Sompong spat. "Fool! To believe he could take my father's place! When Wu Fat brought back the General's ashes from the Cameron Highlands, I swore to avenge my father's murder. Vukrit died with his back against that post, right in this very hut, and he cursed me as I fired the gun. Now the General's men follow me. All my life I have tried to be worthy."

"I wonder if the General would agree," Oliver Krane said thoughtfully.

Stefani met his eyes for an instant. His insouciant mask had slipped. Why?

Sompong reached for Wu Fat's rifle and turned it idly on Oliver. "We understand each other, Mr. Krane. We understand the nature of face. The destruction of one sort of honor demands the death of another."

"Getting biblical? An eye for an eye?"

Sompong ignored him. "Wu Fat, untie the woman."

The soldier sliced through the ropes with his knife. Stefani felt the blood tingle painfully into her fingertips. Wu Fat lifted her to her feet and propelled her toward the door.

"Going to kill me yourself?" Oliver inquired genially.

Sompong shook his head. "First I want to see you put a bullet in Ms. Fogg's brain."

Stefani's knees buckled and she sat down abruptly in the dirt. Wu Fat hoisted her back to her feet like a sack of flour.

Ankana screeched with laughter. Then she pulled a packet of cigarettes from her leather jacket and inquired, "Last smokes, anyone?"

"Sorry, Stefani," Oliver muttered.

"Why, old thing?" Stefani told him as she stumbled past. "It's just the high-wire act, isn't it? Without a safety net."

10

The Cameron Highlands,
Easter Sunday 1967

The air was chill as Jack Roderick loped down the winding road toward the Tanah Rata golf course in his dark blue suit, the briefcase with his entire life's fortune swinging jauntily by his side. It had been a cool weekend—the weather of late March oddly reminiscent of Scotland, with its showers and sudden fogs rising over the scattered cottages and elaborate English gardens. The British had built this hill station cheek-by-jowl with the jungle and tea plantations because of that weather: it was a haven from the oppressive tropics of Kuala Lumpur. Rapacious vines encroached on the scrupulous plots of roses.

For a time during the war the Highlands had been overrun with Communist guerillas, and the darker rumors of the expatriate community still infested the jungles with pygmy tribes and mercenary bands. Carlos commanded one of these, as he had done somewhere in Southeast Asia ever since his flight from the Grand Palace twenty-one years before. Vukrit Suwannathat might have overrun one encampment in Chiang Rai, but the General had moved south, into Malaysia. Carlos never forgot the hill country of the Golden Triangle, or the hidden shrine to his dead wife, a woman named for a river.

A breeze whipped through the low-lying scrub, and Roderick shivered. After two decades in the moist heat of Bangkok, he could not adjust to Tanah Rata. *Nerves,* he thought. *Christ, you've done this sort of thing all your life. Snap out of it—*

But never, in all his life, had it mattered so much.

When, three weeks before, Carlos had left him standing alone on the terrace in Bangkok to decide his son's fate, Roderick went sleepless until dawn. He'd thought of night drops over North Africa. Of training in Ceylon. Of his youthful arrogance at being a warrior, his unswerving belief in Right. He felt again the irrational love for the OSS—that happy band of brothers—and how ready he had been to die for men like McQueen and Billy Lightfoot. He thought of the hero named Ruth and the curious way in which his life had diverged from the one that Pridi Banomyong had planned.

He considered Rory, both the boy he had abandoned and the man who was dying with courage and pain. He thought of his grandson, Max, as he had been four years ago—and the way the boy's dark eyes had widened as he'd stared at the blood on his grandfather's face.

Is life more valuable than honor? He recalled, suddenly, the schoolboy taunts Rory had endured—Joan's description of a necktie swinging from the bedroom light fixture. Rory felt passionately that the shadow of cowardice was not to be endured. If he gave way to extortion, Rory would never forgive him. But he could not bear to know that he might save his son—and allow Rory to die. He carried too much guilt already.

"Tell Ruth he can have his blood money," Roderick had said, when at dawn Carlos reappeared like a ghost. He pressed a crumpled envelope into the General's hand, scrawled in childish pencil. Max had written to his father from Lake Tahoe, and when Rory was declared MIA, the letter had been sent on to Jack. "And see that Rory gets this."

He sent young Dickie Spencer to the bank for all the money in the world. He signed the draft of his second will, leaving everything to his heirs instead of the people of Thailand, whom he had decided to betray. He tried not to think of Rory, dying by degrees. He did not see Fleur for almost a week, but when she appeared on his doorstep as inexplicably as she had gone the night of Carlos's visit, he asked her to stay with him. He craved distraction. He was inattentive and remote, and he knew that he hurt her. She did not again raise the subject of flight to the United States.

*   *   *

Rose Cottage, where he had spent this Easter with Fleur, belonged to friends of Alec McQueen. Roderick had visited the Marshalls before, in Singapore; they had dined in turn at his house on the khlong. It had not been difficult to press them for an invitation to their summer home in the Cameron Highlands. Roderick drove south with Fleur on Holy Thursday, and reached Rose Cottage on Good Friday afternoon. He impatiently waited for Carlos's signal—a red smear of paint on a rock near the golf course. Two days passed in growing tension, in fitful walks and abrupt conversations, Fleur staring at him uneasily and the Marshalls pretending disinterest.

He had seen the splotch of crimson paint that morning as he walked to Easter service in the little town of Tanah Rata. The meeting time with Carlos would be between four and five o'clock that day. After an impromptu picnic, during which Roderick glanced perpetually at his watch, the Marshalls and Fleur declared themselves tired and lay down to rest. Roderick poured himself a drink in the silent living room. He lit a cigarette, and left it burning in an ashtray.

Now, at the foot of the road, he hastened his step. The exercise felt good. The end of waiting felt better.

In the slanting light of late afternoon, the jungle loomed at his right hand like an emerald wall. Roderick had a map of the local hiking trails in his pocket, with Carlos's meeting place marked. The first cutting swerved perpendicular to the road and ran skittishly into the underbrush. He glanced over his shoulder: the hillside and surrounding landscape were empty of life. He struck into the path in his supple leather shoes, a gesture toward Easter Sunday. Carlos would laugh. *I had forgot that men dressed like that, in places like these.*

The path dwindled as he walked, the air sharpened, the light dimmed. The canopy overhead was broken by the startled wings of birds. Roderick had chosen this hour and place because it was certain to be deserted, and offered Carlos protective cover. The intense loneliness, however, he had forgotten. He had not considered tigers. He walked on, feeling the cold sweat on his back, suppressing the urge to whistle.

Perhaps twenty minutes passed in solitary trudging. The briefcase felt awkward in his hands. How must he look to anyone watching: an urbane and distinguished figure in his Thai silk suit. This was a landscape for combat fatigues, for thick boots and army packs. Shadows swallowed the path behind him. Even the birds were silent, now, and Roderick wondered why Carlos's men were not heralding his course from the surrounding trees, as they had done in Chiang Rai ten years earlier.

He stopped dead, the back of his neck prickling. Not only darkness filled the gap behind him, now. Someone was following.

"Hello, Jack."

He turned, fingers clenched on his briefcase.

A towering figure in U.S. Army green, broad and hard as a side of beef.

"Billy," he said, bewildered. "What are you doing here?"

"Gotta ask the same of you." Lightfoot shambled toward him, two others behind—privates, by their uniforms. All three carried automatic rifles.

Roderick glanced farther down his path into the welling dusk, and caught a movement in the underbrush. Of course. Lightfoot would have thought of that—of the mad impulsive plunge a man might make into the jungle. He said, "You're a long way from Khorat."

"And you're a long way from Bangkok, old pal. Care to tell me why?"

The figures he'd glimpsed ahead were approaching, now. He would shortly be surrounded. He considered a sidelong dash. Useless. One of the soldiers would be sure to fire.

"We've had some intelligence, Jack, that a pack of Commie bastards are hiding out in this jungle," Lightfoot said cannily, "run by an old warlord, code-named Carlos. They're planning to bring the revolution right to the outskirts of Kuala Lumpur. You know anything 'bout that?"

"Not a thing." *Abort the meeting, Carlos. Turn around. Go home.*

"That's a load of crap, Jack. You always take a walk in your civvies at this hour of the afternoon?"

"You think I'm a Communist, Billy?"

"What I think is that you'd better talk fast. What's in the briefcase?"

The second group of soldiers stood twenty yards away, now, and recognizable: regular Thai Army troops. "Do you fellas have permission to maneuver on Malaysian soil?"

Lightfoot held out his hand. "Give that case to me."

One of the privates stepped forward with his gun leveled. The Thai soldiers closed the gap ahead. It was Field Marshal Vukrit Suwannathat, however, who wrestled the briefcase from Roderick's fingers.

When the combination lock on the thing would not open, one of the privates shot it off with his gun. A dull, pinging sound, like nails thudding into a coffin.

"You see?" Vukrit cried exultantly to Billy Lightfoot. "I *told* you. One million U.S. dollars. The warlord Carlos was to carry this into Hanoi."

"Jesus Christ Almighty, Jack," Lightfoot muttered hoarsely. He stared down at the money, which gleamed sickly in the jungle light. "The Legendary American, aiding and abetting the Viet Cong."

"It's not what you think."

"I didn't want to believe it." Lightfoot's anger and disappointment were scorching. "No American with your record of service—no man with a son shot down in this war—would sell us out to Uncle Ho. That's what I told the minister, when he came to me with his tale. I had to see for myself."

Fleur, Roderick thought despairingly, *you've betrayed me again. Why tell Vukrit? Why now?* "Rory's a POW in the Hanoi Hilton, Billy. The money is his ransom. You'd do the same for your son, given the chance."

"I'd have died first, and so would any boy of mine," Lightfoot replied thickly. "And if you believe for one second that poor kid's still alive—Hell, you been played big time, Jack. The Viet Cong spun you a tale. All they wanted was your cash. And like a fool, you brought it to them. You realize what this means? You'll be tried in the States for treason."

"Rory's alive. If you don't believe me, ask Carlos."

"Carlos is done talking." Vukrit's voice was smug. "We raided his camp last night; he was never a competent fighter. But he told us, eventually, how to signal you. It was almost the last thing he said before he died."

"You son of a whore," Roderick said tautly. "I don't believe you."

Vukrit shrugged. "You can see his body if you like."

* * *

It was not many minutes farther down the path to the place on Roderick's map where he had been supposed to turn, and strike off alone into the thick vines that tangled about the ankles, groping like a blind man toward a clearing where no paths led. Here the huts had been erected, their roofs covered with leaves; but the place was deserted, now, except for the few men Vukrit had left to guard it.

When they reached Carlos's camp it was quite dark, and Roderick stumbled between the two Thai soldiers who frog-marched him through the brush. A great desolation welled in his heart: *Rory my boy, Rory you're lost, and Carlos is dead.* Carlos had been tortured and he had died with the shame of betrayal on his lips—he had told Vukrit of the rock and the red paint and Jack's intended course through the jungle. To think of this—and to think of Rory, who would never know how his father had tried to save him—was agony.

As he was hauled into the clearing, one of the soldiers lit a torch: the flames soared under the jungle canopy. Seven bodies lay sprawled in death on the ground; but not, Roderick thought with satisfaction, a fifth part of the General's men. The bulk of Carlos's troops must have escaped.

There would be no money sent to Ruth. No release or salvation for Rory. Bitterness and loss filled his mouth with ashes.

"We left Carlos inside that hut," Vukrit told him with a smile. "Look at his body well. This is how the Thais deal with traitorous dogs."

Roderick lunged for the man and knocked him heavily to the ground. He beat at Vukrit's face with his fists, his breath tearing in his chest. He was sixty-one and he smoked too much and his doctor nagged him about his heart—but he was filled with the violence of blasted hope, the lifelong hatred of Vukrit and men like him and the knowledge of the lives they had destroyed.

Rory, my son, my son—

He felt Vukrit's nose collapse under his fists and the wet smear of blood and he heard screaming; then a soldier hauled him to his feet and a gun was pressed to his temple.

"Kill him," Vukrit screamed from the ground where he lay, writhing in pain. "Kill him, I say!"

The last thing Jack Roderick saw was Billy Lightfoot, standing rigidly at attention, an expression of sorrow on his face.

*   *   *

Two days later, when the search for the Silk King was at its peak and more than two hundred men swarmed through the clinging underbrush, Major General Billy Lightfoot—Commander of U.S. Forces, Khorat—flew a phalanx of Army helicopters into Malaysia to join in the search for his old friend.

More than one reporter thought it singular that at a time of warfare in the region, a foreign military service was allowed to violate Malaysia's airspace; and it seemed unlikely that a helicopter would be able to discern much through the dense canopy of the Highlands jungle. But Lightfoot ignored his critics and flew into Malaysia anyway and was much admired for his dedication to Jack Roderick. Billy had always been a man for whom duty was the highest calling.

He flew directly to the clearing in the brush that had once held a military encampment of no particular political orientation. It was deserted now but there was evidence of fighting in recent days. Lightfoot set down his helicopter and ordered two of his men to lift the body that rested, as though sleeping, in the doorway of one of the abandoned huts.

The Army chopper swung away to the east. It was a matter of half an hour by air to the China Sea. Roderick's body turned twice in an arc of sunlight as it tumbled through the sky, like a man who had jumped without a parachute. It slipped soundlessly into the waves.

11

Hanoi,
April 1967

There came a night—the seventy-first slash on his prison cell wall—when Rory Roderick was left alone. No guards came to bind his arms together and hang him from the torture-room ceiling. No one shouted abuse through his door. He was only conscious of the passage of time because he was very weak, now, from raging fever and dysentery, but he understood that the night continued without interruption, unmarked even by sleep, and he was thankful.

There was tapping on the walls around him, some of it urgent. He listened to the letters as they unreeled, but he was too exhausted to make sense of them or to respond. In his right hand he clutched a filthy scrap of paper. It was his letter from Max.

—I'm learning to ski now that we've moved to California and my coach says I'm pretty good. Mom's scared I'll hit a tree but I tell her I'm not a baby. I'll take you over all the jumps I've found in the woods when you come home. You know how to ski, right, Dad?

Rory thought of that brief week in January, a lifetime before, when he had swerved off the trail at Stowe to hide in the woods, and prayed that his father wouldn't find him. The fear and the weakness seemed laughable, now, but he was glad that Max loved the speed and the challenge of the tortuous pitch, as he never could. Max would make Jack Roderick proud. Rory felt a great and forgiving peace toward the father he loved and no longer needed to understand. He closed his eyes and slept.

They came for him at dawn, shouting at him to *get up, get up,* although they knew he could no longer stand. In the end it took three of them to drag him into the courtyard where the old French guillotine from the glory days of the Maison Centrale had been resurrected for Jack Roderick's son.

"Where is Ruth?" he asked them, as he fell at the foot of the thing.

"Ruth has failed." The chief guard spoke with contempt and Rory understood now that the price of Ruth's failure would be his death. "He is sent home to Beijing in disgrace."

Rory gazed across the courtyard. There the rest of the Americans were assembled, their faces white and startled, their bodies thin as martyred saints. He recognized Beardsley, the boy from Indiana, and saw the tears on his cheeks.

He could not have walked away from them all, a free man, and held his head high. He closed his eyes instead and saluted, in his mind, the image of his father.

The blade screeched as it was drawn upward. The guard beside him grunted with the effort; the winch, it seemed, had rusted. There were stars bursting behind his eyes and one of them had the face of Max.

Rory tightened his hand on the letter, and thought of snow.

12

Stefani found the sunlight blinding after the shadows of the hut. Dazed, she blinked at the sea of faces and her entire body trembled with the effort not to show the terror that consumed her.

Wu Fat gripped her arm tightly. Sompong yelled something brief and biting in Thai, and the General's men came at a run to surround their prisoners. She had no time to estimate the number of guns pointed at her and Oliver Krane. Wu Fat forced her to kneel; she swayed and felt the world slipping sideways until the old soldier jerked her upright again.

Sompong positioned the rifle Oliver held, thrusting the muzzle against the raw skin of her cheek. Oliver's nerveless hands dropped the gun and Sompong swore, bending to retrieve it. Stefani's breath was shallow and desperate. *I will not think about it.* She would not listen for the click of the trigger. She would keep her eyes trained on the jungle brush beyond the clearing. There were orchids in the trees. They would be the last bursts of color she saw.

Except that one of the trees rose upward, and in the brilliant half-life of fear she thought it was a man, covered in leaves with branches on his head. Sompong had stopped talking, now. Raising the rifle again. Would he kill Oliver Krane after he made Oliver shoot her?

The tree advanced. As she watched, hysteria bubbling in her brain, other trees joined it—all racing now across the open clearing of the encampment. Shots rang out and the General's men wheeled and dived into the dirt, their guns trained on the shifting forest, hoarse curses torn from their throats. Oliver Krane lay facedown in the grass with his hands flung protectively over his head; Ankana tripped on her stiletto heels; and Stefani screamed with laughter. Her shrill madness blended with the cracking of rifle upon rifle.

Wu Fat barked an order. Then the old soldier's arm flew upward and his body jerked violently. He fell over on Stefani, crushing her beneath his weight, forcing her downward into the seared jungle brush. The shock of it finally slapped sense into her brain. She bucked upward with savage strength and crawled out from under his corpse, hand over hand, through the kicking feet and the strafing bullets, toward the open door of the hut.

As she reached the threshold, a shot tore a splinter of wood from the door frame. It stung her cheek, drawing blood. Aged teak was no protection against firepower like this—the hut would surely prove a deathtrap in the end—but she could not bear the chaos behind. She thrust herself forward.

Someone else had done the same.

He lay, gasping for breath, propped against the pillar that had been her tether post that morning. Sweat poured from his face and pooled in the gap exposed by his shirt collar. His right hand was pressed over his stomach, and blood, purple and thick, welled between his fingers. In his left hand was Wu Fat's rifle.

Stefani waited for Sompong to level the gun, to finish the execution he'd started minutes before, but instead he raised the muzzle to his mouth. The long barrel wavering in his trembling grip.

"No!" she screamed.

The protest was explosive, startling him enough that he dropped the rifle. She stumbled across the hut and seized the gun.

Sompong stared up at her. Even in the gloom she could see his eyes, riddled with pain. His chest heaved. He tried to stand—tried to do battle for the weapon—but the effort ended in a crouch, Sompong on his knees at her feet.

"Kill me, then." The words came like the rasp of a dying heart. "Take your revenge."

She held the barrel steady, inches from his ear. She was overcome, in that moment, with an anguish so fierce it felt like an iron fist to the ribs. Max—the man she might have loved beyond anyone, given time—Max, whose unflinching gaze swerved from nothing, no matter how difficult or brutal. She thought of the Legend with the silver hair and the fathomless eyes, a white bird on his shoulder. Of the father Max had lost too soon, his wings dipping in the sun. The Roderick men: brilliant, lost, believing in and demanding justice.

She looked down at the man clenched in pain at her feet. And let her forefinger find the trigger.

It was Rush Halliwell who found her there, twenty-three minutes after the last shot was fired.

She stood defiantly in the center of the hut with a smear of dirt on her face and a gun in her hands. At her feet lay Sompong.

She had torn off his shirt and made a clumsy bandage, but the wadded cloth was dark with blood.

"Holy Christ," Rush muttered. "You killed him."

"It's what he wanted. But that's too easy. I want him shamed. I want him tried. I want him called *murderer* before the whole world." She handed Rush the automatic rifle. "I want Sompong to live."

Later, as they sat in the C130 transport plane waiting for takeoff, Rush stole a look at her as he adjusted the harness of his jump seat. She was already strapped in and staring mutely at the warnings printed in block capitals on the fuselage interior. The huge propellers thundered to life, and the uninsulated cabin was filled with the roar of gears and power. There would be no conversation, now—and it was just as well, Rush thought. Stefani looked as though she might tip over in a slight breeze. He was light-headed with exhaustion himself.

Pulling off the raid on Sompong Suwannathat's base had required whipcord nerve and ceaseless concentration. No joint U.S.-Thai exercise—even in the name of interdicting the drug trade—could be sprung without warning on the Thai Ministry of Defense. He and Marty Robbins had pressed the issue far into the wee hours of Friday night, with the

Prime Minister, the Thai head of drug enforcement, the American ambassador and the director of the FBI—who appeared at the embassy via
satellite on a secure videoteleconference screen. The case against
Sompong was viewed and reviewed to the point of idiocy, the Thai government officials expressing regret and dismay with a world of disbelief
in their stiff smiles. Rush paced the corridors in frustration, his patience scored raw.

Marty got the green light and a transport full of troops at 4:17
Saturday morning.

The entire raid required forty-eight minutes, from the point when
the jungle commandos moved into position, until the moment when
Sompong and his men surrendered. The Thai drug-enforcement team
claimed full credit for the speed and efficiency of its planning. Sompong's
downfall would be broadcast live in a matter of hours.

Rush had held her back when she tried to fight her way onto the
field helicopter that airlifted Sompong to a hospital in Chiang Rai. She
seemed convinced that the minister might escape—and her passion to
see him in handcuffs bordered, Rush thought, on obsession.

Whereas she had barely glanced at Oliver Krane as he walked coolly
up the C130's rear gangway with Marty Robbins.

"He goes free?" she asked.

"Krane's been cooperating with the FBI for months," Rush told
her. "He's part of an active investigation of illegal arms racketeering.
He'll tell you the story, I'm sure."

"Oliver always has a story." Contempt and weariness in the words.
She had been one of Oliver's stories herself, after all.

"You're free of him now."

"Am I?"

Her voice was incredulous—mocking even; and he understood that
she was changed from the woman he'd met at the Oriental's cocktail
party days ago. She would never walk in all the bravado of innocence
again.

When he asked, in the taxi from Bangkok airport, if there was anything she needed—anything he could do—she answered only, "I want to
go home."

"We can arrange that." He hesitated. "It might take a day or two.
We'd like a complete account of your experience. Everything you
know."

"All right then. Let's work a trade." She stared at him challengingly. "I still don't know how Jack Roderick died. I'd like to hear the truth. Because of Max."

"I might be able to help you there."

"You'll take me to see Sompong?"

Rush shook his head. "Get some sleep tonight. We'll visit my father tomorrow."

13

Bangkok, Then and Now

When he tore the piece off the press wire in the *Bangkok Post* newsroom that night—March 27, 1967—Joe Halliwell's chest tightened and for a moment he could not believe the name he was reading. *Jack Roderick.* Lost in the Malaysian jungle. It was Easter Monday and the Silk King had been missing for thirty-one hours, the story would have to be written immediately and the presses stopped, and by sunrise tomorrow the entire city would be talking of nothing else. But first Halliwell must call Alec McQueen at his home and rouse him from sleep and tell him the news as one old friend to another.

"Assign the damn piece," McQueen barked through the tatters of his sleep, "and get the hell on a plane. I want you in the Highlands by dawn, you hear?"

Joe had gone out of the newsroom as though his mother or his wife or his dearest child lay dying in a hospital somewhere and he had taken the last flight to Kuala Lumpur from the airport. As the plane hurtled south and then the hired car lurched north, he had believed that he would arrive to find Jack strolling out of the rainforest canopy with a careless grin and a wave for his supporters.

By Tuesday morning, when he pulled up in Tanah Rata, the beaters had worked their way through twenty square miles of jungle. He stood for a time on the hillside above the golf course—the logical starting point for any search, because Jack must have started there himself—and took a few photographs. He talked to the cook who worked in a nearby cottage and who claimed to have seen a man walking downhill on the night of the disappearance, but the glimpse had been fleeting and the cook could not say whether the man stuck to the road or not. He talked to the local cop in charge of the search and to one of the beaters who was having a cup of tea after walking for nearly twenty hours, and to the cleric who had said Easter Sunday service for Jack Roderick and his friends. He found the caddy who had been cleaning clubs at the course but had failed to look up from his task long enough to note a solitary walker. He cajoled the woman who delivered flowers to the Marshalls at Rose Cottage and the grocer who supplied milk twice weekly when the couple was in residence; and only then did he turn toward the cottage itself.

The Marshalls were nice people but bewildered and clearly out of their depth. They had known Jack Roderick as a social acquaintance, a Bangkok personality, a friend of a friend—and they knew Fleur Pithu-vanuk, Jack's companion, not at all. When they had awakened from their nap the day before and discovered Jack gone, they had seen no reason to worry. He'd been restless all weekend, they said.

"You're a personal friend?" Mrs. Marshall asked Joe. She was a plump woman with washed-out eyes. "Then I don't mind telling you I'm worried about Fleur. She's so quiet. And she won't leave her room."

He had gone to her then, and found her sitting motionless in a chair with her eyes fixed on the window.

He's not lost, she told him, *and he's not coming back. I made sure of that.*

It took him fifteen minutes to get the story out of her. He listened without his pen or his paper and he listened with a building sense of doom. By choosing Jack's mild-faced friend as her confessor, Fleur condemned them both to a lifetime of lies.

Ten years earlier, when Fleur betrayed Jack Roderick for the first time, it was a simple matter of selling the Silk King's secrets to the man who held Fleur's neck in a noose. Vukrit Suwannathat had power of the crudest kind—power to support or arrest, to elevate or to destroy.

He threatened the livelihood of Fleur's father and brothers, he held the future of her clan over her head. She did what Vukrit told her to do and was thankful when he wearied of raping her body.

"In August of that year I told Vukrit that the man he had sought most of his life—his brother-in-law, Carlos, a fugitive from justice—held camp in a village near Chiang Rai," Fleur told Joe Halliwell. "But when Vukrit went to attack him, Carlos had fled. Vukrit looked like a fool. He returned in a rage. He called me a trickster and a whore and he had my father arrested and my brothers' businesses seized. My family disowned me and I went alone to the south, where I filled my rice bowl as best I could. I never asked Roderick for help. It was impossible to see him again."

She understood how Jack had tested her—providing false information of the meeting, in perfect detail—and that he'd suspected she would pass everything on to Vukrit. She had betrayed both men in different ways.

But there was still the secret Fleur guarded, year after year: when she fled in sorrow to the south, she carried Roderick's child. The last day she spent with Jack—the picnic at Ayutthaya—she already felt the sickness of pregnancy.

"My son brought me no honor," she told Joe Halliwell. "The people of the village guessed that I had never married, although I called myself a widow. It was obvious from his birth that my child was a half-breed bastard of a *farang*. But I loved him all the same. He grew tall and strong, and his eyes were green."

When the war in Vietnam swept over them, and the boy needed schooling, she grew desperate at the poverty of her village. She told herself that no son of the Silk King should be raised in the dust, but still she was afraid to see Jack again. Until the day when the newspaper reported that Rory Roderick—a Navy flyer, Jack's son who had grown up in the United States—had died in the wreck of his plane. She gathered her courage, then, and made the journey back to Bangkok.

"I meant to tell him," she said to Joe. "I meant to show him the child of my heart. I hoped that if he knew he had fathered a son—a boy to replace the one he had just lost—he would marry me and take us to America, where we could all be safe. But the very night I went to fall on my knees before Jack Roderick, the man named Carlos came back."

She had turned her face from the window, then, and stared at Halliwell. Her eyes were dark with malice.

"To ransom that grown son of his—the pureblood *farang* he'd abandoned in America—Jack was prepared to give everything he owned. His house. His business. His princely fortune. I watched how he burned to redeem his Rory—and I saw that he spared not a thought for me. He did not even know when I left his house that night. My bastard child would mean less to Jack than the old white bird he kept on his shoulder. I had waited too long—and my hope was dead."

"And so," Joe Halliwell told Rush and Stefani as they sat in the sunlight of his back porch, "Fleur left Jack's house and went in search of his worst enemy. She informed Vukrit that she had seen the man named Carlos, and that Carlos planned to meet with Roderick in the Highlands of Malaysia to collect a king's ransom which would save his son from the Viet Cong. Vukrit could swoop down and kill the man he had hunted his entire life, and if Roderick died in the fighting—so be it."

"Ruthless," Stefani mused. "She must have hated—or loved—Jack beyond reason."

"Men had used poor Fleur for so many years. I think she enjoyed having the upper hand, for once."

"But if she told you—a reporter—she must have known you had an obligation to write the truth."

"She knew that I had always loved her," Halliwell replied baldly. "You can't stare at a woman with longing, as I did for years, and have her fail to see. She knew that I would protect her. It was Suwannathat, after all, who'd killed Jack—though no one would ever prove it. Fleur was just Vukrit's pawn."

"I wonder if Roderick knew—as he died—what she'd done."

"Jack was no innocent." Joe's eyes were filled with old grief. "Betrayal got Fleur nothing, in the end. The money Jack had brought into the Highlands vanished—presumably into Vukrit's coffers. Fleur drowned herself not long thereafter, in the waters of the khlong."

"But what happened to the child?" Stefani asked. "Roderick's half-Thai son?"

Joe Halliwell glanced at Rush, who placed his hand on the old man's shoulder.

"Joe adopted me. He called me his boy. He was no Roderick in my mother's eyes, but at least he was *farang*. He could take me to the States if life got too rough. She knew Joe would never betray her secret, Stefani—because it was *my* secret, too."

14

Oliver Krane bent to study the placard that described the enormous terra-cotta vase—a central piece in the museum's current exhibition, *Two Thousand Years of Southeast Asian Art.* This was the show's opening day, and the crowds that flowed and parted the length of the exhibit hall were staggering.

" 'Dated 1000 BC,' " Oliver murmured, " 'discovered at a hearth site in Ban Chiang, near the Laotian border—meticulously restored from the merest shards.' Hmmm. And exactly who did the restoring, I wonder? A man named Khuang, late of the Thieves Market?"

The faintest smile curled the corners of his mouth. It faded, however, when he caught sight of the woman standing three yards from the display, her eyes fixed on his face. Her expression was forbidding; but at least, Oliver decided, she had consented to come.

He had tried and failed to catch her attention repeatedly since his return from Bangkok. For three weeks he had employed his usual methods: opera tickets delivered by a famous tenor; an exquisite meal composed by a sought-after chef in her very own kitchen; her portrait freshly painted by the *artiste du jour*. She had ignored them all, and with each failure the zest had dwindled from Oliver's life.

But this morning, when Stefani Fogg opened her door to retrieve the morning paper—there was the white cockatoo waiting in its six-foot cage, with a pass to the Met show tethered to one claw.

"Ms. Fogg, is it? You *have* made yourself scarce." He peered at her mockingly over his glasses.

Stefani offered no word of reply.

Afraid she might turn and run, he walked toward her. "I owe you an apology. I deceived you, my dearest Stefani, from first to last of this sordid little tale; and although I had my reasons, they cannot be considered excuses. The threats to your person were shocking. The possible consequences, unthinkable. I am seared with remorse, and humbly beg forgiveness."

"You would have killed me if necessary," she returned, in a voice so low he strained to hear it.

Oliver shook his head. "Remember, ducks, how strenuously I resisted Sompong's representations in that hut. At no point did I admit to having employed you to work against him. When he placed that rifle in my hands I dropped it rather than fire. I confess that I had no further notion of how to effect our rescue—but happily your embassy chums rendered that moot."

"In other words," she retorted, "you got lucky. But too many people died for your little game, Oliver. You and Sompong, with the *Risk* board wedged between you."

"The man had his boot on my neck. He'd murdered my old friend Harry. I went hat in hand to the FBI, and they treated me as a father would a son. *Oliver, old boy,* they said, *do your best to entrap the cunning little sod and we'll back you to the end.* And so I laid my plans."

"Max Roderick was convenient. I was convenient. You used us both."

"And I *abase* myself, for all my sins. As a gesture of good faith and apology, heart, I've brought you this." He held out a small pouch made of Thai silk, bound with a braided tassel.

"No more gifts, Oliver."

"But this already belongs to you! Part of your inheritance. Dickie Spencer found it, inside a massive limestone head of the Buddha. He was packing it for shipment to New York, and the thing fell out in his hands."

"Spencer—that *bastard*. He owes me a hell of a lot more than this—"

"As he knows. He asked that I send this on, with his thanks for windmills tilted."

"He should be on his knees praising God he's not in a Thai prison. I could have had him arrested. Accessory to kidnapping."

"But you didn't?"

She gave him a long look. "I might need his . . . gratitude. When I come into my inheritance."

Oliver smiled and nodded. "A patron-client relationship. How very Thai of you, Ms. Fogg."

She unwound the tassel. Inside the silk pouch was an envelope, penned in a difficult hand. *To be opened in the event of my death.*

"This is some sort of document. It's been notarized."

"There was a marvelous old gemstone stored with it," Oliver told her. "A cabochon ruby. But that's been returned to its niche in the Buddha—you'll find *him* a few yards farther on. Won't you stroll with me through the exhibit, my dear? It's time we discussed your future."

"My future?"

"You *must* have thought about your next post. Where would you like to go? Argentina? Istanbul? St. Petersburg?"

"You can't be serious. I didn't come here today for a job. I came for the *truth*. I want to know exactly how Max died."

"Ah," Oliver said mournfully. "Poor Max. I was forced to put him *hors de combat*, as it were, to placate Sompong. But Jeffrey Knetsch, God rest his soul, was an immense pain in the ass. He fiddled with his friend's skis. Max wasn't supposed to die without my help."

"*Help?*"

"His position obviously required some sort of assistance. He was in the gravest danger, heart. From my conversations with Sompong, I knew that the minister was determined to make an end of Max's life. He had ordered poor Knetsch to do his worst. I informed Max that he would never be safe from Sompong Suwannathat—or his chums—until he was officially dead."

"Informed him—"

"You're being very obtuse." Oliver shrugged. "All Max had to do was head out alone to the cliff edge that night. Send Knetsch back for something at a calculated moment. I was waiting nearby to shove the chair off the ridge and help Max down the mountain via the tramline, before anyone discovered the suicide. Max had achieved enough strength in his legs by that time to walk with assistance. We got safely on our way to Moutiers while Knetsch was still summoning the alpine rescue johnnies.

"The only thing that troubled Max, really, was how much danger his apparent death placed *you* in. But he could tell from your letters that you'd grown in confidence over the previous few months. And I assured him I'd keep an eye on you. Neither of us expected Sompong to take you as seriously as he did. We never dreamed you'd become such a target."

Stefani gripped Oliver's arm so fiercely he winced. "Are you saying Max is alive?"

Oliver turned, and let his gaze fall on a massive stone head of a reclining Buddha that rested, like a meteor fallen from the sky, at the far end of the room.

"I understand that was one of Jack Roderick's favorite pieces," he murmured.

But she was already fighting her way through the crowds that jostled the length of the exhibition, toward the serene gaze of the limestone deity and the blond-haired man who stood by it, waiting for her.

AFTERWORD

In October 1999, I flew to Thailand with my husband, Mark Mathews, in search of a legend.

I had long been fascinated by the life of Jim Thompson, who settled in Bangkok after 1945, revived the moribund Thai silk industry, founded a company that thrives to this day, served as the first chief of U.S. intelligence in Bangkok and disappeared without a trace in the Cameron Highlands of Malaysia on Easter Sunday, 1967.

I began my search for Thompson at the Oriental Hotel, the gracious and evocative Bangkok institution that dominates the banks of the Chao Phraya. Thompson had lived for over a year at the Oriental in the late 1940s and had briefly served as part owner before founding his Thai Silk Company. The Oriental Hotel remains, for me, the epitome of Bangkok experiences. In the book-lined Authors Lounge, I was offered tea and chocolate cake by one of the most beautiful women in Bangkok, the elegant and charming Ankana Gilwee, who first joined the hotel's staff as a young girl and remembered the days when Thompson had lived there. Ankana graciously shared her memories of the man and the postwar period, and I am indebted for her welcome and her kindness.

She should, in no way, be confused with the character of Ankana Lee-Harris, who shares merely a part of her name.

I owe thanks to Dean Barrett, a fellow writer who suggested I speak with Harold Stephens, one of the last great adventurers and writers of Southeast Asia. Steve, as he is known, had worked as a reporter for the *Bangkok Post* at the time of Thompson's disappearance in 1967, and took part in the search for the Legendary American in the Cameron Highlands. He was purposefully reticent regarding Jim Thompson and the mystery of his death, and offered my most cherished bit of advice: *Don't write this story. People have died because of it.*

It was my acquaintance with Harold Stephens that proved vital in securing seats on a Royal Thai Air Force C130 transport plane out of Hué, Vietnam, where we were trapped together for five days in November 1999, during the worst flooding to hit central Vietnam in a century. While waiting for the waters to recede, my husband and I played endless rounds of cards with Steve, Joseph McInerney, the Chief Executive Officer of the Pacific-American Travel Association, and Dr. Craig Hedges, an American doctor donating his services to the hospital in Hué. Sunathee Isvarphornchai, Director of Public Relations for Thai Airways International, agreed to airlift us out of Hué in company with her delegation and press corps; without her extraordinary assistance, we might be swimming home still. We owe a deep debt of gratitude to all.

I would also like to thank Chase McQuade and his wife, Marilyn, for their generosity with family history and their support for this book. Mr. McQuade is Jim Thompson's great-nephew, and shares his famous relative's fascination with Asia. He related what family memories of Thompson he could, as well as discussing the aftermath of Thompson's disappearance; at every turn, he expressed his enthusiasm for the novel in progress.

Stefani Fogg and Jeff Knetsch donated their names to principal characters in this story for charitable purposes, and I appreciate their willingness to be dragged through a complex tale, cast into danger, manipulated without their consent, and in one instance, killed. Neither has profited from their association with the story, but the charities they supported are deeply grateful. They should never be confused with the characters their names represent.

My thanks go out to those members of the Central Intelligence Agency's Publication Review Board who read this manuscript prior to publication; and the remarkable Kate Miciak, Vice President and

Executive Editor at Bantam Dell Publishing Group, without whom my work would be much impoverished. Kate's patience, vision and intelligence inform every project I pursue.

The Secret Agent, while inspired by the story of the Legendary American, as Thompson is still known, diverges from strict biography in numerous ways. Although married and divorced immediately after the war, Jim Thompson never had a son, and the extent of his espionage activity after 1948 remains in fierce dispute. Most of the Thai characters are fabrications, with the exception of King Ananda, Prime Minister Pridi Banomyong and Field Marshal Pibul, three men who dominated Thai history in the post Second World War period. Similarly, the character of Alec McQueen is clearly based upon Thompson's OSS field-mate and *Bangkok Post* founder Alexander MacDonald; but my character should never be confused for a portrait of that distinguished journalist.

My solution to the mystery of Thompson's death—or Jack Roderick, as he is known in these pages—should not be read as anything but fiction.

For those readers who wish to consult a biography of Thompson, I would suggest William Warren's *The Legendary American: The Remarkable Career and Strange Disappearance of Jim Thompson* (Boston: Houghton Mifflin Company, 1970). And no trip to Bangkok is complete without a visit to Jim Thompson's House—that remarkable museum on the banks of the khlong.

Francine Mathews
Golden, Colorado
June 2001